THE PEEP SHOW

INA LOUISE JACKSON

Pine Lake Books
Canada

978-1-926898-58-2

Pine Lake Books
West Guilford
Also available in eBook format
eISBN 978-1-926898-57-5

THE PEEP SHOW
FORWARD

FRED KADIGAN

: Sometimes bad things do actually happen to bad people.

NO SCAVENGING

: Like the sign says, you should not take things.

INTERMISSION

: Now I lay me down to sleep if I have a nightmare instead of a dream, I pray the Lord to wake me before I start to scream.

COUNTY ROAD 507

: There are other places to dig a home's foundation, than on ancient burial grounds.

TROLLING

: Internet chat rooms can lead to fun, or not.

There is this white thing on the ground up ahead. As we close in we sense it is a sheet; A bed sheet with a good sized hump under it. Closer still, though we seem to be moving slower, we see the white sheet is not exactly white. It has pastel flowers with large stains. Brownish coloured stains not unlike, say dried blood. And the good sized hump more or so resembles a body. A human body? Maybe. We are now standing over the sheet. Our flesh starts to bead with sweat. Our limbs shake. Should we dare look? We glance around peering this way and that; though we are the only one there. We bend stretching out our hand, grasping the corner with our fingers. We slowly start to peel it back further and further ... until we gasp in utter horror and scream and scream and scream. Then scream some more.

But is not that why we walked over to it in the first place?

There are four sheets and a slight intermission here, care to enter and take a peep?

FRED KADIGAN

Dedication

For Fred
The devil made me do it!

Prologue

Beware the blue moon that shines bright.
For it casts shadows that loom and follow us.
Allowing our sins to walk beside us
Once again ...

Ina Louise Jackson

FRED KADIGAN

Sometimes ...
The more things change, the more they stay the same.

"YOU GOD DAMN LITTLE FUCKER! GET YOUR SKINNY GOOD FOR NOTHING ASS BACK IN HERE!" Lloyd Kadigan screamed. He leaned out the window; watching his son run full tilt across the lawn, hop the fence, and dive headfirst into the hay field. "F ... R ... E ... D ... D ... I ... E!" Lloyd screeched. He shook his head withdrawing, sitting back down to dinner.

Fred could feel his heart drumming in the back of his throat. It was beating faster than his feet were running. His mother must have told his father sooner, rather than the later she had promised. He ducked into the chicken coup, slamming the door shut behind him.

"How is Sable doing, anyway?" Lloyd asked. He swiped his bread at the last of his mashed potatoes and gravy, scooping it up. He doubled the bread over, cramming it all into his mouth, filling it beyond capacity.

"The Doc said she's goin' have a mighty big scar on her forehead. She will be in hospital for a spell. But, she'll be okay," Mavis said.

"What about the burns?" Lloyd asked.

"It was just the bottoms of her feet."

"What in hell is wrong with that damn fucking boy?"

"They was playing cowboys and Indians. Freddie was the Indian."

"For fucking Christ's sake!" Lloyd pulled his lips into his mouth quickly shoving them back out, making a hollow touting sound. "When ever did an Indian rope up a cowboy, or in this case cowgirl, to a bale of straw, light it on fire with a propane torch, and shoot arrows at their head? ... Real arrows at that!"

"He's only six. He don't know any better."

8

"And might I ask where you were when all this hoop-lah was going on?"

Mavis looked down. "I was hanging the laundry." She folded her hands neatly in front of her on the table, weaving her fingers together. "I thought the burning smell was the leaf pile I'd lit up a might earlier," she added, more so for self-defence.

Lloyd smacked the palms of his hands on the dinner table, bouncing his plate. "If this shit doesn't beat all," he said. He pushed himself away from the table.

"Go easy on him," Mavis said.

"Yeah, right!" Lloyd walked across the kitchen to the bullwhip propped up against the far wall. He picked it up, slapping the handle on and off his palm, speckling his sweating flesh in an odd array of glowing red half-moons. He booted the screen door open. "FREDDIE," he yelled. "I got a great big surprise for you! ... Come out! ... Come out! ... Where ever you are!" Lloyd hid the whip behind his back striding in the direction of the hay field.

Fred had settled in for the long haul, curling up in the straw at the far end of the coup. His taut breaths huffed out of his open mouth with loud thumping rasps that seemed to collapse back into his ears. He closed his eyes, counting to himself. He had gotten to one-hundred-fifty right on the nose when something snapped over the far side of the coup. It was a pure, crisp, clean sound like a dry twig stepped upon by a heavy boot. His eyes shot open, whipping back and forth in the darkness, seeing nothing but blue-black murkiness, fuzzing and fading at the edges of his vision.

There was another snap, louder, closer. Then another ... and another. The last snap seemed slower, more deliberate, and drawn out. It crackled and bounced into the boarded walls, lurking in the air above his head.

Saliva squirted from under his tongue filling his mouth. He swallowed hard. He suddenly found himself wishing he had hidden someplace else. He bolted knocking the door open with his fists. It smacked off the window, breaking the panes. He dashed for the tractor, crawling in and under, ducking behind its immense front tires.

The coup door banged back and forth like it was caught up in a wind torrent, but there was no wind. His eyes bulged, ringing themselves in white. He swam out from under the tractor, flaying his arms, propelling himself through the dirt on his belly. He took off through the barnyard in a dead out run, turning once to look behind him. He rounded the corner abruptly halting, bouncing off the stationary figure, laying himself out face first into the dirt. He smiled at the figure pulling him up, all at once relieved, bullwhip or not.

'It stood in the darkness waiting, watching.'

'At Eight'

"MOMMY!" Susie yelled. "Mommy, I can't find the kittens." Susie was down on her hands and knees, frantically searching through the mishmash on the front porch.

"Maybe," Mavis said. "The mommy kitty moved them. They do that sometimes." Mavis joined her daughter in the hunt.

"But the box isn't here mommy!" Susie plopped down in the middle of the floor and started to cry. "Mommy! ... I want my kitties ... I want my kitties," she wailed.

Mavis pulled the towel she had given the mother cat to birth on from under the old wicker chair. How it got there was beyond her. She had checked on the cat and kittens but all of an hour ago. The box, blanket, mom, and kittens were all together.

Susie picked up the bowl of cream she brought out for the mommy cat. Teardrops rolled off her cheeks splashing into the warm cream. It circled and swirled making tiny side-by-side eye-like whirlpools. Susie cradled the bowl against her little chest. "Mommy, where's my kitties?"

Mavis scooped her daughter up in her arms. "We'll find the kits. Don't you worry your pretty little head none," she said. Mavis rocked Susie back and forth planting soft kisses atop her head.

Fred smacked the last of the dirt with the back of the shovel, flattening it out. He could not hear the mewing any more. He groped through his pocket, fetching the pack of his dad's smokes, lighting one up. He slung the shovel onto his right shoulder strolling confidently towards the shed. He smiled, and then snickered. 'That'll teach the stupid little bitch for snitching on me,' he thought. The more he mulled it over the funnier it became. He roared with laughter.

A wind born out of the stillness whistled, swirling, biting at his back. The hay swooned, rolling, huffing. The little downy hairs on his neck all stood to attention at once, prickling his skin into rows of hives. He hesitated. He glanced behind him; first to the right and then the left. There was nothing. Still, he walked a little faster. The hay whipped and whisked making low, drawn out whoosh noises like it was speaking in some unrecognizable language. His skin chilled, wetted and goose bumped. He gulped, glancing again over his shoulder. The hay field seemed as if it had come alive. It thrust sideways, rustling, bending, and parting, offering up a direct, unencumbered path to the newly formed earthen patch.

He launched the shovel sideways into the field, suddenly running at breakneck speed for the house.

'It stood in the hay field waiting, watching.'

'At Fourteen'

"YEE ... HAW!" Fred screeched. He put the pedal to the metal. He was going to win this one hands-down. The car fishtailed, rounding dead-man's curve.

"FREDDIE! ... SLOW DOWN!" Judy screamed.

"HUSH UP GIRL!" Fred shot back. He swerved, passing on the right hand shoulder.

"FREDDIE!" Judy tugged at his right arm, pulling it from the wheel.

Fred gave his girl a dirty glare, forgetting about 'Bigbee's hump'. All four wheels left the road, going air borne. The car snaked and zigzagged as it came down bathing both sides of the pavement in kaleidoscopic coloured sparks. The car bounced, popping the front two wheels back into the air. Fred gunned it, spinning the back tires, too hard, too fast. It jerked, slid sideways, tipped, rolling three times. It went down and over the embankment on its roof, coming to an abrupt halt in a stand of maples.

One of the boughs bent doubling over in half with the force of wood versus metal. It pulled, tangling in the twisted alloy, weakening, snapping. The branch all at once reinvented itself. It launched up into the air like a mammoth wooden spear, bolting straight through the passenger side windshield and out the rear window, severing and taking Judy's head along as its trophy.

The car Fred was racing did not stop. It did not even slow down.

Fred crawled from the drivers' window cursing a blue streak. His arm was broke. He rubbed at his chin. Judy was as Judy was. He could get another girlfriend. But damn, that car of his daddy's was really something. He could not get another one of those.

He climbed up the embankment, walking backwards down the soft shoulder, holding out his right thumb.

A wind came out of nowhere, whispering, hopping through the tops of the branches, swaying them, curving the boughs towards him.

He picked up his pace. Something rustled alongside him like leaves being disturbed by ... he didn't know. His eyes bulged. He peered into the woods hunching his shoulders.

The wind lowered, filtering through the leaves, whirling, smacking him in the face. There was another rustle, closer ... Then another.

Fred turned and beat it for home.

'It stood within the trees waiting, watching.'

'At Sixteen'

"Come on Tam ... Let's do it," Fred coaxed. He undid her bra.

"I've never done it, this way before," Tammy said softly. "Freddie, you haven't done told me, you love me yet."

"Okay ... Whatever ... I love you then," he said.

"Really Freddie? You love me?" Tammy's eyes sparkled.

"Yeah sure. Take your panties off and open your legs real wide."

"Go slower Freddie. You hurting my bum hole." Tammy bumped the stick shift with her left knee, knocking the car into neutral.

"It always hurts the first couple times ... You'll get used to it."

"How you know this? You done said I was the only one?"

"I ... I ... read it someplace," Fred said. He was lying through his teeth. He figured she was too dumb to catch on. "Hush now girl, let me get it all the way in."

The truck jerked and jarred from the movements inside, coaxing the tires into a slow roll. It veered from the drive onto the lawn picking up speed as it went backwards down over the hill. It plummeted into the front veranda, lodging on top of the bottom three stairs.

Neither noticed.

The parents of the thirteen-year-old woke.

"Come on baby," Fred whispered. "Tilt up to me." He put his hands under her butt, pulling her close. "Let's get this hole dripping too," he said.

The windows were all the way down in the truck.

A swift breeze wormed and whirled through the grass, working its way towards them, all at once shooting through the window, nipping, gnawing at their salted, damp flesh.

The truck swayed side to side.

Fred stopped mid thrust. He narrowed his eyes into slits, searching through the night shadows playing in the darkness.

The breeze picked up momentum, whooshing, circling, and encasing the truck. It rocked, tilting like a seesaw, sliding them back and forth across the front seat.

Fred stiffened. His flesh pricked in over sized goose bump like welts. He swallowed rapidly, gulping air. His tongue flipped up to the roof of his mouth, cementing itself in place. He grabbed the door handle, wrenching it, flinging the truck door open as his blood thudded and hammered at his temples.

Tammy left his thoughts.

He jumped from the driver's seat, tumbling ass over teakettle, rolling through the damp grass. Something cold and hard shot out of the dark ramming his temple. His head jerked sideways. A hollow click sound followed. Fred froze. He knew that sound ... All too well.

"Freddie," Tammy's father said. He shook his head adamantly. He furrowed his brow, first studying the naked sprawled out boy on his front lawn, and then his naked sprawled out daughter on the seat of the truck. He pierced his lips drawing and curving them slowly into a sneer. He ground the barrel unsparingly against the boy's skull.

Fred's temple ringed the metal in bright red.

"Hope ... You ... Brought ... Your ... Sunday ... Best ... Boy!" he said.

'It stood in the shadows waiting, watching.'

'At Thirty-Four'

"What the hell you trying to tell me Tam?" Fred asked.

"I done told you," Tammy retorted.

"Then, d ... o ... n ... e ... tell ... me ... again," he said. He drawled his words mocking her on purpose.

She didn't notice. But she never seemed to notice stuff like that. Or much of anything else. She was not the brightest bulb in the pack by far. He rolled his eyes plopping his feet up on his desk.

"I told you! It's time the boys, done got their own room!"

"It's a two bedroom house. In case, you hadn't caught that. Just where we going get this other room from? ... Outer space?"

"I don't care! Just, get it!"

"Why?" Fred picked up an old girly magazine flipping through the tattered pages.

"I tells you, when you come home." She waved her index finger back and forth in a silent warning at one of the boys. He was jittering up and down in the corner, instead of standing to attention as she had told him. She eyed the other boy. He was standing like a statue in the opposite corner. Face forward, nose still pressed against the wallboard.

"Oh for Christ's sake," Fred said. He threw the magazine into the garbage can. It went over spewing its contents half way across the doublewide industrial trailer.

"Christ had nothing to do with this!" Tammy said.

"TAM," he shouted. He was tired of the crap. Looking after the kids and the house was her job. She needn't be running to him with every little thing all the time, like she always did. He couldn't care less. Hell, if truth were known, he'd never cared from the get go. Not keeping it in his pants, way back when, had been the biggest downfall of his entire life.

"Just spit it the hell out, will you? I have to pull a double. I won't be home till tomorrow and by then you'll have forgot, like always." He slid the window all the way open, sticking his arm out, swaying it back and forth in the dead summer air.

"Not this I won't," she said.

"For Fucks sake! I am going to hang up. I'm too busy for this shit Tam."

"All right. Have it your way. But ... you best be sitting on your ass! Cause if you ain't, you're going to come down hard on it."

"ENOUGH, ALL READY!" he yelled.

"I caught, Jimmy and Billy ... doing Val," she said.

"What?"

"I caught, Jimmy and Billy, doing Val," she repeated.

His mouth dropped. "You mean having sex?"

"Yep! The same way we do's it when you brings that pal of yours from the poker games over after you've had a dry run."

"You're kidding me?"

"Nope! Not kidding you! They had her spread wide and all opened up. One was taking her from the back the other from the ... the front," Tammy stumbled over her words.

Fred hunched his shoulder, hugging the receiver to his ear. He knuckled his hand resting his chin, smiling a king's smile. Those two peepholes he had drilled a might back had done wonders. His boys were learning well. Coming along mighty fine, they were. A chip off the old block. Using their ten-year-old sister was neither here nor there to him.

Something thumped, strained and hollow.

The trailer door suddenly slammed shut.

Fred threw down the telephone. He swivelled round in his chair popping his head out the window.

A breeze that wasn't there moments ago danced and spun along the gravel drive, halting outside the trailer as if it was calibrating its next move. It all at once whirled, circling, twirling, and kicking up dust and debris into his face.

He opened the door stepping out.

A wind whooshed past him, leaving miniature spinning dust storms in its wake. They sparkled and flickered in the sunshine as they whirled round and round like toy tops before veering off into the lawn, dissolving and settling down amongst the manicured green into oblivion.

He did up the top button of his shirt, setting his shoulders square, warding off the rising goose bumps under his skin.

Something thudded, hard and heavy like ... he could not place the sound. He scanned the lot. There was nothing. He was alone.

He walked around the trailer.

The wind shifted, following him, skipping and playing in and out of his shadow.

Something pounded.

He stopped.

He glanced behind him, suddenly unable to swallow. He suddenly found himself back where he had started with no recollection of running like a fifth grader full of sugar cookies in a twenty yard dash. He bent over putting his hands to his knees, chest heaving, drawing in long breaths.

The trailer door whipped forward, then back, slapping off and on the doorframe.

He watched, mesmerized.

The door creaked, then sprung open, groaned, then snapped back against the aluminum siding of the trailer. It pinged, echoing, bouncing the sound across the empty lot. It stayed stationary, then launched forward, halting mid-way, flapping to and fro as if it was made of paper, then thundered into the frame, slamming shut.

Wind rushed him, encircling, encasing him head to toe. He felt something, something unexplainable in words.

The wind gusted, died, gusted again. It filtered lower and lower. It churned by his boots skipping underneath the trailer where it took up residence, howling and growling like a penned up wild animal.

He ran for his car. Jumping in ... Jamming it in gear ... Gunning it across the lawn ... Drilling it for home.

'It stood in the grass waiting, watching.'

'At Thirty-Six'

Fred pulled back the bolt opening the chamber. He loaded the shell locking it down. He pulled the hammer back, waiting, controlling his inhaling and exhaling. He rested the barrel of the twenty-two on the side of the metal feeder.

The show doves swooped and circled enjoying their mid-day flight. They glided crossing paths. Exactly what Fred had been waiting for. He held his breath pulling the trigger, picking them both off in one single shot. They fell like stones to the barn floor, landing on top of one another. He sauntered over giving them a swift boot. They slapped against the wall breaking their necks, up ending, slumping over in slow motion like wet dishrags.

He roared in laughter.

He picked up the cage and threw it in the back of the old truck, parking it at the rear of the house, just in case.

He strolled into the kitchen fetching the telephone. "Hey Cindy," he said. "Put Tam on will yaw?" He drew his hand across his mouth wiping off his grin. Fred heard his name mentioned in between the high pitched, female bantering, shuffling, and clunking.

Tammy gave the wall clock a quick glance. She was not near ready. She held the receiver between her chin and shoulder, intent on threading her needle. "I not quite ready yet to comes home," she blurted. She pulled the thread through the underside of the material, knotting it. "I needs about another two hours before you fetch me. Oh Freddie," she said. "You got to have a look see at all the things we's made before we goes," she chattered away with all the details.

Fred looked up at the ceiling, whistling softly, rolling his eyes as she trailed on and on and on. He smiled. This was going to be much better than he had hoped for. Maybe a ten pointer? He started to laugh.

"We's got the backgrounds all done and painted up. They look real nice. The costumes are cut out and ready for sewing. Cindy even made matching little capes to the doves' headdresses from the left over materials. I can't wait for the fair tonight. I thinks we's got a good chance of winning ... Freddie? ... You there? ... You haven't done said a word ... Freddie?"

That was his cue. He sighed loudly into the receiver. "I don't know how to tell you this ... but ... I ... I," he stuttered on purpose hoping she'd clue in and cut him off.

"Tell me what?" she broke in.

He smiled.

"Freddie?"

"I got some bad news," he said. He kicked at a piece of straw on the kitchen floor, trying to stifle his laughter. This was better than pulling a twenty-dollar bet and winning sixty.

"What?" Tammy figured the Power Company had come and cut off the hydro again. She'd had three telephone calls in the last two weeks wanting a heap of money they didn't have.

Fred took a deep breath. He sucked in the sides of his cheeks, hollowing them pushing his lips out like a fish blowing air bubbles.

"Well? What Freddie?" she asked.

"I went out ... I went out to feed the doves, at noon, like you asked me and ... and ... and ... they were gone."

Tammy dropped her sewing. "Gone? What do you mean, gone?"

"Gone ... You know, gone ... The cage was open and they weren't anywhere to be found." He coughed on purpose.

"NO! ... DEAR GOD! ... NO!" Tammy screeched. "THIS CAN'T BE! ... NO! ... NO!" Tammy dropped her head, wailing and sobbing. "Ar ... are ...yo ... you sure?" she asked.

"Yep, I'm sure," he said. "I looked all over for them, for a couple three hours, I did." He cupped his hand over his mouth, holding his lips together. He didn't want to blow it now. He had never wanted to go to that damn fair in the first place. When his friend had dropped by an hour ago with an invite to a Jack and Jill, all night poker game, he had made his mind up. He was not going to that fair, and neither was she. The twenty-two made crossing the T's and dotting the I's real nice and easy.

"Why don't you stay at Cindy's for the night," he suggested. "It'll do you the world of good to be with another woman for a spell." He chuckled to himself. Being with another woman for a spell always did him the world of good.

"I ... I guess. I could," Tammy said, through tears.

"I'll drop by in the morning and get you," Fred smirked. He punched his free hand up into the air, mouthing a triumphant yes at the ceiling.

He went upstairs showered, changed, and fetched his new cowboy hat from in back of the closet where he had it hidden. It was by far better than a telephone payment. He went back into the kitchen grabbing his keys from the table.

Tammy never went in the barn. If perchance she did, before nature took its course, he knew nothing from nothing. He would ditch the cage somewhere on the way to the game. There were too many feathers with hide attached stuck in the wires. He'd had one hell of a time getting them out of that damn thing. He dumped out the flour jar pilfering through the grocery money and shoving over three-quarters in his pocket.

The kitchen light hummed and flickered, blinking once then went out.

He flipped the wall switch. It clicked dully. He thumped it with his fist.

The switch let out a snapping, popping sound, then silenced.

Something hissed outside like a tire suddenly going flat.

He glanced out through the open window.

The overhead light exploded, showering the kitchen with thin jagged spears of glass.

He ruffled his hands through his hair, dislodging glass, slicing the flesh of his fingers wide open. They instantly erupted spouting and dripping like a tap with the washer gone. He whirled round in circles spraying the worn, spent linoleum flooring. It gleamed as if new, showing off its bright red Polka-dot splashes.

A wind churned down the drive, making a swift left. It howled and battered the upper windowpanes, rattling and shaking them as it dove through the screen into the kitchen.

Fred braked as if he had been lassoed and hogtied. He stared, mouth open. His breaths drawing hard and long.

The kitchen door whacked open. It thundered, wailing into the wall, poking the doorknob clear through the plaster.

He bolted. His feet sliding and gilding through the glass and blood like an ice skater with training wheels. He swayed sideways, twisting up like a pretzel. He went down. Cold tremors shot along his spine, stabbing and prickling him like he was under attack by an army of angry fire ants. His breath puffed out onto the floor, frosting the linoleum. He clambered on his hands and knees out through the door onto the side porch.

He stole a look back over his shoulder into the kitchen. It was way past dark. It was black. Like something had blotted out every trace of daylight. He hunkered down, turning, his hands cold, his knees trembling, slithering backwards, pushing himself with his hands. He misjudged the distance, passing too far over the first stair edge. His weight teetered back and forth. He lost his balance, flipping over doing a backward somersault. He tumbled like a rag doll down the wooden steps, doing a face plant into the grass.

Elongated willowy shadows crept after him. Following, mimicking his every movement, crawling forward slow and steady, like a black and white art film shot in slow motion for effect. They slunk and wiggled, snaking down and over each stair. They wound and coiled through the grass and up onto his hands, rubbing together, pooling into dark masses that seemed to settle down into his flesh. He pulled his hands underneath him, pressing them flat.

A wind bounced and whizzed across the lawn. He lifted his head. His nostrils twitched like a mouse finding a discarded piece of fresh cheese ... He could smell something. Something pungent yet sweet, like rusted tin layered with salt pork. He squinted, scanning the grass, suddenly halting; his eyeballs bursting from their sockets.

Underneath the apple tree laid two feathered gray lumps. Their wings lifted, rising and falling in the wind. It was as if death was giving him an up close and personal 'hello, howdy do'. Gone but not forgotten can translate to many, many things.

Fred's tongue sucked into the back of his mouth in a long drawn out silent scream.

He sprung to his feet taking off in a dead run down the drive like the devil himself was after him.

'It stood by the porch waiting, watching.'

'At Forty-Eight'

"What we going do Freddie?" Tammy's forehead crinkled like tissue paper, creasing, folding its self into worry lines.

"Everything will work out. It always does," Fred said.

"But ... It's well passed a year now, since you done had work. We got no power, no telephone, no much of nothing. And we got another one of those legal like letters, from the bank about not paying's on our house." Tammy dropped her head sniffing, wiping at her eyes.

"Don't you worry your pretty little head none. You hear?" Fred put his arm around her, drawing her against him.

She snuggled up close, trying to form a smile, giving his cheek a kiss. "You's been saying that to me all my life Freddie. I 'member the first time you ever done said it to me. Do you?"

Fred shook his head back and forth, but he knew. It was one of the starters of a night he would never forget. How could he? How could he forget having a loaded shotgun rammed into his head. Or getting hitched the very next day, with the same loaded shotgun as one of the ushers. Right up close and personal like.

Tammy grabbed onto his hand, locking her fingers through his. "It was the nights my daddy caught us in the truck. Member?" she laughed. "Who would have thought we were blessed with a miracle that night."

"Blessed with a miracle?" he asked.

"Yeps ... Jimmy," she said.

"If you say so," he replied. He would have used much different words to describe it, if it were up to him, like cursed or damned to name but a few.

Red lights glinted on and off the passenger side mirror. "What's flashing backs there?" Tammy asked. She turned peering out the back window.

"Ambulance or something, I think," Fred said. It was coming up on them fast. He slowed and pulled over to the shoulder.

A fire truck whistled by.

"Hope they's not going, to our house," Tammy said.

Fred shot Tammy a quizzical look. "Why in hell would you say something like that?"

"Cause ... just cause," she said.

He opened his mouth, closed it, and then opened it again. He shook his head. "Cause ... just cause?" he repeated.

"Yeah ... Cause just cause," she retorted. She grew her eyebrows into one solid line, giving him a sideways glance.

"And you mean what exactly?"

"I told you's!" she said. She knew he had understood what she'd meant. It was as he called it, self-explanatory.

"I know. Cause just cause," he quipped.

"You went down into the cellar before we's left," she whispered.

"Yeah, so?" He had forgotten his wallet on the saw table.

"What did you's do down there," she asked.

He gave her a look.

Tammy pressed on. "What's did you do?"

"I got my wallet," he said. He turned facing her.

"Nothing else, Freddie?" She did not gaze away like she usually did.

"If you fucking must know, Miss Private Eye. I turned off the stupid oil lamp you keep on down there. There's no need for it. It burns up too much oil, leaving it on like you do." He suddenly kicked himself for using the burn word.

"You turned off my lamp?"

"Yep."

Another fire truck tore up behind them, whipping past so rapidly it resembled more so a long red streamer than anything else. They threw open their doors, jumping from the car as if both their movements were choreographed. They bounded towards the front of the car. All four eyeballs straining and pulling, shooting from their sockets, following the tail lights of the truck as it disappeared from sight.

A third fire engine whizzed by. Tammy walked over to Fred, placing her hand on his arm. "You's wouldn't never lie to me? Would you?"

"Nope," he replied. He wasn't lying.

He had turned the lamp off just like he said. Turned it off, turned it down, just words really. It was all the same. If the flame was too low to see, it was technically off to the naked eye. He had turned it so he could dump some of the oil out onto the papers. He'd decided it was too full. And after deciding that, he had moved it over to the wooden table

24

where all the papers were. The old dried out table just below the drapes. Before shall we say, accidentally bumping the knob with his elbow, turning it back full on. It was terrible how incredibly hot that thing got; scorching, incredibly hot.

A fire rescue truck screamed by.

Tammy turned, searching Fred's eyes.

He smiled, wearing his best mask. "Shall we go darling?" He patted her bum giving her a wink.

"Yeah ... I put the rabbit in the stew pot out back in the fire pit before we's went to town. It should be about done cooked now."

She'd had the laundry out on the line. The line was rope and stretched from the far side of the house to the pit and back. The clothes were already bone dry when they left.

"I have no doubt," he said. He burst out laughing, getting back in the car and pulling onto the road.

One second the air was as dead as doornails and one could see for miles and miles. The next, the air was whipping, whirling and churning. Rattling to beat all hell like an old washer gone out of sync, throwing dust devils up and down the road as far as the eye could see.

Fred slammed on the brakes, blinded.

"What the fucking hell?" he said. He rolled down his window sticking his head out. A dash of misplaced air, cold and frosty darted in, working at his legs, turning them numb and clunky like oversized stale marshmallows. He rolled up his window quicker than lightening could hit a man holding up a steel umbrella in the throes of a summer thunderstorm. He stared wide-eyed into the dust cloud.

It whirled like a vortex, blending the dirt and matter vacuumed from below and churning the air into a smooth as silk mocha latte.

The car swayed, rocking side to side.

Fred's throat grew thick grapes, which jiggled side to side, blocking his airway. He choked and gasped thudding his fist into his neck. Something warm drizzled down his throat.

He turned to Tammy. She was just sitting there in the passenger seat, browsing out the front window like all this had happened a million and one times. This was now a million and two. She was smoking away on her cigarette, drawing long and hard, puffing it out into little doughnuts that floated and hovered just above her head. She seemed oddly oblivious to all around her. Even him. Like he wasn't there. Or she wasn't there. Or ... he didn't know.

He caught something out the corner of his eye. Something dark. Something floating. He shot himself forward, leaning into the windshield. He extended his eyes straining them to the ninth, staring, searching, and scanning for the something. He knuckled the dash. His eyes watered. He was sure there had been ... something. He tucked his lips into his mouth. Seconds drawled like hours. And then there it was again. The something ... Dark, shadow like, floating.

"TAM! ... TAM! ... DID YOU SEE THAT?" he screamed. He shot his arm out pointing at the windshield, knocking the heater off her cigarette. It fell down into the foot well, slipping in between the pages of the newspaper.

Tammy sat as she was, sucking in and out smoke.

Fred reached over, shaking her by the shoulder.

She tussled back and forth like the dead.

"T ... A ... M ... M ... Y!" he yelled.

She didn't move.

Fred felt like he was caught in the middle of a sideways illusion, where nothing was as it should be. The wind whipping, shaking and biting at the car didn't seem ... Tammy sitting beside him puffing smoke didn't seem ... There was that missing word again. There was just something.

He jiggled himself up and down. He bounced in the seat. He pounded the dash. He stomped his feet. He had to ... to get out of whatever this was.

Flames sparked, hissed, and sprouted, growing in the foot well between Tammy's feet. She didn't move. She did not even look down. She just sucked in and blew out, sucked and blew, over and over like a dime store elephant ride jammed with too many quarters.

His eyes slung shot around the car. He could smell the burning rubber bottoms of her runners. Blue flames shot up, twisting in and out of the foot well. He tugged and pulled at her. She was like a leaden weight. The flames grew, jumping and sparking on and off her knees. He twisted his hands into her sweater trying to jerk her from the seat. She fell over rolling and sticking to the side of the seat like an oversized slimy dew worm.

"TAMMY! ... I'M GOING TO GET US OUT!" he screamed.

He flung himself against the driver's door, struggling and fist fighting with a handle that didn't want to open. He kicked at it. It held fast. He rolled down the window, propelling himself out, elbows flapping like a bird with clipped wings. He spun in the wind, coming down hard.

He humped his back, scampering in large circles on his hands and knees.

The dust devils howled and whistled.

He couldn't see anything. The car seemed gone. His hands slipped into cool strands. 'Grass,' he thought. He about faced, holding his one arm off the ground like an alien probe. He hopped, shuffling and bouncing forward like an animal with three legs. He swung his arm blindly back and forth in front. The dust devil tracked along with him, swirling, encasing him within its thick pea like soup.

Stones and twigs pelted off his forehead and cheekbones. Stinging, grinding and cutting through his skin. He brought himself to his feet stretching out his arms, swaying them side-to-side.

He banged into something hard. Something hard, hot, and smooth. He surged forward, throwing himself at the car. He groped, running his fingertips back and forth, up and down, like spiders crossing a hot plate. He found the door, then the window. It was back up. Back up and shut tighter than hell. He searched for the door handle. It was gone. He backed up booting the door, time, and time again. It made a hollow pinging sound, denting in.

He stepped back. "TAMMY! ... TAMMY!" he screamed. "WHERE ARE YOU?" 'She has to have gotten out,' he thought. She had to have. Just like, he had.

He leaned into the car, wiping at the brown shit coloured dust, clearing a swatch of glass. He pressed his face to the window. Tammy's face pressed back. His mouth dropped wide and full, drying on the spot, turning his tongue into dried up old road kill.

Horror furrowed across his forehead. He stepped back. The interior was totally engulfed. Fire blazed from everywhere.

He froze.

Tammy smiled. She curled her index finger in and out, motioning him to come.

He shook his head, snapping his eyes shut re-opening them.

She drew back from the glass patting the seat beside her.

He slapped his palms into his temples. His eyeballs felt as if they were spinning in circles. He watched in terror as her hair caught fire, fizzing, twisting as the flames shot upwards. She just sat there smiling, the sweetest of toothy smiles. Her face caught fire. The skin steamed and curled, blackening like old shoe leather. Still she smiled.

He hit the car, thrusting his weight into it. He bounced back like a kid's slingshot. He rammed it again. Time, and time again he pelted it. The edges of his clothes blackened and singed.

The car was an inferno. He bent pressing close to the still intact window. Tammy was sitting facing him. Her clothes were gone. Her skin was gone. Her eyes were gone.

Smoke curled off the top of her head and out her ears, nose, and mouth.

He started to scream and scream and scream. Screaming, even as he stiffened and fell backwards, hitting the ground hard and heavy, and stirring up his own personal dust devil. It swirled and danced in and around, and on top of him as he left this world.

Something dug into his rib. He groaned. Something rammed him again, hard. He rolled onto his side bringing his knees to his chest, curling into a ball.

"FRED! ... FRED! ... FREDDIE!" Tammy screeched. "YOU'S DEAD OR SOMETHIN?" She knelt down beside him shaking the living daylights out of him.

His eyes shot open. They stung and itched. He rubbed at them. His arm jerked up and down. He squinted starry eyed at the figure leaning over him. It was backlit by the sun. He couldn't make out the face.

Tammy shook her head.

Fred pushed himself to a sit. His eyes closed in and focused.

"Tam," he beamed. "You're okay!"

"Why ... wouldn't ... I's ... be?" she asked. Her pained tone went by unnoticed.

He chucked his head back and forth. To her, to the car, back to her, back to the car. The car was covered end to end in thick brown sludge. It looked old and used up like it had seen better days. He opened and closed his mouth in rapid silent pops. He pointed at the car.

She took a step back, looking down at the ground, shaking her head again.

He raised both his arms, pointing with his index fingers first to her, then to the car, then back to her, mouthing silent words.

She looked at him as if he had downed a whole bottle of crazy pills.

"You ... you ... yo ...u ... you were in th ... the ...car ... an ... and it ... it ... it was ... was ... on ... fi ... fire."

She cut him off. "Don't needs to tell me's about it. I was there. I gots the lumps to prove it," she said.

"No ... n ... o ... no ... it," he stumbled. He clicked his tongue against the roof of his mouth. He did not seem to be able to spit the words out into the open. He tried again and failed. "You ... sur ...sure ... yo ... you're ...o ... okay?" he asked gulping and sputtering.

"I'm the one that's should be asking you's that! You's the one that plum drove off the road, into the ditch. Hooting and hollering' nonsense' 'bout seeing stuff in the winds like some crazed madman. Screaming at the top of your lungs like a girl as we's went down and overs the bank, into the swamp." She leaned over to him giving him a stiff poke in the chest. "We woulds still be stuck down in there's, if that farmer lady hadn't come by awhile backs and pulled the car."

Tammy smacked her lips together giving him another one of those looks. The one that translated into, you are a crazed idiotic lunatic. She turned, walked back to the car, and got in. She lit a cigarette, puffing away on it, staring out the windshield.

Fred rose to his feet. Went back down, and then rose slow and easy using his hands. His knees vibrated and shook, wobbling his weight back and forth, as he stumbled towards the car.

He opened the door and slid into the driver's seat. He cupped his hand over his nose and mouth. He could smell something. Something putrid, something sickening sweet with a sulfur over-lay. Something that ... he stopped thinking.

He rolled the window down. The crank fell off. It clanged hitting bare metal. The rubber foot mat was gone. The carpeting was gone.

He glanced over at Tammy. His mouth jerked sideways then hung like an old swing, twitching like a dog with tics.

Her shoulder length honey brown hair was all of an inch, black, crispy and frizzled. Smoke was whisking out from her eyes, ears, nose, and mouth.

"Shall we's go home darling," she whispered. She put her hand on top of his. It was cold and hard and repulsive in a way indefinable to thoughts. She clenched her fingers around his. The skin slid off, plopping and splatting into the console. She scooped it up, smacking it down into place. She slowly turned his way, and then smiled.

His open mouth rounded, wide and full, screaming screams he did not comprehend as his own. He slammed his body into the side door. It opened this time. He tumbled from the car, paddling himself along the ground using hands and feet that seemed more like dead flopping fish than anything else. He was still screaming, at least until he backed himself smack dab into that big rock, smashing his head off it.

A bright red 'SUV' with the words 'Fire inspector'" printed in bright yellow along the sides and back, tore past.

Tammy crawled across the car, planting herself into the driver's seat. She had never driven before. Couldn't be that hard.

She started it, turned the wipers on, clearing the brown silt from the windshield. She put it in gear, pulling out onto the highway. She turned off at the baseline side road, following the sound of the siren. She lit another cigarette.

'It stood off to the side waiting, watching.'

'At Fifty'

"Happy birthday fast Freddie," Sam said.

"Thanks."

Sam gave Fred a knuckled shot in the arm, grinding it in. "Say? ... Did you know there's an eclipse today?"

"Really? Didn't know. What time she be?"

"About four p.m., they say." Sam plopped his oversize body into one of the many swivel chairs. "So how many babes you got lined up to celebrate your fiftieth? One for each year?"

"I wish ... I wish." Fred gave him an 'awe shucks' grin snapping his fingers.

Sam leaned into him, lowering his voice to a bare bones whisper. "Humour me, Freddie. How many belt notches did you get this week?"

Fred held up four fingers and two thumbs.

"Not too shabby old man. Not too shabby at all." Sam plucked a doughnut from the box, settling down into his seat. "Hear from Tammy?" he asked.

"That bitch hasn't called once since she ran off," Fred said. He smiled. He had been telling the same story so long he'd come to almost believe in it. Convincing everyone she had left for another man had been the greatest thing since sliced bread for him. It had gotten him invites to all sorts of things. Even brought in money when he had added the bullshit about her cleaning out the bank accounts they never had. It wouldn't have been near the same if he'd said, 'she' ran off cause I seem to have '"Spells"' every now and then.' He laughed aloud.

Sam licked the jelly off his fingers, smacking his lips. "How long's it been now?" He reached for another doughnut.

"Just about two years."

"Wasn't he a might older than her?"

"A might? Try thirty years on for size!"

"Jesus!" Sam shook his head back and forth. "He must have something. Money? A big fucking dick?"

"None of the above, so the kids have said." Fred checked out the clock, and then looked out the window.

"How old are the kids now?"

"Thirties and late twenties."

"Shit, time does fly huh Freddie?"

"Yeppers." Fred sauntered over to the hut door. "Come walk with me. I got to make my rounds."

"I get first dibs on any good stuff." Sam grabbed the box of doughnuts, following Fred out into the lot.

"Hey it's my birthday, I get the good stuff," Fred retorted.

They trailed across the empty lot, crossing the grass and entering the outdoor luncheon area.

"You know ... It never ceases to amaze me how many of the workers bring and dump off their own garbage. What do they think? We don't notice?" Fred hauled the bags out from the waste bin.

"It costs money now, if you have more than two bags Freddie," Sam said.

"Yeah ... well ... maybe so. But I'm a security officer not a damn waste recycler." He dragged the bags over to the industrial waste bin throwing them up and in.

A soft mew curled out, echoing and resounding, playing Ping-Pong back and forth into the metal sides of the bin.

Sam climbed up the side rails. "Hey there's a half grown cat in there. I'll get the ladder."

"The fuck you will," Fred laughed. He clambered up the other side, hurdling in two more bags, hitting it on purpose.

The cat screamed in distress.

"Watch this," Fred said.

He unlocked the side door of the container picking up a handful of broken bricks, winging them one by one at the cat. He connected twice. The first split the top of its head wide open. The second smashed in its face from the nose over, knocking its right eye loose from the socket.

The cat wailed in agony. Its hair darkened and clumped, as blood bubbled through and over its tiny body.

Sam swayed back and forth mortified. He clung onto the topside of the bin with one draped arm, the other outstretched pointing, as if frozen in time and space. His open mouth hiccupped in long drawls of air then contorted into a horrid grimace. His popping eyeballs whipped back and forth as if seized by some force that was hell bent on making him look until vomit rose in his throat.

Fred jumped from the bin, opening, bending the door backward, stepping just off to the side.

The cat circled, hunched, making a mad dash for the doorway.

Fred lifted his right foot off the ground as if cued, hauling off and booting it dead center between its front legs.

Its terror filled wails seared and burnt the air leaving a see-through vapor arch of jet stream as it spun round and round like a top. It rammed into the metal wall staggering back and forth like a disoriented drunk, wetting itself, collapsing in a tangled heap.

Fred stood still and silent, like that cliché, 'Silent as a church mouse,' had his name plastered all over it.

The cat slowly rose, limping and humping itself in the direction of the door.

Fred waited, watching, tensing like an experienced hunter scoping out its prey from a cull beneath the underbrush.

The cat drew nearer.

Fred white knuckled the doorframe. Eyes glued to target. As the cat crossed the half way mark on the door stopper, he jerked hard and fast, winging the door shut, severing its tail in half.

The cat shrieked and screamed in short ranting bursts, shrilling, pitching and changing tones like something not of this world. It dragged itself up under a board, leaving bright red trails in its wake.

Sam was still topside, seemingly welded in place, as if he'd become part and parcel of the bin. Fresh doughnut vomit dribbled down the metal interior decorating it.

Fred picked up the cats tail, examined it, and then tossed it up and in. It made a soft thunk as it landed. It rolled like a sausage coming to rest against one of the garbage bags.

"Yo ... you ... a ... a ... bett ... betting ma ... man Sam?" Fred had started to laugh so uncontrollably he was having trouble spitting out his words. He slapped his thighs trying to get hold of himself.

Sam did not reply.

Fred dug into his pocket pulling out a five. "Closest to picking the time of death wins the pot. What do you say?"

Sam pulled his arm from the rung, descending with legs that did not seem to bend at the knees, and feet that wobbled and slipped right clear of their shoes.

"You got a fiver?" Fred shielded his eyes looking up at him. He was starting to wonder if the old coot was going to make it. He was wavering back and forth, slipping and sliding like some used up old rummy. "We on?"

Sam's legs gave way. He bounced, free forming it from the ladder, hitting the ground hard, landing in a twisted up pretzel like heap.

Fred bent into him offering his hand.

Sam swiped it away. He rolled up onto his side, gathering his knees up under his chest. He turned slapping his palms on the ground, heaving up his body butt first.

"Hey, we good?" Fred fanned the five-dollar bill in front of Sam's face.

Sam stared Fred in the eye not masking his loath and disgust. He shook his head.

"What are you some pussy-ass hose? It's only a fucking good for nothing cat. They're a dime a dozen."

Sam didn't say a word. He got in his car and left.

Fred stood with his hands on his hips cussing at the old man under his breath. The car faded into oblivion. "Ah who needs you anyway, you fucking used up goof." He turned and walked back to the hut.

The cat screamed and cried for the better part of two hours. The tortured pleas waning and muffling as the hot sun beat relentlessly into the metal.

Fred did not go back to the bin. He didn't do another round. He closed the window, turned up the fans, and watched the TV, counting down the hours until quitting time. At quarter of four, he punched out his time card. He'd discovered soon after starting this job, if he waited until exactly three-forty-five p.m. on the nose, held his time card in the machine sideways and folded over the corner, it would punch six p.m. He fetched his belongings, bolting and locking the hut door.

He opened the driver's door, throwing his things in the back seat. He put one foot in, paused, cocking his head in the direction of the bin straining, listening, grinning, when he heard nothing. He drove through the front gate and pulled the heavy chain through the rungs, snapping the lock shut.

The hut door whipped open. Its hinges squealing as it roared backwards, catching and banging in a thunderous boom as it struck and fitted to the underside of the window.

Fred's mouth dropped like a fly swatted from the air by a brand name swatter. His bottom jaw hung limp and loose like it was made of wet putty. He stared at the hut, not believing what he was seeing. He felt like his tele-prompter was from the wrong set. His upper body swayed back and forth stiffly like his limbs had been splinted and his feet had cemented to the pavement.

He was sure he had locked the hut. Dead sure. He glared at the open door. It seemed to be grinning, drawing on him, as if daring him to take a step towards it. Its dark, open, rectangle shaped mouth seemed to stretch and widen, taking on the eerie familiarity of the something's in sci-fi flicks. The something's that always skulk just out of sight, lunging when your back was turned, swallowing you whole. Keeping you just barely alive, in a place where there was no heaven or hell. The place where you would' pray for death, not caring which end you went to, as long as you went.

The sweat of his cold palms seemed to have turned to slime, oozing and growing through and around the keys and ring. The sweat of his cold palms seemed to have turned to slime, oozing and growing through and around the keys and ring. Without warning, they slid from his grasp hooking onto the fingertips of his right hand. He pawed at them with the other, peeling away layer after layer of glop. The flesh of both abruptly numbed as he fumbled and groped, making him feel like his hands had been swapped out for a discontinued plastic line of cheap mannequin's. The keys all at once dropped, spattering out grunge as they hit the drive, ring down, keys arrow straight and vertical as if staking a claim.

A wind erupted from a crack in the black top, whirling like a mini ant size tornado, tracking like a hound towards the key ring. It circled them gluing on a topcoat of dust, lifting, flipping, and tumbling them into the long grass of the ditch and beyond. It hissed whirling, collapsing into itself, and then disappeared like it had never been there at all.

He froze. His breath puffing in short bursts matching the interior rhythm of his chest. His eyeballs, as if by their own accord, seemed to magnify, zoning in and following the key-napper's trail. They jolted back and forth from his hands, to the gravel drive, to the ditch and back, like a recording needle stuck forever in a divot.

He did not look for the keys. Terror had set in. The same nameless terror that always set in, the one that simmered on the back burner his entire life, the one without a face or name. The one he had paid therapists thousands of dollars to whisper in his ear, that it was not real. But it was. He knew it was.

He did not ask any questions' either. Like how a locked door could open. Or, how a wind could rise from a crack and turn into a tornado, small but still a tornado, and tumble a key ring laden with twenty some metal keys as if it was a feather.

He arched his body sideways, ripping and tearing it free. He jumped into his car, snapping the door closed on his left shoe, catching it, sending it hurdling into the air as he raced from the lot. The shoe shot forward coming down like a cannon ball, smacking into and shattering the car windshield turning it into a massive glittery spider web.

Fred stomped the brake, fish tailing the car. He blindly groped for the shifter. His hand knocked something into his lap; Something soft ... something warm and almost gooey. He cupped it, lifting it. The one end stuck as if it had clamped onto his hand. A scream rose, then choked off in his throat. He opened and shut his mouth in mocking silent screams that dried his mouth and gorged his tongue full of blood.

He flung the drivers' door open, his feet running before they even hit the ground. He bounded in a zigzag motion down the open roadway.

The cat's' severed tail broke free from his skin. It bounced and rolled merrily down the painted centerline dogging his every movement.

'Four p.m.'

The total eclipse of the sun commenced right at the dot of four as predicted, reaffirming that age-old pact of totality, 'The total eclipse ... the time when God himself looks the other way.'

The sky moved, working against itself. Swirling the blue to gray, dulling, casting midnight hazes, blackening.

The shadow stood on guard, backlit and illuminated. The dark figure bent and dug inside the enormous bin. The sky pitched into obscurity, sucking them into the blackness, obliterating them both from sight. The figure seized and pulled the half-grown cat, freeing it out from under humankind's filth.

The figure clutched the barely breathing cat to its chest, drawing and pressing it close. "There ... there my little one. I have come to take you home," the figure whispered.

The cat whimpered.

"Shhh ... Shhh now." The figure lovingly stroked the top of the half-grown cat's head. "Remember ... Promises made ... Promises kept."

The cat snuggled up close. It turned its tiny head upwards gazing upon the figure's' face. It mewed, single, compliant, softly.

The figure cradled the cat, rocking it gently.

The cat purred.

The figure smiled.

The cat relaxed, fixating and drawing into the radiating warmth within the figure's' eyes. Its limbs went limp and splayed. Its breath laboured, shallowed, and then stilled.

The figure bowed, dropping to one knee, bending its head to its chest. Silent tears trickled from its cheeks. The shadow followed suit, grieving by the figure's' side. They spoke as one, reciting, rendering the prayers for a soul lost in the shadows to emerge into the light. The figure drew the endless knot upon the half-grown cat's forehead with the tip of its index finger. The eternity symbol sparked and danced, glowing in radiant hues of blue not known by man. It flared, and then dulled, leaving a blue hazed smoke filled outline that drew close, threw thin wisps, and dissipated.

The figure rose from the bin clutching the stilled cat and walked across the grass into the weaning darkness of shadows that came alive nodding as it passed. The figure glided smooth and easy, not disturbing the ground beneath it, disappearing in between the last few remaining remnants of night as the sky struggled above, rolling in navy waves that washed out into gray.

Its shadow followed close behind. But, not too close. It had made that mistake ... once.

"My Lord!" The figure held the body of the cat out in its arms. "I speak whilst he not watches. Is it time?" the figure asked.

The figure stood motionless, in the shadows, waiting, watching.

The skies whirled the gray to baby blue, sparkling, and relighting the world.

It stood waiting for the sign.

Twilight broke early, showing off a moon that grew a face and spoke. Then clouded and bloodied.

The figure smiled, pleased. It turned and walked stealthily through the forest in the night breeze to the burrowed place. It swaddled the cat in a pink blanket placing it gently within an oak box. It moved across the marsh to a stand of thickets. It followed the trail through to the meadow, crossing it and coming out into a clearing. It walked along the stone pathway up and over the hill.

The figure's shadow followed obediently, counting out the three hundred paces as it had done many times before, pausing as the figure opened and went through the gates of the massive burial grounds.

The figure walked in steadfast silence down the white picket fenced rows that separated the plots, stopping, opening the gate with the marker 'Kadigan'.

If I were dead, would I be gone?

Just like falling asleep?

I wonder...

'Monday'

"Hey Freddie. You seen that new temp the boss hired?" Kenny's mouth dropped. He stared wide-eyed at Fred.

"What?" Fred did not meet his eyes. He gave himself a quick glance in the mirror tugging his hat forward, covering up the new two-inch wide band of silver-gray that ran through his hair.

"You okay?"

Fred squirmed, pressing his back into the chair. He forced a smile. "Yeah, why?" He cleared his throat on purpose.

"Man, you look rough." Kenny punched his timecard clocking in. "Get it on a little too much on the weekend?" He picked up the morning paper.

"No ... nothing like that. I ... I ..."

Kenny cut him off. "Fuck, Freddie you look like you haven't slept in days."

"I hav ... havn ... I haven't," Fred stuttered.

Kenny rubbed his chin. Fred was unshaven and still in the same clothes he had worn at the last shift change. He smelled worse than a burst sewer pipe full of shit. His uniform was crumpled and torn and stained with helter-skelter blotches of ... red-brownish ... something's. If he did not know better, he would have sworn on a stack of bibles, the ones on his upper legs were dried blood. "You sure, you're all right?" he asked again.

"I ... I'm ... yeah ... I'm okay," Fred said. He wasn't, not by a long shot. A shudder struck his spine. He quaked side-to-side closing his eyes, the haunting events of Saturday surfacing and smacking him hard in the face.

Kenny pulled a flask of whiskey from his jacket pocket. He threw it down on the desk in front of Fred.

Fred downed it in four gulps.

"Feel better?"

Fred grinned and nodded. He shoved Kenny's management proposal across the desk. His name was scrawled under Kenny's.

"You've come around to my way of thinking huh?" Kenny asked.

"Yeah," Fred lied. He had his own reasons for not wanting to be alone every other Saturday. "They put two of us on together all week. So why not on Saturdays too? And like you said, for safety sake, there should be two."

Fred could feel the whiskey setting in, sending his nightmarish terrors back to where they lived when not thought about. He crossed his legs and stretched. His thoughts jumped, piggybacking Kenny's first sentence. He footed his chair over to Kenny's desk. "What was that you were saying when you came in?"

"Oh yeah, that new temp the boss started today." Kenny rubbed his hands together. "If I wasn't married! Well I tell ya!"

"That good huh?"

"Better!"

"And," Fred paused laughing. "Just how have you come by this important tid-bit of information? Huh? Tell me that will you?"

"I stopped by the main plant this morning on my way in. I had a screw up on my pay. I stuck my head in the office on my way out, and there she was. A pure vision. Want to know more?" Kenny clasped his hands together leaning into Fred like a kid just bursting to tell a secret.

"Tell. Do tell."

"It'll cost you a coffee and doughnut," he grinned.

"Both?" Fred adjusted his cowboy hat.

"Yep! Both!"

Fred searched his pockets pulling out the leftover five from Saturday. Something clawed out of his thoughts, hurdling itself into the air, biting down hard into his neck. He turned up his shirt collar pressing it tightly to his skin. He hunched his shoulders, knocking it loose.

"Well?" Kenny asked.

The muscles in his neck twitched. Fred looked back behind them. He bent and glanced under the hut. "Got another flask with you?"

Kenny poked it into Fred's hand.

Fred unscrewed the top, downing it. He wiped his mouth on his shirtsleeve.

Repeating himself seemed to be the lesser of two evils. Fred was acting weirder than a fruit cup full of jelly. He just did not want to go there. "Well?" Kenny asked again.

"Okay! Okay!" Fred draped his arm over Kenny's' shoulders. They sauntered across the lot towards the coffee truck.

"She's gorgeous," Kenny laughed. It was a fake laugh but still a laugh. He examined Fred. Those two flasks held a twelve ouncer.

"That's it?"

Kenny grinned; Fred's speech was slurring at the edges.

"Come on spill the beans," Fred insisted. He fanned the five in front of Kenny's face. The whiskey plus the empty stomach was working wonders. No thoughts, no feelings, no nothing.

"A coffee and two doughnuts now?"

"Okay." Fred scooped a small fist full of loose change from his pocket.

"She's a brunette. Just like you like them."

"That's it?" Fred slapped Kenny on the back spilling his coffee. "Come on! You got me all sparked up!" Fred grabbed his crotch feverishly whacking it up and down at Kenny.

"You ... want ... it ... all ... huh?" Kenny drew out his words on purpose, taunting his friend. Fred was suddenly like his old self.

"Yep! Spill your guts!"

"Late thirties, early forties maybe. Did I say ... knock out dead gorgeous?"

Fred's eyes were glazed and wide like a kid's when pressed up against the store plate glass window hoping and dreaming of owning that vintage baseball cap. The one on the stand, front and center. He nodded at Kenny, hanging off every word.

"Slim, but not too slim. Beautiful deep blue eyes. Sexy smile. No ring on her finger. But there's just one thing."

Kenny drew out his lips, narrowing his eyebrows, starring directly at Fred.

Fred grabbed Kenny by the arm. "What? What is it?"

"She's classy. Probably out of your league, Freddie boy!"

"We'll see. We will see."

'Later'

"Mack Industries, Gord speaking," the boss said.

"Hey Gordie! How you keeping?"

"Good. Good Fred. What can I do for you?"

"I was wondering if I could stop by after last break and pick up a case of safety glasses. Ours is low."

"I can drop them off in the morning. I'll be by that way."

Fred cursed under his breath. He paused, drumming his fingernails into his desktop. He had to think fast. "I have a whole list of stuff we need out here," he blurted. "I wanted to pick it all up at the same time."

Gord burst out laughing. "Come by tomorrow morning at ten Fred. She's left for the day." Gord shook his head. That guy never once ceased to amaze him, when it came to scenting out a woman. He swore he was half hound dog.

Fred grinned, a Cheshire' cat grin, holding and relishing in it. He said his good-byes, picked up the full case of safety glasses, walked over to the trash bin, and heaved them in.

'Tuesday Ten a.m.'

"How do you take your coffee?" Fred asked.

Lilith turned. "I don't," she replied.

Fred raised his eyebrows. "You don't?" he questioned.

"No ... I don't drink coffee," Lilith said.

He smiled in amusement. He leaned back against the wall, across from the front counter giving her an obvious once over. She was even better than Kenny had said. He was getting stiff just looking at her.

"By the way," Fred titled up his chin, shoving himself from the wall, extending his arm over top of the counter. "I'm Fred. Fred Kadigan, from the north plant."

She ignored his gesture. "I know who you are," she replied.

"You do?"

She smiled. "Yes I do," she reaffirmed.

He stepped forward, splaying his legs sideways, bending in half, putting his elbows on the counter. He rested his chin in his palms. "And how might that be?" He gave her a sultry wink.

"I've been told all about you," she laughed. "Or I should say warned." She reached over freeing his left hand from under his chin, offering up a warm gentle handshake. "I am Lilith," she said softly.

"Lilith? Really?" He continued on, not skipping a beat. "Isn't that a name right out of the bible?"

"Yes," she said. "Isaiah thirty-four- fourteen and Lilith shall repose thee."

"You know the bible?" he shrieked with a child's delight.

"Some," she replied.

Fred clasped his hands together, beaming ear to ear. "Well. Well if that doesn't beat all to hell!"

"I beg your pardon?"

"Oh nothing. It's just I am quite religious."

"I know that too," she smiled.

Fred leaned into her, lowering his voice to a whisper. "Is there anything you don't know?" He scooted closer. "L ... i ... l ... i ... t ... h," he drawled her name rolling his tongue saucily back and forth.

She smirked, bypassing the question. "Now that we're properly introduced, Mr. Fred Kadigan. I'll have a tea with double cream, if you don't mind?"

"My pleasure," he said.

'Tuesday Afternoon'

"Good afternoon Mack Industries. How may I assist you?" Lilith tucked the telephone receiver into the crook of her neck, freeing her hands to file the remainder of the reports.

"How may you assist me Lilith? My Lily of the valley ... You don't mind me calling you Lily do you?" Fred tossed his cowboy hat onto the desk leaning back in his chair smiling. This was his eleventh call to the office over the last few hours. Gord had been the recipient of ten hang-ups. He knew the office did not have call display. He was safe and sound. "Hum ... m ... m,' he said. "Now that's a loaded question if I ever heard one," he chuckled. "How may you assist me? Well, well, now. Let me think. Quite a few ideas are coming to mind already."

"Mr. Fred Kadigan," Lilith scolded.

"I like the way you say my name."

"You do, do you?" She filed the rest of the papers away and sat down. It was a minute to six p.m.

"I was hoping I'd catch you before you left for the day."

"You did. What can I do for you?"

"Oooh ... Lily," he whispered unzipping his fly, peeling at the band of his briefs.

"Yes?"

The locked hut doorknob twisted back and forth. A loud series of heavy raps followed suit. Fred snapped the elastic waistband back into place, zipped his fly, peddled his chair over to the door, and opened it. Gord was standing on the stoop with the box of safety glasses he had forgotten.

"Can I call you back in a few minutes?"

"I do have to be going. If you don't mind, maybe we can talk another time?"

"Sure okay. But before you hang up. I wanted to ask you something."

"All right."

Fred took a quick scan of Gord.

His lips were drawn into his mouth, puckering it up in an odd left angled slant, which ran from his chin to his nose. His cheeks were puffing in and out like a cartoon chipmunk. The tip of his right hand index finger was waving back and forth from under the front edge of the cardboard box in the 'You naughty boy! I caught you red handed!' gesture.

"It's okay," Fred said slowly. He wrinkled his brow in disappointment. "I'll ask you tomorrow."

"Oh, okay then. Have a good night Fred Kadigan."

"And you." Fred replaced the receiver.

"FREDDIE!" Gord growled.

"Come on Gord. It was only a friendly phone call."

"Really? And might I remind you of the company policies regarding friendly phone calls placed from known deviate employees?"

"Deviate now am I?" Fred raised his legs, crossing them in midair thumping his boots down on his desk.

Gord belly laughed. "If the shoe fits? And we both know first-hand it does!"

"Come on Gordie."

"Don't come on Gordie me, my boy. She's so far out of your league." He opened his eyes wide framing them in white. "So far," Gord paused on purpose, pointing back and forth across the length of the lot with extended arms. "So ... damn ... far!"

Fred lifted his chin in defiance, disguising his amusement. He plopped his cowboy hat back on, standing and adjusting it in the mirror until it acquired the perfect tip. He puffed out his chest oozing 'I'll show you' smugness, and 'You better put your money where your mouth is.' "You think so, do you?" he asked his voice cocky and brash.

"I know so, fast Freddie ... I know so. You might as well quit while you are ahead. You are not going to get another notch on your belt off of that one. She is a real lady. Not a," he paused, drawing his fingers over his chin. "Let's just say,

47

she'd not what you're used to." Gord narrowed his eyes to thin slits driving home his point. "Besides," he continued. "She'll only be around until Gloria gets back."

"Well ... well then ... I better get right on it, or, should I say her." Fred wet his lips, spat into his palm and rubbed his hands together as if the plan was seeded and ready for take-off.

"Freddie, I think you'd be best off leaving this one alone."

Fred pushed himself away from the desk. "Why? Don't you think I got it in me to bag this one?"

"No, quite frankly I don't. But it's not just that, I ..."

Fred cut him off. "Ah Gordie, you got no sense of the sport anymore! You've been out of the game and married too long!"

Gord held Fred's eyes, studying the hormone over-loaded childlike glee flashing around in there. This was not high school and the woman was not a toy. He shook his head. "I'm going on home. My supper's probably getting cold."

The etched laugh lines on Fred's face drooped, curving downward as if a magic wand had been whisked through the air in front of his face. He ran his tongue over his lips wetting them. "Gord?"

"Yes Freddie."

"All kidding aside. This one is something. Really something. Special. A keeper ... I can just feel it."

"I wouldn't Freddie."

Fred grinned a 'know it all' smile. The same kind the cat that ate the canary always seemed to have smeared across its face before the owner came into the room and choked the living daylights out of it making it spit it out on the floor.

Gord scraped his tongue with his teeth, avoiding all the things he wanted to spit out. He closed the hut door, walked towards his car, got in, and left the yard, his thoughts doing double time. 'What a piece of work that guy had become ... If he'd been female he would have been branded the town slut.

Worse, if there was such a thing.' Gord pulled his visor down warding off the bright sunshine. He cleared his throat on purpose. 'This time,' he mused. 'That old boy is going be skinned, drawn, and quartered, just for starters.' He could just feel it. He smiled a toothy grin, which quickly turned into a grimace. He nodded reaffirming his convictions, as he continued with his thoughts. He for one could not wait to see it happen. Freddie' sleeping with his sixteen-year-old daughter at the Christmas party, drunk or not, had been and still was, unconscionable. "So Lilith, my dear," he said. "I'm counting on you to bring it on! Bring it all on! I pray you take that bastard down and put him in his rightful place. Once and for all." He lowered his voice to a whisper. "We're all counting on you love. We're all counting on you," he repeated. He turned in his driveway.

'Wednesday'

Fred crept into the front office, and placed a hot steaming take-out tea with double cream on the front counter. He stood motionless not saying a word.

Lilith hung up the receiver and placed the message in Gord's in-box. The strong over-done after shave had whisked along the walls sucking in and out of the office filtration system from the moment Fred opened the foyer doors. She turned, sauntering over, plucking the cup from the counter. "And what did I do to deserve such a kindness?" she said.

Fred tipped his hat. "By being you my dear." He pushed the top half of his body across the wooden counter, closing the distance between them. "I can't get you out of my head," he whispered. "After I met you yesterday you became so much more to me than just some beautiful lady."

"And just what did I become than, a?" She put her finger to her lip pausing, jesting. "A frog?"

Fred burst out laughing. He ran his index finger down the back of her hand. "Lily would you go out for dinner with me on Friday?"

Lilith raised her eyebrows cloaking her amusement. "Go out for dinner! With you? Hum," she made her lips disappear as if deep in thought.

"Ah come on ..."

"Okay," she said turning up the corners of her mouth. "B ... u ... t," she drawled. "But only if it's Dutch."

"No, no. My treat."

She moved her hand from under his wandering finger. "No! Dutch!"

He grinned.

"Well?"

He studied her. "Is that' the only way?"

"It is," she affirmed. She leaned into him close and personal. "And," she paused allowing her breath to filter across the skin of his ear lobe. "It's' only dinner. There is no desert," she whispered.

He smirked. "You beat me to the draw darlin'."

"As I said previously. I've been warned about you Fred Kadigan," she laughed.

"Really now?"

"Really," she countered.

"Well then, do tell," he quipped. He was so close, too close. He could smell the scent of her perfume mixing and sweetening her skin. He could feel the soft warmth of her. He suddenly so wanted her. He wanted her more right that minute than he had wanted anything or anyone in his entire life.

"How about," she withdrew from his personal air space taking a step back from the counter. "How about," she repeated. "We save that conversation for over dinner? Shall we?"

"Deal!" he said. "So, where do you live darlin'?" He pulled the office notepad across the counter, retrieving a pen from his shirt pocket. "So I can pick you up Friday?" He uncapped the pen. "Better give me your phone number too. You know, in case," he paused giving her a devilish grin accompanied by a wink. "Something comes up or you know."

She reached over and touched his nose with her right fingertip. "Pick me up here at six-thirty," she smiled, looked directly into his eyes then added the word darling finishing off her sentence.

His mouth fell open. His face flushed. He felt like a twelve-year-old school boy overwhelmed with his first crush. His knees wobbled. All he could manage was a stiff nod. He felt like he was about to drown in those brilliant deep blue eyes looking into his.

'Friday'

"Do you want anything to drink before dinner?" Fred asked.

"A tea would be nice," Lilith replied.

Fred turned to the waiter. "Two tea, please."

The waiter nodded, disappearing through the crowed dim lit restaurant.

"So ... my mystery lady ... tell me something about yourself. You far from home?"

"You take a person too far from home, they get lost."

Fred scrunched up his face rubbing his hand back and forth across his lips seemingly deep in thought. "You far from home?" he asked again.

Lilith smiled. "I am not lost, if that is what you're asking."

He pierced his lips together. "I ... I don't understand what I'm trying to ask anymore," he laughed. "You're a smart one aren't you?"

"I wouldn't say that. So, Fred Kadigan, tell me all about you," she said.

"Want to know why they call me fast Freddie?"

51

"Sure."

"I got a speeding ticket on the way to work years back." He rubbed his hand across his lips again, all at once apprehensive. Gordie was right. This woman was out of his league and, absolutely beautiful. He cleared his throat, jiggling his feet up and down under the table like a five-year-old. "Wa ... wasn't what you thought was it?" he asked meekly, stuttering from nerves.

Lilith smiled. "No," she replied. She licked the tip of her finger then marked the air in a number one sign. "That's one for your side," her smile broadened into soft laughter. "Tell me some more about yourself sir."

Fred ran his hands up and down his vibrating thighs. He was beyond nervous. He freed one hand gulping down his tea. He was in total awe that this lovely creature would take any interest in him. Usually all his dates did was talk non-stop about themselves. He usually couldn't get a word in. But here he was being asked to talk. Talk about himself. He shook his head gulping in the heavily flavoured restaurant air. "You ... you, want ... want me to tell you about myself?"

"Yes," Lilith replied.

"You sure?"

"Yes, but of course."

"Okay, where do you want me to start?"

"Where ever your heart desires, Fred Kadigan."

"I think my heart started when I laid eyes on you."

Lilith smiled in appreciation. She reached across the table and placed her hand gently atop his. "That's very sweet of you to say dear sir."

He took both her hands in his. "No ... no ... I am serious. I think I'm falling hard for you."

"Well before you fall too far," she quipped, withdrawing her hands from underneath his. "Tell me more of you."

Fred tapped the tabletop with his thumbs drumming it lightly. He wondered if she had changed the tone of the conversation on purpose or if it was accidental. Or maybe it was just his nerves playing tricks and he was reading in too much where he shouldn't. He firmed his footing, stopping the jiggles, trying to relax. "I thought you knew all about me?" he teased.

Lilith laughed. "Maybe I do. Maybe I don't," she jested. "Come ... come now ... tell me your life story." Lilith leaned closer putting her elbows on the table, placing one hand on top of the other resting her chin. She gazed directly into his eyes.

"What do you want to know?"

"Everything," Lilith replied.

"I was born and raised a country boy." He could feel his heart pounding in his chest. Her intent gaze was unnerving, making it difficult for him to concentrate. He felt like he was being studied somehow by some higher power. Like a science experiment.

Lilith cocked her head slightly to the side, a small smile appearing on her lips.

He watched her lips broaden then relax into a cute little pout. The deep blue of her eyes seemed to be pulling at him in a way indefinable in words. He gave himself a shake, starting again. "I was born and raised a country boy. Bet you didn't know that?"

Lilith reached and flicked the brim of his cowboy hat with her thumb and index finger. "Never would have guessed," she replied.

He all at once relaxed, pouring another tea, sipping it slowly. He drew closer to her. "Okay I'll tell you. But trust me there's really not much to tell. I'll bet you'll have more."

Lilith grinned.

"I was born and raised about fifty miles from here. We had good times and hard times growing up. I was a little on the wild side when I was young," he paused finishing his tea, returning her intent gaze. He silently kicked himself for saying he was wild when he was young. What a stupid thing to say to a woman of this caliber.

"You still are so I hear," she whispered.

It was his turn to smirk. He was instantly so darned honoured just to be allowed to sit and talk, and be seen in her company all the buttons on his shirt could have popped. "I'm not boring you?" he asked.

"Not at all. Go on."

"I got married young, had three kids. I always wanted my own family. They are grown up now. I'm a grandpa twice over. I was religious when I was young, and then left the church for a spell but I found my faith again. I am a devoted catholic."

"Devoted for a reason?"

"Put it this way, I really needed to reaffirm my faith."

"Enough said."

"My wife left me over two years ago for another man. An older man," he paused. A chill swept over him; like she somehow knew the untruths he was spinning. The untruths he had told so many times it had become embellished fact. He gazed at her glorious eyes, so warm so soft so intent and oh so intelligent. He squared his shoulders.

Lilith flipped her hand palm side up motioning him to continue.

"As I was ... was saying. My wife left me just over two years ago for an older man. That hit me really, hard. I cried every day for a very long time. She was my whole world and I guess I haven't been quite right since."

"I am sorry to hear that."

"Thanks, thanks a lot. You don't know how much it means to me to hear you say that." He sniffed then fumbled with his dinner napkin sending it to the floor.

Lilith handed him hers.

"So tell me fair lady, how did you end up here?"

"I was searching for something," she said.

"Did you find it?"

"Yes I did."

Fred reached across the table cupping her hands in his. "I've been searching for something too," he said soft and low.

Lilith smiled.

"I think I've found it too." He cast his eyes into hers. The penetrating blue seemed to still be tugging, pulling, drawing him in, draining his body, mind, and soul. All sense of time and space seemed to cease. He drew close to her. "Want to come to my place for a night cap?"

"All in good time Fred Kadigan."

He almost fell off his chair. It was not what he had expected, not by a long shot, nor was it an outright no. He licked his lips going for broke. "Your place then?"

Lilith did not hide her outright amusement. She chuckled openly. "How about we go back to the plant," she said.

"You want to go back there?" Fred rubbed his hand across his pocket feeling for the lump of company keys. He beamed with outright delight, he had them. "You sure you want to go back there?" he asked again. He laughed aloud. He felt like kicking up his heels in salute of the 'Irish', he'd found the pot at the end of the rainbow.

"Yes."

"How come the plant?"

"For starters, my car is there."

"Oh," he looked down at the table all at once feeling foolish. Whatever was he thinking? This kind of woman would not entertain one single thought like the hundreds he was letting loose inside his head. "Oh yeah. I forgot. See what you do to me," he whispered. He stroked the back of her hand with his baby finger.

"Will I see you again?" he asked. He motioned for her car key to unlock the driver's' door. They slipped from his hand pulling the rental tag loose. It glided down and under the car unnoticed.

"Will I?" he asked again.

"You can count your rosary beads on it Fred Kadigan."

Fred watched the taillights until they were no more, not realizing he was holding his breath. He flipped his lucky coin in the air. It landed heads up. He grinned. He was one lucky son of a bitch.

'Monday Mid-Day'

"Good afternoon Mack Industries. How may I assist you?" Lilith said.

"Lilith, I need a really big favour."

"Yes, but of course Gord."

"Would it be possible for you to run the company truck over to Freddie's house late this afternoon?" Gord grimaced. He wished he did not have to ask this of her but he was in a bind. The meeting had run behind schedule. "I won't make it back till late from this here meeting and," he hesitated, glancing at his watch.

"Say no more," Lilith reassured. She grasped for a pen and paper. "Please give me the directions."

"Okay, turn right when you come out onto the main road. Follow it to the little town at the bottom of the hill. Hang a left. Go until you find a road called Melody Bay. Hang another left and go about two miles. Freddie's place is on the right. It is a white brick bungalow with a rail fence. You cannot miss it. It's directly after a small gravel outfit."

"Got it," Lilith said.

"Want to repeat it back?"

Lilith read off the directions.

"I appreciate this."

"Anytime."

"Leave a might early. Okay?"

"Will do."

"And make sure, Freddie gives you a ride back."

"Not to worry."

"Can't help it. The man can be a bit of an ass at times."

"It's all under control."

"Thanks again. Oh, Lilith, I almost forgot. Did the exterminators show up yet?"

"No, not as yet."

"Would you mind giving them a quick call, if they haven't shown up by the time you're ready to leave? The number's on the pad on my desk."

"Not at all."

"I do apologize for this."

"You have nothing to apologize for. Sometimes things just happen."

"Well, it's not ideal working conditions. Not by a long shot. I have never ever seen anything like this in my fifteen years here. There seems to be more and more of them every day. Like they are, breeding and doubling their numbers overnight or something. Christ, they're coming out from under the floor tiles, the electric sockets, crawling up the walls, hanging off the ceiling and fixtures, plugging the filtration system. Hell, they have clogged the drains in the restrooms. I just don't get it. I have never seen an infestation of flies like this in all my born days. The place is just ... just swarming with them!"

'Monday Afternoon'

Fred was leaning against the rail fence when Lilith pulled up. He held up a portable telephone. "I thought you might be calling," he said. He opened the driver's' side truck door.

She smirked.

"You just keep on amazing me Lily," he cooed.

"Really?"

"Yep. You're beautiful, smart, hot, and you ... you," he hesitated reacquainting his senses with her sweet scented perfume. He so wanted to take her to bed and ravish her.

Lilith waved her finger back and forth in front of his face. "You're a naughty one," she quipped.

"Hey I didn't say nothing."

"It's what you were thinking Fred Kadigan."

"You know what I think too. Do you?"

Lilith smiled.

"Okay smart ass! Tell me what I was thinking!"

She stepped close, very close, running her fingertip along his cheekbone. "Sometimes the best way to hide the truth is to keep it in plain sight," she whispered.

He rubbed his chin, his puzzlement stretching ear to ear. "I don't get yaw."

She stepped back pointing for him to watch her eyes. She slowly lowered them to his bulging crotch.

"Oh," he smirked.

"Want to come in? I found my teapot this afternoon and went out and got you some cream."

Lilith glanced at her watch. It was almost six p.m. "Sure," she said.

"You take just cream right? No sugar?"

"Yes."

Fred boiled the water and poured it into the teapot to steep. "So, what do you think?"

"Of?" she asked.

"The house? Me? Work? Take your pick."

"Work is fine," she replied.

His eyes danced and sparkled. "You're a sassy one! Aren't you?"

"I wouldn't say that."

"What would you say then?" he countered. His smirk was as broad as the horizon. He was standing toe to toe, doing damn good too. He was proud of himself. He did have what it took.

Lilith made her lips disappear into her mouth, and then shoved them back out, the corners turning up. "Depends," she replied.

"Come sit with me, at the table." He plunked down the cream container, two mugs, sugar, and the teapot.

"Would you have a spoon?"

"Jesus Christ! You expect a lot, don't you?" he taunted. He got up, retrieved a spoon from the sink, washed and dried it. He crisscrossed the kitchen, purposely ending up directly behind her. He moved close pressing into the back of her chair. He leaned forward, bending, encasing her chair, placing the spoon beside her mug. He exhaled, depleting his lungs, sucking in her delicately perfumed scent. His head lightened and spun in slow circles. He drew his fingers through her hair. It was like an angel's', downy soft and silken. He struggled with himself, forcing his body from the chair.

Lilith smiled.

Fred sat across from her.

Lilith slowly shook her head back and forth, her eyes glittering with entertainment.

"So," Fred began. He was feeling pretty perky and more like his old self than he'd felt in a long while. "So," he repeated. "What do you want to do with me? Any thoughts?" He pushed his chair sideways stretching out his legs, crossing them.

"Yes, a few."

"Well then, my dear 'Lily Of The Valley', I must be doing something right. Am I?"

"That's one way of putting it."

He reached across the table seizing her hand in his. "You must know that I really, really, r ... e ... a ... l ... l ... y like you?" He did not wait for an answer. "You are the first woman I've met that stirs something so deep down inside of me that I can't even find words for. Do you believe in God, Lily?" Again, he did not wait for her to speak. "I do and I believe he has brought you to me. You are just so different from everyone else. You're like a precious gift." This time he waited, giving her space to join the conversation.

"There is a higher order to things, even though it's fashionable to love chaos," she said.

59

He didn't give way to his lack of understanding. He'd caught she had said, there was a higher order. And that was more than enough. He scooped up her other hand, cupping them together within his. "You're all I think of. You fill up every minute of every day. I want to get to know you. Inside and out. I think you are the one. The one I've been waiting for all my life."

"What is meant to be, will always find a way," she said.

"You ... you think we were meant to meet and be?" He could feel his face flushing; this was better than he had ever hoped and longed for.

"Most definitely."

"Can you stay for a while? Dinner? A movie? Hot tub?"

"I cannot stay today. However, tomorrow is the blue moon. I cannot think of any night more perfect for a hot tub."

"Tomorrow?" he asked. His voice shrilled in excitement. "You'll come back tomorrow?" He reached under the table and pinched himself just to make sure he was not dreaming.

"Yes."

"Tomorrow it is! Want to know a secret?"

"If you like."

"I don't really like the dark."

"The dark is enchanting."

"I don't like the dark," he whispered back at her.

She smiled gently. "Then we will have to have special things happen tomorrow evening."

Fred raised his eyebrows. "Hmm is that a promise?"

"Yes," she said.

'Tuesday Evening'

"Hello Fred Kadigan."

"You did come!" Fred's voice pitched with excitement.

Lilith nodded.

He glanced downward at the decking. He was sure his nervous energy had beaten a path. He had been outside for hours, pacing end to end with the telephone receiver stuck in his shirt pocket. He had rehearsed the words 'Another time then,' repeatedly until he could say it with no obvious air of let down in his voice. "You really did come," he reaffirmed, unable to help himself.

"Of course. I said I would."

"Do you always do what you say?"

"Yes."

Fred crossed the wooden planking accidentally knocking over the plastic bag full of fly rid tins. They spewed across the decking rolling off and the over edges.

Lilith picked up the one lone survivor handing it to him.

He gulped, clearing the excess saliva from under his tongue. 'God damn nerves,' he thought. He swallowed again. "You know it's the damnedest thing." He threw the tin over the railing onto the lawn. "After I got back yesterday from dropping you off. The house was overrun with flies. Thousands of them. If I did not know any better I would swear someone dumped them playing a prank on me. But even that's stretching it." He dipped his head feeling his cheeks flush in embarrassment and then continued, not meeting her eyes. "They were crawling on the windows, the floors, the walls. They were damn well everywhere. It was as if the house had fallen under one of 'God's Plagues.' Like right out of the bible scriptures."

Lilith remained silent.

He hesitantly chuckled swishing his bare feet side to side. "I wanted to surprise you with a real nice barbecue for dinner, before the hottubbing." He gazed past her feeling like a five-year old kid. "But ... living hell, the things are even inside the fridge." He curled his toes into the planking, took a deep breath, and then continued. "They must have crawled in through the cooling system on the back of it or something. I thought the cold slowed those things down, you know made them stupid. But not these ones. They have gotten into everything. Even, doubling up like they're breeding on the food."

He shifted his weight, his nerves jumping front and center. He felt like a fool. "I rushed to the corner store and bought every container of fly rid they had in stock. Came home, closed everything up, and sprayed. But it didn't have any effect." He drew the tips of his fingers across his lips. "When I went to power up the hot tub, the breakers for the whole damn house blew. Everything went out, hot tub and all." He knuckled his hands. "When I opened the control panel, it was like it was alive. I have never seen so many flies all in one place. The breakers were so stuffed full I could not flip ... flip them back. I ... I ... swear they've tripled in the last hour."

"Not to worry."

"You don't mind?"

"Not in the least."

"You sure?"

"Fred Kadigan," Lilith tutted. "I didn't come for food or lights, I came for you," she said.

Fred could feel the blood rustle in his veins. It shot clear up from his toes to the top of his head. He was beyond flattered. "The hot tub is still pretty warm, not hot but ... but," he stuttered, then stopped mid-sentence, unable to remember what he was saying. He pursed his lips together, shaking his head slowly back and forth. He raked his eyes over her as she put her carry bag down. She seemed to grow more radiant every time he saw her.

"Warm is good," she said.

Fred chewed on the inside of his cheek. She was so above anyone he had ever been with. Even talked to for that matter. She was so poised, so graceful, real down and outright first class. He whipped his tongue over his top teeth. He snapped his fingers. "We're good to go then."

"Yes, indeed."

"You ... you can change in behind of the house if you like."

Lilith shook her head back and forth.

He squeezed his eyes into slits, cocking his head off to the one side. Shivers gunned up and down his spine. He was almost sure. Almost sure there was more said with that headshake than just not going behind the house. He had to ask. "You did bring a suit for the hot tub, didn't you?"

"No." She smiled slow and deliberate.

"You're my kind of girl! Come over here!" Arousal took wing pitching his anxiety attack to the back burner.

Lilith casually walked towards him.

Fred draped an arm coolly around her shoulders. He pointed skyward with the other. "You know, it really does look bluish." He slipped his arm down to her waist drawing her close, giving her a squeeze. "So, that's your blue moon huh?"

"No. It's actually yours Fred Kadigan."

"Mine?"

"Yes, yours," Lilith replied.

"Girl if you only knew what you do to me." He moved in behind her wrapping both his arms tightly about her middle. He pulled close, gently swaying his body back and forth across hers leaving little to imagination. "Sometimes when I see you smile at me, I kind of get the feeling, that maybe you're thinking about doing to me what I'm thinking about doing to you." Fred dropped his head, filtering his breath back and forth along the edge of her jaw line.

Lilith smirked.

Fred's eyes darted to the empty deck chair. He had meant to bring them out earlier. "Shit!" he exclaimed. "Give me one second darlin', I'm going to brave the flies to dash in the house and fetch us some towels."

"Take your time," she said.

"Wow! Did it ever darken up fast." He set the pile of towels down on the bench. "Good thing there's that moon."

Lilith was on the far side of the tub, facing him.

Fred slipped out of his shirt and shorts, not taking his eyes from her. He grinned. She had changed out of her clothes while he was in the house.

She looked like a smoking hot, glamour goddess from a movie poster. She was wrapped in a dark coloured, hooded, full length robe. The hood was down, spilling onto her back and shoulders, bunching her hair forward. The robe was tied loosely about her waist, the lush velvety material draping, hugging her curves, and descending the length of her legs, where it pooled about her feet.

He drank her in absorbing everything, from the strands of hair whisking gently back and forth in perfect tune with the night breeze, to the folds of fabric stroking and caressing her bare feet. Her flesh where exposed seemed to glisten and glitter. The round moon at her back fully encased her silhouette, outlining it with a dark navy blue line that faded at the edges where it radiated into an aura of delicate pastel rainbow hues.

He beamed. "You know something darlin'?" He rocked his weight using the balls of his feet. "With the moon back lighting you like that ... you ... you look just like an angel. An angel sent by God out of heaven." He wiped the excess saliva that had beaded in the corners of his mouth with the back of his hand. He was so awe struck; it was starting to scare him. He had done nothing but think of her every waking minute since he met her. He had never fallen this hard and fast for anyone in his life.

"I wouldn't go that far," she said.

"Well then," he paused, crimping his fingernails hard into his palms making sure this was not a dream. "Well then," he repeated. "How about I just call you my angel?"

Lilith smiled. "Going to remove the remainder of your clothing? It might prove cumbersome."

Fred shimmied out of his underwear faster than a raging bull hit with a prod. "So, my angel, my beautiful angel, you going to drop that there robe of yours?" He winked, and then smiled slyly. "It too might prove cumbersome." He beamed, proud of himself for using her words back at her. "Hmm darlin'?"

She ran her fingertips over the tie, loosening it, opening her robe at the middle.

He watched transfixed, mesmerized as if suddenly bewitched.

Lilith released the tie. She inched the robe from her shoulders.

Fred gasped. Her beauty was so over-powering, so magnificent, so utterly imposing that it rattled his core right through to his soul. His knees wobbled in circles, and then side-to-side shattering the quiet night air with loud quacks and thuds as they knocked uncontrollably against one another.

"Come closer," Lilith said.

Fred reached down steadying his whacking knees with his hands. He shuffled slow and awkward. His limbs and feet seemed full of lead. He pushed and guided his legs towards her wobbling side to side like a man that had just come indoors from a numbing, blinding blizzard.

Lilith liberated her robe. It flowed to the decking, landing in folds about her ankles. Her porcelain skin shone and danced as if dozens of miniature strobe lights illuminated her from within. Her shadow laying off to her front right, swayed and arced as it drew out across the decking, completing the perfection of the moment.

Fred flash froze, over taken by raw emotion. He was out of his league. Tears formed and fell from his eyes. "You're ... you're the ... the most gorgeous thing I've ever laid ... laid my eyes on." He started to weep.

A light breeze churned the air, waving the grass and fluttering the leaves of the trees.

Lilith motioned with her index finger for him to draw nearer.

Ina Louise Jackson

He instantly obliged, staggering around the tub.

Lilith nodded in approval. She gestured for him to halt as they came face to face.

Fred's back was to the tub. He pinned his calves against it, in a vain attempt to steady his weight. His legs were bending and wobbling as if they were made of elastic bands.

Water splashed from the hot tub, kissing his backside.

He swivelled his neck, gazing down into the tub admiring the wavy imprint of her shadow glistening and sparking in the waters as it playfully rolled from side to side.

He gave little thought to proper proportions or equations. Nor did he contemplate swirling waters without power or rationalize the placement of shadows. Lilith, his Lily, his angel was all there was. Was all there would ever be.

Without warning, his rubber-band legs gave. His body deflated, slithering and folding in equal lengths as if he had ready-made perforations. His head spun and lightened. He puffed out short loud bursts of oxygen, sounding more like a hot air balloon with a malfunctioning shut off valve than anything human.

He slammed butt first down on to the tub's edge. He glued his fingers up and under the rim. His head bobbed up and down then shook side to side. Everything, suddenly surreal.

Lilith smiled.

He tilted his head searching the celestial dark blue eyes gazing upon him. They seemed magnetic, all consuming, in ways there were no words for.

He dabbed his tongue from behind his bottom front teeth, to the roof and sides of his mouth. Saliva seemed at a premium. The fleshy insides felt like old wet cardboard about to flake apart. He gulped swallowing balloons of air. He knew he was acting bizarre but could not stop himself. He opened and closed his lips omitting a solitary squeak.

"No need," Lilith said.

He closed his eyes feeling relieved. Somewhere deep inside he could feel she understood. Understood him on a level no one else ever had. No one else ever could. No one else ever would.

"Stay as you are," she said. "Keep your eyes closed. I have something to surprise you."

"For ... for ... m ... me?" His voice was clogged, raspy, and uneven. "Rea ... really?" he sputtered. He could hear the waters of the hot tub hitting and splashing as it blustered back and forth behind his back. He could feel the warmth of the spray as it flew up dampening his hair and skin. Again, no thoughts crossed or plugged into his circuit board. "Something for me? For me? A surprise?"

"Yes," Lilith replied.

The soft breeze changed to a satiny wind that seemed to steal in and out of the deck furniture and play peek-a-boo in the shrubs.

He pressed his weight shifting his body mass. His right hand splayed crab-like as it skirted sideways along the underneath rim of the tub. Frigid air nipped at his fingers. Without warning, he suddenly felt uneasy, almost fearful. Lilith left his thoughts. He drew a breath and held it, puffing out his cheeks like a chipmunk.

The uneasiness took root and grew. He could feel something. Something not right, something out of place, unnatural. He stole a glance out the corners of his eyes, first to the left then the right. He froze, his edges freezer burning. Beside his right sat a shadow figure. Not two feet from him. Its head was cocked as if it was examining him in minute detail. Fright trembled his lips. He snapped his eyes shut, his body goose bumped then shook uncontrollably. He death gripped the rim. He tried to calm himself by forcing deep long breaths in sets of tens.

'Get a hold of yourself old boy,' he instructed himself. 'You're just seeing things again.' He forced more breaths. He sucked in his cheeks rounding his lips blowing out invisible air bubbles. He lifted his right index finger snaking it to and fro antenna like circling the air. His flesh numbed and stung, the air seemed colder still, like he had been pitched into the dead of winter.

"Are you ready?"

Startled, he slammed his knees into one another. His mind had betrayed, him going off into one of his 'Spells,' leaving Lily, his beautiful Lily, behind.

"Are you ready?" she repeated quietly.

His shoulders unhitched as the smooth silkiness of Lilith's voice infiltrated into all his being, erasing everything that had come before in its entirety.

"Are you?"

He let go of the rim clasping his hands together, knitting his fingers. "Yes! Yes! Yes!" he chirped. He bounced up and down on the edge giddy with anticipation like a three-year-old on Christmas morning. "I want it! ... I want it! ... I want it!" He giggled, and then stopped as heat swarmed his groin. The start of a massive erection sprouting from between his open legs, changing the shape and texture of his childlike thoughts into something dark, full of anticipatory lust. He rubbed his hands together. "You have something? To surprise me? Going to do something to me?" he cooed.

"Yes. Indeed," Lilith retorted. "Open your eyes Fred Kadigan."

The wind culled, whooshing back and forth against his flesh. His skin took on hives, rippling and standing the hairs on the back of his neck to attention. The water behind him simmered in small rounds, the edges rolling, starting to foam as it bubbled and whirled into a slow boil.

Fred lifted his chin in the direction of her voice. A cool snip of air winged past. He stiffened, fright resurfacing.

"Open your eyes Fred Kadigan." Lilith took a single step toward him.

Her voice was soft, warm, closer than he had expected. His fear retreated under his skin where it manifested into shooting spouts of perspiration. He opened his eyes.

Lilith was but a mere foot, foot and a half at best.

He twitched then electrified. His body jerked and jarred, short-circuiting as he became over-whelmed with the nearness. His left shoulder drooped slumping his body into an awkward odd shape. If he could have lifted his arm he could have touched her, caressed her exquisite body. But he could not move. It was as if he had been cast in quick drying cement. He grated his teeth, trying to work his lower jaw. The cement held.

"Fred Kadigan! Behold!"

The air coloured, bluing like the hues in faded opaque denim. It swirled then rippled in waves. It slapped into his skin biting at it, fissuring it, layering the insides of the wounds with sea salt. The air expanded then contracted, drawing in and out as if it had come alive and was breathing as Lilith's wings stretched out.

Fred's lungs huffed, hissing and spurting, emptying themselves of their own accord. His eyeballs protruded profusely, bulging from the sockets as if they were two oversized marbles. He gasped. His mouth slanted off side. Its bottom swayed back and forth like a gate with a broken hinge. His arms fell to his sides. His hands dangled loose and free on appendages that seemed crudely taped together. His breaths laboured, blowing shallow streams of steam that hiccupped like each was going to be his last. He gazed transfixed, lost in time and space.

Lilith drew her lips back, showing the whites of her teeth, careful not to show the tips of her elongated canines. She flapped her wings like a bird preparing for flight, halting, arching them wide and full.

The edges of her winged silhouette pulsated with a colour of blue he had never known. The moon's back light cast rays of light through her opaque feathers, distorting the black-blue to silver gray.

This part of the 'something to surprise' went by him unnoticed.

She grinned.

Fred surged forward like a man possessed. He dropped to his knees, accepting without question, clasping his hands in prayer. "Oh my God! You're an angel!" he blubbered. Tears streamed down his cheeks, catching and pooling in his wide-open mouth. "I knew you were special. I just knew," he cried. "What did I do to deserve this? Oh my ... oh my good God," he wailed.

"You are most deserving. Trust me Fred Kadigan," Lilith said. "Trust me," she repeated.

Fred crawled to her side, stretching his arms out and up to her in praise.

Lilith bent over him, surrounding, shielding, swooping him within her wings. "Fred Kadigan! Behold! 'The Golden Rule,' Mathew seven-twelve! Therefore all things, whatsoever ye would that men should do to you, do ye even so to them: For this is the law and the prophets." She released him. There was no smile.

A gale force wind whipped through the treetops growling, reeling, tipping and slashing them side-to-side. It corkscrewed; whirling and gusting, picking up momentum as it spiralled downward. It surged, encasing him, ripping his feet out from under, tumbling him backward, flipping him head first into the hot tub. The water whirl-pooled, penned, pulling and sucking him towards the base where the under current took over lashing and ramming his skull ruthlessly into the metal drain.

His chest tightened, restricting, he twisted like a pretzel. He righted himself snapping his feet off the bottom, propelling his arms in circles. He struggled, kicking and lurching against the water as it grew increasingly more turbulent. He tossed about like a broken child's plastic toy caught up in a rushing storm drain.

Dull aches surged and racked his hips as he slammed against the porcelain bottom, his entire weight bouncing uncontrollably up and down as if he was a fishing bobber without a sinker. He opened his mouth. Water rushed, doubling his tongue backward carrying the tip down his throat. He gulped and choked in the hot liquid. His lungs became heavy and full. He forced his jaw closed with his palms. Over-size air bubbles shot from his nose. He dropped his feet, frantically pedaling for the bottom. It was nowhere. The tub all of a sudden seemed twenty feet deep. He pivoted his body, flapping like a salmon caught in a current. He streamlined like a missile bringing his arms to his sides, propelling his feet in turbine fashion.

He tilted his head trying to scan the surface. His unprotected eyes stung and burned, blurring the dark outline of something perched above. Something perched above, watching him.

He closed his eyelids rubbing furiously. He squinted his eyes into slits re-opening them. He could not focus. He squirmed closer. Terror's fright leapt, clawing up his spine to the back of his neck. His eyes shot full, round and wide of their own accord. The something dark perched above, watching, was leering toothy and full.

The current sucked at him, towing and pitching him head first into the base. Terror sidelined into survival. He spun his body in circles, kicking wildly stretching out his arms, pleading to whatever it was above, to be pulled free.

Its smile seemed to broaden.

Fred's fingertips broke the surface. Frigid air nipped, frostbiting, colouring them a pukish off white. All at once, a fiery pain surged throughout his inner thigh. Then there was another and another and another. His skin gave, splitting and tearing. He could feel heat seeping from his body. As the pain turned to agony, his head started to reel in tight dizzying circles, heaving his stomach. Streams of bile shot from his throat into his mouth, coating his tongue as it pooled, building and over loading until it spewed out from between his clenched teeth.

The water boiled red.

He lurched forward, smashing his fists wildly. He grabbed at a stair. He fell short. Something tore at his back, at his feet, at his hamstrings. The red deepened, churning, frothing with dark coloured wide ribbons that paled as they swept past in the current.

Horror collided with fear. Panic infiltrated. He was far from alone.

Something whacked his elbow. It surged sideways then turned coming straight at him. His eyeballs shot from the sockets, time slowed to a standstill, his mouth opened, forming the first of a long line of inaudible screams. A tiny cat-like skeleton hooked into his skin embedding scalpel sharp claws deep into the flesh, anchoring itself as its mouth scissored through the meat of his forearm. It gnawed with razor sharp teeth, swinging its jaws back and forth rhythmically as if they were demonic saw blades.

Blood burst, pumping and spurting, dousing, coating its off-white cranium in deep burgundy slime as it continued to sink its teeth deeper and deeper into the muscle. Three more joined sucking, latching, and tearing into his battered flesh like mutated skeletal leeches. Their jaws worked cruelly together as they sought out and gnawed clear through the bone.

Guttural scream after scream bubbled through the raging water, breaking the surface in 'Rice Crispy' like pops and cracks as his severed forearm twirled and tussled through the water. It upended, fingers waving lazily in all directions as it descended into the murky depths, skeletons in tow.

Thick green vomit blew from between his parted lips like an erupting volcano, firing bacon chunks and heavy string bean leftovers' into the water.

He pitched sideways as something hard, cold, razor sharp jetted into his side. He doubled in half. Sheering agony fanned his body, torturing and twisting. Coaxing, contorting spasm after spasm as his skin stretched out in knots. The unabashed torture intensified as it burrowed beneath his skin. He could feel his flesh betraying him as it pulled tightly at the intruder, closing and wrapping it within.

He somersaulted, and then bobbed in the water surfacing, his mangled half arm pissing out bright red blood torrents in all directions. The streams hissed and spit, throwing long steaming vapours into the air. A dense copper stench hung like a cloak over the tub, dipping and arching as it followed the trail of the ripe red streamers.

His mouth unroofed, bubbling out gob after gob of mucus filled blood. He groped at his side. He wrapped his fingers around the protrusion. He yanked pulling it free. The wound collapsed inward leaving gaping raw edges. They flapped, swelling with water, turning up as if smiling. Long red fibrous tentacles sucked in and out of the wound, twisting and turning as if they were performing a ritual based macabre waltz.

He manoeuvred the shaft bringing it eye level. The words 'Least we never forget ... Sable' scrawled in his mother's handwriting scorched his eyeballs. Imprinting and tunnelling into the dark memories he kept under lock and key. A cold sick sweat sprang across his forehead, foaming the water. He froze stiff. The arrow he had shot his sister with so long ago whipped in circles, riding the whirl pooling ripples, until something caught hold, stretching out tiny skeletal paws, climbing aboard.

He unlocked. His body trembled. His hair stood. His mouth opened and closed in silent rapid successions. The screams came slow and long, pitching and heaving as churning water vaulted down his throat. He suddenly stilled. His legs rose and arms spread. He floated on his back, dreamlike, eyes open, blood oozing.

Without warning, he bolted sideways. He rammed hard into the stair steps, slipped away, and then rammed again. Something was at him, something much larger. He could feel it clawing, tearing, and biting its way up his backbone towards the back of his neck. His skin ripped and stripped free like tissue paper.

He swung blindly with his arm, batting side to side over his head. It connected. A dark gray mushy something tumbled through the water, stopped, hovered then turned, as if taking aim. It surged its legs in unison propelling itself directly for his face. His throat bubbled out silent scream after scream after scream, as the decomposing cat tore and slashed making mincemeat of his cheeks before embedding its sixteen claws.

His hanging mouth all too quickly filled with dislodged maggots as the cat continued its unrelenting siege. They greedily wiggled in between his teeth, under his tongue, and down his throat feasting on remnants of leftover vomit. He swung wildly his fingers poking holes clear through its rotting flesh. He clutched at its tail. The stump slid through his hand like it had been freshly oiled.

The water surged then rolled with a single whitecap. The tub sides groaned and thundered as it smashed and slapped against them. As if cued, the cat pulled its head, mouth wide, its one eyeball staring profusely into his. It turned its head side to side. It jerked its paws free, releasing his flesh.

The cat swam lazily back and forth almost as if it was gloating.

Fred flayed his arm and legs, bobbing himself sideways.

The cat halted directly in front of him. Its back surfacing, its legs splayed, paws treading. Four skeletal kittens and mother cat of bones joined, forming an impregnable lineup. The arrow surfaced and sloshed lazily back and forth with the current. Two doves long since raped of flesh and plumage swooped and dipped back and forth through the spray overhead.

Fred's heart slowed, thundered, and missed beats. It echoed, bouncing throughout his body as if he was made of tin. His blood thickened. His pumping wounds ceased, weeping only bead-like pink watery dribbles all too quickly swallowed up and consumed.

He watched unable to flinch a muscle, transfixed by horror as the line broke and formed a semi-circle that started to close. He could hear high-pitched screams of terror, but did not equate them as his own.

The circle tightened. One of the kittens rushed, biting down, taking away his index finger at the knuckle.

Fred bellowed in agony as his eyes flickered of their own accord from skeleton to skeleton. The corners of all their jaws had an upturned slant, as if they were grinning. His mind slipped a clog and rotated. One single wire sparked, connecting, allowing simple one word thought. It played out in front of his eyes in large black and white teletype. "Death ... Kittens ... Death ... Cats ...Death ... Birds.' There was no connection, nothing. His mind sidestepped flashing small home movie snippets. 'A little sister shot with an arrow, a mother cat and kittens buried alive, doves shot, a house fire, a half grown cat tortured and left for dead.' Fred quaked side to side. His mind grew feet and fled, racing ahead of the rumbles as they cracked and tore at the very fabric of his being.

His heart quivered, shaking as if revolting. It became irregular, slowing, thumping like a washer out of balance. Paralyzing lightning bolts exploded from within, traveling through his body with the speed of sound, claiming his left side. The side with the stump arm. He tremored like he was being shook by some invisible force. Half his mouth drooped. He floated face down. His heart hiccupped, shuddered, spitted, and then regulated. He rolled his limp arm and legs splashing in the water.

The toothy smiles grew, drawing out into horrid grimaces as they surrounded.

He buckled, dropping his legs, feet flipping, treading water. His head awkwardly bobbed, sucking in and out of the waves. A dove swooped, landing on his skull. It started to peck and peck and peck. His eyes ringed with white. He held his breath. He flapped his arms, his stump savagely splashing. Pink foam started to leak from under the rollers as the pecking continued and the slashing and ripping started. Pieces of flesh and fat laden meaty chunks rose to the surface, floating, swishing back and forth, sliming and sticking to the tub sides.

He tilted side to side. One of the doves lost its balance, tumbling down onto his forehead. It slid as it scrambled to its feet. It dug in, balancing, perching on the bridge of his nose. It turned its head, flapping and prepping its wings as if admiring itself in the wide black pools of his eyes. It brought its head back, then thrust forward, ramming its beak clean through and out the other side of his eyeball. It made a hollow popping sound like a ripe purple grape being whacked as it ripped from the socket. The dove tilted its head, choking back its prize, devouring it in one gulp. It rolled down its throat descending into its rib cage where it promptly fell out between the bones splashing into the water.

Fred's drawn out howls took on an inhuman overtone as they pierced through the wind. Sheer agony racked over every inch of his body like long fingernails being drawn over a squeaky-clean chalkboard. Green, foul smelling bile dribbled down his chin. Blood spurted in torrents from the gaping hole in his abdomen where a tiny skeletal kitten pulled and yanked, feeding the water foot after foot of gray-brown sausage like links.

Darkness filled with little effervescent sparks peeled in on him. The pain dulled and dissipated.

Suddenly he was spinning in circles, his body high above the water. His looped intestines lay flat against his torso, drooped down to his knees, wrapping round them twice leaving one long loop as if about to be tied and knotted in place.

Lilith smiled. She gave him a slight shake.

He stopped rotating.

Lilith readjusted her grip, tossing him over to her other hand. She wrapped her fingers tightly about his neck just under his chin. She inclined into him. "Genesis two-seven," she said. "And the lord God formed man of the dust of the ground, and breathed into his nostrils the breath of life; and man became a living soul." She drew him close. "What a mistake that was! Whatever was he thinking?" She tutted, giving him another shake, swivelling her head back and forth in disgust.

She dropped him into the water.

He hit bottom, popping up headfirst.

She squatted on the rim watching him jostle back and forth, smiling as she observed the veil of death crawling across his face. She tossed her hand in a half wave silencing the water.

She grabbed him by the hair towing him towards her. She lifted his head and shoulders from the water.

His eyes fluttered then focused.

"Fred Kadigan, I am aware you've probably been fearful," she paused shifting her weight, folding up her wings. A mass of black feathers swirled then surged downward covering his head and shoulders.

Horror furrowed across his eyes.

She smiled.

He tried to pray but could not remember how.

Lilith's' smile broadened into laughter. "Pay no mind. It happens every time. They will grow back. They always do." She brought him closer. "Praying won't help you," she whispered. She moved him back in front of her. "Now, Fred Kadigan as I was saying."

His head dropped, flopping to the side.

She doused him in the water twice.

He gasped, sputtered, and then stared directly into her eyes.

"That's better," she said. "No going off just yet. As I was saying Fred Kadigan, I am aware you have probably been fearful your little Judy was missed. Forgotten if you will." Lilith scooted him closer. "After all it's not every day one gets into a vehicle accident and a tree bough severs their girl's head," she said quietly against his ear. She stretched back out her arm. "No mind," she said pausing, ruffling up what was left of his hair with her other hand. The arrow floated past. Lilith recited part of the inscription. "Least we never forget." She gave a backhanded wave at the tub and the water immediately obeyed, rolling into white caps, boiling and bubbling with hell's fury. Again she laughed.

Lilith raised herself to a stand clutching Fred. She leaned over the tub, tilting her hand side to side, swinging him back and forth until he was dead center.

"Least we never forget," she said again.

She released him.

Fred dropped, disappearing into the spray of the white caps, bobbing helplessly like a cork. His body smashed violently against the sides. The skeletons commenced where they left off, tearing and ripping to their heart's content.

His open mouth screamed silent scream after scream after scream after scream.

Lilith turned towards her shadow.

It was still perched on the stair railing of the tub staring intently into the water. It lifted its head, nodded in obedience, and then backed away. It quickly gathered the towels, clothing, and its mistress's carry bag. It threw them into the tub. The surface water swirled and lit, throwing flames, sparking the air.

Lilith motioned it to come.

It complied, standing two paces from her left shoulder.

Lilith bowed her head.

The shadow followed suit.

They spoke as one. "Philippians four-eight," they began. "Whatever is true, whatever is honourable, whatever is right, whatever is pure, whatever is lovely, whatever is of good repute. If there is any excellence and if anything worthy of praise, dwell on these things, Fred Kadigan."

The water drew, sucked in and out dousing the flames. It surged and frothed, then stilled.

The ground rumbled, heaving, rupturing, earth quaking.

The hot-tub base exploded with a deafening charge, shattering. Porcelain missiles launched through the water at lightning speed, carving and flaying Fred's flesh into ribbons as the water started to whip in circles sucking itself into the open ground.

A pair of skeletal arms surged from the earth. A headless vertebrate popped and swivelled, lunging on cue as if guided by some demonic sonar implant.

Fred twisted and bounced as Judy's slender claw-like fingers closed, embedding one by one in and through his ankles.

The water corkscrewed, spiking as it churned red-black.

Judy twisted her fingers ringing Fred's ankles, snapping and popping the bones like they were dry kindling. The fingers flexed, and then yanked, drawing him deep into the quicksand like earth and swallowing him whole.

Fred was no more.

The shadow bent, harvesting Lilith's' robe from the decking. It placed it about her shoulders, drawing up the hood.

Lilith descended the stairs and crossed the patio stones to the far side of the lawn.

The trees bowed with respect.

The earth tremored, shaking, rocking, rumbling. The hedges fell sideways. The lawn furniture collapsed into one another.

The kittens scurried out from the tub as the mother and stump tail cat flipped up and over the top edge. The doves skimmed the surface taking off simultaneously like two seaplanes.

The deck rattled, shaking, and heaving its screw nails, twisting and snapping in place as the planking punctured through itself.

The tub fissured and cracked, then imploded shattering into thousands of bite sized pieces.

The water bubbled, mixing the earth and stirring it into molten mud as it ruptured splitting wide open. The decking shot outward, like matchsticks lifting and toppling over.

The earth grew a mouth and opened wide, greedily gulping down decking, tub, hedges, and lawn furniture.

Lilith glided silently across the newly formed shoots of green grass where the decking and hot tub once sat. Her robe whisked back and forth in the gentle breeze. The skeletons trailed her.

She extended her left arm snapping her fingers.

The loud snap echoed throughout the night sky.

"Promises made. Promises kept," she said. She walked off into the darkness.

The doves were the first to spasm. Their bones trembling with the sudden re-birth of tendons and muscles. Their bodies coated in downy baby fluff and then grew feathers. They beat their wings savagely, strengthening them as they prepared for flight. The kittens and cats grew lean and brawny, with shimmering coats that glistened in the night rays. They tore across the grass, galloping after her, bouncing and dancing as only cats can do in the moonlight. The half-grown cat waved her little stumpy tail back and forth in delight as she scurried and pounced at the folds of the robe whisking along the gravel roadway. The doves swooped and soared overhead.

A swift breeze wormed through the woods. A branch snapped. The grass rustled.

Lilith smiled.

The wind picked up wavering the treetops.

Lilith stretched out her arm extending her hand. "Come Judith, there is much to make ready ... The skies are whirling ... The moon will soon grow a face and speak," she said.

A warm hand slipped into Lilith's.

They whisked through the darkness. The night shadows came alive, arching and nodding as they passed.

Judy bent picking up one of the kittens. It purred bunting its head against her chin.

Lilith"s' shadow stepped in each of her footsteps; following close behind, but not too close. It had made that mistake only once.

'Wednesday Morning'

"This is me is that you?" Fred's answering machine whirred and clicked twice.

Kenny plunked down the receiver not leaving a message.

Gord poked his head around the door. "Get an answer at Freddie's yet?" he asked.

"Nope, just the machine," Kenny replied. He handed Gord the morning newspaper. "Odd," Kenny said. "Don't you think?"

Gord shrugged, tucking the paper under his arm. He watched Kenny hit the redial button trying again.

"Nothing," Kenny muttered.

Gord leaned against the doorframe. "Maybe he died and went to hell." 'Where he belongs,' he added under his breath. He turned and walked out the door.

Ina Louise Jackson

FRED KADIGAN

Epilogue

There is this saying:
"Sometimes bad things happen to good people."
In Fred Kadigan's' case:
'Sometimes bad things do happen to bad people.'

NO SCAVENGING

Dedication

For George: Bless your heart for
Mispronouncing the sign.
God speed
1942 - 2005

Prologue

You cannot see the pattern,
If all you see is the first one.

Ina Louise Jackson

NO SCAVENGING

Sometimes ... That, that is not known, is best left that way.

'October 13th, 1885'

'Port Smith Daily Times Newspaper' excerpt from headline:

Grizzly Massacre at the Wood's family farm. Local authorities concluded the assault must have taken place at least two days prior to the gruesome discovery by the Wood's neighbour Mr. Fielding. The times of deaths were estimated based on the state of decomposition of the remains. Details of the deaths are withheld due to the sensitive nature. There is speculation a drifter may be responsible.

It is reported that not one single member of the Wood's household survived, including the family dog and all farm animals. A large mass of body parts believed to be pieces of Mr. Wood's torso and limbs was found lying beside a freshly dug four foot deep hole where it appears he unearthed some sort of artefact. It is presumed this was the reason for the massacre.

The artefact, is thought to have been contained in an ornately carved wooded cage, which it is assumed was pried open with Mr. Wood's shovel. Local archaeologist Mr. Stemple, has preliminarily dated the age of the wooden cage to be approximately 3000 to 3200 BC and of Egyptian origin. While there appears to be an inscription along each frontal column, translation at this time is deemed unnecessary.

Burial services for the Wood's family will be held Tuesday at noon, weather permitting.

The local sheriff has announced a hundred-dollar reward will be posted tomorrow morning for anyone with information leading up to the arrest of the presumed drifter.

'October 2nd, 1886'

Excerpt from 'New West Peachtree Press News:'

Authorities today reported the once bustling community of 'Port Smith' to be deemed a ghost town. The coroner has concluded the bones scattered throughout the town appear to be of mainly human origin.

The area has been completely sealed off while demolition is in progress. Once the levelling is complete, all will be burned in one massive site. The erection of a stone memoriam in the town's honour is planned for spring. Donations can be deposited in the tin drop box inside the Mayor's front office.

The county sheriff has noted one curious item; an ornately carved wooden cage in the middle of Main Street.

'October 15th, 1886'

'Daily Sincoe News Express': extract from front page:

A reliable source has indicated a hundred mile quarantine in all directions has been imposed upon the 'Port Smith' sector.

It has been confirmed that all life forms within the vicinity are deceased, people, animals, and wildlife alike. The source also indicated portions of what is believed to have been an adult male, although identification was near to impossible due to the desecration, was found near a freshly dug crater sized hole up on Cable Ridge where a wooden cage of some sort was being unearthed or buried.

An eyewitness to this account had also come forward though now is unavailable for comment, as is the reliable source. Both proceeded to the area the day before yesterday and have yet to return.

It is suspected some form of plague or virus has infiltrated the district. Water and soil samples have been sent for analysis.

Action, Reaction, Consequence, Recourse ...

'October 20th, 12:00 p.m. present day'

"How long is the site going to be shut down?" The man in the blue truck asked. He thumped the steering wheel with his middle and index fingers in frustration.

"Oh, just for the morning," the landfill attendant replied. "Nice backhoe you dump guys got."

The attendant shrugged her shoulders giving the mustard yellow machine and the massive mounds of muck it had unearthed a sideways glance.

The man in the truck backed, pulled a three-point turn, and then drove off.

'October 20th, 2:00 p.m. present day'

"Think we'll see a bear?" Miles Miller asked his father.

"Don't know. Might be a tad early," Jack replied.

Miles pressed his lips against the back window making fish smooches. "Are we there yet?" he asked. He blew into the middle of each print steaming the window up into an oddly patterned frosted glass pane.

Jack and Susanna Miller held one another's eyes. Jack's mouth drew into the cat that ate the canary' smile. He had beaten her out, winning with ten minutes and counting to the question, 'Are we there yet?' Susanna had bet on fifteen. He was going to enjoy Chinese tonight after all. If she won, it would have been Italian. He turned his head to her, winked and gave her hand a squeeze, slowed and flipped on the indicator turning down the roadway into the dump.

"Daddy! ... Daddy! ... See any bears? ... See any? ... Do you?" The five-year-old jerked his dad's headrest back and forth, as he pulled himself to a stand. He climbed over the seat plastering his face up against the windshield. "See any? See any?" He whipped his head side to side, as if his neck was made of rubber. "See any Daddy?" he asked again.

Jack pulled the truck over to the office rolling down his window. "Any bears out?" he asked the attendant.

"Nope ... Funny though, at this time of year they are usually here by now ... Maybe all the commotion and noise scared them off." The attendant motioned over to the backhoe.

Miles sighed, plopping down between his parents. He folded his hands together "I wanted to see bears," he said almost too quiet to hear.

Susanna fished through her pocket pulling out a grape lollipop. She leaned over pressing her lips against her son's forehead. "We'll come back again next weekend," she said softly. "Maybe we will see some then." She wiggled the lollipop flag like into the crevice between Miles' thumbs.

He instantly started unwrapping.

Jack gave the attendant his free pass for the load of construction materials. His gaze drifted to the machine "What are you building?"

"A new retaining wall." The attendant separated the tab from the pass handing the bottom portion back through the window.

Jack smiled; 'Another good use of his taxes.'

"We have to dig a base, so I'm told," the attendant added.

Jack eyed the mammoth square cut boulders. "Building it out of those I presume?"

"Yep."

"Must have cost a pretty penny?"

The attendant shook her head back and forth. "Don't know sir, I only work here part-time."

"Well, have yourself a good day now."

The attendant smiled and gestured him on.

Jack put the truck in low gear, climbing the steep hill to the construction pile. He gave the attendant a backhanded wave then rolled up the window, before parking at the bottom of the pile.

Susanna grabbed onto the back of Miles' sweatshirt as he skipped hurriedly past. He abruptly slung shot backward into her thighs. "Hey young man slow down, you can get hurt in here. Stay in sight okay?"

"Kay."

"And ... And ..." She turned him around, bent, looking him straight in the eyes. "Don't ... I repeat don't touch anything," she adjusted his baseball cap. "All right?"

He nodded, walked three paces, and then ran full tilt hopping on top of a pile of old mattresses, bouncing side to side.

Susanna frowned watching him bob up and down. "Good alternative to a trampoline I suppose," she muttered. The cooled October air nipped at her fingertips. She rubbed her hands together, made them into fists, blew into them, and then placed each deep within her sweater pockets warming them.

"Jack, just look at all those lawn chairs." Susanna walked closer taking a better look at the gigantic pile.

"Yeah I know. Something isn't it?" Jack flipped down the tailgate, off-loading the truck.

Susanna lifted a chair from the pile giving it a once over "They're in perfect shape. Makes' you wonder why people would throw them away. They look like they're brand new." She took down another rolling it over; it still had the store's tag attached to one of the slats. "Look, this one is brand new." She shook her head in disbelief as she shoved the chairs back into the pile.

"Want them?" he asked. "They'd look great on our back deck."

Susanna pointed to the big red and white sign a mere five feet from them. 'NO SCAVENGING by orders of Saren County. Video surveillance in place. BI-law No. 341 strictly enforced.'

Jack chuckled openly. "You see a video camera anywhere?" He swept the yard with his arms.

"Well, no but ..."

Jack cut her off. "Ah come on," he grinned. "Let's live dangerously." He walked over and picked up one of the chairs.

"Mommy! ... Daddy! ... Look what I found!" Miles' screeching voice pitched and hollowed like an over eager fan running from the tunnel back into the stands at a baseball game.

Susanna put her right hand to her forehead, folding her thumb neatly under at a cross-angle. She scouted the lot whirling in circles. Miles seemed to have vanished. "Miles? ... Miles? ... Where are you? ... Miles?"

"Mommy! ... Down here! ... I'm down here! ... Come look what I found!"

Seconds later his blue jeans clad backside poked up over the top edge of the tremendous mountain of dirt alongside the backhoe. "This ... would ... be ... great ... for ... Buffy," he huffed in short strained bursts of breath. "Just ... wait ... till ... you ... see ... it ... Mommy."

Miles splayed his legs, firmed his stance, and jerked hard. He fell backwards landing on his rump. The wooden cage flew out of his grip, up ended, rolling itself at a feverish pace down and through the gooey earthen sludge. It landed with a loud plop spewing muck in all directions.

Cold chills swept up and down Susanna's spine. She flipped up her hood pulling the strings taught.

'Boom ... Ra ... Ta ... Tat ... Boom ... Ra ... Ta ... Tat,' shot through the air carving it in two equal halves. It spun like a miniscule dust devil launching directly into Susanna's left ear, played one set of Ping-Pong inside her head, then exited out her right. She flicked her eyes side-to-side questionably and then glanced back behind her. She shook her head grabbing the drawstrings of her hood, double knotting them under her chin. She looked behind again. ""Right ... Okay then, I'm losing it,"" she quietly whispered.

Miles expertly skied down the hill on his runners, crouched, and then rolled onto his side purposefully tumbling himself twice before reaching bottom. "Isn't it neat Mommy?" He grabbed onto the cage pulling himself to a stand.

"You want this? ... This?" Her tone shrilled, then grew hoarse. She cleared the frog out of her throat, swallowing hard. Her oesophagus spawned another in the four short paces to her son. She forced a cough. "You want this thing? ... For Buffy?"

"Yeah! ... Wouldn't he just love it?" Miles ran his hands across the topside of the cage. "Wouldn't he Mommy? Its big, roomy, and neat looking. I could get him a bunch more stuff and a hammock too!"

Susanna swallowed hard again, suddenly unable to answer. She folded her arms wrapping them snugly around her chest, backing. For some obscure reason, all she wanted to do at that moment was just get the hell out of there and go back home.

"Daddy isn't it neat?"

Susanna did not smile like usual, at her son's quick change. The old 'When one doesn't respond immediately try the other,' had been learned very early on with this kid.

Jack flipped the cage over inspecting it.

Susanna physically jumped, spooking. She hadn't noticed Jack beside her. When he right-sided it knocking some of the dirt free, she fanned her arms pointing

90

desperately to the sign. She shuffled her feet, her unsettled feeling turning fearsome in a way indefinable to words.

"Hey! ... You were about to lift the lawn chairs." He gave her a devilish grin.

She hugged her body tighter. "I ... I ... was ... was n ... not!" she said in garbled hoarseness. Her tongue had dehydrated, anchoring itself down in behind her front bottom teeth. She pried it loose thrusting it into the inside of each cheek searching for shreds of moisture. The skin poked out in round marble like humps mirroring one another, staying transfixed, puffed like they had been flash frozen. Susanna, more than anything else, resembled a crazed character from one of Miles' Saturday morning cartoons that had been pumped full to the brim with helium and was about to blow.

Jack slowly cocked his head to the side narrowing his eyes. "Would you care to repeat that?" His mouth did not smile.

She poked her cheeks back in place with her thumb and middle finger. Worked her mouth with her hands opening and closing it in rapid successions, and then repeated herself. "I ... Was ... Not!" she said, chirping out each word separate and apart.

"Yeah right," he retorted. His eyes hung on her face studying her.

"I was not," she countered again. She pointed over to the sign once more. "It's not right! ... And ... And ... That sign's there for a reason ... You know! ... And ... And besides we'll get caught," she said quickly, abruptly.

His expression softened. "You done?" His dimpled smirk could have lit up the night sky.

"Yes! ... No! ... One more thing!"

"Y ... E ... S?" He drew out the one word reply long and slow forming and contorting his lips purposely into an odd array of shapes.

"Just, just what are we teaching our son? ... Tell me that will you?"

"We are teaching him about salvaging for the common good," Jack replied his smirk turned broader.

"You're impossible!"

Susanna stared at the cage. It was heavily clumped and caked with old and new dirt and some sort of gray crud that resembled dried cement. She poked at it with the tip of her sneaker. Her foot numbed, her leg prickled with thousands of pins and needles, like it had been weighted down with five hundred pounds for hours upon hours, and then suddenly freed. She wilfully dragged her outstretched limb from the cage, pulling and tugging at it hand over fist. It felt leaden and awkward like it belonged to someone else ... Someone dead. A shudder rocked her body. She zipped her sweater. "I don't like this thing," she said quietly. She bit at her lip, chewing it in the middle.

"Isn't it neat Mommy?" Miles squatted down in front of the cage jabbing at the dirt clumps with a stick.

She stared at the cage. She took in a huge breath gulping it back like a man dying of thirst. 'Isn't it neat Mommy ... Isn't it neat Mommy?' repeated inside her head, bouncing like a new glossy rubber ball, smashing into things. 'Isn't it neat Mommy? ... No, Miles it is not neat ... I do not like it ... I do not like it one bit ... Why don't I like it? ... I don't know ... I just don't ... No sir ... Don't like it at all ... It's ... Its damn well horrid ... Yeah right! ... I'll just get on this. I'll pitch it all out in one long babble complete with the waving arm gestures and big cow eyes so my husband and son can both look at me like I've just grown three heads, maybe four if I pull it off good'.

She shifted her eyes to the chairs, to the sign, then back to that cage. She shuffled over to her son, her feet rebelling as if they'd suddenly acquired a mind of their own, flipping and painfully bending back her toes binding them up underneath like a 'Japanese concubine.' She slowly lowered herself, kneeling beside him. Her skin immediately broke into a cold sweat.

'Boom ... Ra ... Ta ... Tat ... Boom ... Ra ... Ta ... Tat ... Boom.'

There it was again. She glimpsed nervously around her. "What the hell is that?" she asked.

"What Mommy?" Miles replied mindlessly, still jabbing away at the dirt clumps.

'Boom ... Ra ... Ta ... Tat ... Boom ... Ra ... Ta ... Tat ... Boom ... Ra ... Ta ... Tat.'

"Don't you hear that?" She slowly glanced over one shoulder, and then the other. She detailed the office, the people, and the vehicles searching for a point of origin. Nothing out of the ordinary.

"Hear what Mommy?" Miles asked again.

No sooner had the words departed Miles' lips when everything changed, abruptly, completely, like all within had been clicked on pause by some giant being's remote control so they could go off and make a sandwich. The silence chilled to the bone, unnerving and playing off your senses, introducing perplexity like some impenetrable fog, blotting out, covering and concealing all things alive and all things not, declaring this peculiarity the site of the earths' newest gateway to unnaturalness. Not a frog croaked, bird chirped, nor leaf rustled.

Susanna unconsciously leapt, springing like a frightened animal too close to a sudden downed 'UFO.' She brought her feet up under her, intertwined her fingers in the hood of Miles' sweatshirt bouncing them both backwards frog-like. She hunched her shoulders, dropped them, hunched again. Her flesh felt as if it was crawling round in circles inside her sweater.

"Hey guys." Jack placed his hands on their shoulders.

Susanna lurched forward, startled, swaying as if she was made of elastic.

Jack tightened his grasp. "You all right?" he whispered.

Susanna did not answer.

"'Okay, maybe I'll just leave well enough alone,' he thought. He started over. "Hey guys ... Tell you what?"

"Wh ... a ... t?" her voice wavered and squeaked. She cleared her throat; it seemed to have grown some sort of thick gooey fuzz.

Jack's eyebrows rose, growing together. He ran his tongue along the outside of his bottom lip. Susanna was acting a little odd ... Who was he kidding, She was acting a lot odd ... Maybe, he ran his tongue over his bottom lip again, maybe, it was just the residue from the creepy movie they watched last night. It was set in the woods and here they were, surrounded by them. Nevertheless, he did not see any half-dressed cannibals carrying axes, not a one.

He slid his hands from their shoulders wrapping them both in a bear hug. He kissed Susanna softly on the cheek. Her skin felt cold, clammy. "So guys ... what do you say, Mommy ... You go talk to the attendant and distract her and I'll throw some of the chairs and the cage in the box." He walked in reverse over to the truck, grabbed the tarp flapping it back and forth. "Who's to know?" he added.

Susanna brushed at the dirt on her jeans. She stared up at the sign. It seemed to have gotten closer, as if it had jumped poles so it could intentionally loom and eavesdrop. "I don't know ... I just don't know about this." She glanced apprehensively around her. She sidestepped slow and cautiously over to Jack. "There's," she lowered her voice, and then gestured toward the cage. "There's ... There's something about that thing ... I just don't lik ... like." She had to voice her feelings. It was eating away at her insides like an oversized worm in an intestine. She scrutinized Jack's eyes.

He sucked the air drawing it between his teeth. His gaze turned stone cold. His facial features masked, not divulging any hint of emotion. It suddenly reminded her way too much of the adult male faces that came and went, with her mother's beckoning, in early childhood, sending her to her room without supper. She glanced at the ground.

The five seconds of silence that passed between them seemed devoid of life, deafening beyond measure and an hour long.

"Oh come on!" Jack unexpectedly blurted. "Live dangerously for once," he coaxed.

Susanna looked up shyly, feeling as if she had all of a sudden been dismissed by her homeroom teacher after serving part of a detention. 'Whatever,' she thought sweeping his reaction off. She switched veins. "But, but ... It's stealing, isn't it?" she said quietly.

"Think of it as recycling," he quipped. The usual softness in his eyes was still missing, but his mouth smiled.

"I don't know ... I ... I ... I." She stopped mid-sentence. She was losing this mini battle, if that 'is what it was. She heaved a sigh. Underneath it all his heart was in the right place, as it always was. Her irrational, 'I don't like the thing,' lacked a viable base that could be formed into some sort of logical explanation. Nor could it even be turned into anything other than a stupid explanation of something unexplainable. Nevertheless, whatever the cause was, or wasn't, she did not like the thing.

He put his hands on her hips gently pivoting her half a turn, facing her toward the office. He held out both his arms in the arrest position. "Go on over. I'll be responsible for the deed, if we get caught." He smiled then gave her a slow deliberate wink.

She hated when he did that. Those winks always melted her like a pot full of butter over high heat. Always had, probably always would.

He gave her back a pat. "Come on ... Go ... Our Chinese is a waiting."

"Please ... Please, please Mommy." Miles joined the cause, each side of his pouted little lips showing off his father's' expertly cloned dimples. "Please ... Please can I have the cage for Buffy? ... Pretty please Mommy?"

She squished up her face sucking her lips into her mouth, camouflaging her smile from view. She swished the tip of her tongue on and off the roof of her mouth. There they stood, side by side, the big one and the little one, the two greatest joys and loves of her life.

She strode off in the direction of the office.

~~~

"We'll here it is, all cleaned up and ready for Buffy." Jack crossed the bedroom setting the wooden cage down, cornering it evenly into the walls directly across from Miles' bed. "It sure is a beaut after you get all that muck and crap off." Jack dragged his fingers slowly across the ornate carvings.

Miles took the ferret from his metal wire cage, gave him a kiss on the head and placed him in his lap. He propped the wood door open, then started placing Buffy's dishes, litter pan, and toys inside.

Susanna watched from the doorway. She unconsciously began tapping her left foot to a slow, odd, tribal like rhythm broadcasting from inside her head. "I don't like this ... I don't like this one bit ... I don't know why I don't like this ... But I don't," she said low, grated, off key. Her mind repeated her words, hurdling and throwing them at her like darts.

Jack joined her, draping his arm over her shoulder. "You know," he whispered. "I almost threw the thing into the truck and headed back to the dump with it. I had one hell of a time getting all the crap off it. And to compound matters, prying that damn door open. It was as if it had been sealed shut or something, took me an hour."

Susanna forced a smile that more so resembled a scowl than anything else. Her psyche, hand selected from his words, picking some, 'The thing ... Hell of a time ... Damn door open,' adding some, 'With the ... Will now ... Give you ... One.' It tumbled them in a clear plastic bingo ball until they formed a sentence it could spit out on red ticket tape in one line. 'The thing with the damn open door will now give you one hell of a time.'

"I wish you had thrown the thing into the truck and headed back to the dump with it too," she said. Her flesh seemed to squirm then goose bump, standing the hairs on the back of her neck to attention.

"For Christ's sake," Jack sneered.

"Christ, I don't think, has anything to do with that thing," she replied in lifeless monotone. Her left foot still tapped, scoring out the repetitive rhythm as if she had been born to it. 'Boom ... Ra ... Ta ... Tat ... Boom ... Ra ... Ta ... Tat.'

"What' in heaven's sake is wrong with you?"

"I don't think heaven has anything to do with it either." She ducked out from under his arm taking a step back. Her goose bumps had grown and mutated into giant hives. She could feel them under her tee shirt, puffing and filling with hot fluid, stretching her skin taut.

"Jesus," Jack scoffed.

"I told you! ... I don't like that thing!"

"It's just an old cage."

"No, it's not!"

"Then ... What is it? ... A set of dishes?"

"You're an ass!"

"So you say, sometimes," he quipped. "You really don't like it?"

"No."

"Care to tell me why?" The corners of his mouth were starting to go up.

"No, I can't."

"I see ... Is there something about the lawn chairs too then?"

"No!"

"No?" His grin turned into a hearty smile.

"No ... I said no."

"Why not?"

"Cause, they're only chairs."

He seemed more amused by the second. "And this isn't only a cage?" He gestured with his left arm in the direction of the cage.

"No, it's not!"

He dragged his hand over his mouth trying to contain his laughter. "Come on now ... Don't get all ruffled up ... Maybe," he lowered his voice out of Miles' earshot. "If you'd quit with all those horror movies and stupid documentaries on paranormal stuff you're always watching on television, which by the way seems to be starting to affect you." He leaned closer dropping his voice to barely a whisper. "And not in a good way might I add. Then maybe a cage would just be a cage ... Think about it?"

Susanna glared at him cold, hard, her eyes widening to the max. He had just graduated from an ass to an asshole. She shifted back into the small hall. Her left foot as if cued abruptly stilled from its unwitting drum beating. She leaned against the bathroom doorframe, stretching out her legs, crossing one over top of the other preventing entry into her personal space.

Her foot quivered, restarting its tapping. She started to hum then sing, chanting in short huffs and puffs, rhythmic and tribal, reciting words that held no sense or meaning to her. "Droom-Vloofi ... Droom-Vloofi ... Droom-Vloofi ... Droom-Vloofi," she wailed. She accompanied herself drumming the wall with her fingernails 'Boom ... Ra ... Ta ... Tat ... Boom ... Ra ... Ta ... Tat ... Boom ... Ra ... Ta ... Tat ... Boom.' Each ticking second seemed to intensify, collapsing into itself as she drummed the beats of the repetitive rhythm. She flattened her hand using her palm as a make shift tom-tom knocking it on and off the wall, hardening and pulsing it into bangs and thumps. She swayed her hips stiffly side-to-side like a voodoo captive caught up in the throes of possession. She drummed harder and faster, both feet flipping, tapping, and fighting off the sudden urge to set a blazing campfire in the hall way and dance round it naked with her hair stuffed full of eagle feathers.

A shadowy contour whisked across the inside of the cage. In the blink of an eye it was there and gone. Unnoticed in time and space.

'Boom ... Ra ... Ta ... Tat ... Boom ... Ra ... Ta ... Tat ... Boom ... Ra ... Ta ... Tat ... Boom.' She swung her hips bending her knees, rolling and rounding her sways. "Droom-Vloofi ... Droom-Vloofi," she sang.

"Ahhh!" she squealed, ramming into the doorframe. Paralyzing pain seared through her hip joint and down her one leg. She grabbed at her hand cherry picker like with the other hastily forcing it from the wall. 'Where in hell did all that come from?' she mouthed silent, shocked with herself.

The rhythmic infusions hollowed, subsiding far too quickly into background white noise, taking along the anomalous words letter by letter. Her eyes flashed side to side then straight ahead, zoning in on the cage. Alarm crept across her forehead. Her toes lifted, bent, starting to tap. She cemented her feet to the floor. Her fingers curled, flexing in and out, in and out of their own accord. She shoved her hands into her pockets.

She pressed the thumbs and index fingers of each hand hard into one another taking a purposeful deep breath. She held it for a count of ten then released, performing an anti-anxiety breathing tactic. She repeated the process five more times until she felt the onset of calm drift over her.

She wished she could just start this entire damn day over. It had been, at her insistence that they all went to the dump in the first place. She wanted to get rid of the construction materials from building the two-piece bathroom off the family room a month back. She could have easily lived with it for another week or two, or three or even four. If only she had just baked the chocolate cookies like Miles had wanted.

She angled her head back purposely thumping it hard into the wood of the bathroom door. She closed her eyes enveloping the darkness, drawing it inside. Immediately ... The cage ... That retched cage ... floated past in living colour, sailing along mindlessly, effortlessly, atop a black sea, it's mast trailing that awful red and white sign 'No Scavenging by orders of Saren County' along for the ride. The sign dipped then spun, flapping and slapping against the mast like it was caught up in a wind current. It tore and tattered, then commenced dripping blood red, oily ooze down through the riggings and onto the wooden rungs. It gathered then pooled into the water, swirling and engulfing the cage.

'Boom ... Ra ... Ta ... Tat ... Boom,' battered her left eardrum.

She jolted, snapping her eyes open.

'Boom ... Ra ... Ta ... Tat.'

Her brow beaded with perspiration.

"Are you okay?" Jack asked. This was the second time he had asked a question ... The same question ... On the same day ... Knowing it would be the same answer.

Susanna shook her head in a slow no.

He held his hand to her forehead. "You're really not all right are you? Do you want me to get you a glass of water?"

"No."

Jack's mouth had already started to form the first syllable of a long string of words, which would form into sentences and questions, when Miles' voice filtered in, drawing his attention.

"Daddy? ... After supper can we go to the pet store and get Buffy a hammock and some new stuff to play with?" Miles stroked Buffy's head then placed him into the wooden cage. He fastened the door.

"Sure," Jack replied. He glanced at Susanna, she had moved away from the bathroom doorframe.

"Great, I'll get my piggy bank."

"It's okay. It is on Mommy and me. We ..."

Susanna cut Jack off. "Maybe we should put Buffy in his old cage until we get back home," she spoke so rapidly the words almost needed decoding. She rushed the cage, swept out her arm and stretched out her hand towards the door. Her fingers immediately burned, sizzling and popping as if on fire. She shook her hand, flinging it back and forth and up and down furiously blowing on her flesh as if she was dousing flames. She went at the door. "What do you think guys?" she said without turning. She jerked at the latch reefing it back and forth. The fastener seemed riveted in place. She booted it with her foot driving the corner of the cage into the wall.

"Mommy! ... Mommy! ... You're going to scare Buffy!" Miles squealed.

Susanna threaded her fingers through the cage door rungs, anchored both feet on the cage spacing them equal distances each side of the hinges, raising her body off the floor in the process. She heaved for all she was worth. Her hands slipped, springing off like old fashioned 'Slinky' sending her down onto her rump a quarter ways cross the room. She hurriedly rolled, righting herself, swiftly crawling on her hands and knees towards the cage.

Jack stepped in her way road blocking her route. "You're acting a little bizarre dear ... Don't you think?" he whispered.

'Boom ... Ra ... Ta ... Tat ... Boom ... Ra ... Ta ... Tat.'

Her eyes widened like saucers. 'There it was again! ... Can't he hear it? ... Can't they hear it?' She butted his legs with her head trying to ram past.

'Boom ... Ra ... Ta ... Tat ... Boom.'

She lifted her head, eyes probing the room, 'Television ... off ... Radio ... off ... Computer ... off ... Game systems ... off.'

'Boom ... Ra ... Ta ... Tat.'

Her eyes fused onto the cage. She jerked one hand from the floor putting it over her mouth. 'It's got to be that thing,' she thought.

'Boom ... Ra ... Ta ... Tat.'

Her mouth pressed into her palm opening and rounding. 'On my God ... Oh my God ... It is that thing!'

She rose to her knees. "CAN'T YOU HEAR THAT?" she shouted. Her eyes whipped feverishly from Jack to Miles and back.

Jack and Miles exchanged glances, and then in unison turned towards her, staring blatantly as if she had just morphed into a pink and black winged elephant.

"Hear what?" Jack asked. He cleared his throat on purpose.

'Boom ... Ra ... Ta ... Tat.'

"THAT!" she screeched. She lifted her arm swinging it toward the cage. "THAT BOOM ... RA ... RA!" she screamed.

"What?" Jack repeated.

'They can't hear it,' she gasped. 'They can't hear it? ... Oh my Lord God, they can't hear it!' She pulled Jack's legs apart wriggling through them toward the cage. She yanked and jerked at the door.

Miles grabbed onto her hand easing his fingers through hers. "He's okay Mommy. Really he is. Look see," he pointed at Buffy. "He's sniffing around."

Her eyes locked with Jack's.

He instantaneously mouthed, "'what in the hell is wrong with you?'"

She choked on the dry lump sitting on the back of her tongue. 'What in hell is wrong with me?' she thought. 'What in hell is wrong with you?' She reefed the cage door with both hands. The cage drew towards her. 'What ... In ... Frigging ... hell?' Miles had closed it so effortlessly mere minutes ago. 'Why won't the Goddamn thing open now? ... Why? ... Oh, Lord why?' She tugged hard, feverishly, brutally raking the cage back and forth along the floor.

Jack and Miles without a word caught her under the arms, sliding her across the floor backward toward the hallway. She turned her head watching the ferret over one shoulder. He was digging in his food bowl scattering bits of food into his bedding.

She grasped the doorframe. "WAIT! ... WAIT!" she blurted. "We have to get him out of there and say the Droom-Dro-Dra." Her eyes expanded in disbelief, she had no earthly idea of what in hell she was saying or why she was saying it.

"The what?" Jack asked.

"The Droom-Dro-Dra." There, she'd said it again. Her mouth had opened and out it had come, again. 'Oh my God ... What in hell is wrong with me?' She dug her fingernails into the palms of her hands. 'Is this a dream?' Her nails broke into the flesh. She winced in pain. 'Pain? ... Pain! ... No ... Not a dream ... Oh God help me!' She choked, coughing and sputtering out the sudden over flow of saliva.

"What?" Jack repeated.

He compressed his lips against his teeth. He shook his head. 'They already had more than enough fruit loops in the house; though they were all safely tucked in the kitchen cupboard, at least as far as he knew. Had she had too many this morning and was now in sugar overload? Or, maybe too much coffee, or stepped in toxic waste at the dump? He didn't know ... Whatever the hell she was going through was far beyond him. He was going to phone their family Doctor Monday and make an appointment for her.'

He looked down at her. She was still latched onto the doorframe, knuckles white, eyes crazed. "What the hell are you even saying?" He motioned for Miles to get his jacket.

"We have got to get him out of that thing and say The Droom-Dro-Dra," she replied. She'd said it yet again. She'd spoke and there it was. 'Again? ... AGAIN! ... What on earth?' She popped her index finger into her mouth ringing her tongue with it. 'What the hell am I saying? ... A ... A?' The words were not there. 'Okay ... Okay ... This is not a dream ... It doesn't make sense, but it doesn't matter ... All that matters, is that animal has to come out of that thing ... And now! ... Maybe if I just act nonchalant? ... They'll come around and we can get him out of there.' She smiled up at Jack, ran her hand through her hair, patting it back into place in an attempt to appear unfrazzled. "I ... I."

He cut her off. "A Dream-Do?" he rapidly blurted. "The ferret has to have a dream." He hesitated then added, "whatever." He had no idea of what she was saying or why. He took a long pause carefully planning his next words. "Susanna please, I'm begging you, cut it out ... You are acting like a nut case ... Worse actually ... The ferret is fine ... He'll be fine all the time we're gone and he'll still be fine when we get back." He put his index finger to his lips as he did for Miles when he wanted him to shush, draped a sweater around her shoulders, and pulled her to her feet.

Jack threw on his sweatshirt, plucked the keys from the table, and locked the door behind them.

~~~

A veil of utter stillness fell over the home. Not like the usual silence when the humans were not within the walls, it was more so the cessation of sound when the descending darkness is consumed by evil; Much like depravity and inertness when it slithers into a soul and takes it over.

'Boom ... Ra ... Ta ... Tat ... Boom ... Ra ... Ta ... Tat ... Boom ... Ra ... Ta ... Tat ... Boom.'

The ferret held his left front paw up. His ears rotated and tweaked. He sniffed the air, whiskers twitching. His eyes plumped, darkened, his body grew taut. The fur along his backbone hoisted to attention. His heart rate doubled.

'Boom ... Ra ... Ta ... Tat.'

He lowered his haunches, stretching out, streamlining, his back legs tensing, feet pushing, nails scraping. He thrust forward launching himself like a missile through the air, his legs in full motion, galloping before they hit the ground. Round and round, faster and faster he circled the cage, blurring his outline at the edges. He collapsed on his side, chest heaving, tongue dipping out the side of his mouth. His broadening eyes whipped side-to-side, up, down, back, and forth.

'Boom ... Ra ... Ta ... Tat ... Boom ... Ra ... Ta ... Tat."

He raised his head tucking his front legs into his chest. He pivoted onto his stomach bringing himself to a stand. He buckled and went down, repeated and then stood. He drew backward, hunching into a ball, huddling into the far corner of the cage. He trembled and vibrated as his fright sidestepped giving way to terror. Small clicks and clacks rang and clanged, penetrating into the eerie silence, changing it up as his body knocked and thudded uncontrollably off and on the wooden side rungs.

His mouth gaped, distending, elongating as it let loose a lengthy series of high-pitched startled squeaks as he suddenly skidded across the cage floor. His tongue curled, jamming into the roof of his mouth. His tiny body quavered, shaking and vibrating his core. Without warning, he shot up into the air, twirled and spun like a top. His eyes widened, abruptly protruding from their sockets like over ripe grapes about to burst, his four legs out stretched. Unexpectedly, the spinning halted with a snap like the ride had suddenly slipped a gear. He swung side-to-side, suspended mid-air, as if invisible wires had been plunged through his body and out the top of his skull by some macabre puppeteer.

He began to rotate counter-clockwise, slow, purposefully, as if something was examining him in minute detail. His shrill frightened chirps gave way to long vile scream after scream, as his ribcage started to dent in, concaving and compressing, folding back into itself. He pitched side to side in spasms of agony. His bowels let go. He spewed urine. Without warning he pivoted and then started to whip violently from one side of the cage to the other, smashing into the rungs as if some giant invisible hand was using him to play a game of spatter ball. His terror filled screams pitched and hollowed as they echoed off the bedroom walls and closed windows. Blood started to bubble and spurt from his body, chunks of hair and flesh flew through the air and out the rungs, highlighting the bright blue walls in pink, red, and brown. His burbled breaths heaved, separating the squeals. Deep black heart blood pumped up through his oesophagus and spurted out his parted lips, abruptly dulling his screams to throaty gurgles.

The pitching ceased. His body juddered down and up like wire springs had been implanted in his hind legs. His tail started to turn and twist, wrapping around something that wasn't there. A crisp pop, followed by a snap, resounded. His body rippled and curled as his tail separated, dropped, up ending as it hit bottom. It rolled across the cage, soaking and sopping up everything in its path like a cadaverous sponge.

He again rocked, side to side, back and forth, his profile hazing and changing in shape and form. His screams droned to fluffy gurgles, then hisses, as the light started to leave his eyes, his bones cracking, splintering, and shattering as he was pressed pancake flat smearing into the rungs, out the other side and beyond. His constricted ribs made a crackling kind of popping sound as they sprung through his flesh, inverting like an umbrella in a violent windstorm. They caught on the wood rungs, hanging his unmoving carcass midway up the side of the cage like fresh meat in a packaging plant set out for final inspection. His bashed in skull sprouted pockets of curly gray tentacles which dangled loose and free on the one side of the cage as did the spliced flesh of his chest cavity, torso and four boneless limbs. On the opposite side lay the rest, more so resembling raw minced meat mixed with red jelly and slivered almonds then anything that was once alive and breathing. Clumps of fur-covered flesh ringed the cage bottom, walls, and floor. A bloody pelt, once attached to his back in the form of soft tissue and gleaming coat, lay halfway across the room near the garbage pail.

The veil of absolute stillness returned over the house, reaffirming that old saying 'Silence is golden.' However, if someone listened very carefully the silence and quiet had voided its ticket, becoming noiseless in an unnatural kind of way.

The cat, Libby, was noiseless too. Still beyond life, eyes half dislodged from their sockets, hair from bridge of nose to tip of tail standing straight, erect beyond measure.

She had been asleep, curled up deep into the cushion of her favourite chair by the window, long since tired of watching her playmate scuttle about investigating his new surroundings.

With the second, 'Boom ... Ra ... Ta ... Tat ... Boom ... Ra ... Ta ... Tat.' Her eyes had flashed open, growing huge and bulbous as she stared spellbound through the rungs at her galloping companion furiously flying in circles, a shadowy transparent substance weaving in and out, under, around and through his every movement as if taunting him. She had risen on all fours as he fell onto his side distressed, his chest heaving and shuttering. Her tail had twitched and bristled as the substance crept from beneath him, growing denser and denser as it rose. She had growled low, steady, as it had slithered about the cage, then stopped, turned in her direction, pressing itself against the rungs, fixating upon her.

With the third, 'Boom ... Ra ... Ta ... Tat ... Boom ... Ra ... Ta ... Tat.' Her tongue had flipped up and down in a full-blown pant as she leapt from the chair, crossed the bedroom, and ran straight up the dresser spraying piss like a yellow jet stream. She had seized when she reached the flat plateau, her body flipping and flopping on its side like a fish out of water. She shuddered and quaked, her heart retracting in spasm after spasm, beating a rhythm like an upright vacuum with a fur ball stuck in its roller belt. She continued the tremors, with oddball wobbles and jerks, drawing out and stiffening inside the final grand mal spasm as her fright, fear, panic, and terror twirled its swizzle stick blending the deadly doses with the last whispers of breath exiting her lungs. Her nose blew out mucus filled air bubbles, her blood thickened, reversed flow, backfilling and coagulating. She collapsed in a heap, toppling off and over the back edge of the dresser, landing like a sack of potatoes in behind the dresser to be served up later for the encore.

~~~

"Buffy! ... Buffy! ... Wait till you see all the stuff we got you!" Miles ditched his jacket, ran through the living room and down the hall into his bedroom. "Buffy! ... Buffy! ... Look Buffy!" He flipped the light switch. His body congealed. His mouth rounded. He screamed and screamed and screamed and screamed.

Susanna bolted, running through the house like a rabbit chased by hounds. Jack hopped the sofa running on her heels.

Susanna's mouth opened and closed in dry, rapid succession, uttering silent screams. She grabbed the bedroom doorframe, anchoring her weight. Her body swayed, pivoting back and forth on her toes. The walls and floor looked like they had been spray painted red by an amateur painter who neglected to shake the tin. The space smelled of feces and urine, with a dense copper overlay. There were small and large furry flesh chunks about the room like something had played dodge ball using an axe. What was left of Buffy hung dispersed through both sides of the cage as if something had attempted to strain the bones from his flesh by jamming him through the narrow rungs. His bloodstained head drooped onto his chest, his popped eyeballs hung by thin cords, his open mouth curled at the outer edges forming a horrid half moon.

Jack teetered back and forth beside Susanna. Repulsion and horror trickled down his throat settling in his limbs. His open mouth salivated, abruptly sputtering liquid surrounded air bubbles, which popped against his chin like water-filled balloons. He shut his eyes willing his appendages to move.

He thrashed forward bumping Susanna's doorframe stronghold. Her knees wobbled in circles. She collapsed against the wood.

He pushed past, scooping up his son, gathering him into his arms. He turned Miles' head, pressing his face hard against his chest. He caught the hood of Susanna's sweater twisting it through the fingers of his free hand and yanking her with him as he slowly backed into the hallway. His knees knocked with each step, rotating and threatening to buckle. He bounced off the bathroom door, stood motionless, drawing in breaths that seemed encased in shattered glass, and then sidestepped carefully crossing one foot over the other over the next as he veered right.

"He ... Her ... Here," he stuttered. He jerkily removed his hand from Susanna's sweater hood. He opened and closed his mouth attempting to squeak out something audible. His tongue slipped from the side of his mouth, shock infiltrating and infusing making him suddenly deaf and dumb. He couldn't speak, his body trembled, his hands vibrated, his throat had a lump the size of a golf ball. He dropped Miles on the bed. He forced his own mouth open with his hands, pushing and fingering his lips. "Yo ... y ... you st ... st ... Stay wit ... With Mil ... Miles i ... In our ro ... Room." He turned and shuffled out the doorway; dragging his feet with each step as if they were dead and about to fall off. He closed the door behind him.

He stood with his back pressed into their bedroom door counting under his breath; he could not remember what came after twelve. He started over. "'One, two, five, six, seven, eight, seven, ten,'" he stopped and stared at the hall light. He did not want to leave the security of the door and go into that room. He tried counting one more time aiming for a hundred. He gave up at five.

He coaxed one leg forward using his hands, and then the other. He scuffled his feet, minding them one by one as they sluggishly moved with an off kilter robot-like rhythm.

Without warning, they flipped sideways just before the door opening, filled with lead and refused to move. He directed his gaze to the floor examining the baseboards. It suddenly seemed as if they all had been cast into a reality horror show where the viewer's got to vote on who they thought would lose it first. 'Vote for me,' he quipped silently. His lips sketched into an askew smile. "I'm going to be you're it guy ... Lay your money on me," he said. He stretched his arms wall to wall, grinding his palms in semi-circles. He gritted his teeth. "Christ, Jesus Christ! ... Come on Jack pull it together." He pressed into the wallboard swinging his weight back and forth, then pushed and released, flinging himself past Miles' bedroom door.

He compelled himself to fetch a garbage bag, pail with hot soapy water, towels, and scrub brush. His legs quavered, knocking his knees against one another as he entered the room. His left foot skidded across the flooring, going out from under him. He halted, flapping and waving his arms, teetering and rocking, almost going down. He lifted his leg tilting his runner up. He crumpled his face. Something indefinable had stuffed into the treads.

He dropped the cleaning supplies, drew out his fingers flexing them, and then slowly peeled it away. It stuck to his fingertips sliming them. He shook it loose. It fell in slow motion landing hair side up; it's under carriage splatting when it hit the floor; Watered down red liquid oozed from all its four sides, quickly connecting and forging an outline. Vomit rose in his throat. He cupped his hands over his mouth. His throat burned as he swallowed it back down. His wide unblinking eyes focused downward, gluing themselves onto the tiny fur pelt beside his foot. If he did not know better, he would have sworn the entire back of the ferret had been surgically stripped with the precision of a scalpel.

He rocked back and forth. The room suddenly felt like it was rotating. He lifted his head. The cage with its bloody bounty came into full view. He boosted his weight balancing on the balls of his feet, taking in and blowing out structured breaths in a vain attempt to regain back the little composure he had left. He gave himself a shake.

He silently counted for a fourth time. Why was he counting? He didn't know. He never had before in his life. 'One, two, three, four, five, six, seven, eight, nine, ten,' he smiled; he' got it. "Ready or not, here I come," he said. He put one foot in front of the other walking slowly and deliberately towards the cage like this type of movement was a newfound skill and required immense effort and concentration.

He stood soundlessly in front of the cage. It almost looked like it was grinning, pleased that he stood before it paying homage. He booted it driving it hard into the wall.

His mind clicked on like it had been on pause, bypassing play, rewinding to an earlier conversation as if it had to make a point ... "I told you! I don't like that thing' ... 'It's just an old cage' ... 'No, it's not." He choked off his thoughts before the "I told you so" could surface, reach out its icy arm, extend its hand, and slap him.

"Okay ... Jack ... Old Man ... Let's get this done," he said. He could hear the drone of Susanna's voice soft and gentle, comforting their whimpering son in the other room. He selfishly wished it was him held within her arms, cocooned within her motherly warmth and security being assured everything was going to be okay.

But ... It never would be okay. Never again would it be. How could it? Buffy was no more. Gone, butchered into ribbons. The questions... 'How?' ... 'Why?'... did not surface.

He scanned the horror. 'Departed but not forgotten,' something inside him chirped. Tears rolled and dropped from his cheeks as he jerked the cage from the floor and carried it through the house into the garage. They'd had the little ferret a year longer than they'd had Miles. He was as much a part of the family as anyone. He dropped the cage.

He cleaned and mopped the bedroom erasing all the telltale signs of wickedness. It seemed so much more than death. It was like the epitome of evil. Something one would read in a horror novel or see in a motion picture. He surveyed the room. It was as it was before, minus the ferret.

He went out the kitchen door avoiding the garage. He grabbed the shovel from the garden shed and crossed the backyard to the flower garden. It was here Buffy loved best. He dug a hole and erected a crude two by four cross. He went to the garage, dropped to his knees and crawled across the floor to the cage. He wiped the blood away from the latch he had installed. He fidgeted with the mechanism; it seemed as if welded in place. He pried at it with a screwdriver. The latch held. He got out his hammer, striking the door time and time again, skipping the cage across the garage into the wall from the force of the blows. He studied it, gnawing on his lip. He retrieved his handsaw, setting it on top of the cage as he dragged it from the wall. He centered the blade on the rung adjacent to the latch. He pressed his weight down into the saw as he worked it back and forth against the wood. The blade bent and wobbled, grating and shrieking like the wood had suddenly petrified. Seconds later, he was holding two halves. He examined them, fitting the two together. It was as if the metal had turned to paper and ripped. He pulled his drill from the rack, plugged it in and commenced drilling out the lock. The bit snapped and flew across the garage floor.

"All right have it your way then," he said. He strolled across the garage whistling as he pulled the sledgehammer from under his workbench. "This one's for you Buff," he said. He drew the sledge back like a baseball bat. He firmed his feet, wielding with all his might. The latch popped, releasing with a high pitched, metal grating into metal, hiss.

He reached for Buffy, pulling away what looked to be a piece of his ribcage. He cursed under his breath. The ferret seemed part and parcel of the cage, welded into the rungs. His skull crushed to the point of pulverization, its gray matter mashed like lumpy potatoes with roots. Half his body on the one side and half on the other, parts of him bore more of a resemblance to play dough than anything else.

He fetched the towels he used to clean Miles' room, laying them out neatly in front of the cage. He rooted through his toolbox for his snippers and pliers. "I'm sorry little guy ... There's just no other way," he said.

He kneeled in front of the cage, his mind disconnected, his mouth set in a tight grimace as he cut, pried, and pulled Buffy piece by piece from the rungs. He rolled the towels, wrapping him tightly within, and placed the bundle in an old wooden hatbox he had been planning to refurbish. He stroked the top gently with his fingertips, tucked it under his arm, and walked across the garage.

'Boom ... Ra ... Ta ... Tat ... Boom ... Ra ... Ta ... Tat.'

He stopped mid-stride, leg extended. His skin chilled, goose bumping. He turned slow and careful like he was atop a slippery log about to cross a stream. He skimmed the garage in minute detail, not overlooking as much as a nail. His eyes latched onto the cage. It was as it was; the piece de resistance true unadulterated horror; the ultimate triumph of evil, in the most primitive of fashions. He waited, head cocked, straining, and listening. His breath rasped in the silence. The silence of death. Whatever he thought he heard was not making a second appearance, if it had even made a first.

He buried Buffy.

He whacked the cage door with the hammer closing it, took it out behind the garage carefully picking it up from the top, for reasons he dared not bring to the forefront. He turned the water on, put his thumb over the end of the garden hose creating a make shift power washer, blasting it full force. He booted the cage repeatedly, tumbling it up into the garbage at the side of the drive.

Its door had not quite caught and latched from the hammer blow. Close but no cigar. It sat a hair's breadth off latched. Barely ajar in other words but ajar, unlatched, its day old clasp poking through into the adjacent trash bag taking up residence within the rest of the refuse.

He sat outside on the stoop, in the dark, staring off into space while smoking a stale cigarette from his stash. His three-year old stash he'd put up under the eave when he was trying to quit smoking. Stale or not the cigarette went down good as gold, like savouring that whiskey you bought and put away 30 years ago; Pure perfection. He butted what was left of the filter into the bricks and pinged it off into the lawn.

He stared at the cage. Hating it like he'd never hated anything before. In the morning, he would take it over to the fire pit and torch the thing. He went back into the house forgetting to close the garage door, flipping on every light as he passed. He stopped at his son's room, reached in and flipped the wall switch squelching the overhead light.

He put both his hands on the doorknob, slowly turning. The television was on, whispering in a barely audible tone. Susanna was staring out the window. Miles, curled into the tiniest of balls was asleep in the middle of their bed. The skin of his still wet cheeks sparkled and danced in the dim lighting. Susanna did not speak for the longest time. He stood motionless, waiting.

"Miles was asking for Libby. Could you find her for him?" Susanna didn't turn from the window.

Jack backed out of the room silently, much the way he entered, closing the door, turning the knob slowly and methodically, using both hands until the click.

He walked back through the house calling out the cat's name. He stopped and stared at her full, untouched food bowl. He opened all the kitchen cupboards where she loved to lounge. No Libby. He drew his fingers across his lips thinking. 'The cat and ferret played together all the time. Have for years. She couldn't have done this ... Could she? ... No way,' he answered. He tilted his head back and forth in slow motion, tucking his tongue in behind his lower front teeth, opening and closing his mouth clicking out odd bouts of

Morse code. "No way in hell," he said. "The two of them slept together, for Christ's sake." He suddenly hated himself for thinking such a thing. He searched the house, top to bottom; Still no Libby. Even her litter box had not been disturbed. 'She has to be curled up sound asleep somewhere,' he thought. He hunted down all the places where she might have hidden away, coming up empty. He could not return to that room without her. He plopped down on the family room sofa, crossed his arms over his chest, tilted his head back and stared at the ceiling. He'd wait her out.

~~~

"They stand at the fringes of reason. They transcend understanding. They come in numberless forms and are far more sighted than angels are. Together they form the source of all secrets."

Susanna turned slow and purposeful from the window zoning in on the television.

"They are everywhere, in every section of our world, and in every moment of recorded history. Demons and deities are invisible for the most part and can inhabit places or things. One need not believe in, hear of, or see them, to become afflicted. They lurk, crouch, hide, slip into, hover, and follow, shape-shift, and trespass. Some even serve as portals to sacred ground. They can be summoned, and concealed. Some are reported animalistic in nature, baring fangs, with ferocious attitudes, acting out chilling horrific prophecies for all whom come in contact."

Susanna repositioned the bedroom chair directly in front of the television.

"Demons, and other incredible entities, the layman's guide, will continue after these brief messages."

She glanced at Miles. He was sound asleep. She drew closer to the television.

"In all cultures, subversive spirit-demons are reported to lurk about specific spots or be contained within objects. Limitations throughout time have been imposed on this specific sect of demons by Sorcerers and Gods alike; corralling them inside specialized containment units. This group is neither alive nor dead until we open its box where its invisibility rests. The implications of opening such a unit are to unleash unthinkable pure evil. There have been many documented cases throughout history, of dire consequence. For a complete list go to our website under specific sect / limitations."

Susanna hurled herself from the chair, grabbed the laptop and typed in the website. She scrolled through the pictures and lists, the television humming in the background. She clicked on case thirty-five, 'The Wooden Cage.' She studied the picture, dismissed it, and went back to searching. Case fifty-eight, 'Scrolled Box Pre-Dynastic Egypt.' Her jaw dropped. The picture was a spitting image. The wood ... The ornate carvings ... The frontal columns.

She read the case study aloud. "The box like cage was first photographed in 1885 at the site of a grizzly massacre and again in 1886 in the midst of a ghost town affiliating it with a series of inexplicable events, which are notated within the three following editorials reprinted in their entirety."

Susanna cupped her hand over her nose and mouth breathing through her fingers. She quickly scanned the articles, words jumping on and off the pages as if they were intentionally smacking her in the face. Her voice dropped to an inaudible whisper.

'October 13th, 1885'

'Port Smith Daily Times Newspaper' excerpt from headline:

Grizzly Massacre at the Wood's family farm. Local authorities concluded the assault must have taken place at least two days before the **gruesome discovery** by the Wood's neighbour Mr. Fielding. The times of death were estimated based on the state of decomposition of the remains. Details of the deaths are withheld due to the sensitive nature. There is speculation a drifter may be responsible.

It is reported that **not one single member** of the Wood's household **survived**, including the family dog and all farm animals. A large **mass of body parts** believed to be pieces of Mr. Wood's torso and limbs was found lying beside a freshly dug four foot deep hole where it appears he **unearthed** some sort of **artefact**. It is presumed this was the reason for the massacre.

The artefact, is thought to have been contained in an **ornately carved wooded cage**, which it is assumed was pried open with Mr. Wood's shovel. Local archaeologist Mr. Stemple, has preliminarily dated the age of the wooden cage to be approximately 3000 to 3200 BC and of Egyptian origin. While there appears to be an inscription along each frontal column, **translation** at this time is **deemed unnecessary**.

Burial services for the Wood's family will be held Tuesday at noon, weather permitting.

The local sheriff has announced a $100.00 reward will be posted tomorrow morning for anyone with information leading up to the arrest of the presumed drifter.

'October 2nd, 1886'

Excerpt from 'New West Peachtree Press News':

Authorities today reported the once bustling community of **Port Smith** to be deemed a **ghost town**. The coroner has concluded the **bones** scattered throughout the town appear to be of mainly **human** origin.

The area has been completely sealed off while demolition is in progress. Once the levelling is complete, all will be burned in one massive site. The erection of a stone memoriam in the town's honour is planned for spring. Donations can be deposited in the tin drop box inside the Mayor's front office.

The county sheriff has noted one curious item; an ornately carved wooden cage in the middle of Main Street.

'October 15th, 1886'

'Daily Sincoe News Express': extract from front page:

A reliable source has indicated a **hundred mile quarantine** in all directions has been imposed upon the Port Smith' sector.

It has been confirmed that **all life forms** within the vicinity are **deceased**, people, animals, and wildlife alike. The source also indicated portions of what is believed to have been an adult male, although identification was near to impossible due to the **desecration**, was found near a freshly dug crater sized hole up on Cable Ridge where a **wooden cage** of some sort was being unearthed or buried.

An eyewitness to this account had also come forward though now is unavailable for comment, as is the reliable source. Both proceeded to the area the day before yesterday and have yet to return.

It is suspected some form of plague or virus has infiltrated the district. Water and soil samples have been sent for analysis.

Susanna cleared her throat returning to reading aloud, her voice pitching and shrilling as she went. "The existence of the box is documented as early 3200 B.C. and of pre-dynastic Egyptian origin. It is said that this very demon was carried up from hell by Lucifer himself. It is believed the master sorcerer, Droom, to bind the demon spirit, Vloofi, whose name should never be spoken alone aloud, created the box. (The only contradiction to this is notated on the frontal top doorframe of the box.)

"In 1887, two French anthropologists were hired to translate the texts on the frontal columns. Though discounted by some as outrageous and bizarre, the translations were encrypted, having made reference to the old rotations and orbits of planets in our solar system that stemmed from 'Siros Mythology', Chantstem, and other associated variables involving 'Stonehenge' to name one."

She cleared her throat again. "In 1901 another translation was commissioned from a husband and wife team, though never completed due to their untimely demise. (Their bodies were found desecrated, strewn in a three-foot wide span encircling the examining table on which rested the wooden box.)"

'This group is neither alive nor dead until we open its box where its invisibility rests ... The implications of opening is to unleash unthinkable pure evil,' mockingly whisked round inside her head, mimicking the voice of the television announcer. She tensed and hunched her shoulders. "Droom-Vloofi," she whispered without thinking.

She trailed the words with her right index finger as she read the remainder of the case study silently.

It is notated because of the massive amounts of blood drawn into the fabric of the rice paper documents, that not all translations were recoverable. What remained are as follows.

'October 12th, 1901'

> Time 9:34 a.m.
> Script Translation: Pre-Dynastic Egyptian
> - Left frontal column: SOMETHING ... V ... L ... WICKED ... O ... O ... THIS ... F ... WAY ... I ... COMMETH.
> - Right frontal column; 'Droom-Dro-Dra.' Droom, Dro, Dra, Dratf ... Droom-Vloofi ... Dro, Dra, Dratf ... Floom-Floon ... Dro, Dra, Dratf ... Bracth ... Dro, Dra, Dratf.
> - Top frontal doorframe: Droom-Vloofi.

Penned Notes:

> - Right frontal appears to be a chant with direct relevance to the master sorcerer Droom.
> - The name Vloofi is made mentioned in the 'book of the dead.'
> - The box is categorized as a containment unit.
> - Research from the 'book of the black earth' recounts evil entities being summoned from their gauze of invisibility, by voicing the sorcerer's name in conjunction with the demon's name. It further details sacraments and binding rituals for containment units. IE: Chant to be voiced (by the one that knows without knowing) once in a sacrament to ward off penetration of depravity. To be voiced twice for ritualistic purposes recited (by the ones that know without knowing) in conjunction with a doorway seal, a ½ and ½ mixture of blood and beeswax.

- Research documents from the A.F.T.C. museum in Egypt are in the process of being forwarded for comprehensive study. The gist of which suggests, two separate evils, the first confined within the unit lays a stage three demon, second beyond the doorway of this containment unit is a portal with a direct link to hell. Thus, the box should never, under any circumstances, be opened. To do so will unleash sheer unadulterated evil.

Susanna's mouth arched then rounded in a silent scream. Her heart rumbled and thundered in her ears. Case number fifty-eight was right up close and personal. She launched herself from the chair, her feet running before they hit the ground.

"JACK! ... JACK!" she screamed, racing through the main floor of the house. "JACK ... JACK ... DID YOU CLOSE ... IT ... JACK?" Her voice upped two octaves. "WHERE IN THE HELL ARE YOU?" She ran out into the garage and back into the house. "J ... A ... C ... K!" she shrieked. "Jack, where on earth are you?" She sunk to the floor, put her head in her hands and cried.

Throaty growls whistled through the open kitchen window.

Her flesh prickled and goose bumped. She crawled across the kitchen floor, used the edge of the table to bring herself to a stand, and pressed her face into the screen. The wind seemed to be whispering her name. She strained listening, cocking her head side to side. The hair on the back of her neck stood.

Another growl, low, threatening, paced, crept out of the darkness.

She pushed against the screen, denting and forming it forever into a 'Face-o-gram.'

The growls intensified.

"Something," she said. "Something's not right ... Something's very wrong," she continued, silently repeating the two sentences that should never be put together. 'Something not right ... Something very wrong.' Yet there they were. Together. Crystal clear. Not even fudged at the edges.

More growling, deep, guttural, drawn, hissed through the wind as if slicing it in two.

Susanna nodded. "Yes," she said. "Something's not right ... Something's very wrong." She punched out the screen, and jumped. She crouched like a runner waiting for the whistle to commence the race, pausing, listening for directions.

The neighbour's dog had long been awake; its heart racing and thundering in its chest like it was preparing to explode. Its bristled hair formed one solid line front to back. Low throaty growls burped from its throat. It backed, drawing its tie-down chain beyond taut.

The wood of the cage, still water soaked, glistened in the moonlight.

The dog bared its teeth, and then snapped. The metal anchor pole wavered, arching as if preparing to bend as the dog inched his body farther and farther back into the yard. The dog humped his back, hunching, turning, jerking and scrambling, whipping back and forth.

Susanna's directions came; she dug in her left foot sprinting across her walkway. She drop kicked their backyard gate open, grabbed the post, swinging her mass around onto the neighbour's side pathway.

The dog silenced at once. It picked its front foot off the ground, as if pointing. The dog cocked its head, turning and swaying it from Susanna, to the cage, back to her, back to the cage, and then back to her.

Her eyes trailed the dog's head.

The wind whisked, grunting and groaning as it began to falter and fade, before disappearing completely in amongst the grass. The unexpectedness of the silence seemed deafening and unnerving. She was almost sure she had heard it call the dog's and her names as it wrinkled into the blades of the lawn.

'Boom ... Ra ... Ta ... Tat ... Boom.'

The dog froze. Susanna froze. In unison they twisted, their wide eyes fixating on the cage.

The cage rocked, gentle and synchronized like it was dancing for their enjoyment. They stared, mouths open, totally enthralled.

'Boom ... Ra ... Ta ... Tat.'

The dog squealed and howled, erupting into the stillness, curdling it into shock waves. It dropped its front haunches, and then sprang into the air. All four paws hit hard, thundering against the ground as they came down simultaneously. Its nails dug in deep, anchoring its weight as it pulled and strained against the tie. Its collar compressed, grinding into the flesh of its neck, carving a one-inch pathway. Blood bubbled; sprouting into miniature rivers as the dog frantically twisted and jerked, side-to-side, and thrashed back and forth. The dog's collar made a high-pitched pop as the buckle snapped in two. It tumbled backward, yelping, scrambled to its feet, snorting through its nose, and then raced across the yard. It tunnelled through the fence in one fluid motion, ears flat and tail horizontal. The dog's body thinned, drawing into one streamlined trail as it fled through the fields disappearing from sight.

Jack grabbed the corner of the house, his feet still in motion. His runners squealed across the cement walkway leaving burnt rubber flakes in their wake. Susanna's eyebrows rose of their own accord at his sudden appearance. She stared, her surprise and shock in full view.

'Boom ... Ra ... Ta ... Tat ... Boom.'

The universe repeated itself verbatim.

Susanna froze. Jack froze, filling in for the dog. They both in unison twisted, their wide, white ringed eyes fixating on the cage.

The cage rocked, frantic and synchronized like it was performing for their enjoyment. They stared, mouths open, totally mesmerized.

'Boom ... Ra ... Ta ... Tat.'

The cage slid bumping the bricks, angling as if some invisible hand had given it a shove. The top corner swayed, rocking the cage gently like a new mother with babe in arms, as its bottom diagonal corner pivoted in perfect sync.

Jack opened and closed his mouth, gulping in huge bubbles of air. His mind and his eyes seemed to be malfunctioning, sending messages that did not compute.

Susanna and Jack stared, mirroring one another in body and thought. The only difference was small, his mouth was open, her closed.

The dog and Susanna had done much the same, minutes ago, but the dog had done the smart thing, beat it the hell out of there; A much more superior action than to still be standing before the cage, staring.

The cage swung, picking up momentum as if happy and about to snicker behind their backs. The wooden rungs sparkled, glinting with coloured hues like a comet's tail streaking across the night sky. The door was ajar just enough of a smidge to allow moonbeams to reflect and glow off its new metal latch.

'This group is neither alive nor dead until we open its box where its invisibility rests,' a voice sounding like the television announcer's piped out from in her head ... 'Until we open their box' ... 'Until we open their box,' the voice prompted, repeating and whirling the same five words at her like they were caught up in a scratch. 'Until we open their box' ... 'Until we open their box' ... 'Until we open their box.' Susanna's eyes widened, growing like overripe grapes. The voice silenced. She lifted her arm in slow motion, hung it horizontal, pointing in the direction of the cage.

"THAT GOD DAMN FRIGGING DOOR ISN'T SHUT!" She screamed.

The cage door, as if cued by Susanna's screaming recognition, burst fully open. Horror slid into the lines on their foreheads, pitching its tent in preparation of a long stay.

"JACK!" she shrieked. Her other arm moved of its own accord, gluing itself to the other reinforcing her pointer. "FOR CHRIST'S SAKE!" She lifted her left heel from the pavement. It slammed itself back into place. She couldn't move. "JACK! ... OH MY GOD! ... OH MY GOOD GOD! ... SLAM THAT THING SHUT! ... BEFORE IT'S TOO LATE!"

He sprang towards the cage. He grabbed the door, wrapping his fingers over the edge. He whipped it. It thundered against itself the latch miscuing. It jolted shuddering side to side then lashed backward, then forward again like a bird preparing for flight, beating its wings.

"DO SOMETHING!" Susanna yelled.

Jack threw himself at the cage. He rammed the door. The latch receiver bent. He reached inside clawing at the mechanism. Without warning, his wrist pivoted like it had been unhinged. Blood flew from his hand spattering the rungs as something he couldn't see bit down hard, pulling, tugging, dragging his forearm inside. His teeth clenched as he let loose a blood curdling squeal, his elbow and upper arm succumbing to the cage. His rolled shirtsleeve turned dark and muddy as it soaked up the spouting streamers of blood.

Susanna flung herself on top of him, wrapped her arms around his chest, pulling. She smashed her teeth together, wrenching and hauling, moving him backward one painful inch at a time.

Something latched onto his finger, burning and clamping it down like it had been shoved into a vice, tugging against Susanna. The skin of his finger peeled from the flesh folding over top of his knuckle. Blood sprayed, coating the air as he was dragged back into the cage.

"OH NO YOU DON'T!" Susanna screamed. She dug her heels in, straining, tugging, and heaving with all her force, tearing him loose. He flew backward like snapped elastic, knocking her down, intertwining their bodies, rolling and bouncing them like rubber balls into the fence.

Susanna clamoured to her feet and raced toward the cage, ramming it, knocking it level. She kicked the door jamming it into itself.

The metal latch squealed as it drove against itself raking into the mechanism, closing, shutting. The all-important popping sound of the tongue locking down missed from the equation.

She humped her back, pawing herself backward like a four-legged animal, collapsing on top of Jack. Their eyes joined. Neither spoke. The terror furrowed in their brows speaking volumes.

'Say ... The Droom-Dro-Dra ... Say ... The Droom-Dro-Dra,' rolled around inside her head in a voice that sounded like the television announcer.

It flew by unnoticed.

Susanna used Jack to bring herself to a stand. She pulled and dragged him to his feet, hung his battered arm around her neck, and guided him towards the house. He moved slow and clumsy, unsure of his footing, like a man that had been out on a bender all night. She tugged him into the garage, up the steps and into the kitchen, slamming and locking all doors behind them.

She plucked him down into one of the kitchen chairs. Blood dripped to the floor, having taken up most of his shirt. Long ribbons of skin were folded like perforated paper sections about his one hand and forearm. He felt cold and slimy like a two-day-old fish from the market. She ran to the bathroom returning with scissors, antiseptic, tape, gauze, and bandages.

She stripped his shirt, snipped away all the loose tattered skin, and doused his wounds with an overabundance of antiseptic. He hissed in agony, expelling hot air from between his teeth as the antiseptic started to penetrate and foam. He opened his mouth breathing hard and deep, filtering and weaning out the pain. His eyes strained, focusing on her face as she played doctor.

Finished, Susanna shoved the supplies to the far side of the table. His eyes were still on her. She knew he was searching her for some form of logical explanation to the unexplainable.

"Television," she said, her voice devoid of any tone.

He narrowed his eyes. "Television?"

"Yes," she replied.

'Demons are neither alive nor dead till we open their box where their invisibility rests,' the voice that sounded like the television announcer quipped from somewhere inside her head ... The one and the same from the show, 'Demons, and other incredible entities, the layman's guide.' It was as if he had packed a suitcase and moved into her mind at the completion of the show.

"We should get you to a hospital," she said.

He shook his head back and forth.

"No? ... Are you sure?"

He nodded.

"Television?" he asked again.

"Yes," she affirmed. She did not explain any further. What was she supposed to say? It was case 58. She was sure of it. The box notated as, 'Scrolled Box Pre-Dynastic Egypt.' The one Miles had pulled from a hole at the dump. The one that had made noises only she had heard at first. The one they had placed their pet in to be slaughtered. The one that had scared the neighbour's dog. The one that had just dragged his arm into it and had started to rip it to shreds. The one that had danced mockingly before their eyes. Yep, case 58. Though the word *television* was singular, it seemed to neatly sum it all up and was better than saying ... You're going to think I'm crazy but I am way ahead of you 'cause I've already been thinking that as a good sounding alternative here.

"Let's get you to bed," she said quietly. She got him to his feet. She pointed him in the direction of the bedroom.

He stood motionless like he did not understand. Susanna moved in behind him steering him through the house, down the hall, and into their bedroom.

Miles stirred. His face crinkled. Tears flowed. He held out his arms. Susanna swept him up, rocking gently.

"Mommy, can I have Libby?"

"Of course, sweetheart." She dabbed at his wet cheeks with a tissue.

"Jack, did you find her when yo ... u?" She stopped mid-sentence.

Jack was curled in a foetal position on the floor beside the bed holding his forearm, eyes staring blankly. He looked transparent and plastic like a department store mannequin.

"Never mind," she whispered. She tossed the blanket from the bottom of the bed on top of Jack, covering up his head in the process. He didn't move.

She tucked Miles into the middle of their bed, propped him up with all the pillows, turned the television to the cartoon channel and left the room, closing the door behind her.

She tiptoed through the house calling out for the cat, shaking the kitty treat bag. The final lap of her search brought her to the place she did not want to be; her son's room. Cold shills swept up and down her spine as she reached in and flipped on the lights. She stepped in, her legs moving slowly and stiffly, as if they had lost their knee joints.

She stopped in the doorway scanning the room in its entirety like a snake testing the air with its tongue. Her eyes drew on and off the far wall, where the dresser sat. Something wasn't right. Something was wrong. There they were again. Those words. 'Something not right ... Something very wrong.' The ones that shouldn't be together. She closed her eyes and reopened them. Something was very wrong. The books, the airplane, the green army men, were gone. All gone, as if they had been whisked away to outer space never to return.

Susanna willed her feet toward the dresser, weaving back and forth like a psychiatric patient on too much medication. She ran her fingertips back and forth across the top, pausing, drawing slow circles around the gouges she did not remember being in the wood. She backed across the room. Pulled the chair out from the desk. Dragged it over to the dresser, climbing aboard. She inched her feet over to the inner edge, leaned over the top of the dresser and looked down.

Libby looked back, staring profusely with wide glazed over eyes, protruding and lifeless, her fur, sticking straight up porcupine like. She looked as if she had been flash frozen and cast inside an ice sculpture. Her mouth was open, her teeth bared in a foreboding grimace.

Susanna dropped the treats; Libby would not be needing them any longer. She flicked off the lights and returned to the bedroom.

Jack had uncurled under the blanket, making him resemble a covered up corpse more than anything else. She bent to study his chest. It rose and fell. She scrutinized the damp spot on the blanket as it sucked in and out of his mouth. It smelled sour.

"Find Libby?" he whispered without so much as an involuntary twitch. His voice seemed full of gravel and not his.

"Yes, yes I did," she replied.

"Bringing her in?"

"No. No I'm not." She watched his mouth close and the blanket concave, settling against his lips, sticking to them. She studied him for the longest time, standing over him, counting and matching her breaths to his. His didn't seem right. She stopped her thoughts before those two sentences met and formed yet again, for the third time. "Something not right ... Something very wrong."

129

Her eyes swept over her sleeping son. He did seem right. She slumped into the bedroom chair. She brought her knees up to her chest, wrapped her arms around them locking her fingers, and plunked down her chin, closing her eyes.

The next day came and went as quiet and humble as any Sunday with Miles camping out in their bed and Jack laid out on the floor beside it.

The neighbour had ventured over twice looking for his dog. Each time, Susanna had dutifully listened to the tale, chewing on her bottom lip, showing concern in all the right places; the battering of their resodded lawn; the bent ground tie pole; the broken blood soaked collar.

She had held fast, not flinching or trying diligently to offer up the truth. 'The truth shall set you free,' bounced around inside her head. 'Really? ... Are we sure about that? ... At least their dog is still alive.'

She had refuelled Miles, once with two pieces of plain toast and once with soup and crackers. Jack had mumbled a slurred no to the toast, and been unresponsive to the offer of soup and crackers.

His chest still rose and fell.

When afternoon started to slip away, Miles asked again for Libby. She trotted off closing the door behind her, counting down the minutes on the kitchen that clock she figured it would take a five year old to assume one was doing his bidding. She returned and told him she had not found her. 'Never lie when the truth will do,' her mother had always said. And ... no she had not found her, she'd bypassed his room with the chair pulled up to the dresser where Libby lay behind stiff and quiet.

She bathed and crawled in bed beside her son, leaving all the lights on.

Jack was, as he was, laid out on the floor beside the bed on his back. The blanket covering him head to toe. His chest still, rose and fell.

~~~

Susanna awoke with a start, sitting straight up. She retched, vomit rising into the back of her throat. Her eyes stung and burnt. The air was vile, as if injected with some form of plague. It swirled, forming layers of putrid, constricted fog like particles she could see and touch and smell. She retched again. She cupped her nose and mouth.

"What the hell is that?" She drew air in and out of her hand, re-circulating her own breath.

She lunged from the bed slamming the slider window open. She fanned the air swearing it rippled in response. She sat back down and reached over, tapping Miles. Her fingers made little hollows in the replacement body pillow. She whipped the covers back. He had even swapped out his head, aligning his foam basketball perfectly.

'That little scamp,' she thought. 'Now where on earth has he gotten off to?' She dropped her guard smiling. She instantly retched. "Holy hell,' she muttered. She double cupped her nose and mouth using both hands. She swung her feet from the bed walking round the other side.

"Jack! ... Oh my God! ... Jack!" Green slimy grunge had infiltrated the blanket fibres outlining his bandaged arm to perfection, sprouting and growing fuzzy fungi in thin bean sprout like wisps.

She folded back the blanket using her thumb and index finger. She vomited yellow mucus filled bile.

His arm and hand were alive, crawling with hundreds of little off white, plump maggots. The stench was overwhelming.

She vomited again.

"We ... we've," she sputtered coughing and choking. "We've got to get you to a hospital ... Jack? ... Jack?" She crouched down beside his head. "Jack? ... You in there?"

Silence.

She grasped the top of the blanket lifting the corner from his head. Her hand trembled, shaking and vibrating like an old blender crushing ice as she slowly started to peel

131

it away. His hair uncovered first, it was disarrayed and clumped like small haystacks and smelled of wet earth. His forehead came second, the skin off white and puffy like someone had injected water into it, a lot of water. Next were his eyebrows, once dark, now speckled with silver, as if he had aged thirty years over night. They were stiff and taut and crusted with mustard coloured dandruff, like he hadn't washed over the same amount of time either.

She took a deep breath, holding it, fear crawling up her spine. She uncovered his eyes. 'His eyes ... Oh my Christ ... His eyes!' They were open, dried and wrinkled like a tee shirt forgotten, left wet in the washer until next week's washing. She whipped the blanket back over his head.

"Oh my God," she said. "Oh my good God!" She sat on the floor beside his head rocking back and forth. "What should I do?" She rocked harder. "What to do? ... What to do?" She trailed her eyes up and down his body trying to keep it together.

His chest still rose and fell.

"He needs a hospital," she said for the second time. "Yes ... yes he does," she reaffirmed. "And fast," she added. "Yes ... Yes I know ... I'm on it."

She sprang to her feet, rushed through the doorway into the hall, slipped, and went down. She palmed the floor, something slimed under her hands. Her lips rumpled in disgust. Maggots, squished, creamed flat maggots. Her eyeballs ogled her hands, jumped to the floor, then trailed into Miles' bedroom, where they marched in two sets of two neatly formed rows disappearing under the dresser. Where they were coming from, she didn't know. Where they were going she knew. She swivelled her head, looking back over her shoulder. 'Correction,' she thought. Where they were coming from ... Yes, she did know ... Jack! ... They were coming from Jack ... And going to Libby.

She clambered to her feet using the wall, her eyes never leaving the trail of humping maggots divided off into four separate lanes like that of a busy congested highway; Two rows travelling the one way, and two travelling the other. The only thing missing was the centerline.

"WHAT THE HELL IS GOING ON IN HERE?" she screamed.

She booted it into the kitchen. The telephone was gone from the holder. She depressed the button, waiting for the shrill locator beeps.

Nothing.

"MILES," she shrieked.

"Yes Mommy," he said. He slipped from behind to in front of her.

She jumped, startled.

"Want some?" He offered up the huge salad bowl filled to the brim with cereal and milk.

"No!" she snapped.

His mouth wrinkled and vibrated. His wide innocent eyes brimmed with tears.

"I mean no," she said soft and gentle. "No thanks honey."

"Did I do something wrong?" he sniffled, and then wiped at his eyes.

"No, no sweetheart you didn't." She felt like an ass. It was not his fault that his father was on the floor, arm crawling with ... with those things. Or the cat was deader than a stone behind his dresser.

She bent, pulling him against her, cuddling him and his gigantic cereal bowl. 'I'm about to lose my goddamn mind. But ... first, I have to call an ambulance, and then I can lose it. Oh wait no I can't, I have to bury the cat,' she thought. Her eyes flashed to the empty phone receiver on the wall.

"Sweetie?"

"Yes Mommy."

"Have you seen the phone?"

"Yes Mommy."

She drew her hand across her lips, wrong question. "Do you know where it is?" The right question.

"Yes."

"Where?"

"In the garage."

"In the garage?"

'This is taking too long,' she thought. "Do you know where in the garage?"

"No."

'Think like a five year old. Think like a five year old scared his Mom is going to get mad.' "How do you know it's in the garage honey?"

"Daddy had it talking to his friend before we went to the du ... mp." He scuffled his bare feet back and forth, wishing never gone.

"You go on back downstairs now and shut the door behind you and don't come out for any reason ... okay?"

"Okay. But Mommy?"

"Yes? ... What?" Susanna was already half way down the garage stairs.

"There is no door to shut."

"That's okay honey, just shut it anyway."

Miles shrugged his shoulders, went to the top of the lower level's stairs and pretended to shut the door that was not there. He jumped down the stairs two at a time, spilling cereal and milk as he went. He curled up on the sofa, centered the bowl between his legs, dipping in his spoon in and out watching television.

Susanna searched through the garage tossing and dumping everything the telephone could be under. She could not find it. She suddenly stopped and turned grinning, shaking her head. She was losing it. If she had found it, it would have been dead anyway. What was she thinking? Its beeper had not gone off which meant it was dead. 'Dead like Buffy, dead like Libby,' socked around inside her, making all the hairs on the back of her neck stand and poke through the fabric of her sweatshirt.

She grabbed the garden spade off the rack, flinging it into the back yard as she passed across the walkway that separated the neighbour's house from hers. She banged on the side door.

"Hey Susanna," Celia propped the door open with her foot.

"Hi, Can I use your phone? Mine is dead," Susanna said.

'Dead ... yes dead. Dead like so many things in your house,' the voice inside said.

"Just stop it right now!" Susanna blurted. "You're really getting on my nerves ... Shut up will you? ... You're supposed to be thoughts! ... Not slip in here unnoticed, and strike out on your own! ... You got that?"

Susanna watched her neighbour's eyes widen. She pursed her lips tight together, and then smacked them with the flat of her fingers. "Whoops," she shrugged her shoulders. "I'm having a bit of a bad day," she whispered. "Can I just use your phone?" she shuffled her feet side-to-side then bounced up and down heel to toe. She opened her mouth drawing her lips back from her teeth pretending to smile.

Celia stepped back. "I'll get it for you." She closed the door behind her locking it.

"Thanks," Susanna said to the back of the door.

"Here," Celia handed her the phone. "Just knock when you're done."

"Okay, thanks," she said again to the door. "Jesus, what in hell is with her?"

She leaned against the side of Celia's porch, crossed her legs at the ankles, and punched in 911.

'Oh boy ... here we go. I can't wait to hear this one,' the voice piped.

"Shut up, just shut up!"

'Just saying.'

"By the way you should gargle with some salt water you're starting to sound a little hoarse."

"911. What's your emergency? Police? Fire? Ambulance?" the male voice on the other end of the telephone asked.

"I need an ambulance."

"For yourself?"

"No ... My husband."

"Name?"

"Ah ... ah," she suddenly could not remember.

"Is he there with you ma'am?"

"No ... No, he's at home. Look, he really needs an ambulance!"

"Where is home ma'am?"

"Next door."

"Your address ma'am?"

The receiver slipped through Susanna's fingers. It plummeted to the decking, bouncing twice before rolling into the planter.

'I thought you needed an ambulance, why you playing bouncy ball? ... Fine ignore me ... You are on your own then ... And by the way, just in case you haven't noticed you're not doing too well,' the voice whispered.

The words and voice were clear as a bell. It was the television announcer. He had moved in. How he had gotten into her head was shrugged off with one shoulder lift.

She dashed after the phone, retrieving it, fumbling it, losing it again. She took a deep breath, sauntered slowly over to it, looked both ways then snatched it, clutching it with both hands tightly into her chest.

"Are you still there ma'am? ... Ma'am?"

She jostled the receiver to her ear. "JACK!" she blurted. "My husband's name is Jack. Jack Miller and we live at 1430 Lakeshore Road and 'God Damn It!' He needs an ambulance! Now!"

"See, I don't need you! I'm fine!" she said to the television announcer.

"You don't need an ambulance ma'am?" the male operator asked.

"No ... I mean yes. I'm just talking to too many people," Susanna was speaking so fast she sounded like a chipmunk.

"Okay ma'am, simmer down. First things first. Do you need an ambulance?"

"Me? ... No ... My husband ... Yes."

"We just need to take some information. Before we start, is he breathing all right?'

"Yes," she replied. 'His chest still rises and falls.'

"Now then ... What seems to be the proble ... m?"

She cut him off. "He needs help. He's ... he's ... he's." She wanted to say 'Something's not right ... Something's very wrong.' She bit her tongue, 'Oh dear God somebody help me! ... Help me! "He's hurt," she said. "Is the ambulance on its way?"

"No ma'am. Not as yet. We require some additional information before we dispatch. We need ..."

She cut him off again. "Look! ... He hurt his forearm and hand Saturday night. Now it's severely infected. She omitted the parts about him lying beside the bed on the floor, not moving for over a day and a half, eyes shrivelled like raisins, stinking like rancid meat, arm leaking green crap and crawling with maggots. They would find out soon enough.

"You want an ambulance for a hurt arm ma'am?" The operator covered the phone receiver, leaned back in his chair, and mouthed 'I got a live one here ... Full moon tonight?' He smiled, deciding to play her along. "How did his arm get hurt ma'am?"

"A cage."

'Demons are neither alive nor dead till we open their box where their invisibility rests,' the announcer whispered slowly. She switched the phone to the other ear. She could hear muffled laughter in the background.

"How hurt is it?"

"ARE YOU SENDING THE GOD DAMN AMBULANCE OR NOT?" she screeched. Her voice echoed back through the telephone. She chewed her lip. They had her on speaker.

"Yes ma'am. We have to."

"How long?"

"Hard to say ma'am." The operator scrawled not required across the report in red, putting it in his out basket.

"Good. Thanks. As long as it is coming." 'Please God ... Let his chest still be rising and falling.' "I'm going to go bury the cat now."

"Pardon ma'am?"

"Nothing," she muttered.

She depressed the off button, throwing the phone against Celia's door. She had said to knock when she was done. She hadn't said how. 'Bitch,' she thought.

~~~

Susanna pulled Miles' dresser from the wall. She folded Libby's favourite blanket around her tucking in the edges. She buried her next to Buffy. It had been slow going with the garden spade but the alternative had been moving the thing at the side of the house, the thing pretending to be a cage ... 'That horrid thing!' ... to retrieve the shovel from behind.

She returned to Miles' bedroom fully armed, bug-rid spray bomb, vacuum, room deodorizer, and mop bucket.

The maggots were everywhere, inching mindlessly like a flock of sheep without their shepherd. She held the spray tin a foot off the floor, depressed the button sweeping her arm side to side. They wriggled in place holding onto life. She sprayed again. They jiggled, stretched out, wriggling faster. She dropped the tin, lifted her feet one at a time reciting right, left, right, left, marching around the room, stomping and mushing them into the hardwood. She hooked up the vacuum running it across the flooring.

She stood in her bedroom doorway water bucket in hand. Jack's chest, 'Still rose and fell.'

She wet mopped Miles' room, opened all his windows, and then closed the door.

"One, two, three, four, five, six, seven, eight, nine, ten, ready or not here I come," whisked in through the open garage window. She exhaled noisily as she rang out the mop and hung it on the rack to dry. Celia's day care kids were outside for their morning recess period. Monday was always the hide and seek play exercise. Teaching them to count Celia would say. Susanna had always secretly thought it was a good way to get them out of her hair while she peeled potatoes for fries. That was also a Monday thing. Homemade fries with ketchup for lunch.

She checked out the time. A half hour had passed since her call for the ambulance. 'Any time now,' she thought, 'any time.'

More counting, followed by laughter and high-pitched shrieks of delight bounced around the garage walls.

'Boom ... Ra ... Ta ... Tat ... Boom ... Ra ... Ta ... Tat.'

Susanna stiffened.

The shrieks shrilled, pitching into screams ... Scream after scream after scream.

'Boom ... Ra ... Ta ... Tat ... Boom.'

Cold chills swept over her. She flew from the garage her runners screeching across the pavement in the direction of the cage. Her eyes bulged from their sockets as time transcended to slow motion 'deja vu.'

The cage was not empty.

'Boom ... Ra ... Ta ... Tat.'

"GOD HELP US!" Susanna screeched.

She reached for the door. Her fingers felt on fire. She shook her hand up and down, blowing on her flesh. She yanked at the latch. It seemed riveted. She booted it with her foot driving the corner of the cage into the bricks, tossing Celia's daughter Judy from one side to the other.

Judy stared straight ahead, head tilted, mouth wide, tongue extended, belting out terror filled howls and shrieks. She backed into the far corner of the cage.

Susanna lunged putting all her weight behind her, pulling, and wrenching on the door.

It held fast.

She picked up the cage slamming it to the pavement. Time and again she repeated her motions, thundering it to the ground.

"KIDS ... INSIDE ... NOW!" Celia screamed. She slammed the kitchen door shut behind them. She tore down her steps paring knife and potato in hand. "STOP! ... STOP!" She shrieked. "SUSANNA ARE YOU INSANE? ... STOP IT RIGHT NOW!" She grabbed Susanna's sweater ripping the sleeve at the seam. "LEAVE MY CHILD ALONE! ... YOU'RE GOING TO HURT HER!"

"Your child is going to die if we don't get her the hell out of this thing!"

"WHAT?"

"YOU DEAF? ... JUDY IS GOING TO DIE!" She rapped the cage into the wall, heaving it again and again and again trying to spring the door.

'Droom-Vloofi,' teletyped across in front of Susanna's eyes.

"Droom-Vloofi," she whispered through her teeth.

A shadowy contour whisked across the inside of the cage. There and gone in the blink of an eye.

Susanna cocked her head, something incomprehensible on the surface, sinking in and storing below the layers of reason.

Celia lunged at Susanna tackling her.

They both went down beside the cage.

"MOMMY! ... MOMMY! ... HELP! ... HELP! ... IT'S BITING ME!" Judy screamed. Her hand washed in blood. Her arm pulled, straightening as if something was tugging on it. The skin from her wrist to her elbow ripped open, the thin layers of muscle and tendons popped, steaming the cool air like a boiling pot of water without a lid.

Celia's mouth gaped in shock. Warm wet blood dripped from her face ... Her daughter's warm wet blood.

Susanna struggled like a person possessed, pushing, shoving, untangling herself from Celia.

"I ... TOLD ... YOU!" she screeched. "I DAMN WELL TOLD YOU!" She rocked the cage door back and forth, picked it up and rapped it into the wall as hard as she could.

Judy jostled like a rag doll. A bloody rag doll.

'Boom ... Ra ... Ta ... Tat.'

Celia's eyes flashed at warp speed to her daughter, to Susanna, back to her daughter. Her brain kick started. Susanna was trying to help. She gulped swallowing air, choking on it as if it was made of over-sized gumballs. Her face flushed. "SUSANNA! ... DO SOMETHING!" she squealed.

Susanna stopped dead. She stared Celia down. "WHAT THE HELL DO YOU THINK I'M DOING?" she screamed back.

"But ... But ... It's not working."

"I KNOW! ... I HAVE EYES TOO!"

Susanna slammed the cage to the ground again. Nothing. She booted the cage in front of Celia. "You keep hitting it against the ground. I'll be right back." Susanna ran into her garage, retuning seconds later with an axe.

Judy screamed in short horrific bursts, her mouth closing and opening as her index and middle fingers jerked, severed, and flew across the cage.

"STAND BACK!"

Celia dropped the cage. She jumped backward. Susanna swung the axe, hitting the latch dead center. The door thundered open.

Susanna flung the axe into her yard.

It abruptly boomeranged, coming back at herself and Celia as if piloted by some unseen force. They ducked as it whizzed past, cutting a swatch of air directly over their heads. It twirled, upending, planting itself blade down in amongst the rose bushes.

Celia grasped Susanna's arm. Her hand trembled and vibrated. Panic had succumbed to terror, furrowing deep lines into her brow. "Oh my God," she sobbed.

"God has nothing to do with any of this ... Trust me," Susanna stated.

'Demons are neither alive nor dead till we open their box where their invisibility rests,' the announcer silently flashed before her eyes, using cue cards.

Susanna dropped onto her hands and knees in front of the cage. She lurched forward, wedging into the doorway, arms extended, grasping for Judy.

Judy eyes whipped side to side, up and down, back and forth, like she was watching something. She drew back, plastering herself against the far side of the cage.

"JUDY!" Celia screamed. "FOR CHRIST'S SAKE! ... GO TO SUSANNA! ... GO TO SUSANNA!"

Susanna pushed with her feet. She pivoted her shoulders, rocking them back and forth, straining against the door opening, trying to fit farther through. She felt like 'Alice' with no mushrooms, she was just too big. She swung her hands, fingers hooked like claws, swiping side to side.

Judy held her breath concaving her stomach in. She pressed hard into the rungs.

Susanna pushed with her feet gaining an inch of ground. She swiped, snapping her fingers closed on empty air.

"J ... U ... D ... Y! ... WHAT IS WRONG WITH YOU?" Celia wailed.

Judy's eyes rolled back, her head drooped, she scooted forward, zigzagging across the cage bottom. Her arm raised in swift jerks, like it had been embedded with an invisible pulley system. Her hand with the two fingers and a thumb spewed and blew blood out into the air as it flapped up and down in a mock bye-bye wave.

Celia clamped her fingers to her face, digging in her nails, screaming and howling.

Judy's body rammed the back rungs. Her head jolted upright. She trembled and vibrated, her eyes thumped in circles around the cage. Her mouth gaped, rounding as she started screaming horrid and guttural. She skidded across the cage. Shot up into the air and spun then halted. She swung side to side then began to rotate counter-clockwise, slow, purposeful, as if something was examining her.

"MOMMY! ... MOMMY! ... IT'S GROWLING! ... IT'S GROWLING AT ME!" Judy howled. She belted from one side of the cage to the other, smashing off the rungs. Without warning, she dropped her arms, and legs splaying and twisting as she hit the base.

Susanna bashed, clutched and grabbed, tearing away particles of Judy's clothing.

'Boom ... Ra ... Ta ... Tat ... Boom ... Ra ... Ta ... Tat.'

"MOMMY! ... IT'S ON ME! ... MOMMY! ... H ... E ... L ... P!"

Judy's ribcage dented in, compressing and folded inward. Her mouth bucked out watery blood bubbles.

"WHAT THE HELL IS GOING ON?" Celia grabbed onto Susanna's leg with a death grip. "I DON'T SEE ANYTHING! ... THERE'S NOTHING IN THERE! ... IS THERE?"

'Boom ... Ra ... Ta ... Tat ... Boom ... Ra ... Ta ... Tat.'

"WHAT ON EARTH IS THAT?" Celia wailed.

Judy's bladder let loose. Her jacket and sweater shredded into long ribbons. Hunks of skin and flesh separated and flew through the rungs as if something was biting off chunks and spitting them out. The pieces of Judy splattered as they hit the pavement.

"IT'S EATING ... M ... E!" Deep rich heart blood spurted from Judy's mouth.

"SUSANNA, HELP HER! ... DEAR GOD HELP HER!" Celia howled.

Susanna broke from the cage. She lunged at Celia's hand shaking it, twisting it, freeing the paring knife. She threw herself at the cage, stabbing and slashing the air.

Judy rocked side-to-side, blood spouting from her nose, eyes, and ears, flesh flying in all directions.

Ina Louise Jackson

Susanna opened her mouth, wailing the words stored below layers of reason. "DROOM-VLOOFI! ... DROOM-VLOOFI!"

A dark semi-transparent shadow lifted out from under and around Judy's body.

"DROOM-VLOOFI! ... DROOM-VLOOFI!" Susanna screeched. She wielded the knife stabbing repeatedly into the form.

An inhuman squeal rocked the air, rippling it. Black blood gushed, fouling the atmosphere.

Susanna stabbed and slashed and stabbed and slashed.

The shadow spun, hovered, then darted across the cage, circling Judy's slumped body, slowly, methodically, like it was inspecting its kill. It shot straight up whirling and spiralling, and then turned hanging motionless as if studying its opponent in minute detail.

Without warning, it warped at Susanna's hand, wrapping, squeezing, and constricting, abruptly disappearing from sight.

Susanna's scream was long and blood curdling. She dropped the knife. Blood burst and flew from both sides of her hand. She whipped her arm from the cage clenching her fist. She held her hand to her face scanning it. It was punctured clear through. 'It bit me ... The damn asshole thing bit me. ... HOLY HELL!' she silently screamed.

'Sing! ... Sing! ... Sing now,' the announcer blurted.

She looked at her hand again, shaking it.

'You must sing! ... SING! ... SING NOW!' The announcer screamed. 'Droom, Dro, Dra, Dratf ... Droom-Vloofi,' the announcer sang.

Susanna's eyes widened, her mouth dropped. There was a voice singing inside her head. A male voice ... Singing?

'Dro, Dra, Dratf,' the announcer continued. 'Floom-Floon ... Dro, Dra, Dratf ... Bracth ... Dro, Dra, Dratf,' done the announcer said.

Her eyes flashed across Judy. She was in the far corner of the cage, still beyond measure, doused in so much blood she more resembled a mock up child horror movie prop than a real life little girl. Her eyes were open, head twisted, slumped awkwardly off to the side, arms bent at the elbows, legs splayed.

'Her chest doesn't rise and fall.'

Susanna grabbed the rungs, her blood dripped, beading and absorbing into Judy's. The cage rocked and vibrated. She firmed her grip. More blood dripped.

High pitched screams and squeals pierced the air. Something inexplicable wormed through her, adding itself to the something incomprehensible already in storage.

Susanna's parted lips stretched and formed a grimace. She gritted her teeth, lifted her lips, baring her teeth, focusing on the cage. 'Lost your dinner did you?' She swung the cage, flipping it over onto its side, jerking it up and down.

Judy rolled out.

'First things first or there'll be more Judy's rolling out.' Susanna kicked the cage with a vengeance, tumbling it back into the garbage heap. She went after it booting the door shut. The metal latch drove home popping into place.

'Quick ... Say ... The Droom-Dro-Dra,' the announcer said.

It didn't register.

"CELIA CALL 911," she yelled.

Celia did not move. She seemed glued in place, crouched on her knees, mouth open, eyes wild, fingers entangled in her hair.

'Her chest still rose and fell.'

Susanna grasped hold of Judy's body. It was chilled. She slipped off her sweatshirt, wrapped it around Judy, placing her into Celia's lap.

Judy's dead weight slid from Celia, turned, and flopped face down on the pavement. Celia's eyes trailed her daughter, staying transfixed as they widened and bulged from their sockets.

Susanna ran into Celia's house, grabbed the phone dialling 911.

"911. What's your emergency? Police? Fire? Ambulance?" The male voice on the other end of the telephone asked.

Susanna swallowed hard. 'Oh no, not him again!' "I need an ambulance."

"For yourself?"

'Here we go,' she swallowed again. "No ... for a little girl."

"Name?"

"Judy."

"Last name?"

"Ah ... Ah ... It's hard to think right now."

"Take your time ma'am."

"Anderson, I think. Yes ... yes it's Anderson."

"Address?"

"1432 Lakeshore Road." Susanna bit the inside of her bottom lip. 'Should I dare? ... Yes! ... Yes!' "Can my husband and the child share one? Our address is 1430 Lakeshore Road. His hasn't come yet."

The operator sifted through his out basket retrieving Susanna's call request. He smirked. "Oh it's you again. I kind of thought your voice sounded familiar." ... "Before we start, is the child breathing all right?'

"No," she replied. 'Her chest doesn't rise and fall.'

"No? ... Please state the problem?" he asked matter of fact. He leaned and switched his phone to speaker again.

"The problem? ... THE PROBLEM?" Susanna repeated raising her voice. "STATE THE PROBLEM? ... SHE'S NOT BREATHING ASSHOLE!" she yelled.

"Okay ma'am and you're sure of this?"

Susanna clutched the phone to her chest. 'God please help me. Please give me strength ... and God please let Jack's chest still be rising and falling, unlike Judy's whose isn't.'

She inspected Celia. Still glued. She glanced at Judy. Still face down.

"Are you there ma'am? Ma'am?"

"Yes," she said. "And yes I'm sure she's not breathing," she added before he could ask it again. 'Where in hell do they get these assholes from? ... Raise them from sea nymphs?' "Are you sending an ambulance?"

"Yes ma'am. It's already on the way."

'Thank God,' she mouthed.

"Ma'am, the child breathing all right yet?"

"No."

Celia was too close for her to say the words lying across her tongue. 'She's dead, dead like Buffy, dead like Libby.'

"For our information sheet would you care to explain what happened?"

"Sure, she, I assume, crawled into the cage and ..."

The operator cut her off, "the same cage that hurt your husband ma'am?" He leaned over, slipping the first and second reports into the fax, pressing the send button requesting police back up. This wasn't a live one, this was a loose cannon.

Susanna could hear sirens. She put down the phone. She stared across the lake. Bright lights flashed in between the buildings. They were coming. 'Thank God they are finally coming,' she thought. 'Thank you,' she mouthed.

"Celia," she crouched down beside her. "Help is coming." She put her hand on Celia's back patting gently. "They're coming now," she said softly.

Susanna stood motionless beside Celia. Her eyes caught the flashes as they rounded the corner and started to cross the causeway. She trailed the two cruisers, ambulance, and fire truck as they tore down the middle of the roadway, went straight through the red light, then slowed and turned into Celia and her shared driveway.

147

Ina Louise Jackson

The police officers rushed from the cruisers, all four moving in unison as if they had been pre-primed and synchronized.

Celia didn't move. Still glued, crouched, mouth open, eyes bulging, fingers entangled in her hair.

Susanna watched as their stone cold expressions riveted in place. Their mouths struggling to remain closed, fixed, as their eyes flashed over the six-foot blood-bathed circumference. Now a six foot crime scene that looked like an overdone, blood sprayed, flesh chunked, staged background for a zombie horror movie featuring, Judy, laying on her face. Dead Judy ... Dead like so many things around there. Celia, so glued in place she was white and shiny at the edges, and herself.

Susanna flicked her eyes across the pathway to the side of her house. The cage, 'the thing responsible' lay silent and still, almost dutifully silent and still, in amongst the garbage heap. It seemed cloaked in a veil of innocence, there on its side, door closed, in amongst the dark green plastic bags as if nothing had happened ... Nothing had ever happened ... Nothing ever would happen.

She ran her eyes across the locking pin making double sure, then the latches. If she hadn't known better she would have sworn the door latches were different; Different style and colour of metal. She bit at her lip studying, comparing both sides of the latch hinges, as they seemed to stretch out and turn at the outer edges, turn up into a gloating sneer. Her eyes widened. They were! ... The Goddamned thing was! She was sure of it. Case fifty-eight, was sneering to beat hell!

One of the officers stepped forward, snapping pictures. Another approached Susanna drawing out his pad and pen. A third bent down beside Celia. The fourth turned Judy over and then motioned to the fire and ambulance attendants.

"Name," the police officer asked.

"Are you taking my husband too?" Susanna blurted. "I called for him over an hour ago. He needs help so badly." Her eyes brimmed with tears.

"Name," the officer repeated.

"My little boy is in the house ... alone."

"Name?"

"Aren't you listening to me?"

The officer snapped his pad shut. He took a step forward. "Where is your husband ma'am?"

"In the house ... He's in the house."

"Then your little boy's not alone. Is he," he said coldly. He flipped his pad open. "Name?"

"Susanna Miller," she said slowly.

"Your friend's name?" The officer pointed toward Celia being helped to her feet by the third officer.

"She's not really my friend. She's just my neighbour."

The police officer lifted his eyes from the report.

Susanna abruptly stiffened. His stare was hard, unnerving. She pursed her lips tight together. Saying Celia was not a friend was definitely the wrong thing to have said. "Can we start over?"

The officer's eyebrows arched. "Your friend's name?"

"Celia Anderson."

"The deceased girl's name?"

'The deceased girl! ... THE DECEASED GIRL! ... You mean Celia's little daughter lying on the pavement face down in a blood pool?' "Judy," she replied. "Judy Anderson," she added, beating him to the next question.

Her eyes flickered across Judy's body, halting on her one hand. The one with the pudgy white wiggling lumps. 'Maggots? ... Is that maggots?' She leaned forward watching as they humped and slumped towards the sleeve opening, stretched out flat and slithered underneath the material, disappearing from sight. 'Oh my good God ... It is! ... Holy hell ... It is!'

Susanna tented her fingers over her nose and mouth attempting to conceal her horror. She looked from the officer, to Judy, back to the officer. "Did you get the ... the ... the name?" she stammered through her hands.

He nodded.

She flexed her fingers, removing them one by one from her face as if some unforeseen force was plucking them free. She looked around the police officer. Three more cruisers had joined the flock bringing the sum total of emergency vehicles to five cruisers, one ambulance, and one fire truck. She watched as the officers and attendants formed a tight huddle, their voices melding and buzzing like the drone of workers bees in a hive.

Susanna continued answering the officer's one and two word questions, mirroring them back, replying with as few words as possible.

She watched over his shoulder as the huddle fanned and separated. Everything was moving as if a slide show, frame-by-frame in slow motion. Judy lifted onto a gurney and zipped up in a light purple fake velvet body bag. Attendants dressed in white lifting the legs out from under the gurney; Wheeling it down the drive; Loading it into the ambulance; Closing the doors; Leaving with no flashing lights. She watched two police officers help the now hysterical Celia over to her deck steps. A third following close behind, studying the blood soaked pavement as he walked. She watched all three sit with Celia, writing, talking, looking her way, much too often as Celia cried and gestured with her arms. She watched one of the officers depart the stairs, cross the pathway, and bend over the cage examining it. She watched the paring knife along with bits and pieces of Judy slide from between the rungs and tumble onto the ground as he picked it up. She watched the knife go into a clear plastic bag by a gloved hand.

"Ma'am would you like to tell me in your own words, what happened here?"

'What? ... What?' Susanna stared right through the police officer. 'Was that a question? If it was, then the answer is no ... No, I most certainly would not! ... No ... No ... and no.'

"Ma'am?"

"Yes."

"Ma'am, would you like to tell me in your own words what happened here?"

There it was again. The same question. By the same officer. The one that suddenly seemed ten feet tall and built like a brick shithouse. The one that just ran his hand over the leather strap of his gun holster. "Pardon," she said. She cleared her throat on purpose.

He repeated himself drawing out his words, like he was talking to a mentally defective primate.

Susanna shuffled her feet. 'Oh ... My ... Good ... God.'

'The truth shall set you free,' the television announcer offered.

'The truth shall set you free?' She repeated inside her head. 'Does it? ... Will it with a ten-foot high brick shithouse of a cop in your face? ... Nope! ... Not a snowballs chance in hell.'

"Ma'am?"

"Um ... Um ... Okay," she said. "Judy was stuck, well not actually stuck, trapped would be a better word. Anyway, Judy was in the cage and the door was shut, but I did not see that part, I was in my garage getting the dead, the dead ..."

'They look like noodles, say noodles, Noodles ... Noodles ... Noodles' the announcer interjected.

"Maggots out of my mop."

'Oops too late,' the announcer quipped.

"Sorry did I say maggots, I meant noodles," she shrugged her shoulders. "Maggots ... Noodles ... Whatever right?" Susanna was speaking fast and furious, too fast and furious. Her eyes locked with the officers. "Anyway ... where was I?"

"Maggots and noodles," he said flatly.

"Ah ... Yes ... So I was in the garage washing my mop ... Did I already tell you that?"

The officer nodded.

"Well, anyway I was in the garage," she reached and touched his forearm. "As you know, and Judy was locked in the cage outside screaming but I didn't know that till I heard her scream and then the cage made that noise you know Boom ... Ra ... Ta ... Tat. Then I knew," she paused. 'God, help me. This is not coming out right. It is coming out all wrong.' Those two sentences were too close to forming and meeting again. Something not right ... Something very wrong.

"Then you knew?"

"Yes I knew," she said. Susanna went up on her toes peeking at the officers note pad. The page was blank.

"Continue please," he said.

"Well, then I ran outside and tried to get Judy out but the door wouldn't open. Then Celia came and Judy starting getting hurt, so I took the paring knife from Celia and I stabbed and stabbed trying to get it off her. Celia was right there with me, she'll tell you. She'll tell you ... And then ... when ..."

The police officer cut her off. "She already did ma'am." He nodded to the officer just off her left shoulder. "Please be informed you are under arrest for the murder of Judy Anderson."

Her arms were grabbed by the elbows ... pivoted behind her back ... her wrists handcuffed. The police officer behind her pushed into her back moving her in the direction of the cruisers. The other officer walked beside, informing her of her rights.

A detective walked by with a pry-bar.

She swivelled her head.

He picked up the cage.

Her eyes widened like flying saucers coming in for a landing. "NO! ... NO! ... DON'T!" she screamed over her shoulder.

The detective sprung the door.

"YOU DON'T KNOW WHAT YOU'RE DOING!" Susanna screeched. "NO! ... NO! ... NO!" She lashed back and forth.

She slipped from the officer, turning, running back down the driveway. "CELIA! ... CELIA! ... YOU KNOW! ... I KNOW, YOU KNOW! ... KICK IT SHUT! ... KICK IT SHUT! ... TELL THEM THE TRUTH CELIA! ... I DIDN'T KILL YOUR DAUGHTER! ... TELL THEM!" she screamed at the top of her lungs. "TELL THEM!"

'Boom ... Ra ... Ta ... Tat ... Boom ... Ra ... Ta ... Tat."

"OH MY GOD NO!" Susanna yelled. "NO! ... NO!"

The two officers bolted after Susanna.

'Boom ... Ra ... Ta ... Tat.'

Celia's eyes widened, ringing with white. They hung on the cage.

"CELIA! ... I KNOW YOU CAN HEAR IT ... I KNOW YOU CAN HEAR IT TOO ... KICK THE GOD DAMNED DOOR ... CELIA!"

Susanna's feet went out from under her. Her face smeared into the pavement. Her body flattened, weighted down by the two officers. She couldn't breathe.

"Shut up," one of the officers whispered into her ear. "Just shut the hell up."

They plucked her from the ground, stuck their batons hard into her ribcage and forced her toward the cruisers. They bypassed the first and second cars, shoving her into the back seat of the last one in line. They locked and slammed the doors.

"What a hell of a weapon she is," the one officer said.

"Why don't you get her the 'H' out of here? There's plenty of us to wrap up," the other said.

The front door of the cruiser opened and shut. The officer adjusted the mirror. Started the engine. "Face forward ma'am," he instructed.

Susanna was turned in the seat, staring out through the back window, her eyes pasted on the cage.

"FACE FORWARD," he yelled.

Susanna didn't move.

'Demons are neither alive nor dead till we open their box where their invisibility rests,' whispered the television announcer from way inside her head.

'Well, it's open,' she retorted silently. 'Again,' she added.

The officer eyed her intently. "Face forward," he said again. He shook his head. He put the cruiser in gear.

'Boom ... Ra ... Ta ... Tat.'

Cold spikes shot up from Susanna's spine. She opened her mouth gasping for breath. She turned her head. The officer's window was a quarter down.

'Boom ... Ra ... Ta ... Tat.'

The officer instantaneously checked both side and rear view mirrors.

'It's not a coincidence. He hears it. I know he does,' Susanna thought.

'For sure,' the announcer added.

The constable edged the cruiser out to the end of the drive. He flipped on the left turn signal.

Susanna twisted, turning back toward the cage. It seemed to be vibrating. 'Demons are neither alive nor dead till we open their box where their invisibility rests ... They stand at the fringes of reason. They transcend understanding ... Some are reported animalistic in nature, baring fangs, with ferocious attitudes, acting out chilling horror like prophecies for all whom come in contact,' the television announcer said.

The cage door flapped of its own accord. Back and forth, back and forth like it was speaking in code.

Susanna's eyes flashed onto the barrage of uniformed people. No one seemed to notice.

'Demons are neither alive nor dead till we open their box where their invisibility rests,' the announcer piped.

'Enough already ... With that ... Tell me something different,' she reflected back at him.

'Everyone's going to die,' he quipped.

The cage rocked and pivoted, opening and closing its door. 'Boom ... Ra ... Ta ... Tat.'

She booted the back of the seat. "CAN'T YOU HEAR THAT?" she wailed. "EVERYONE'S GOING TO DIE!" she screamed at the top of her lungs.

The cruiser pulled out onto the roadway.

"PLEASE ... PLEASE ... GO BACK AND SHUT THE DOOR!" she screamed.

She threw herself at the side window. "GO BACK! ... GO BACK! ... She kicked the back of the officer's seat with both her feet. "SHUT THE DOOR! ... SHUT THE DOOR, she shrieked.

The officer totally ignored her. She might as well have been invisible, not there. She turned backward and watched the cage becoming smaller and smaller, turning miniature, a dot, and then disappearing all together.

'Gone but not forgotten,' the announcer said.

She booted the back of the front seat again. "GO BACK! ... GO BACK," she wailed.

He pulled off onto the shoulder, turned and sprayed her in the face with pepper spray.

"Bastard," she cried, her eyes instantly watering, puffing, blinding. "Why did you do that?" She clamped her eyes shut, doubled over, rubbing her face back and forth across her knees.

The officer drove on as if he was the only one in the vehicle.

She kicked the seat out of temper. "Die then, see if I care," she muttered. She kicked the seat again.

"Keep it up and I'll do it again."

"Oh, you can talk," she scoffed. She bent and rubbed her eyes over her knees again. She cleared her throat. "How long will I be blind?" she asked quietly.

"Twenty to thirty minutes. It depends," he said.

She leaned forward, pressing her face against the wire cage. "Can you please send an ambulance for my husband? ... And take my little boy somewhere safe?"

He eyed her via the mirror. She appeared so harmless. Sounded crazed but appeared harmless. "Look ma'am, your neighbour said she hasn't seen your husband in days, or your little boy for that matter."

"Please, please he needs an ambulance ... he ... he's," she paused.

'Come on say it,' the announcer dared. 'Say he's lying on the floor in the bedroom, hasn't moved for almost two days, has shrivelled raisins for eyes, stinks to high heaven, and is crawling with maggots.'

"He's very sick," she finally said.

The officer worked his jaw back and forth checking his teeth in the mirror. "We'll check on him ma'am. They're both in your house?"

Susanna nodded in the direction of his voice.

"Are they alive?"

"You're an ass."

"A murder calling me an ass, well doesn't that beat all?"

"I'm not a murderer," she said calmly.

"So you all say ma'am. So you all say." He pulled into the small police station lot across the lake and turned off the cruiser.

The front door of the cruiser opened, and then slammed shut. The back door opened. A hand firmed around her upper arm. "Turn sideways, ma'am," The officer helped pivot her into the opening, placed her feet on the ground, pulled her to a stand, and guided her towards the station. "There's a step here," he said.

She heard a door open.

"Another step ma'am," he voiced. "Okay you're inside. Come along quietly now. I'm going to place you in the interview room." He backed her against a chair. "Sit here ma'am. I'll be right back."

She heard the thud of a heavy door closing and locking. Her arm muscles strained and ached from being in the same backwards position for so long. The skin of her wrists burned, she could feel the rawness inside the tight metal cuffs.

She sat still and silent, eyes shut, head cocked, ears pricked, straining to pick salvageable words from the outer office muffled two-way radio conversation.

The door latch groaned. Susanna opened her eyes. A blurred blue uniformed figure approached. A chair squealed across the tiled floor. The officer sat, plopping a tape recorder and file folder onto the table that separated them. She smiled ever so slightly, her vision was returning.

He opened the file spreading papers across the table. He eyed her briefly then reached and clicked on the recorder. "I'm just going to take the preliminaries. I go off duty in twenty minutes. Another officer will be doing the interview."

Susanna nodded. She was still stuck with the same asshole that had sprayed the pepper spray and driven her across to the station. 'How lucky ... Not.'

"Please state your name for the record."

"Has my husband been sent to the hospital?"

"Name for the record."

"My little boy ... Has he been taken somewhere safe?"

"I ask the questions here."

She lurched forward, pressing herself tight against the table. She locked her eyes with his. "Did you people shut that damn thing's door?"

The officer drew his fingertips across his lips. "Name," he repeated.

"I want a lawyer ... And my phone call ... please."

The officer glanced at the wall clock. He shuffled the forms into the file folder closing it. He picked up the recorder. "For the record, the accused is currently hostile and uncooperative." He clicked off the tiny machine.

Susanna raised her eyebrows. "That's a lie," she stated.

He didn't say a word. He drummed the tabletop with his fingernails, smiled as if he was suddenly God, and stood. He plucked the folder and recorder from the table, pushed in the chair and exited the room, locking the door behind him.

'Prick,' she mouthed.

'I second that,' the announcer voiced.

She grinned. At least she was not totally alone. She had the announcer. An oddball relationship at best, but at least it was something. For whatever it was worth ... Real or not.

She scanned the room. Bare ... except for the small, square metal table and three dilapidated chairs.

She stood and made her way over to the metal door with the window. She pressed her face into it. 'One way glass? ... Nope ... Normal.'

The officer's back was to her. She watched him scrawl something in red across a piece of paper, slap it down on top of a folder, 'Hers,' she presumed, put on his jacket, pick up keys, and leave via the front door.

"Okay," she said. "Now what?"

She ran her tongue over her lips, wetting them. This was nothing like she had anticipated. She had presumed she would be subjected right away to the good cop/bad cop routine like on the reality television shows. With the standard, 'Why did you do it? Why would you kill a little girl? Did her mother help? Was it a plan between the two of you? Why do you hate little girls?'

She slumped against the door watching the traffic going by on the main street through the outer office windows. She had been taken no farther than the old rickety police station in her own town. The 'open only when a volunteer constable donated his or her own free time' police station. 'Not much for the area's newest child murder,' she sneered.

She pressed her forehead into the window. She'd been left unattended, with hands cuffed behind her back, in a small locked room, no phone call, no lawyer, no nothing. She watched the street colors start to fade, signalling night was approaching. She scraped her teeth backward over her tongue. Not one ambulance had skirted by, nor one emergency vehicle of any kind.

She prayed Jack's chest still rose and fell. She prayed Miles was safe. She bent her head and cried. She knew deep down inside neither prayer stood a hope in hell of ever being heard. How could they? She couldn't even clasp her hands together. Susanna slunk to the floor, rolling onto her stomach. She squiggled up tight behind the door. She turned her face into the room, closing her eyes.

~~~

Susanna awoke to the sound of sirens. She fumbled in the blackness, humping like an inchworm, working her body until she was able to stand. She pushed into the glass. More sirens, shrill and piercing. She shifted her weight pressing closer, flattening her nose against the glassed pane. The outer offices desk telephones lit in unison, all glowing a see through plastic orange as they started to ring. And ring and ring and ring.

A black and white, big city cruiser, siren blaring, white-blue lights flashing, whizzed past. Then another. Then another. Then another and another. Then two ambulances running side-by-side, taking up the entire roadway. Then another cruiser. Then ... nothing.

'Demons are neither alive nor dead till we open their box where their invisibility rests,' the announcer said.

"Would you quit saying that! ... For God's sake that's all you say."

'Is not,' he countered.

"Is too," Susanna, replied.

She stayed glued to the window waiting on the return trip of the cruisers and ambulances. She watched and waited as the exercise played out into futility.

She strained her eyes into tiny slices, aiming them along the walls of the outer office scoping for a wall clock. It was way past dark. Too dark, almost unnatural. 'A perfect ending to a perfect day,' she inwardly scoffed.

She wobbled her legs on purpose crumbling her body to the floor. She went down on her side. The one handcuff hooked onto something, pulling itself sideways, slicing fresh wedges into her already raw flesh. She rocked her weight back and forth, twisting and pulling her hands.

It held fast.

She slammed her teeth together, tugging and turning. She abruptly shot forward, sliding and skidding across the flooring like a car trying to brake on black ice. Something metal bounced along with her keeping her company, pinging as it lunged into the wall.

She slithered snake like, about facing, pushing her weight along with her feet. Her head rammed the metal door. She scooted sideways. Something poked into her shoulder. She inched backward, coming face to face with the screw-less, bent, metal door sweep.

The telephone rang again, loud and full. She smiled, she might as well be in the same room. She stretched out on her stomach, pressed her ear against its newly formed outer office listening device, staring blankly into the door. She closed her eyes as sleep found her for the second time, erasing away all and everything.

The telephones started to ring. The front door unlocked. Male voices talked over one another, the pitches and tones thundered off the walls echoing along the ceiling.

Susanna's eyes popped open. 'Daylight ... It's daylight,' she mouthed. She lifted her head, her vision rotating counter-clockwise around the interview room. She climbed the wall with her eyes connecting with the clock that read '7:00 a.m.' "I'm still here," she said sullenly.

'Yes ... Yes you most definitely are,' the announcer confirmed.

Susanna dropped her face into the floor tiles. 'God? ... Please let Jack's and Miles' chests still rise and fall ... And God? ... Please can you help me too?' she said under her breath. 'If ever I needed you, I need you now,' she added.

The telephone rang again.

Susanna pushed her ear tight into the sweep opening, shadowing and concealing it.

"Yes ... Yes ... Can you repeat? ... Repeat again? ... Again?" Billy swallowed back the sudden lump in his throat. "Yes ... Yes ... Take backup ... Yes of course ... I'll take Ed with me ... Separate patrol cars? ... Yep ... Leaving now." The officer dropped the receiver as if it was made of red hot coals. He stared mouth gaping, watching it bounce across the desk into the open drawer. He fumbled with fingers that shook and vibrated, finally retrieving the receiver.

"Ed ... Suit up ... There's a bad ... A bad ... one on the causeway. One of ours." Billy's voice pitched and wavered.

"Okay Billy ... I'm a coming ... I'm a coming."

"Ed?" Billy shoved his hands into his pockets fidgeting with his change. He motioned for Ed to step back against the steel interview room door.

Susanna pushed sideways into the flap, flattening her ear against the opening.

'Eavesdropping at its finest,' the announcer piped.

"Shush," she whispered. "Something's up."

"Apparently the crash is a bad one. Just want to ... Want to." Billy stammered his voice unsteady, wobbling uncontrollably. "Want to ... To give you a heads up. The Sergeant said to ... To pack up our ... Our strong stomachs."

Ed grew his eyebrows together. He had never seen Billy shaken.

Billy stepped close, dropping his voice. "Stu ... You know Stu Wadley?"

Ed nodded.

"Stu ... apparently was transporting the cage from over at that ... That crime scene. The one where the little ... Little girl got murdered."

Ed nodded again.

"Well ... He ran off the road on the causeway, or got ran off the road, no one knows. But, they think some kind of animal has been at him. He's all ... All shredded up," Billy drew his fingers down the side of his face.

"Shredded up?" Ed repeated Billy's last two words throwing them back at him.

"Yeah ... He's ... He's ... He's," Billy hesitated trying to form the Sergeant's words he'd had repeated three separate times into something tangible. He couldn't. He gulped back another lump, blurting the words verbatim. "He's all over the outside of the windshield, both sides of the front passenger door, the dash, and back and front seats of the vehicle and he's crawling with maggots." He sucked in a deep breath, he had said it, he had actually said it, somehow. "But, the thing ... The thing is, all the windows are rolled up with the safety locks on and the doors and trunk is locked." Billy paused, drawing his fingers down his face again. 'Animals that could roll up windows, and lock doors after they were done eating you?' Cold chills swept up and down his spine. "The Sergeant has instructed us get over there pronto, tarp it, wait for the tow and escort it over to the compound and say nothing."

Susanna's mouth gaped. Her stomach tumbled. It suddenly hurt to breathe. "I told them," she whispered. "I told them to shut it." She rolled onto her back.

'So you did,' the announcer said. 'Many, many times, might I add.'

Susanna could hear shuffling and banging. Then voices talking rapidly, vying for space, and tumbling over one another. She caught footsteps, then the heavy thud of the front office door. Then, drawers being open and closed.

'Have they forgotten me? ... Should I tell them I am here? ... I don't know what to do?'

'In my grandmother's words, God rest her soul, when you don't know ... don't!' The announcer offered up.

Susanna took too deep a breath sputtering and bubbling the excess out her nose. "Okay," she said. "I won't," she confirmed.

The office telephone sounded. She listened to another one-sided conversation, more shuffling and banging, running footsteps, then the thundering of the front door once again. Then there was nothing, like the room had suddenly become a void.

She stared at the ceiling tiles. The silence, the pin-drop silence, was deafening. She snapped her teeth together. The clacking buzzed and danced through her ears. She counted the tile rows, the joins, the half tiles, the bubbles in the overhead plastic light cases. She watched the second hand of the clock calculating with it.

At ten-thirty a.m., something broke the silence. 'Fluttering or ...?' She cocked her head tilting towards the peep-holed opening, listening. 'Another flutter ... Mail? ... Mail being dropped through the slot?' She strained taking note, as if she had been born with spider-senses. No more flutters. Just nothing ... and more nothing.

At eleven a.m., the silence broke again. 'Grinding,' like metal against metal. Then cracking and scuffling almost like someone walking. The clanking of glass, water running, the smell of packaged coffee. Then a faint clicking. Then more clicking. 'Clicking? ... Clicking? ... A computer keyboard? ... Yes, yes ... That is it.' Seconds later, there were low mutters, and then the squeaking wheels of a desk chair rolling back and forth followed by muffled footsteps. 'Someone has unlocked the door, come in, made coffee, and turned on a computer. Someone is out there,' she thought.

'Brilliant deduction ... Sherlock,' the announcer quipped.

'Shut up,' she shot back.

Abruptly the lock on the interview room access clacked, the handle turned, and the door popped and thrust forward. Susanna grunted, curling her knees up into her chest as the pain of the body slam rippled through her.

"Oh my goodness," the gray-haired woman said. She raised her hand to her mouth. "Oh dearie, I'm so sorry. I did not know anyone was in here. Are you all right?"

Susanna nodded. She squiggled away from the door.

The woman slowly filtered her eyes over her, stopping at the handcuffs. "Oh my," she said. "Honey, sit tight." She reached down tapping Susanna's shoulder gently. "I'll be right back."

The woman withdrew leaving the interview door propped open. She scuffled through her desk drawers, talking away out loud to herself. "Animals ... Animals in blue uniforms they are ... They just have no concept of human dignity ... That poor sweet girl locked up like a dog ... I wonder just how long she's been in there? ... Now, where are those keys? ... Ah ... Here they are." She hurried back over to Susanna. She squatted, unlocking and removing the handcuffs.

'Go on ... look,' the announcer prodded.

Susanna folded her legs underneath her, brought her arms round, and pulled her bitten hand directly in front of her face, flipping it back and forth examining the punctures. No green grunge ... No fuzz ... No maggots ... No nothing ... Just holes. The something incomprehensible together with the something inexplicable wormed up through from below the layers of reason. 'The Droom-Dro-Dra,' she mouthed. She smiled ever so slightly.

'Here! ... Here!' the announcer shot out. 'Finally!'

Her smile broadened. She folded both her hands into her lap, alternating rubbing the raw skin of her wrists with her thumb and middle finger.

"Oh my Lord," the woman said, disgust showed in her tone. "Come on out of there, and sit." She motioned to the chair beside her desk. "I'll fetch the first aid kit." The woman disappeared down a corridor.

Susanna plopped into the padded chair relishing in its comfort.

"Would you like a bottled water dear?" the woman called out.

Susanna opened her mouth and squeaked. She cleared her throat and tried again. "Yes, yes please," she said. She studied the front door, unlocked.

'I saw that,' the announcer said.

Minutes later the woman returned. She handed Susanna the water, quickly snatching it back and opening it for her.

"Thank you," Susanna said.

"Don't mention it dearie," the woman's gaze was soft and warm. She opened the first aid kit, setting out antiseptic, antibiotic cream, and gauze bandages.

Susanna's thoughts flew to Jack. She had done this very same thing but a mere three nights back. 'Please let his chest still rise and fall.'

The woman tended to her wrists suddenly stopping, grasping Susanna's right hand and examining the four punctures. She ran the side of her thumb across them. "Did a dog bite you hon?" The woman doused the holes with a liberal amount of antiseptic, dabbing up the excess fluid with a cotton ball.

"No," Susanna replied.

'Going for the plain and simple ... Not bad ... Not bad at all,' the announcer said.

"Cat?"

"No ... I'm really not sure what it was."

'Never lie when the truth will do ... I am impressed ... My hat's off to you,' the announcer piped.

Susanna's gaze drifted across the woman's desk. Receptionist name-plate ... stapler ... telephone ... in - out baskets ... 'empty in - out baskets' ... pens, pencils ... a white file folder with a sticky note; the words hostile and uncooperative scrawled across it in red ink. Her folder, her white sticky-noted folder filled with lies.

The woman wrapped Susanna's wrists and put away the kit. She slid the white folder with the sticky note off to the side, accidentally knocking it to the floor. She reached, picked it up, opened it, shuffled through the blank forms, muttered, ripped it in half, and threw it in the waste bin.

"Why they leave blank folders around is beyond me." The woman said more to herself than Susanna.

Susanna's eyes shone.

"Feeling a little better dear?"

"Much."

"So honey, let's get to your paper work, so you can go home." The woman rifled through her desk, pulled out a form while picking up her pen. "I always fill them out by hand before putting the report in the computer," she whispered. "So why are you here sweetie?"

Susanna smirked. She tilted her head back. 'Thank you God ... Thank you.'

'Well you did pray,' the announcer said.

"It is a misunderstanding really. My dog ... my dog went ... and ... and."

The telephone rang. The woman held up her index finger. "Just a sec, honey." The woman covered the receiver then whispered to Susanna giving her directions to the rest room if she was in need of it.

Susanna rose, repeating her words in her head. 'Go through the door between the filing cabinets, turn left, not right that way goes to the Captain's office. Go down the hall turn right, not left that goes to the outside door. The light switch is on the upper left hand side.'

The telephone rang again. "Police," the woman answered. "Pardon? ... Repeat?" her voice shrilled, quickened, pulling up and parking itself on the borderline of hysteria and mayhem.

Susanna stopped dead, her hand constricting and freezing on the outside doorknob. 'Something's not right ... Something's very wrong.' She turned her head, focusing on the telephone conversation.

"The girl here? ... What girl? ... No ... No ... No ... There's only a young woman whose dog did something?"

There was a long period of silence.

Susanna opened the back door. She stayed transfixed in the light of day, both arms extended, hands grasping the doorframe, waiting for the receptionist to tell her more about the words that should never come together. 'Something not right ... Something very wrong.'

"Repeat? ... Repeat again? ... No ... No ... No, no one radioed in ... All dead? ... Just a minute ... Let me grab my pen ... For Heaven's sake! ... My hands are shaking so bad I can't write ... Goodness! ... I dropped the pen ... Okay shoot."

Another long period of silence.

"Let me read this back ... Everyone, excuse me ... all life forms ... forms from the residences ... all ... all the residences ... sorry ... known ... known as 1430, 1432, 1434, 1436, 1438 Lakeshore Road obliterated ... scattered ... I'm having trouble, wait please. I think I'm going to be sick."

Retching ... Muttering ... Coughing ... Retching.

"I'm Back ... Let me start this again. All life forms, human and animal alike have been obliterated, and are notably deceased. The location of the desecration ... desecration ... sorry," Retch. "Let me start that last sentence again. The location of the desecration is Lakeshore Road ... numbers 1430, 1432, 1434, 1436 and 1438 inclusive. Ed Thompson and William Wood have been identified via their nametags to be the mutilated carcasses on the front lawn of house number, 1430. Also the lives of twelve city officers, identification pending," Retch ... Retch. "Sorry ... has been ... been compromised as well as six ambulance attendants."

Another long period of silence.

Susanna dropped her arms, her body bending and collapsing like it was designed with pre-determined perforations. She slithered out onto the stoop. She grasped her chest ... she couldn't breathe.

"Horrid, just horrid! ... Susanna Miller? ... Never heard of her ... Nope! ... As I said, just the young woman with the dog issue ... Someone needed an ambulance at 1430? ... And 1432? ... When? ... Before the massacre? ... Yes ... Yes ... No one in the home of 1430? ... No, Jack Miller? ... Drag marks? ... Maggots? ... MY WORD! ... Little boy? ... What is left of the Miller boy is in the county morgue? ... Oh I see ... Yes ... Well pieces." Retch ... Retch. "I have to go home."... Retch ... "One more thing? ... The cage? ... What cage? ... Oh that wooden thing? ... Yes it is at the vet clinic already ... The name? ... McLeay's Veterinary ... Yes, yes ... No, it's just across the way here ... No I don't know what time it came in ... All right ... I'm gone then."

Susanna could feel her heart revving inside her chest, shuddering and skipping, like a race-car being primed by an unknowing amateur before the next heat. She shook back and forth as it pulsed off rhythm and palpitated like it was about to explode and send sharp razors of shrapnel through her entirely to cease her existence. She shut her eyes in preparation, waiting.

Torment prevailed, it didn't explode and she lived.

Her head flopped down in defeat. Everything in her world was gone. Her animals ... Little Buffy, Adorable Libby ... Her people ... Her son ... Her husband Jack ... Gone, missing? ... Was he the drag marks?

She clutched at her ribs; she could not feel him any longer inside her heart. 'His chest doesn't rise and fall.'

The bellowing clang of the front office door shutting thumped and banged through the hallway walls. Susanna sat cross-legged sobbing for all she was worth. Thunder roared overhead. Rain started to pelt. She lifted her face skyward.

The tears and drops ran as one, washing her in minute waves. The concept of time shut down, allowing for rejuvenating and spirits rebirth.

The old was gone ... The new had arrived.

The thunder bellowed. Sheet lightening streaked, lighting the sky with wide bans of blue-white light. Hail beat onto the earth.

Susanna rose. She descended the wrought iron stairs. Walked twenty paces crossing the back parking lot; Halted, turned left, Stepped underneath the awning. Reached, she reefed the knob, popping the door beside the sign that read 'McLeay's Veterinary Clinic Employees Only,' wide and full.

She stepped in.

The distinct odour of copper hit her like a ton of bricks, as if it had been lying in wait for someone, anyone. 'That thing is in here,' she mouthed.

'Indeed,' the announcer agreed.

She flicked the light switch with her thumb. Nothing. She grinned. 'Stupid is as stupid does.' She should have known better.

'Hey ... Isn't that from a movie?' the announcer asked.

'Yes ... Yes it is,' she replied.

She walked through the small back room, her footsteps resounding, turning larger than life against the backdrop of the eerie silence. An unnatural eerie silence, much like the kind put in horror movies to prickle the hairs on the back of the audiences' necks.

A ribbon of dull gray, the only light source, stretched across the far wall as if attempting to mirror the overcast sky.

She entered the recovery room.

What was left of a large, dark coloured dog strewn throughout a wire recovery pen and across the floor; its flesh peeled ribcage hung midway up the side. Farther up pockets of curled gray tentacles sprouted and dangled from the wire mesh.

'Déjà vu anyone?' the announcer said.

Susanna carefully waded through the mincemeat obstacle course. Something popped under her runner. She halted, lifting her foot. A mushed brown eyeball fell from the tread.

The next room in line was the operating room; Spotless, ready and waiting. Without thinking, her fingers snatched an empty hypo from the wall mounted equipment table. She shoved it deep into her back jeans pocket.

'That know without knowing,' the announcer whispered.

Stealthily, she moved through the top floor of the clinic. It was devoid of life, sound, lights; a private ghost town, at best.

She turned, about facing in the outer reception, food for sale, area. Something dripped wetting her hair. Something cool. She looked up. Blood smacked onto her cheek. She backed two paces. Big beaded, round balls of blood dropped from the outer edge of the upper most food bag as if being coaxed along by a nylon line. She climbed up the bags, coming face to face with the clinic cat. If she had been any closer they could have swapped breaths, if its chest ... 'Still rose and fell.'

It stared blankly, one glazed eyeball rotated towards the ceiling, the other focused straight ahead. Its lips were pulled back from its teeth in a horrid grimace like it had died just before the scream. It lay draped over the bag, front limbs loose and free. Its entire back slashed end to end, the backbone missing.

She let go of the food bag, dropping down into the middle of the blood pool, splattering it everywhere. She smirked, 'Just what I needed ... War Paint.'

'Are you all right?' the announcer asked.

'What do you think?' she countered.

'I would be inclined to say ... no,' the announcer replied.

'Ding ... Ding ... Ding ... You win the prize ... Right you are!' Susanna laughed aloud. Sanity seemed at a premium.

'Is there a limit to the terror and horror one can endure?' She wondered. 'Who knows,' she thought.

'You just answered your own question. You do know what they say about people who answer their own questions don't you?' the announcer asked.

'Say it and I'll rip you right out of my head here and now,' she said.

'Funny thing ... I suddenly can't remember,' the announcer whispered.

'Wise,' she mouthed. 'Very wise,' she repeated.

Susanna retraced her steps through the clinic. She scanned each room in detail. 'It has to be in one of these,' she thought. She navigated carefully through the recovery room trying her best not to desecrate the dead any further. She pivoted her feet, whirling in a slow circle, suddenly stopping.

"Snap ... Crackle ... Pop," she said, sneering. She reefed the basement door open. Glooms blackness, utter complete obscurity poured from the opening. She sniffed the air, her nostrils flaring from the dense metallic overlay. "Ready ... Or ... Not ... Here ... I ... Come" she whispered.

She descended the wooden stairs, edging her feet methodically, one after the other, over and down. She stretched out her arm, running her left hand along the damp brickwork as she went. She could feel her breath fogging back against her skin. She counted out the steps, abruptly stopping on the eleventh step. 'Most basement stairs are a set of twelve ... Are they not?'

'Yes,' the announcer confirmed.

'Thank Jesus,' she sighed. She shoved her one foot over the edge, stepping down. She felt with her toe. "There's another stair! ... Wouldn't you damn well know it ... This pathway to hell has thirteen stairs."

She stepped down then slid her feet forward. They scuffed across concrete.

'Susanna?' the announcer whispered.

She stopped dead. "Yes."

171

'I'm here for you ... Remember that ... Okay?'

"Okay."

'Susanna?'

"Yes," she said.

'You can do this ... You know without knowing.'

"I'm so glad you think so," she replied, sarcasm showing through the cracks. She sucked in air, deep and full, in through her nose, exhaling out through her mouth. She repeated the process, following the cleansing rituals of old to fortify her blood stream.

'You can,' the announcer reaffirmed.

Susanna took one last breath, held it, squared her shoulders, firmed her footing. Look out ... Look out ... Wherever you are ... I'm coming to get you!' she mouthed. She stretched her arms out like feelers, put one foot in front of the other walking heel to toe through the blackness.

Thunk.

'What in hell?' She shook the pain from her arms. She held her hands palm forward patting them back and forth across something cold, hard, smooth, big. Her left hand knocked against metal. She danced her fingers backward and forward across its dome, and then closed her hand, turning until it clicked.

She pushed the door open.

The stench coursing out of the hellish oblivion was over powering. She retched, abruptly cupping her hands over her nose and mouth. Then ever so slowly, she removed a finger at a time allowing the smell to infiltrate and rot out her primary receptors, nullifying the overwhelming urge to vomit.

She started moving again, both arms extended horizontally from the shoulders. The air seemed to be dampening and chilling by the second. Her fingers suddenly bent backwards. The walls appeared to have closed in. She could touch both sides. 'A corridor,' she thought. 'I'm in a corridor.'

'Yes you are,' the announcer confirmed.

She ran her fingers along the concrete blocks, her feet moving slow and paced, her open mouthed breaths the only audible sound. Her fingers splayed. She hesitated, feeling out for bearings, running her fingertips up and down. 'Wire mesh?' She pressed the flat of her hands into it. 'Yes ... It is ... The kennels ... I am in the kennel area.'

She continued moving, slow, careful, steady, straining, feeling through the darkness. The dry concrete under foot abruptly changed. Her foot slid. She picked it up, put it back down. Something crushed, popped, squirted underneath her runner.

'We both know what that is,' the announcer said.

Susanna nodded in agreement.

She refocused her thoughts, picking up where she left off. 'There should be an outside door.' She passed a wooden wall. More wire-mesh, more wood, more concrete.

SMACK!

'That's one way to find it,' the announcer quipped.

'Shut up,' she shot back.

She fanned her fingers back and forth hitting the doorknob on the first try. Her hand turned, her arm shoved. She stepped outside. Thunder boomed and growled. Lightening streaked. The skies opened. Torrents of cold rain pelted out huge drops that stung her flesh. 'Perfect,' she mocked, under her breath. 'Just perfect,' she repeated.

Wind howled through the trees bending the tops. The door banged shut. She picked up a small tree branch. Jerked the door wide, jamming the branch into it. She backed from the opening. Closed her eyes. Held her arms skyward, and waited.

'If I may be so bold ... Just what are you doing?' the announcer asked.

"Waiting for the lightening to strike me dead," she said flatly. "The way things are going I figure I'm about due."

'Not going to happen,' the announcer said.

"And ... Why the hell not?" Susanna stretched her arms out further.

'It's sheet lightening,' the announcer said matter-of-factly.

She smiled ever so slightly, pursed her lips, and then sucked them into her mouth. She slowly about faced, stepping back through the doorway.

The overcast sky filtered into the darkness, mutating and re-arranging it into long wisps of shadows that did not seem to replicate anything inside. Everything within was doused in gray, in varying degrees like it had been all hot washed together in some super-sized laundry machine, brought back, and laid out. The puddles of dark gray-black, wet shiny slime that oozed from every pen, meeting and blending in the middle of the alleyway like the great lakes tributaries, the medium grayish bits, pieces, and hunks of tufted things, the light gray, long, shiny, curved, thin branch like things.

Silently she back-tracked walking down the center, lifting her feet slow, precise, purposeful, not so much as making a sound or ripple. The bottom door loomed into view. She slowed, turned right; rounding the corner she had bypassed on the first trip through the dark.

Light became a premium, and then totally vanished as she turned another corner. 'This thing is a U shape,' she thought. She again stretched her arms out feeler-like putting her feet heel to toe, navigating her way through the darkness. Her fingertips tricked across another wooden wall, more wire-mesh, wood, and concrete.

The air seemed to change, dimple. She abruptly stopped. She cocked her head, holding her breath, careful not to create a ruffle in her own brand of silence.

A miniscule clack floated past. Then another. If she hadn't halted, holding her breath, it would have been missed, camouflaged by her own footsteps.

'What is that?'... Susanna held her arms close to her sides, creeping forward in slow motion, listening, computing.

Clack ... Clack.

Louder this time, more distinct.

The darkness seemed to give up ahead. She stole along the walls, stopping and starting liked a seasoned huntress, rapidly closing the distance.

Clack ... Clack ... Smack ... Clack.

She moved fluid, stealth like following the noise, freezing in place when it stopped, continuing when it clacked.

Clack ... Clack ... Smack ... Smack ... Clack ... Chomp.

Her lips pulled from her teeth forming a horrid sneer like smile. She nodded her head. 'Something is eating.'

One wall ended. 'Another corridor?' She slithered to the edge, eyeballing it. Her sneer turned full and toothy. 'Nope ... Not a corridor ... An offshoot with a dead end.' Her smile turned lethal. 'An offshoot with a dead end and a window to light the way.'

The sounds ceased.

She pulled back immobilizing, slipping herself under the radar of detect-ability. She had to be sure. There was no room for mistakes.

Clack ... Slurp ... Clack ... Smack ... Smack ... Clack ... Chomp.

She flattened into the wall, smearing against it as if part and parcel of it. She inched into the corner. Dropped her right shoulder, slanted her neck just enough to allow a one eyed scan. 'There she be ... In all her glory.'

She pulled back, allowing for a victory smile.

Clack ... Slurp ... Clack ... Clack ... Smack ... Chomp.

'Okay ... Let's scope this out,' she breathed. 'You with me?'

'All the way,' the announcer said.

She carefully, silently returned to the outer edge. Detailing, calibrating, and leaving nothing to chance. One window. Four kennels, doors closed. Straw broom propped, back left corner wall. That thing, the cage, middle of the aisle, door open. Something sticking out of it ground level. 'What the hell is ... that?'

She strained squinting hard, focusing. Immediately her stomach rolled, vomit heaved into the back of her throat. She pulled back cupping both hands over her mouth. 'OH ... MY ... GOD! ... HOLY HELL!' she screamed inside her head.

'Susanna,' the announcer whispered.

She stiffened, stopped breathing, immobilized, as scream after scream rocked through her head.

'Susanna, come on girl, don't lose it, don't do this,' the announcer said.

'Don't do this? ... Don't do this! ... Jesus Christ! ... Didn't you see?' she thought talked.

'Yes,' the announcer said. 'In our heart we knew ... Didn't we?' the announcer added.

'Not that! ... Not that!' she repeated. 'Oh ... My ... Good ... God ... Oh my God ... Oh Lord!'

'SUSANNA,' the announcer screamed.

'Oh my Lord God in heaven.' She bent her head, tears flowing fast and furious.

Clack ... Clack ... Smack ... Clack.

Susanna pressed her palms into the wall pushing her weight on and off it, shaking her head back and forth. She wiped her face on her sleeve. 'I've got to look again,' she thought.

'You already saw,' the announcer said.

'Oh God! ... Oh God!' She hung her head looking down at her feet. 'Yes ... I did ... Didn't I?' she muttered inside her head.

'Yes,' the announcer said softly.

She heaved sigh after sigh, filtering in and out oxygen like a fish out of water. 'Okay then ... Where were we?'

'One window ... Four kennels, doors closed ... Straw broom propped back left wall corner ... Cage middle of aisle, door open,' the announcer said.

Clack ... Slurp ... Clack ... Smack ... Smack ... Clack ... Chomp.

'Do what you will ... Then ... Do what you must,' the announcer said.

Susanna bowed her head in agreement.

She crept to the outer edge of the wall, crouching, timing her breaths, gathering all she was, waiting for that three-second window. She put her right hand to the concrete, heel up, every muscle in her being tingling, twitching, anticipating ... waiting for that first clack and slurp.

'God be with you,' the announcer whispered.

Clack ... Slurp.

She sprang. The air fanned, the edges whooshing. "DROOM-VLOOFI! ... DROOM-VLOOFI!" She screamed.

A shadowlike form lifted from under the kill. It hovered dead center of the cage.

'The three second window, open and counting down,' the announcer breathed.

In one fluid motion, Susanna reached, grabbed and snatched, flinging the severed limb, still sporting its ribbed crew sock and runner, airborne. It splattered against the ceiling tiles, coming back down amidst a dense shower of maggots, blanketing the entire floor in humping squiggling white.

The shape growled, horrid, guttural, and inhuman. It spun, shot straight up, squealed, turned, and grew transparent.

"SHOW YOURSELF YOU BASTARD!" she screeched.

She hit the cage full force, smacking it into the wall. The door swung back, and then forward thundering against its self. Something invisible howled, growled, snarled, and then bayed wolf-like, yowled in short rapid bursts that broke in the middle echoing back upon itself like something not of this world.

"DROOM-VLOOFI ... DROOM-VLOOFI," she screamed again.

The shadow re-emerged, circled, streamlined, and warped straight for the doorway and her.

'A half second,' the announcer whispered. 'Just a half second.'

She leapt, booting the door with both feet. It slammed into itself, closing, popping the locking pin.

The thing battered the door, smearing into it. It spun, turned upside down, darkened, grew dense. It howled with rage, restructuring, flinging itself at the bars, rattling and thrashing at them.

The cage groaned, shaking and tossing like it was about to fly apart.

Susanna squatted, studying it in detail. It seemed to have no defined structure; its shape, changing and reforming every split second. It bashed on and off the door rungs threatening, growling and snarling.

She stood, whirled, back kicking it full on, her hatred seething and foaming out of her like an antacid tablet in a cup with too much water.

The cage bounced, up ending into the left wall corner taking out the broom.

She walked slowly, purposefully to the limb, retrieving it, holding it tight against her chest. "Jack ... Jack," she whimpered. "I'm so sorry ... When they said you were gone ... I didn't think I'd ever see you again." She bowed her head cradling the shin, ankle, and shoe within her arms. She gently rocked it. "I'll do right by you ... I will Jack ... I promise."

She laid the limb on the ground, took off her long-sleeved tee shirt and wrapped the limb within. She twirled the sleeves round and round threading them each through three belt loops. She pulled the material taut, knotting it in place.

She walked through the offshoot, eying both end walls. No doorway. She pivoted, marching back over to the cage. "What a god forsaken place this is," she said.

'It was,' the announcer said. 'Till there was you.'

"Thanks ... I think," she replied. "Well ... shall we get on with this?"

'Lead the way,' the announcer replied.

She jerked the cage from the wall. Picked up the broom, jammed it through the top rungs, centering it. Grabbed both ends, pulling and dragging it with her, backing from the offshoot out into the middle of corridor.

She hesitated then surveyed the aisle way. She studied the concrete floor. The wide swatches of liquid that had pooled and banded together, stretching like a river down the center ... The ten, fifteen, paces at best to the blackness ... The utter complete blackness, that seemed to be leaning, creeping forwards as if tired of lying in wait to play its macabre version of truth or dare with her.

Was the concrete floor rough enough to catch the latch and pop the door? ... Horror 101 ... Yes. "Yes," she reaffirmed. She pulled the broom free, flipping the cage, top siding the door, leaving nothing to chance.

'No! ... No! ... Flip it back! ... Drag it! ... Catch the latch! ... Pop it! ... Pop it! ... Release the thing! ... Be cast down! ... Lay amongst the shredded blood soaked carcasses! ... Become one!'

'Susanna?' the announcer said.

"What?" she snapped.

'Are you all right?'

"No! ... You already asked me that ... It was no then and it's still no."

'Okay, then,' the announcer whispered.

She lodged the broom back through the rungs. Went in behind, grasped the pole ends, reached out and pushed go-cart style. She lifted her feet high, in turn, thumping them into the concrete, splattering her way down through the middle using the lifeblood of the lost as her guidance system.

Dark gray mutated in the darkness, casting long, snarled, willow like giant fingers across the wall. They seemed to coil then stretch, wavering, suddenly alive, opening and closing as if they were anticipating, preparing hungrily for an earthly bounty.

Susanna sidestepped, veering offside, sliding her body along the surface of the left wall as she rounded the U in the corridor.

This day was not one of gifts and fairytales, quite the contrary.

She lifted the cage through the back door opening out into the rain, slid it across the cement pad and onto the wet grass. She removed the tree branch, held the door open with her foot then slowly, purposefully turned towards the cage. She ran her fingertips over the scabbed over punctures on her right hand, smiled, turned back to the opening, shut her eyes and started to sing. "Droom, Dro, Dra, Dratf ... Droom-Vloofi."

'I had been fretting, you might for ... get,' the announcer said hushed, low.

"Never," she said. "Never," she repeated.

'Might I join?'

"From the beginning, then?" Susanna said.

"Droom, Dro, Dra, Dratf ... Droom-Vloofi ... Dro, Dra, Dratf ... Floom- Floon ... Dro, Dra, Dratf ... Bracht ... Dro, Dra, Drat."

"Rest in peace little ones," she said almost too quiet to hear. "May God be with you."

She released the door. It slammed shut, its echo filtering throughout the clinic walls, sealing in the dead.

'I didn't know you were religious,' the announcer said.

"I'm not."

Susanna grabbed onto both sides of the broom pulling the cage up the hill backwards. "Holy Christ," she puffed. "There's got to be a better way."

'Well ... there is your undershirt,' the announcer offered.

"Good thinking."

Susanna pulled the broom from the rungs, untied Jack, took off her undershirt, ripped it in two, tied half onto the one broom end, jammed the other through the rungs, tied the other half on, and then double knotted the two lengths together making a pulley.

She re-tied Jack around her waist, cut across the police back parking lot, and went down into the ravine and up the other side. She crossed the causeway against the traffic along the gravelled shoulder, dragging the cage behind, heading for home in what seemed to be the torrential downpour of the century.

Little rivers sprouted and ran, washing out the gravel on the sloping shoulders, carving out earthen passageways down into the lake. Thunder crackled and roared serenading her, offering up encores of lightening and golf ball sized hail. She started to laugh as the vehicles swished on by, not one slowing or giving so much as a second glance.

'Okay you got me too,' the announcer chuckled.

"Yep ... The escaped convict, clothed in jeans and a bra, soaked to the ass, dragging the crime scene cage by an undershirt and a broom down the side of the road with something tied up in a tee-shirt attached to their jeans, go figure."

She howled with laughter.

Bright yellow plastic police tape stretched as far as the eye could see. It ran just off the shoulder of the roadway from the outer corner of her front lawn, across the driveway and far lawn, repeating the pattern for all the neighbouring homes.

She ducked under, dragged the cage down the drive to the truck, stopped, flipped open the tailgate, and heaved the cage into the box. The dark stains on the pavement and cement stairs seemed as if they were swirling in slow motion as they mixed in with the rain forming the groundwork of gruesome looking puddles. She watched as they spread out, floating up substances that appeared a cross of oil and lard.

Susanna cupped her nose with her hands dry retching as stink from the dried out rot came back to life in the rain.

She walked through the open back gate into her yard. Crossed the lawn, knelt and buried the piece of Jack in the flowerbed beside Libby and Buffy. She bent her head reciting the Lord's Prayer.

The announcer joined, reciting with her.

She lovingly stroked the ground. "Please always hold onto what I said to you long ago ... Not only will I love you for the rest of your life but for the rest of mine as well ... With all my heart and soul, Jack ... I meant it then and I mean it now ... God speed, my love ... God speed."

Susanna rose, standing at the foot of the flowerbed in silence, her hands clasp together, her heart aching. She stood for the longest while then slowly walked to the side of the house, broke off four roses, returned, laying them across each mound of earth, placing the fourth on the flat ground the other side of Jack's. "This is for you Miles," she said softly. She kissed her fingers then blew, sending her love out on the winds, to forever surround them.

She turned, strolled across the back lawn and smiled at her half open kitchen window with the screen missing. She climbed through, changed into dry clothing, rifled through the buffet drawers, snapped a beeswax candle in half and shoved it into her pocket along with her stolen syringe and Jack's 'Swiss Army Knife.'

She fetched the truck keys off the kitchen counter, her eyes abruptly catching and hanging onto a brightly coloured folded paper and pack of matches in the middle of the table. She dunked the match pack into her pocket, and then carefully unfolded the piece of paper. The word 'Burn' scrawled in large letters with black marker.

'Jack's handwriting,' she thought. She clutched the paper to her chest, then folded it dime size and shoved it into her front jeans watch pocket. She hopped out the window.

She backed the truck out the drive. Stopped, lifted the police tape up and over the truck roof, steered up the hill turning right onto the back roads. She wove in and out of the nameless dirt roads heading for the remote isolation of the crown lands. She drove deep within, turned into a field cutting a pathway through the underbrush into the pines, before pulling into a small clearing and stopping.

She climbed from the truck, stood on the back bumper, grasped onto the broom and pulled the cage towards her, grabbing and throwing it off.

She dragged it under a tree, knelt and emptied her pockets. She snapped the safety tip from the syringe, made a fist and drew blood out from the large vein on her hand. She picked up the candle, lit a match, and waved it back and forth under the end heating the wax until it softened. She gathered it, formed a ball, and poked the middle with her finger creating a bowl.

'Half and half,' the announcer reminded.

Susanna smiled. She had remembered. 'Binding ... Ritualistic ... Doorway seal; half and half blood and beeswax.'

'I'm impressed,' the announcer said.

She picked up the hypo, depressed the plunger, filling the wax bowl with blood. She placed it within her one palm, placed her other hand over top carefully compressing it within, then kneaded and formed it into a pliable thin strip. She draped it down the length of the door jam, pulling away the excess and winding it around the edges of the locking mechanism. She ran her thumb over it pressing it firmly into place.

Her eyes flashed across the wording on the right frontal column. "It's the Droom-Dro-Dra,"she whispered.

'Yes ... Yes it is,' the announcer confirmed.

Susanna and the announcer chanted in unison, their voices playing off one another like a carefully rehearsed stage show. "Droom, Dro, Dra, Dratf ... Droom-Vloofi ... Dro, Dra, Dratf ... Floom- Floon ... Dro, Dra, Dratf ... Bracth ... Dro,

Dra, Dratf ... Droom, Dro, Dra, Dratf ... Droom-Vloofi ... Dro, Dra, Dratf ... Floom- Floon ... Dro, Dra, Dratf ... Bracth ... Dro, Dra, Dratf."

The cage vibrated, rocked and pivoted, then thrashed side to side.

Susanna turned from the cage, gathering dried twigs, small branches, leaves, and pine needles. She staked and arranged them underneath the one lone oak tree. She struck a match throwing it in and under, fanning it with her hands as it started to ignite and blow out thin wisps of orange and blue fire. She fired in more lit matches setting the blaze full and high.

She jerked the cage from the ground and tossed it on top. The fire crackled, throwing out electrified sapphire blue streamer like sparks in all directions, smouldering and smoking as it dissipated and dissolved.

She lifted the cage to the side, re-gathered, and repeated the process.

The cage shifted, twirled, turned in circles.

The fire thrust and pushed onto a branch, raging across it onto the bottom rung. It popped and sizzled, abruptly extinguishing as if doused with buckets of water. The flames beneath took cue fizzling, dying in place, huffing and puffing out dense gray smoke.

Susanna folded back half the match pack striking the other. She held the mini-torch against the middle rung. It fizzled and went out.

She pulled her lips back from her teeth in a wicked sneer. "Won't burn? ... Well ... Well ... Now why doesn't that surprise me?"

'There's more than one way to skin a cat ... Isn't there?' the announcer said.

"Yes ... There ... Is," she replied slow and undisputable.

Susanna booted the cage rolling it toward the truck. She spread out her kindling base snuffing out the smoky taggers on. She returned the hypo and candle to her pocket and heaved the cage into the back of the truck. She gunned the gas pedal, put the truck in four-wheel tearing off cross-country heading for the old logging road that criss-crossed the black pavement.

'Think we'll see a bear? ... Don't know ... Might be a tad early.' Susanna could hear her husband and son bantering back and forth, as if they were right there with her. 'Are we there yet?' She could almost feel Jack's warm hand atop hers, see his smile at winning the betting time on 'The question.' She parted her lips looking into the rear view mirror; the back window had started to fog showing off Miles' odd array of fish smooches.

She did not flip the indicator as she turned down the dump road. Nor did she stop for the locked gate. Or slow as she climbed the steep hill, bypassing the backhoe and the sign that read 'NO SCAVENGING by orders of Saren County. Video surveillance in place. Bi-law No. 341 strictly enforced.'

She turned off the truck, jumped in the back, and yanked the cage up and out. She toed the rain soaked dirt with the tip of her sneaker ... 'Soft.'

She smiled walking off toward the office. She pressed her face into the glass scanning the tiny square room. Her smile broadened. It was leaning against a fishing pole in the far corner. She tried the door on the off chance the girl had forgotten ... 'Nope ... Locked.' She backed, lunged and booted the door full force. It splintered away from the frame whipping backwards. She grabbed the shovel, toting it with her as she disappeared up and over the edge of the cavernous hole the backhoe had created.

Two hours later, she re-emerged, shoved the cage over the top edge and down into its newly created eight foot deep grave. She filled it in, smacking the dirt with the backside of the shovel, planting it firmly in place.

She walked back over to the office ... Replaced the shovel ... Closed the door ... Crossed the lot ... Climbed the hill ...

Started the truck ... Put it in reverse ... Backed up to the hole ... Jammed it in neutral ... Slipped out the door ... Went around front ... Dug in her heels and pushed.

The truck inched slow and easy, the back tires giving way sliding the body over, in and down.

She strolled out the dump road, turned north on the county road striding along the soft shoulder, about facing and sticking out her thumb as a vehicle approached.

'October 22nd, one year later'

The waitress put down her polishing cloth, joining the group watching 'The all-time top ten most wanted,' on the suspended ceiling television set.

"It has been a year since the grizzly deaths in what has come to be known as 'The Paring Knife Murders' ... Where over thirty women, men, children, and pets, were deliberately slaughtered and sent to their deaths, mutilated beyond recognition at the hands of the most bizarre slasher in history. This number one spot goes to the female femme fatal ... 'Susanna Miller.' If anyone out there has any information please call our toll free hotline. Your information will always be kept confidential."

"Though no pictures of the accused were ever found, Susanna Miller, according to a reliable police source, is believed to be forty-five years of age."

She smiled; she was thirty-two.

"One-hundred-fifty pounds."

Her smile broadened as she rested her one-hundred-twenty pounds against the center support beam.

"Five-feet one-inch tall."

She broke into laughter stretching out her five-foot, five-inch frame.

"She is reportedly blonde with a short cropped hair style."

She drew her fingers through her light brown shoulder length ponytail. She padded the customer's forearm beside her. "Now what was that order again Rick? ... One medium double-double, fries, a toasted ham and cheese, and a cherry Danish to go?"

"Yep Vivian ... You got it," Rick said.

'Hey Viv ... Make me something too,' the announcer squealed.

"Shut up asshole," she said out of the corner of her mouth.

The announcer broke into torrents of laughter.

She strolled behind the counter humming to herself, picking up the paring knife.

On the far wall hung a plaque, transcribed in pre-dynastic Egyptian ... 'Demons are neither alive nor dead till we open their box where their invisibility rests.'

'October 17th, 5 years later 12:00 noon'

"Mommy ... Mommy ... Over here Mommy," Tommy squealed. "Look what I found down in this hole."

The excavator gleamed golden rod yellow in the bright sunshine. A battered, dirt ridden truck lay on its side directly behind, heavy chains attached to its back axle. A hydro pole lay off to one side, to the other an old weathered sign propped on an angle.

Valerie brushed the dirt from the board. The letters were cracked and weathered but still legible. 'NO SCAVENGING by orders of Saren County. Video surveillance in place. Bi-law No. 341 strictly enforced.'

"Mommy! ... Come Quick ... Mommy!" He poked at the cage with a stick dislodging some of the compacted dirt.

Valerie skied down through the dirt with her boots. She pulled the cage free. It tumbled rhythmically as if its movements choreographed. It glided across the muck, landing on its side directly in front of her feet.

She kicked at it with her boot. Her skin abruptly goose bumped. She buttoned her jacket folding the collar up about her neck. She shuffled her feet back and forth. Cold shivers shot up and down her spine

"Isn't it neat Mommy?" Tommy squatted down in front of the cage.

Valerie knelt beside him. Her hide broke into a cold sweat. She stared at the cage. She took in a huge breath whisking it through her teeth. 'Isn't it neat Mommy ... Isn't it neat Mommy,' sling shooting around inside her head. Her mouth opened, the word 'No' forming about to erupt.

'Boom ... Ra ... Ta ... Tat ... Boom ... Ra ... Ta ... Tat ... Boom.'

She glimpsed nervously around her. "What on earth is that?" she asked.

"What Mommy?"

'Boom ... Ra ... Ta ... Tat ... Boom ... Ra ... Ta ... Tat ... Boom ... Ra ... Ta ... Tat.'

"That."

Tommy stopped poking the cage, cocked his head sideways shooting his Mom a puzzled 'I don't know what you are talking about' look.

Valerie hunched her shoulders. Her body trembled with wave after wave of hot prickles like someone was trying to ram a dinky car with square wheels back and forth across her skin. She wrapped her arms around her middle. She shuddered again. She looked from her son to the cage and back. Her body quavered like some invisible force had hold of her and was wobbling her to and fro.

"Can we take it home Mommy? ... It would be a great fort for all my army guys!"

She waded her feet into the dirt digging it up, flinging clumps off to the side with the toe of her sneakers.

"Can we? ... Can we?"

A cold chill vibrated through her legs. 'Must be coming down with ... with ... something,' she thought. "I don't know," she said quietly.

"Can we please?"

She sighed heavily. For some undefined reason, she did not want any part or parcel of that thing ... she studied it carefully. "I don't know," she said again. She should have just said no and been done with it. She hated saying no to him, when he asked for so little. He was a good kid.

"Please ... Can we?" Tommy tugged at her jacket sleeve.

"Okay honey," she whispered, going against her better judgment.

They both picked a side of the cage, entwining their fingers into the wooden rungs, lifting it in unison, scrambling side-by-side out from the hole.

Valerie plopped the cage into the trunk leaving the lid open. She didn't have any rope. The drive was only a few short miles. Surely to God they would not ticket her for an open trunk. She drove out the dump road stopping at the county road. She looked both ways then proceeded out onto the side-road at a snail's pace.

Out of nowhere, even before the turn indicator switched off, a vehicle was on her like white lightening blasting its horn in demanding bursts.

Her rear-view mirror was blocked by the open lid. She felt the car jar as if the driver behind had driven up her ass end on purpose, bumping and banging her bumper.

Fear riveted her hands to the steering wheel. She veered onto the right shoulder.

The driver behind passed in her lane, horn blazing, middle finger extended.

Her passenger tires caught the gravel. The car started to fishtail. "HOLD ON TOMMY-BOY," she screamed. She instinctively turned the tires in the direction of the skid. The car criss-crossed wavering back and forth, then abruptly straightened.

The wooden cage had gone airborne with the second jerk of the car, zooming up and out effortlessly as if it was born to fly. It up-ended returning to earth and hitting the blacktop with a tremendous boom, toppling its self over and over dead center of the solid white line. It traveled down the backside of the hill in a straight path picking up momentum as it went. It veered off to the right steering itself off the pavement, coming to rest amidst mounds of grass and cattails.

Valerie caught the trunk lid flapping up and down in the rear-view mirror. The trunk lid with the empty trunk.

She smiled.

'October 17th, 12:45 p.m.'

"Hey Alice ... Did you see that?" Taylor slammed on the brakes, rammed the car into reverse, and backed down the shoulder. He stopped on the soft gravelled shoulder, flung the driver's door wide, ran to the edge of the swamp, and bent over.

"What the hell are you doing?" Alice called through the passengers open widow.

"Over here." Taylor waved her over, and then crouched.

Alice stood looking over his shoulder.

Taylor flipped something back and forth. "What do you think?" He dislodged the wooden cage plunking it down directly in front of her feet.

'Boom ... Ra ... Ta ... Tat ... Boom ... Ra ... Ta ... Tat ... Boom.'

Her spine prickled with cold shivers. She glanced over her shoulder at the car. 'The radio button must have been bumped to another channel,' she thought.

"Well?" he questioned. He banged the cage on and off the ground displacing huge clumps of grass, cattails, and dirt. "What do you think?"

"What do I think?" She hunched her shoulders in a silent 'I don't know,' type one answer. She zipped up her sweater. The shivers trading up to a throat lump.

He sat it down, came up behind her, wrapped his arms about her, snuggling. "It's our one month anniversary ... So I was thinking ... Why don't we get that new pet you've been wanting on the way home ... Say a nice angora rabbit?"

Alice's eyes glistened. She swallowed back the lump. She tilted her head back peering up at him. "How about two? ... One for each of us?"

Taylor smiled. "Deal," he said. He threw the cage into the trunk.

'October 22nd'

'Radium River Daily Newspaper' excerpt from headline: Gruesome bloodbath at the Simpson farm. Forensic specialists have concluded the assault must have taken place at least two to three days prior to the grisly discovery by acquaintances of Taylor Stevens and Alice Stevens who were renting the farmhouse. The time of the deaths is an approximation at this time due to the state of decomposition of the remains. Details of the deaths have been withheld due to the sensitive nature.

A large mass of body parts and limbs, believed to belong to Taylor and Alice Stevens, their three dogs, cat and two rabbits, (though positive identification was near to impossible due to the desecration) was found lying to one side of a freshly dug four foot deep hole at the rear of the house. Where an ornately carved wooden cage of some sort was being unearthed or buried.

The remains and the cage have been taken to the city of Woodview for in-depth forensic analysis.

'October 30th'

The van turned onto the old dump road just as twilight stretched across the horizon. It backed slow and purposeful, stopping inches from the crater sized hole. Two police officers exited the vehicle, opened the back door, and removed the wooden crate. The one bent and studied it, running his fingers back and forth across the ornate carvings.

"You like that thing?" asked the other.

"Yeah ... Yeah I do," said the first. "We just got a new pup and ... this would be perfect for him to sleep in."

"Take it home," the second said. He nonchalantly shrugged his shoulders. "Who's to know? ... Forensics is long done with it."

They both smiled, nodding in silent agreement. They picked it up and shoved it back into the van.

"We'll swing by your place on the way back to the station."

The first signalled to the waiting driver. The bulldozer's engine revved as it commenced shoving dirt into the crater.

The old weathered sign tilted back and forth in the wind. The letters were cracked and weathered but still there. 'NO SCAVENGING by orders of Saren County. Video surveillance in place. Bi-law No. 341 strictly enforced.'

NO SCAVENGING

Epilogue

Just because you can't see it ...
Doesn't mean it isn't there.

INTERMISSION

Peanuts,
Popcorn,
Candy,
Or perhaps? ... A dream?

Ina Louise Jackson

THE DREAM

It is what you do not hear that matters ...

"What do you see?" Its three voices blended as one; female, male and male all distinctive, yet together, raspy, inhuman, terrifying in an indefinable way.

His gaze lifted from the back of the recliner where it sat, its head and shoulders miles above the pillowed leather headrest, dwarfing it.

His eyes drew across the window. Nothing but total complete blackness, no streetlights, no illuminated houses, nothing. Even the dim room lighting offered up nothing. No reflections in the glass, no outline, no form, no profile of what sat in the chair. He wanted to step forward, come closer, but unadulterated fright had frozen his limbs, rendering him but a darkened gray statue of the night.

"What do you see?" it asked again.

Once more, his eyes traced the windowpane. "Nothing," he muttered.

It laughed hysterically.

"What is your name?" he asked, the tone of his voice two octaves higher than it should have been. He tried to clear his throat, failing, croaking like a frog.

"Name, name, name ... They're all the same ... Plain Jane ... What's in a name?" It responded brashly.

"What is your name?" he asked again.

"Ching-chang, walla-walla bing-bang," it sang smugly.

"Tell me your name."

"Banana fana fo fana, fee fi mo manna ... N ... a ... n ... a," it answered quickly.

"What is your name?"

"Paddy cake ... Paddy cake ... Bakers man ... Make me a cake as fast as you can."

It all of a sudden raised its right hand, pointing the index finger, swaying its shoulders. Babies began crying, soft and gentle. It raised its left arm, suddenly dipping its head up and down as if signalling to begin. All at once, the tempo of the whimpers picked up. Others joined; newborns, older babies, young children, and older children. It flicked its wrists back and forth, extending the index fingers as if conducting an orchestra as the sobs intensified, strengthened, turned to screams.

His breaths came harder, faster.

In an instant, the screams halted, and it was there. Right there in front of his face. Hunkered down. Its massive, orb like, black onyx eyes staring right through him.

Warm urine spread out in a butterfly pattern across his crotch.

"What is your name?" it asked mockingly. It cackled like a hyena. "Colton, it's time to wake up now," it whispered.

COUNTY ROAD 507

Dedication

For Austin & Lincoln:
Always believe ...
In the possibility,
Of the impossible.

Prologue

Before ... You can connect the dots
You must first find all the dots

Ina Louise Jackson

COUNTY ROAD 507

First appearances deceive many,
The intelligence of the few,
Perceive ... What is carefully hidden.

'Prelude'

The funeral service had been too long for hearts to bear. Gary and Emma Stokes drove home in silence. The urn, as promised, returning so the ashes could be released out into the wind and sky.

'One Year Later'

Emma hooked her arm through that of her husband's. The late summer sun was beginning to set, casting delicate baby pink and blue hued streamers up into the clouds. Sweet, soft breezes fluttered the tree leaves. They stood as they had done so many times before, gazing into the meadow across the road. The scene would have been picture perfect except for the sold sign.

Emma stood alone, silent on the front lawn, sipping her morning coffee. The fog seemed to be creeping from the north, drifting and stretching out in mid high ribbons of dense gray; The kind that gives one, unease, a worming, a penetrating stealth-like un-sureness, undermined with layers upon layers of sinister under currents. As if something were busy weaving an invisible web, dancing it right before your eyes without touching your soul, obscuring all, pulling and drawing at you.

A wind growled overhead, moving swiftly, jumping through the treetops. The howling ran the length of the drive, leapt the roadway then groaned and wailed through the forest on the far side of the meadow in ghostly fashion, not so much as moving a single twig.

'Bad omen,' she thought.

'Day One'

"They're sure wasting no time." Gary's eyes traced over the bulldozer and backhoe.

"I guess that's one way of putting it," Emma scoffed. She didn't like this one bit. As far as she was concerned, they were defiling the earth.

Gary cocked his head to one side, then the other. "I wonder ... When did they bring the machines?"

"This morning," she replied.

He went up on tippy-toes scanning the mountains of dirt. "Foundation's in I bet."

"I think." She made her lips disappear into her mouth.

"Must have went like hell on fire."

"Nope."

"Hummm."

"Nope!"

"Hummm."

"Hummm?" Emma's eyebrows drew together with distaste. "Hummm! ... It's a whole lot more than hummm! ... They came, dug for a few hours, stopped, a whole bunch of vehicles arrived. Everybody went down into the hole; a few came back up, huddled in a circle with arms waving like football coach having a bad day. More vehicles came, unloaded big black duffle bags, everybody and everything went down. Afterwards, they flagged and roped off the hole, all leaving together in a convoy." She paused catching her breath, then added. "It was all over and done by noon."

"Huh."

"Huh? ... Is that all you have to say? ... Huh? ... What does huh mean?"

"Huh," he repeated. He sucked air in between his teeth. "Well ... I guess it's not all that bad."

"Yes! ... It! ... Is!"

He shrugged and moved forward, climbing up onto a boulder.

"A shrug? ... Come on!" She glanced over at Gary. "What's the point of living way out here in the country surrounded by forests and meadows if land is severed and sold, and ... And." Emma pointed to the meadow and knoll across the roadway. "And ... That happens!"

Gary sighed deep and full drawing his hand slowly across his mouth. "Em," he whispered. "It won't be so awful ... Really it won't."

"Yes it will," she retorted. 'Yes it will,' she repeated to herself. She moved closer to him.

"I wonder if any one's been over for a look see?" Gary tented his forearms blocking the sun from his eyes.

"It's a hole. What's to see?"

He stuffed his hands into his jeans pockets. "Foundations can be interesting."

"A hole for a house, can be interesting?" Her lips curled in distain. It was as if he was almost in the conversation, but not quite. For all intents and purposes, he could have easily carried it off all by himself.

"Yes sir," he paused then continued, "good size f ... o ... u ... n ... d ... a ... t ... i ... o ... n." He drew out the last word slow and methodically, finishing off with, "by the looks of it."

"Okay ... I stand corrected," she snorted. The corners of her mouth turned up. "Foundation not hole ... Right?"

He smacked his lips. "Think ... I'll go have me a peak after supper."

"Whatever." She raised her arms. "Boys will be boys," she muttered. 'No matter what their size,' she added under her breath.

~~~

"See you later alligator." Gary gave a backhanded wave.

Emma bit her bottom lip, shaking her head slowly side to side. The wave's directional course was so way off it was

202

not even in the same ballpark. For all intents and purposes, he had just flapped his hand at the barn.

She watched him, detailing his journey with flippant silent commentary as he jogged across the lawn, dipped under the rail fence, crossed the field, bounded over the roadway, scooted through the meadow, and disappeared from sight into the hole. 'Excuse me,' she mouthed. 'Foundation, as the smart ass called it.' She chuckled to herself stepping back through the screen door into the foyer. 'It's still a hole ... A hole's ... A hole ... Is a hole.' She laughed aloud.

Hours passed, the setting sun rested, centered on the horizon between the earth and sky, giving way to an extraordinarily large bright-white full moon.

Emma tapped the flashlight on and off her thigh, shut the front doors, and proceeded across the lawn to the laneway. Grey willowy shadow figures tagged her, dancing and prancing and bouncing in and out of the long grasses of the meadow, ducking and hiding when-ever she glanced over her shoulder like they were all consciously playing a game of peek-a boo.

"Where on earth did he get to?" she said. She flipped on the light directing the beam into the dark swatches hiding from the moon. "Over here?" she said. 'Nope,' she answered silently. She made her way over to the machines, shining the light between the massive wheels and under carriages. 'Nope, not here either,' she mouthed.

She stood motionless, silent, listening through the darkness for telltale signs of her husband. Nothing ... Just the night noises of frogs, crickets, and the little things one couldn't see. She pursed her lips, thought talking. 'Maybe ... Just ... Maybe?' She walked to the outer perimeter of the hole lifting and ducking under the roping, striding to the edge. She shone the light. It sparked off yellow somethings ... Shiny, bright fluorescent yellow ... Somethings.

"What the hell is that?" she said. She drew the flashlight back and forth, slow purposeful. "Tape? ... Plastic? ...

Caution? ... Tape? ... Squares?" She dragged the light along the surface of the tapes, veering up and down the wooden pegs at each corner.

"Pegged off squares of caution tape? ... How ... Very ... Odd," she muttered, leaning forward, squinting her eyes, invoking clarity. "Maybe it's marking, juts of rocks ... Underground springs ... Or ... Or ... Something else," she said. She flashed the beam back and forth giving up the guessing game. "Perhaps it's normal, part of the overall design. Possibly, all house holes." Emma smiled, correcting her wording. "Possibly all foundations were as such." She had never been this up close before.

She curled her toes, digging them into the soil, anchoring her weight. She scanned the interior, moving the light slowly, methodically, an inch at a time, searching for a body shape.

'Pay dirt!' she exclaimed under her breath.

She started the decent.

Gary was sitting with his back to her, cross-legged, in the hub of one of the interior taped off squares. Just sitting there, as if he had taken up residence, like he was one with the dirt, akin to it, somehow becoming part of it.

She scrutinized him as she drew closer. His right arm was moving down then up, down then up, repetitively, never changing or altering the motion. Her brow furrowed in puzzlement raising her eyebrows like a stage curtain, slow and precise.

'Okay ... All right then ... Peculiar ... Yes ... But.' She broke off her thoughts; they had nowhere to go except into the realm of weird.

She stopped directly behind him, coughing on purpose.

Nothing.

It was as if she wasn't there.

She coughed again. Nothing ... No acknowledgement ... No nothing.

She bent over, coming ear level. "Hey you? ... Lose track of time?" she whispered.

Once again ... Nothing.

She moved beside him. Shone the flashlight beam.

Shock infiltrated, the light tumbled from her grasp. Her eyes doubled in size filtering him in of their own accord, making the first attempt to digest before sending it off upstairs.

He looked as if he had bathed in the dirt. He was ruddy black head to toe. The front of his tee shirt was clumped with things that had seemingly affixed, solid chunks ringed in liquid, flaky scraps, flat bits, pebbles, and earth balls ... And ... And ... She didn't know what else.

The scattered loose-knit formation streamed directly down the front of him, from just under his chin to his thighs, like he'd had an overstuffed mouth of soda crackers with peanut butter and marshmallow filling and sneezed it out all over himself. His entire face smeared in grease like dirt; his lips split and crusted, his cheeks bulging, chocked-full, like a chipmunk's just prior to the first snowfall.

"GARY!" Emma screamed. "WHAT THE HELL ARE YOU DOING?"

She grabbed him by the shoulder.

He turned his head to the one side, halted, then to the other, in short swift jerks that resembled a vintage windup doll on its last legs. He grinned toothy and full. Dirt fell from his mouth. He slumped the top half of his torso forward, pivoting his arms up over his head stiffly before lowering them, awkwardly stretching out his fingers like all the bones had been taken out and put back reversed and upside down. He fumbled in the dirt, snatching two handfuls, tightening his hands into fists. He partially straightened, flipping both hands palm side up and opening his fingers. He jerked his hands horizontally, back and forth, spraying dirt every which way, like he was a resurrected three-time zombie.

Emma assumed this was his way of an appeasement. A silent offering.

"No I don't want some!" Her mouth formed into a sideways scowl.

He lurched out his arms, straightening them, poised his hands, clamping them together, ducking his head forward and backward like a turtle popping it in and out of its shell. He all at once stuffed the handfuls into his mouth, plugging his nostrils, slapping and smacking his lips together as if devouring one of the world's finest delicacies.

She shook him. "WHAT ON EARTH IS WRONG WITH YOU?"

He whipped his head, gazing over his shoulder, just as suddenly looking over the opposite. He then faced forward, as if commanded to do so by some unseen presence, folding his hands into his lap. His eyes glazed over. He ceased smacking. Subduing, freezing in place like he had been doused with liquid nitrogen.

"GARY!" Emma screamed.

He tilted his chin, up then down, opening his mouth, working his jaws in a sawing motion, chortling and puking out liquid dirt bubbles that stuck to his chin. He cocked his shoulders swinging and gyrating the top half of his body, and then went back to the business of eating.

Emma starred at him, dumbfounded, horror stealing into the little lines at the corners of her eyes, setting up camp, expanding them, as he devoured handful after handful after handful. Like it was perfectly normal to sit at the bottom of a freshly dug hole, cross-legged in the middle of a caution taped square, gobbling down dirt, under the veil of the full moon.

"GARY! ... GET! ... UP!" she screeched.

Emma reached for him a split second too late.

He pitched forward, flopping face first into the dirt, abruptly manufacturing muffled sloshes and gurgles. He whipped back to a sit as if on a bungee cord, flapped his arms cawing like a vulture over-gorged from its meal and unable to fly, but not wanting to all the same. He calmed, pivoting his face skyward and contorting his mouth in an outlandish series of rapid bizarre grimaces.

Emma's open mouth hung in place, disbelief weighting her tongue like a fishing line with a too big sinker.

He got up on hands and knees, bent his head, prodding and moving the soil with his face.

Emma's eyebrows glued to her hairline. She worked her jaw with both her hands.

"GARY!" she shrieked. "STOP THIS! ... STOP ALL THIS!"

He snatched a glutinous mouthful of dirt, raised his hind end, tossed his head, and shook like a wet dog. He fell on his side, making swimming motions with his arms and legs. He then tucked in his limbs, rolled, right siding, rapidly clambering straight up the sidewall of the hole like a deformed, offshoot version of 'Spiderman.' He humped his spine, straightening his back legs, scampering like a wild animal on hands and feet.

She scrambled up and out, giving chase as he whipped on all fours across the roadway and up their drive.

Emma slammed the front doors behind her, locking them. She tracked the trail of dirt through the house into the kitchen, banged the open refrigerator door shut, accidentally kicking the remnants of a raw minced meat packet towards the table.

'God All Mighty ... What in hell?' She picked up some of the larger hunks, turning them over in her hands. They were torn and shredded as if an animal had been at it. She tossed them into the sink.

A single cold shard peeled from the shudder in waiting, snaking the length of her.

She climbed the staircase, by-passed the bathroom, turned left. Stopped dead.

Gary was on top of their bed, fully dressed, in the foetal position, half rolled in the comforter, snorking, snorting, and hissing out bubbled filth from his nose and mouth that fizzed and popped as it hit the air.

"O ... k ... a ... y?" Emma drawled the word slowly, stretching it into a million dollar question.

She backed down the short hallway wiping the cold sweat of her palms onto her jeans, then retraced her steps halting again in the doorway, peering in ... And ... There he was ... On top of the bed, dressed, foetal position, dirt and all the rest of the frills.

The answer to the million dollar question? ... There wasn't one.

She had definitely seen, what she thought she had seen. She sucked her bottom lip into her mouth pressing down on her flesh with her top teeth. She crept over vigilant and silent, permanently placing her picture directly underneath each in the dictionary.

His body was curled tightly, knees to chest, like a caterpillar on a cold spring day. Both his hands clasped in the prayer position, fingers bent and neatly tucked under his chin. His eyes sealed slits, drawn out pencil thin, appearing more reptilian than human. His skin stained ruddy black like the earth down in that hole. He smelled of musk, dampness, and decay, like a piece of rust laced metal pulled from a manure pile. His fingernails were ringed and caked with muck. His facial features blurred, encrusted and smudged with so much soil he looked like someone else. The spatter directly around his mouth hung from his skin in little red-white ball like adhesions.

She leaned over him. Fanned her hand back and forth in front of his face.

Nothing ... Not even a snort or a dirt bubble. Was he asleep? ... Or comatose? ... Or unconscious? ... Or something else?

She drew out her index finger placing it a hair's breadth from his nose. He was breathing.

She flicked one of the red-white clumps from the corner of his mouth, quickly retrieving it from the bedding. It felt punky and squishy between her fingers. She pulled it apart. 'That looks like raw meat!' She towed the torn package image back to the forefront, shutting her eyes, mentally examining it. 'Ripped ... Torn ... Shredded ... Ravaged ... Herbivore marks ... Lots and lots and lots ... No carnivore's ... No canine punctures ... It had to be him ... It! ... Had! ... To! ... Be!'

She stood alongside the bed, shock gravitating like pintsized yellow ducks at a shooting gallery. Her eyebrows rose. Eggshell white suddenly glistened between her eyelids. Everything started to swim, slow and lazy. She sunk to the floor. Her head knocked against her knees. Her hands clutched at her chest. Her breaths became deep, laboured and troubled.

Emma crawled along the floor, pulled herself to a stand with the aid of the night table, and then made further use of it as a lean-to while she finger-patted her eyebrows back into place. She crossed the room closing the bedroom door behind her.

~~~

She sat in the rocker on the front porch running her fingers through her hair, lost amongst unsettled thoughts, as if she blindfolded and taken to an unknown place and pushed from the top of a waterfall.

She eyed the blackened meadow; staring into it as if it was some separate entity.

'Everything on this earth has a purpose,' rolled out from inside her head, precious teachings from her childhood. She closed her eyes drawing on the words of wisdom, the philosophies handed down through the stories of the elders. 'The Great Spirit; The father of all ... The earth; The mother to everyone.' There was nothing to pull from. The principles

Ina Louise Jackson

made perfect sense. Gary didn't, no matter which way she turned him.

She rose from the chair, slowly moving from the porch to the grass. She tilted her head back until it touched her shoulders, focusing on that unconventional moon. It appeared transformed, fuller, brighter, the vivid white over taken with radiating irradiance. And closer ... Unnervingly closer, like she could reach out and touch it with her fingertips if she really tried.

'Is that ... Causing this? ... That bizarre moon?' she asked silently. People had been known to have bouts of temporary insanity during it, hence the terms lunacy and lunatic. 'Does sitting cross-legged, in the dark, at the bottom of a newly dug hole, eating dirt fit into insanity? ... Or scampering home on all fours? ... Or scarfing down raw meat?' She wrinkled her mouth, answering herself. 'Yes ... It ... Does ... Most ... Definitely ... It ... Does!'

She discontinued the gaze, scuffing her bare feet along the front lawn. Her shadow jumped as if something had poked it hard from behind with a stick, as if prompting it to keep her focus on it and away from the skies. She flicked her eyes over it as it jumped again, swearing she saw its one hand whip side to side then jig up and down, as if a tattle-tale.

She cranked her head back.

That moon ... That oddity ... Seemed like it had seized the unobserved opportunity, discerning it as an open-ended invitation to expand its territory, enveloping and gobbling up all the surrounding stars, rapidly doubling its size.

She opened her mouth, circling her fingers round her lips, probing, studying, watching particles within its inner circumference light, glow, spark, and explode as if someone was up there setting off fireworks. The more she watched the more magical the sparking phenomena became as if a private display for her eyes only.

Her thoughts reverted to Gary. The Gary that was upstairs rolled up in a make shift cocoon, there, but not.

"Well," she said, the word hung mid-air as if it was waiting for the rest. "We'll," she said again, pausing, knowing the remainder of the sentence, wishing she didn't. She sighed heavily. "Back over I go."

'Great ... Spirit ... Help ... Me,' she mouthed.

Emma went back in the house for the flashlight. The space it once occupied was empty. She grimaced showing the whites of her teeth, remembering where and why she had dropped it.

She locked the front doors behind her.

'When one is searching for the reasons of others, one should walk their path' floated inside her head deliberately lagging around as she followed Gary's route. She mentally placed her feet into his shoes, jogging across the lawn, dipping under the rail fence, crossing the field and roadway, scooting through the meadow towards the hole.

She suddenly halted mid-stride, foot poised, ready for its touchdown. Her head swivelled, her neck arched, tipping back of its own accord, as if her body had been secretly cued, to observe that moon again. She stood perfectly still, her three-hundred-sixty-degree reflection shining brightly. She could feel its pull, its tentacle like suckers, as if it had its own agenda to fulfill, an agenda she could become part and parcel of, just like one of those stars.

Emma backed up stomping her feet, breaking free from the inexplicable seduction it was exuding. She bowed her head, shaking it, vowing she could see moonbeams exiting, piercing the ground, driving themselves down under.

"This day needs to end," she whispered through her teeth.

She closed the distance, ducked under the rope, and jumped the edge, skidding through the dirt, breaking small clumps free that rolled and followed, gaining momentum like snowballs rampaging down on a steep hillside, obscuring her tracks as they went.

The moon appeared to follow, situating itself directly over-head, swaying and dancing its rays back and forth, lighting the way like a mammoth, red carpet spotlight. She stole a quick glimpse feeling it was but a ruse, a carefully orchestrated deception to distract her while it made ready to beam her aboard.

That hanging moon bothered and disturbed her in an indefinable way she could not seem to shake. She suddenly found herself wishing for cloud cover, for a rainstorm to beat all rainstorms, and then it would be like Gary, there, but not there.

Emma's eyes flashed over the dugout interior. The flat sides steeper than she had remembered and the hollow a much greater mass. She walked the perimeter slowly. Her right arm stretched out, fingers extended, running along the earthen walls. She lightly scooted her feet, purposely placing her forward heel onto the behinds toes, leaving no footprints. The dirt was oddly warm, almost hot to the touch, like it had spent the entire day sunning on the beach and still was.

She closed her eyes, focusing, channelling, picking up Gary's cross-legged image. She opened her eyes, about faced, walked ten paces, stopped, turned left, walked three paces, stopped, and stepped over the tape.

She crouched, running her hands backward and forward across the soil surface, barely disturbing it. She drew her fingertips in and out of a fresh three-inch round divot where something had been removed. The hole lay adjacent to a bum print. Gary's bum print complete with the brand name tag of his jeans, scored into the dirt.

She fanned her palms over the small dugouts, the leavings of the dining. She raised her right hand fingers to her mouth purposely squishing up her lips as a prelude of what was to come. She took a small pinch of dirt between her left thumb and index finger; it seemed to instantaneously moisten, sizzle, as if leeching from her, nourishing itself on her fluids and warmth. She brought it face level examining it.

'Strange,' she thought.

She rolled it into a ball and popped it into her mouth. Her lips blew from her teeth curling inside out in utter disgust. She flipped her tongue to the roof of her mouth, spitting, thoughts whirling. 'That's worse than awful! ... It tastes like dirt.' She grimaced, catching herself. 'Of course it does ... You idiot ... It is.' She spat again rumbling up saliva from her throat.

Her eyes flickered to the multitudes of yellow plastic tapes, bouncing to each in turn. 'Why did he choose this one ... This particular one to?' She drew up her shoulders, shuddering, finishing her thoughts. 'To dine from? ... Why not one of the others?' She had no answers; not even a smidgeon of a letter.

She rose, ruffled up her hair, gazing again from one area to another. She pivoted sixty degrees taking a small step, then another, then another, all at once teetering off kilter and almost going down as the flashlight rolled and popped out from underneath her heel. She sneered, fetching the light, slapping it into the palm of her other hand knocking the dirt free.

Emma flicked the on button forward, stepped out over the tape, walked to the next square and stepped in. She drew the light tightly over the ground, stopping, squatting. Something was partially exhumed, then left. She sifted the blistering dirt through her fingers. She stroked the protruding metal, smooth, ice cold. She filtered the beam directly onto it attempting to decipher the shape. It appeared to be no more than an old metal jam jar missing its lid and spoon.

She walked to the next, for a second time something partially uncovered, metal, old, like a soup pot lid, once again frigid to the touch. She moved to the ensuing section to find exposed metal arrowheads, angled in a circle, an inch of the shafts uncovered.

Emma continued in and out of each taped area, the lot containing old metal objects, some smooth, others nubby and pitted, all a dull gun metal gray with reddish-orange rust overtones. All of them partially uncovered, and left. All bitter cold like they had been encased in ice and still were. All of the surrounding earth bordering on scorching as if being continuously heated on high.

Nothing seemed out of place, nothing missing from any ... With that lone exception. The one containing the distinctive bum print. Had he taken it? ... Or ate it? ... Or? She didn't further her thoughts, shuddering once again.

She clambered from the hole, remaining just inside the ropes staring down into it. The cast of her shadow seemed to remain below, lurking and wavering and wandering all by its self in and out of her trail. She watched it moving about, swearing it turned and looked at her twice.

'Odd and unsettling seems to have become a common stay this day,' she thought. She wrapped her arms tightly around her middle.

Moments later, she ducked out from the ropes to make her way home, walking then running full out, choosing to travel the lane instead of the fields.

'Day Two'

Emma stepped out onto the front porch, morning coffee in hand. She had slept on the sofa deciding not to disturb Gary. She had heard no stirring overhead and presumed he was still whatever he was, up there.

Saturdays had always been extra special to her, a home day ... With Gary working away restoring the old barn and her scraping off the layers of paint from the ornate woodwork inside the house. But ... Not this Saturday.

She swung her body, using the heels and balls of her bare feet, towards the horizon. A thick enflamed band hovered just above ground level as if a giant had dabbed a paintbrush in vivid red stroking it across the sky.

"Red sky at night ... Sailors delight ... Red sky at morning ... Sailors warning," she said. "Another bad omen," she furthered.

Emma continued the pivot, throwing her shoulder into it to come face to face with the roadway and meadow.

Her mouth unbuttoned, her coffee tumbled.

The county road was littered in animals.

Non-moving wild animals.

They lay over the pavement and shoulders, strewn every-which-way possible, side-to-side, over top one another, head to head, as if a huge truck had sped by in the middle of the night not noticing its tailgate was wide open.

She stood motionless, horror-struck.

"Dead! ... They're all dead!" Her voice croaked and pitched as she whispered the words again and again and again.

Out of nowhere, the wind netted chattering, throwing it her way over top of the tree branches. Faint at first ... Too faint to make out the birthplace. It circled, dropped and channelled as if purposely jolted into whirling through the bush grasses picking up tempo and velocity. She shut her eyes, listening as it gravitated up the hill, all at once establishing recognition.

Human ... They were human ... Humans chattering ... Bundled voices full of glee, hooting and hollering in merriment.

Emma flashed her eyes open, the smile abruptly spilling from her lips, wedging and burrowing into the grasses of the lawn, hiding, leaving nothing but a tight grimace as witness to the ten to fifteen people in various states of dress and undress. Clothed, half clothed, pyjamas, naked. The whole batch dirt covered, as if they had sprouted from beneath it.

They were jumping, twirling, and loping, pack like along the gravelled shoulder of the road. Another cleared the bushes, then one more, following the first, howling and yipping, bee-lining for the others.

Emma watched them, transfixed, unable to break away. There was something about the last one ... The last ... To come from behind the bushes. She slanted her body inclining towards them. Something familiar ... The gait ... The stature.

"NO! ... NO!" She clamped her mouth, covering it with both hands, her muffled screams vibrating and raking the insides of her throat. The back of her tongue grew water chestnuts. She bowed pole-like, as if not weighted to the ground, swaying forward, sideways, backward, on legs that felt like unused rubber erasers.

'NO! ... GARY! ... NO! ... PLEASE! ... NO!' Her screams were silent and full. Her rubber eraser legs vibrated, stretched, gumming at the edges.

She watched them run onto the pavement, fetch and sling the lifeless carcasses up onto their shoulders and across their backs. Their dead weightiness, limp, swaying, tossing the limbs. Their eyes open, black, glaring. Emma trailed them as they ran out of sight behind the bushes in the direction of the small farmhouse next door. Breath escaped through her open mouth at the precise time shock coated in repulsion slithered along her tongue dislodging the water chestnuts into her throat.

Moments later, the hooting filtered back. Everything slowed as if meant for some higher purpose, like movies decelerate, flickering frame-by-frame, loosening round the hot spots, even pausing and stopping so every minute detail could be taken in and inspected.

Yet ... Apart from time standing virtually still, they appeared more frenzied, the hooting and hollering louder, the jumping higher, the joyous pitching of their voices greater, their overall demeanours, beyond exuberant.

Midway to the road they halted, each twirling round in separate circles, hips rotating, arms raised and swaying side to side. They spun round and round to the point of dizziness, staggered back and forth, ran on the spot, knees held high, stilled to a count of five, then jumped in sync, coming together, hooting, smacking one another's hands like they all shared the winning lotto ticket. Seconds later, they were back to twirling and whirling in wide circles, changing it up into skipping as they approached the roadway.

Emma's gaze flickered to the carpet of dead animals, to them and back to the animals, as they congregated and dispersed, continuing with the fetching and slinging and carting off beyond the bushes.

Her open mouth hung off kilter as if threaded wrong. The only visible sign of life was her pivoting clock-like eyeballs, ticking back and forth, following the fetch and release, fetch and release.

A low slung, dark coloured, sedan broke the top of the north hill. It crawled smoothly and methodically, almost mindlessly, straddling the centerline, weaving in and out of the animals as if they were no more than scattered paper bags. The vehicle turned into the meadows makeshift drive and stopped. Two men in dark suits got out, opening and closing the car doors in unison. They walked side by side in the direction of the hole, stepped over the roping, and quickly disappeared from sight.

Emma unconsciously zipped her sweater starting across the lawn. She was going over there.

The forest floor rustled. Something flashed at the corner of her eye. She turned.

More rustlings ... More somethings. The long grasses in front of the trees whip-lashed. The hairs on the back of her neck stood, frosting, biting into her skin like little nettles.

Again rustling ... Camouflaged movements. The unnaturalness spiralled up and down her spine. Something was there, right there. Gathering, in the grass.

All at once, they rose.

She screamed, silent high-pitched screams that echoed inside her head. Her throat dried. Her tongue pasted to the roof of her mouth.

They banded into a semi-circle, marching forward as a unit, placing one foot in front of the other, heel to toe, heel to toe, heel to toe.

She slipped gears, her vision and mind running out of sync, so much so, one was totally missing in action. She couldn't get it, couldn't comprehend.

These ... These ... Things ... Beings ... Spirits ... Human ... Somethings ... Severed at the waist ... No top half ... Rawhide-pants ... Bare-feet ... Striding ... Striding as if alive ... Heel to toe ... Erect ... Pack-like.

Emma's eyes widened, ringed with white. She sidestepped, backing. They advanced, closing.

She crouched, extended her hands, pushing off with her right foot madly dashing between them, taking off into the forest on a dead run.

She could hear them. Hear them ... Rushing ... Running ... Chasing.

She ran the shallow creek bed to the drop off, crossed a fallen log and jumped the cattails, scampering straight up the far bank using tree roots as pulleys, miscalculating she smashed her head into a protruding rock jet.

She slid face down, eyes open, arms extended, legs splayed, like a wet limp dishrag coming to rest half in, half out of the cattails, legs tangled around the log.

There was no further movement. Her open eyes did not see. Within seconds, she was encircled.

The forest silenced. Not a bird chirped, nor a frog croaked, nor a squirrel scampered. You would have heard a pin drop.

A single blade of grass wavered.

"Ichabica!" he said. He stepped from the trees giving a backhanded wave.

All at once, they backed away, dissipating, dissolving into the air.

He scooped Emma into his arms, a faint smile traced across his lips. He strolled through the trees, across a small clearing, and turning right he followed the cobblestone pathway that led to the small stone cottage.

'Day Three'

The Chiricahua Chief waited until the moon was completely covered by the earth's edge, and the afternoon sun, high, before he fetched more wood, and re-stoking the fire.

Emma shifted in the cot, stirring, opening her eyes.

He got up from the rocking chair. "Tea?" he asked, almost too quiet to hear.

She nodded, folding back the firs that smelt of cedar and oak and spices. She propped herself up on one elbow, watching him unreserved, undaunted, unquestioningly as he shuffled back and forth from the old cupboard to the woodstove, where a timeworn blackened kettle wisped ribbons of steam.

He pulled the rocker up to the cot, returned to the stove, fetching two over-size cups filled to the point of overflowing.

Emma sipped the tea slowly allowing the comforting essences to filter up through every part of her being. She fanned the cup leisurely back in forth, relishing and drawing in the mixed aromas of the natural herbs of the black tea, the bergamot, and the vanilla beans. It seemed so heartening, so familiar, as did the one room cottage with its cordial fire sizzling and crackling within the stone hearth.

It was ... As if she'd been there many, many times, sipping tea, spending time, with this noble looking tanned skinned man, with the two gray braids that hung to his waist, and the deep brown eyes that seemed to contain the wisdom of all the universe.

He took of the tea in silence.

When done, he placed the cup on the floor. He pulled the rocker closer, reaching gently he lifted Emma's hair from her forehead where he had doctored the slashed up, golf ball size bump with a mug-wart paste. He examined it, and then folded his hands in his lap, locking his fingers together.

"The burial site of Mother Earth has been exposed," he said. "The iron-mask jar has been exhumed and taken, its mouth unplugged, it is speaking." He flipped his hands palm side down, clamping them, whitening his knuckles. "The nineteen are hearing," he nodded his head. "As you have observed," he stated barely above a whisper. He raised his gray eyebrows, gazing directly into her eyes, hooking into her depths, connecting with a power, indefinable by words.

Emma could feel her chest flooding with air, holding it in as if about to dive and swim underwater, then exhaling long and slow.

He repositioned himself within the chair, withdrawing a hair's breadth, breaking the bond.

She swung her legs over the edge of the cot, sitting upright, folding her hands into her lap, mirroring his first gesture, her thoughts lingering on his words. 'The nineteen are hearing? ... Were the nineteen "the crazies" next door?' She looked upon his face, their eyes once again locking.

He nodded as if reading her mind.

'Yes,' she thought. 'Yes indeed.' Her reflections bounced off and away ... To that odd full moon ... To Gary gobbling down dirt ... To his four legged gait home ... To his eating raw minced meat ... To the carpet of dead animals being carted off by, those people. 'Yes,' she had definitely observed.

She suddenly wanted to use the pause, his pause, to step in, to burst forth in question after question. 'Where am I? ...How did I get here? ...Why is everything familiar? ...Where do I know you from? ...Why does my head hurt? ... And the big one ...What in hell is going on?'

He smiled, patting both her hands; a silent message that spoke volumes.

Her questions immediately took flight, lodging up out of sight amongst the wooden rafters.

The touch ... His touch ... Cool ... Too cool ... Mysteriously, too cool ... Like the frost of winter ... Inexplicable ... As if something far removed, something beyond this time and place sent goose-bumps raking across her back, traveling up and down her spine, spiking into her legs, tingling both her feet.

He withdrew his hands, refolding them into his lap.

Emma granted the space silence.

He spoke slow, unhurried, quietly, pausing randomly and often.

"Must understand the beginning ... To draw aside the veil of unborn time ... For the gift of the future ... While in the present." He dipped his head, repeating the four phrases verbatim.

Emma shimmied to the edge of the cot, drawing closer, listening, absorbing in his words like a dry desert dwelling sponge.

"I am ... Too old a soul," he scrutinized her eye movements with each word he spoke. "There is no death ... Only a change of worlds ... In the generations of time ... The past ... The present ... And ... The future ... All ... Co-exist ... In the spirit world."

Emma's eyebrows drew together, her understanding too deep below the surface, too slow to rise through the levels of comprehension required to grasp.

"I am ... Too old a soul," he whispered.

'What is he telling me? ... What?' she wondered.

He raised his index finger ever so slightly, allowing for the circuitous stillness to crossover. Infuse into her.

She bowed her head, in response. With her lips, she hadn't spoke, much unlike her thoughts. She had not granted herself the space of silence.

The corners of his mouth turned up. His deep eyes grew soft. He unclasped his hands.

"When a child my mother taught me the legends of our people," he began. "Legends ... Of the sun and sky, the stars and moon ... She taught me all things of this world, are of two parts ... Twins ... One good the other evil." He leaned into her, dissolving, obscuring their personal spaces, blending them as one.

"In the beginning, the dead roamed throughout the air. Then one day, the great morning star, Quetzalco, who watched over the air, overheard nineteen of the dead plotting with Quetzalco's evil twin, Xoloz, to embed magic strings into nineteen of the living, blinding them to the dead and allowing them to inhabit their souls and live, life, again, and in return for the magic strings, the nineteen dead promised to seed the earth anew so Xoloz could feast on the newborn's hearts and entrails. Quetzalco rushed to the tell The Creator, who at once placed all the dead under the flat surface of the earth ... Into the underworld. He sealed this underworld with a black obsidian mirror." He paused, traced his middle and index finger across his lips, studying Emma.

She met his gaze, her chest rising and falling free and easy.

He continued. "It was then that The Creator gave Quetzalco, the morning star, a new guardianship as the air was now calm. Quetzalco was to watch over the obsidian mirror ... Especially during the five days of the Waning Moons. For it is at this time that the entire earth draws up close to the sky and humanity can turn against itself, thus bringing the mirror and the chosen nineteen to the surface. Quetzalco kept close watch as instructed, but, as generations of time passed the dead accumulated, and in their abundance the chosen nineteen climbed to the forefront ... Steaming the mirrors under surface and blocking its reflective quality, allowing them to give voice and call to Xoloz for release by burning a hole in the mirror with magic. When Quetzalco told The Creator of the dead's cries for Xoloz, The Creator quickly instructed the sun to burn off the steam, restoring its reflective qualities. Xoloz became incensed, immediately seeking out the sun's evil twin, Nusus, and promising all the blood from the new seeds if Nusus aided in freeing the chosen dead. Nusus agreed, happy to finally be able to quench its endless thirst. Together, they pushed the morning star and sun deep into the rays of night, hiding them from The Creator and taking their place. The next day, The Creator waved good mornings, as always, to the morning star and the sun, but when they did not wave back The Creator knew something was wrong and deceitful ... Enraged, The Creator sent shafts of bright white light across the skies, wounding Xoloz and Nusus for their deception. The Creator then reached from the heavens, found and freed the sun and Quetzalco. Quetzalco plucked Jet and Turquoise from inside the dark rays, bestowing The Creator with a thank you gift. The Creator formed the Jet into the likeness of a frog, casting the Turquoise into the Jet as eyes ... The Creator hurled Xoloz within the Jet and Nusus within the Turquoise. ... Xoloz and Nusus combined their powers, summoning the frog to life and spitting poison into the earth's drinking water. All living things that drank of it died. As the death toll rose, they began a chant ... 'All beware ... Beware the five days of the Waning Moons ... When humanity turns against itself ... And the sun becomes three ... The earth will heave, break the mirror ... Set the nineteen dead free.' The Creator became infuriated and instructed Yoorub, the iron lord, to entomb the frog. Yoorub crafted a round jar that wore a mask detailed like a human face. With eyes, ears, nose, and a sealed mouth so Nusus and Xoloz could hear, see, and breath, but never call out. The Creator gave the jar to Mother Earth who swallowed it face down. Over time, The Creator entombed many more evil twins with the aid of Yoorub and Mother Earth. Mother Earth placed them near one another in a safe burial site ... Through the generations of time the soil became unordinary, for it housed evil. The Creator then instructed Mother Earth to lay a band of consecrated dirt on top and beneath the entombment. The Creator then knelt and drew the world into four quarters, creating different looks for mankind. The Creator gave the Indian Chiefs of Nations additional strengths ... To walk the soft earth, clear eyes to see, wisdom to understand, and the power to face evil winds ... For beneath their quarter lays the entombed burial site of Mother Earth."

He rose, plucked the cups from the floor, shuffling back and forth as before between the old cupboard and woodstove, filling the cups once again to the point of overflowing.

This time he spoke as he drank. "One, must understand the beginnings, of the legends, of our people. I am, too old a soul in the generations of time, to draw aside the veil of unborn time for the gift of the future, while in the present."

Emma's gears turned, piecing the mammoth jigsaw puzzle together, fitting the symbolized words into the blank spaces and empty holes.

He sat in silence, waiting, watching, and smiling. After a time he leaned close, so close she could feel the coolness coming off him.

"The burial site of Mother Earth has been exposed," he softly murmured. "The iron-mask jar exhumed, taken, its mouth speaking ... The nineteen hear." He fitted his fingers around her wrist stroking the back of her hand with his thumb. "I am ... Too old a soul, in the generations of time." He cupped her hand within both his, raised it to his lips, whispering his breath across her skin. "Remember ... In the generations of time ... The past, the present, and the future all co-exist in the spirit world."

He turned her hand over, placing a small round eggshell coloured stone within. He pulled his fingertip across it circling it diligently, and then gently tailored her fingers over it closing her hand, wrapping it within his. "The outline of the stone is round, with no beginning, no end. It is a perfect work of nature, strong and true, its power is endless. ... It is the connection of the earth to the spirit," he said. He released her hand. His warm smile, deepening, broadening. "Sleep is the death of our day. It delivers us into our dreams, which is the gateway to our humanity. It is now time for you to take leave ... My Emma."

His last two words did not register.

He stood, backing slowly, methodically into the middle of the room. Stopped, grew transparent, fading, disappearing soft and easy like a morning fog in the sun's rays.

Her mouth opened, she rubbed her eyes furiously, seconds later, they were all that moved, whipping back and forth through the darkness of her bedroom.

She sat upright, disbelief stamped in big black letters across her forehead. The familiarity of the room seemed to be zooming in and out as if focusing its own lens. She swore she could taste black tea, vanilla beans, and bergamot, yet there was no mug on the side table.

She closed her drying mouth, her nose immediately flaring, drawing in and blowing out huge wafts of air.

The bedside clock read three-thirty-three a.m.

She flopped back down into bed, pulling the covers up over her head.

'Day Four'

Emma stretched, drawing out her legs and tumbling the four cats sideways. They stood, rotated, patty- pawing with their front feet, purring in unison, and then nested back down on the duvet.

She flipped off the comforter, alarm abruptly over-filling her eyeballs as they filtered over the length of her body. She had slept in her clothes ... Yet again ... This was the third night ... The fourth day ... Of the same clothes.

She swung her legs to the floor. Something plummeted from the sheets hitting the wooden plank floor. She bent forward gluing in place; brows arched, eyes saucer-like, gaping at the round eggshell coloured stone.

'The stone of a dream.'

She wiggled her right foot forward, touching the tip of her big toe to it.

'Cold ... Ice cold.'

'The outline of the stone is round, with no beginning, no end. It is a perfect work of nature, strong and true, its power is endless ... It is the connection of the earth to the spirit,' whispered round in her thoughts, repeating as if she was mentally reciting it. She shook her shoulders sending the whispers back into the shadows, where it continued recapping, reciting and recapping.

She picked up the small stone, turning it over in her fingers. Her skin clung and stuck as if wet and the stone pulled from a deep-freezer.

'In the generations of time ... The past, the present, and the future all co-exist in the spirit world,' came to the forefront, again repeating as if she was mentally reciting.

She tucked the stone into her jean watch pocket and sprang from the bed, bounding down the stairs two at a time, abruptly stopping four from the bottom; remembering something her grandfather had said at her mother's funeral as he fitted a rose into her mother's hands.

'What if you had a dream, and in that dream you were in a field of roses, and in that field of roses you picked one, and what if when you awoke you held that rose within your hands? ... Ah what then?'

"How strange a thing," she said. "Why would I remember? ... This? ... Now? ... Right ... Now? ... On the way down the stairs? ... Is the stone? ... My rose?" She raked her top teeth backwards along her tongue. "I must have gone crazy in my sleep," she furthered.

She jumped to the bottom, bounding into the kitchen, flipping the light switch.

Nothing.

She rocked the nub up and down.

Nothing.

The room was like death, silent and still. No clicking of clocks, no humming of appliances, no nothing of nothing, as if they were mere shells of their former selves, to keep with appearances.

She fetched the battery-operated transistor radio from the bottom drawer.

Nothing.

She grabbed the flashlight.

Dead.

She took the battery out. Put it back, shaking the living daylights out of it, flicked the switch forward.

Nothing.

She backtracked through the house, pulling, turning, striking and flicking.

Nothing ... Everything lifeless.

She went into the garage, fumbled with the truck keys, found the one for the ignition, shoved it in, and turned it to the right. She twisted it back and forth a number of times before giving up, leaving the key ring dangling from the switch, swinging awkwardly back and forth like a sign of the times, a new age pendulum signifying the end of powered electricity.

She entered the kitchen glancing at the dark space on the telephone receiver where the red light should have been. The smell of smoke filtered in through the open window riding the lace of the curtain, falling off when the breeze sucked it back against the screen. She leaned into it peering across the front field at the farmhouse next door. She could hear the crackling of wood, see thin wisps of smoke above the rooftop.

She pulled closer. There were bunched voices jabbering in short bursts. She pressed her ear to the screen, fine-tuning the grunts and groans. It was as if they had all reverted to prehistoric cave dwellers during the night.

She had to know...

She slipped out the back door. Cut across the lawn. Jumped the rail fence into the front field; silently jogging through the outer tree line, staying under the radar. She hunched down, squat creeping, slow, and purposeful, drawing tight, not so much as disturbing a fallen twig. She laid low amongst the bushes, her dark green sweater melding, blending her one with the leaves.

The bond fire was huge for the small amount of smoke it was wafting. The flames shot out at forty-five degree angles instead of upright as most. The smoke seemed to tunnel, flip then spiral, throwing out clusters of fire sparks that surged through the air like reddish-white starbursts.

They appeared to be dancing, fuzzily, dizzily round and round and round like the fire was a make believe maypole. Lazily hopping, skipping, leaping, and springing ... Naked ... All ... Buck-naked, with animal corpses draped about their heads and shoulders, frolicking and prancing like little children playing royal palace dress up, adorned in paper crowns and bed sheet robes or in this case rotting dead animals.

Their garbled speech patterns resembled a gruff-like chant sequence not unlike, 'Xoloz ... Nusus ... Xoloz ... Nusus.'

Emma inched forward scrutinizing, watching, observing as they whirled and cavorted, as if the world was their oyster. Their unnaturalness seemed an allurement ... Their flesh, stained ruddy black from dirt, red from blood ... Their faces heavily encrusted with matter and mud and clumped gray debris.

More came ... As if drawn to the primitiveness of light and warmth like moths to a flame.

She counted seventeen of them; Gary made it eighteen. Were there more ... Or was this all, she wondered.

'The nineteen hear,' bounded front and center shoving the rest of her thoughts to the side.

She counted again. "Eighteen, just eighteen," she said a hair above a whisper.

She edged back from her point position in the bushes. 'These people, if that's what they still are,' she reasoned, 'are not wrapped right.' She let her eyes crawl over them one by one. 'Hell ... They're not wrapped at all,' she corrected.

One more came from the other side of the house, a young pre-teen girl.

'Eighteen plus one ... Nineteen,' she mouthed. 'There it is ... The number nineteen.'

She watched intently as the girl turned her back, both arms working, slogging through some sort of pile ... Of? ... Something? ... Something that could not be made out ... Something in amongst, too many other some-things ... Things ... Thingamajigs ... Piles and heaps of indefinable some-things.

The girl seemed to settle on one, stomping her feet joyfully. She draped it over her head, lifting her legs high in a stiff backward march. She whirled about facing, bobbed her head catching whatever it was with both hands. She moved forward slinging it back and forth in front of her chest as if showing it off.

Emma crept closer, focusing on the girl.

The girl threw it airborne, catching, grasping it in one hand, swinging it up over her head, whipping it in circles like a wet beach towel. It all at once flew from her hand, landing three feet from the bushes.

Emma's breath chilled in her lungs. Her gaze whipped from the flying thing that came in for a landing ... To the mounds and piles. Back and forth, back in forth they went, all of a sudden halting. The piles ... The piles of indefinable thingy some-things were dead animals. All dead animals ... Rotting, decomposing, maggot infested dead animals. The brown furry one that lay the other side of the bushes, so close she could have reached out and touched it, was maybe once a groundhog or a squirrel. It was so tremendously mangled and insect infested it was difficult to tell.

The girl jumped forward, fetching and snatching her prize, whisking it up in front of her face, rubbing it over her cheeks and forehead like it was a macabre washcloth. She then opened her mouth, wide and full, abruptly sinking her teeth into its bloated under belly, popping it like a gas-filled balloon. She tossed her head side to side like a wild animal ripping into its prey. She cupped it in one hand, the other digging inside, freeing up the distended intestines. She crammed her mouth full, chewing, smacking her lips, swallowing bird like. She repositioned the dead thing, pulling out one link at a time with her teeth, clamping on, bursting and spattering the insides out into the air.

Emma clutched at her stomach as it rolled and flipped, bubbling its contents, making ready. Vomiting right there and then was not an option. She closed her eyes mentally rocking herself, reopening them just in time to view Gary gather up the discarded intestines, tilt his head back, pop them into his mouth and knock them back as if he hadn't eaten in a month.

She slithered to the ground, backing laboriously toward the tree line where she broke out into a dead run for home.

~~~

Emma sat on the kitchen floor underneath the open window, her back jammed against the bottom cupboards. She unconsciously intertwined her fingers.

'Take something ... Leave something ... Take something ... Leave something.' She worked it over in her mind, pausing, rewinding, and replaying.

'Must understand the beginning, to draw aside the veil of unborn time ... For the gift of the future while in the present.' A smile tracked across her lips. The insider whispers of a dream.

She touched her watch pocket. 'The stone of a dream.'

"Take something ... Leave something," she said. "But of course," she added, nodding, concurring. "I need to go back to the beginning," she said. "Again," she breathed.

She pulled herself to a stand by way of the kitchen sink, squinting through the sunshine, scoping down the hill. The fire was still burning. She was too far away for anything else. "Wonder if they sleep?" She trailed her fingers over her dry lips sinking back down to the floor. She tilted her head, resting it against the wooden cupboard.

'Dusk is better,' she thought. 'I'll start at the beginning, at dusk.'

She closed her eyes.

~~~

Emma fastened the front doors slow and cautiously, barely sounding the click-clack of the locking latch. She ran soundlessly across the front lawn and down the drive hunching her back, keeping her chest low, mimicking a cantering animal.

Her thoughts went to the intestine eating girl. She immediately straightened. She stopped at the paved road gazing toward the farmhouse. Fire still burning, noise minimal, no dancing, no sign of movements, not much of anything.

The road ahead was clear, every animal gone, removed. It was as if they had never been there at all, if one ignored the evidence. The soft shoulders were amassed with far too many footprints for a desolate county road, in the middle of nowhere. Prints spanned each side in odd patterns and designs like they had taken it upon themselves to personally tell the grisly story of what had been.

She examined the farmhouse again before crossing the road. 'Still ... Quiet ... Maybe, they do sleep?'

She bounded across the pavement disappearing into the long grasses of the meadow, popping her head up and checking the house one last time. She felt as if a van carrying the mentally insane got terribly lost on its way to the institution, and in exasperation, the driver pulled over at the side of the road right in front of that farmhouse and just let everyone out to fend for themselves.

She grimaced. And how they were!

There was now red tape across the makeshift driveway the construction vehicles' had fashioned with their coming and going. It was tied haphazardly to metal T-bars, which appeared as if they had been hurriedly jammed into place. The tape ends were triple knotted, the extra lengths flapping in the wind, slapping almost rhythmically on and off the two signs propped against the bars that read 'Debrey's Construction ... Site permanently closed ... Do not enter.'

She smirked. Only a construction crew would tape off a crushed grass roadway, leaving the remainder of the meadow open so anyone could walk, or drive for that matter, around it.

The top of the hole was as before, surrounded with rope, with snippets of yellow plastic ribbons tied here and there. She ducked under, stepping to the edge.

Her breath immediately caught. The entire cavity was blanketed in a dense foggy mist that resembled gruel. Wisps of steam shot up and out through potholes flexing and bending, contorting and reforming. Moisture hit and clung to her exposed skin. She could feel her clothing dampen.

Emma stepped from the lip, methodically, blindly working her way down towards the base. The soil seemed much hotter than she remembered. She took note of the smallest details as they came and went from view, as if she was privy to look at selected things and only for an instant.

The base air appeared denser, more tightly knit than the top and middle layers. She wafted her arms, rippling and scattering the coatings. They blew into one another, overlapping and melding, disclosing the ocean of footprints that lay beneath.

Footprints from fine high end shoes ... Footprints from construction boots ... Footprints from runners ... Bare skinned footprints ... Prints in circles, in criss-crosses, in clusters.

She sneered, she'd just found gold. "They've all been down in here," she murmured.

She followed the circled and crisscrossed prints, whirling her arms fan-like dispersing the fog, examining the clusters. They all gravitated towards the middle. The center core where Gary had sat cross-legged, eating.

She stepped over the tape, crouching, dipping her fingertips into the multitude of handprints camouflaged with footprint overlays. She gently traced her index finger over the beaded crumbs of earth ringing the opening, where something had been removed. She manipulated the soil in the hole, filtering and screening it through her fingers. Rusted metal flakes dropped into her palm.

Archaeologists or museum personal would not have been so crude.

She instinctively knew...

She felt for the bottom, swaying the tips of her fingers off the sides discerning the shape of the empty hole; Cylindrical, rounder at the base. The one side fanned, arched with nubs and small protrusions.

She sensed air displacement and immediately stiffened.

The fog sucked back, blew outwards, separating, rolling, as a holographic image of the historic Chiricahua Chief sitting in his rocker sipping tea drifted slowly forward, like it was atop a platform floated by giant balloons.

'The burial site of Mother Earth has been exposed ... The iron-mask jar has been exhumed and taken, its mouth unplugged, it is speaking,' he whispered without moving his lips.

He took another sip of his tea, nodded, and then abruptly disappeared.

Emma was positive she could smell black tea, bergamot, and vanilla. She stared into the fog.

'The burial site of Mother Earth has been exposed ... The iron-mask jar has been exhumed and taken, its mouth unplugged, it is speaking,' he whispered once again.

"Why is this dream rising?" she asked. "What am I missing?" She ran her fingers over her jean watch pocket feeling the outline of the round stone within. "My stone of a dream," she murmured.

She plunked down, drawing up her legs and resting her head on her knees. Her chest heaved in weighted breaths as she began to pray. "Hear me ... Hear me Great Spirit as I take rest upon my Mother, The Earth ... Grant me the eyes to see, the wisdom to understand ... Grant me a footmark to follow."

She waited for the sign. Nothing came.

The fog overhead darkened, veined and cracked open; Rain poured through drenching her, rampaging down and over in minute rivers, gathering and pooling about her, swirling in little whirlpools before seeping into the depths of the earth.

She rose slowly, decisively, turning, stepping out over the tape. She fanned the fog, all at once skidding, her wet bare feet slipping, sliding and skating. Her balance lost, her legs kicked out from under, flipping her flat onto her back. She rolled, clambering onto her hands and knees, limbs abruptly splaying like a galloping dog suddenly caught on ice.

She face planted.

Emma eyeballed the smooth, shiny blackness up close and personal. It was virtually a mirror and hot. Very, very red-hot.

'He placed all the dead under the flat surface of the earth ... Into the underworld ... He sealed this underworld with a black obsidian mirror,' whispered out from under the foggy haze.

Her flesh felt as if it was about to ignite and burn from the intense heat coming off the ... Black ... Whatever it was.

She tucked her knees up under her, crawling across it as if the devil himself was on her heels.

She plunked down into the soil, mouth open. Her face screwed and wrinkled like an old left over raisin. She rolled her tongue flicking it out of her mouth snake-like, spitting dirt. "They all must be crazy to eat this stuff," she voiced. She spit again, smirking. She already knew they were crazy ... And, not in a good way.

She dug her toes into the soil, pivoting her body in a semi-circle coming face to face ... Once more ... With the hot black shiny surface. She gazed down into it, looking through the smoky opaqueness. It appeared to have many layers, a deepness and complexness, like one of those fancy paint jobs on expensive vehicles.

Her eyes abruptly widened, flashing like flying saucers coming down on a landing pad. Something was under there. Something was under there looking back ... From the other side ... Something ... Horrid ... Grotesque ... Monstrous ... Something ... Not of this world.

She shoved herself backward, smacking face first into the soil, mouth open, again.

She spit, scraped her tongue with her teeth, spit again, stuck out her tongue wiping it with her sweater sleeve. "Crap," she said. "Enough already with the damn frigging dirt!"

She climbed the steep bank exiting the hole; sitting on the rim, gazing straight ahead, legs dangling over the side. She took the stone out of her pocket rolling it around in her fingers, her thoughts taking flight. 'The outline of the stone is round, with no beginning, no end. It is a perfect work of nature, strong and true, its power is endless ... It is the connection of the earth to the spirit.' She held it up, examining it closely.

"Are you the connection?" she asked. "My connection? ... To dreams so real I can smell and taste them?" She fidgeted with the stone giving voice to the rolling thoughts. "It is the connection of the earth to the spirit," she said. "There is no death ... Only a change of worlds ... In the generations of time ... The past, the present, and the future all co-exist in the spirit world," she paused once again fiddling with the stone. "Must understand the beginning, to be able to draw aside the veil of unborn time. For the gift of the future, while in the present," she said.

She studied the stone for the longest time before she shoved it back into her pocket.

"A little slow aren't I?" she whispered out into the fog.

She swung her legs in rapid clockwise circles, halting, reversing, all at once stopping, and tilting her head back. That moon, that peculiar, eccentricity of a full moon was out once again ... For the fourth time, hovering up there, stretching itself, intentionally filling up the night sky. The partial cloud cover hung in low bands making it appear as if snickering. She watched as the clouds pulled, then slowly drifted off.

'It is snickering!' she mouthed. 'It wasn't the clouds ... The damned thing is snickering.'

"This is another day that definitely needs to end," she said.

She left the way she came, dashing, noiseless, unseen.

She strolled through the house, the moonlight sneaking through the windows the only source of illumination. She entered the kitchen, jumped up on the counter and sat beside the open window, listening to the new night sounds of jabbering, clustered grunts and groans, screeching, hooting, chanting, and underneath it all, the crackle of the fire.

Emma swung her legs up on the counter, flattening herself out, laying her head directly beneath the open window. She folded her forearms over her open eyes, crisscrossing her hands, rested them on her forehead, settling in for the night reluctantly serenaded by the live radio show on next door.

'The burial site of Mother Earth has been exposed, the iron-mask jar has been exhumed and taken, its mouth unplugged, it is speaking, the nineteen are hearing.'

"Yes indeed, they most undeniably are," she muttered.

'Day Five'

Daylights first amber rays poked through the laced holes in the kitchen window curtains casting long wavy ribbons onto the back wall. Emma unfolded her arms, shimmied her legs to the edge of the counter, dropping down onto the tile floor. She stretched swaying the top half of her body side to side. She planted her hands on the counter and leaned into the screen, listening past the crackle of the fire.

"All quiet," she said. 'Almost, a little too quiet,' she thought. "Recognizance mission due," she muttered.

She halted, fingers suspended, a hair's breadth from grasping the back door knob, eyes narrowing, squinting, and tearing at the corners as if she had just stepped directly in front of bright-white searchlights. She lifted her head gazing up, immediately shielding her eyes from the devastating intensity.

Overhead ... The sun, the moon, and the morning star ... Hung ... Side by side by side ... Intertwined ... overlapped ... As if hooked arm and arm like the best of friends, their glaring power lighting the earth as if three mammoth floodlights. What little was left of the surrounding sky was drained of all color as if it had been sucked dry.

"How ... Incredibly ... Odd," she said in stops and starts. "Another bad omen?" She asked. "Undeniably," she answered.

She pushed the door closed. Cut across the lawn. Jumped the rail fence into the front field; running the outer tree line as before. She crouched among the bushes coming as near as the natural camouflage would allow.

The fire popped and hissed whisking flames that quickly turned and twisted into smoke-signal spirals that shot straight up into the hazed smouldering cloud hanging directly above it. A few were sitting off to the one side, cross-legged, eyes glazed, staring into seemingly nothing, there but not there. Fire sparks burst and whirled, landing unnoticed in their hair and on their flesh, burning and sizzling, exploding as if mini firebombs filled with shrapnel. They resembled life size, unpainted, dirt covered, clay gnomes rather than anything alive, except for the involuntary movements of their chests taking in and expelling out air.

Others, Gary included, were to the left of the fire, focused on retrieving some kind of dead animal off the ground, tugging it back and forth between them, grunting, groaning, shrieking, and squabbling. Whatever it was, ripped and tore to pieces, and they scampered off in different directions.

Within minutes, Gary returned, followed closely by two others. This time they gathered up something significantly larger, clutching it against their chests as they wound around in a semi-circle, all at once plopping down and laying it across their knees. They worked as one, lifting the carcass to their mouths, ripping with their teeth, digging down in, chomping, chewing open mouthed.

Her eyes drew back in an invisible slingshot, propelling forward, growing feet, hiking end to end over the flesh of it, almost skidding off as the three flipped it over, their jaws, lunging, feasting.

Emma's lungs halted, stuck between breaths as if her life cord had been tripped over, pulling the plug from the socket. Both hands ringed her neck. Her eyeballs flew at lightening-speed retreating back into the sockets fearfully, pulling and tugging at the lids to close as the tattered red cloth with laced edges fell to one side exposing a woman's breast.

She stared with unabashed horror as they tilted the torso, angling it, sending its only arm flopping in the dirt, where it lulled and rolled back and forth like a dying fish after spawning. The wrists adornment, the gold bracelet with the stationed pink and white roses, fell onto the top of the hand, sparkling and dancing as it reflected the light.

She clamped her mouth using both hands; her unruffled screams slamming dead center of her palms. "THEY'RE EATING HUMANS! ... THEY ARE ... EATING ... HUMANS!"

She watched Gary rip away the remainder of bra, shove, push and bat the ones either side, clench his teeth, growl, then nip, tearing their ears, like a mother lion teaching harsh discipline to its cubs. He lowered his head to the breast, whirling his tongue around the nipple as if making love to it, and then plunged, bared teeth slashing it open, gobbling down chunk after chunk.

Beads of perspiration swept her brow, stringing together in a row like fresh peas released from the pod. 'That bracelet.' She had seen it before. 'But where?' she wondered. All at once, she remembered. Glena ... Kindly Glena, who lived at the other end of the road with her grown children. Her sixtieth birthday present, two years back. The one she had been so proud of, showing it off to anyone who had the time.

She hugged her mouth, screaming again. 'THEY'RE EATING THE PEOPLE OF THIS ROAD ... THE NEIGHBOURS?'

Emma speedily backed, rolling into a ball, somersaulting onto her feet taking off at a dead run, the thought ... 'What happens when they've eaten everything,' chasing her, nipping at her heels.

She slammed the back door behind her locking it.

She ran through the house smashing, and slamming windows shut, drawing blinds, latching deadbolts. She pulled the ladder to the attic down, rounded up the cats, placing them within, padlocking the door in place. She gently kissed her fingertips, setting them to the wood of the door. "You'll be safe here," she whispered. She climbed down the ladder folding it back into place, tucking it away out of sight in its cubby.

The spare room closet was way beyond dark. She felt for the light switch running it up and down. Nothing. She scoffed shaking her head. Of course there was nothing. There was no power anywhere else, why would she expect it in the closet. She glanced up at the ceiling. "Somebody help me ... I'm finally losing it here." Her mind flickered to the things next door. "Forget it ... I'm fine," she corrected.

She hiked the blinds to the top of the window frame, a trickle of light glimmered into the closet. She pulled a belt from the rack, dipped her hand into the left pocket of the only woolen sweater, retrieved a key, propelled all the clothes to the front, unlocking the concealed door. She felt along the shelves, recovered a box, shoved the *Puma* hunting knife into its sheath, sliding it onto the belt running it to the right. She gathered one of the ropes fastening a quick release knot sliding it left. She crouched, walking her fingers the length of the floor. Finding the steel-toed boots, ramming the toe end of one into the plate glass until it shattered. She pulled out the *Marine* shot gun and a box of shells, loading seven, pumping one into the barrel, replacing it. She emptied the shell box ramming them into her pockets, slinging the shotgun across her back.

She walked the length of the upstairs hall, pulled a chair under the window, knocked out the screen and climbed up onto the roof. She squatted at the peak nearest the farmhouse, watching, waiting.

The fire roared as before, but now there was a second in behind, smaller more structured. Emma could see a few heads bobbing up and down at the second, nothing at the first.

'What now?' she wondered. She examined them intently. There were four. Just what they were up to? ... Other than the head bobbing ... Seemed, not to be much.

Moments later, some ran from the farmhouse, yipping and yapping more or less barking, as they scampered back and forth on all fours like animals. They darted and scooted about drawing closer and closer to the main fire, suddenly stopping, falling in one behind the other, arching their backs, humping up their backsides, rotating round the flames on three limbs, the fourth forward extended, palm side up, latching between the legs of the one in front. The clutching of one another, the swaying of hips, the open gait of the back legs seemed to carry heavy sexual overtones as if they were performing some ancient fertility rite of passage.

The human train picked up speed circling faster and faster, all at once tipping, falling to the ground on their sides, laying as they landed, connected together like a mutated human caterpillar.

Emma gulped in a giant air bubble, swallowing it whole. She dragged her hand through her hair, disbelief, revulsion, and loathing rolled up into a tight little ball and embedded itself into the back of her tongue.

She stayed, observing, surveying, for what seemed like an eternity with nothing altering; the ones around the main fire, seven in total, still lying on their sides, the four around the smaller fire in back, still head bobbing.

Eight were missing ... Unaccounted.

She hunched her shoulders, the prickles of unease setting up camp at the base of her spine. She went up on her toes, slow, decisively pivoting three-hundred-sixty degrees.

She circled again, abruptly stopping. Something was off.

The bushes that separated the farms, the limbs, pushed apart, some hanging, others broken, the leaves disturbed in an unnatural way. She followed the tree line, and then detailed the long grasses in the front field. The middle held mocked up movements, bending and swaying like caught up in the wind, but there was no wind. She watched as it swooshed, bent, and stilled, swooshed, bent, and stilled again.

She shifted across the peak, bringing herself nearer.

The grass grunted, an arm flayed, three heads popped up, and then dipped down. The mock wind restarted as they crept, awkward and frog-like through the grass in starts and stops.

Their next stop was lengthy as they manoeuvred like sleepwalkers, changing up, rotating uncoordinatedly, bumping into and against one another, regrouping, and aiming for the house.

She reached feeling along the length of shotgun, flipping the safety off.

She stepped back, sitting on her heels, pushing her back into the brick chimney, virtually disappearing as they progressed slow and clumsily up the hill.

"Animals generally don't look up," she whispered.

She trailed them keeping low in amongst the lines of the roof as they moved near, leaving the grass, jamming and squishing themselves through the rails in the fence, planting their bodies face down, slithering on their bellies along the outer edges of the lawn, forming into a huddle twenty some feet from the back door.

The silent cue that spoke volumes.

Emma shimmied along the roof, sat, turned, and grabbed the fascia board swinging in through the window. She stole silently through the house, descending the back stairs. She could hear grunts, groans, and a distinctive rubbing as if they were running the flats of their hands along the board and batten. She mirrored their location from the inside, all at once halting, backing from the living room plate glass window as it thumped and banged and vibrated.

Emma swung the shotgun forward, raising it to her shoulder, firming her stance.

The thunking halted. The rubbing recommenced. She lowered the shotgun, tracking, moving soundlessly, parallel.

Abruptly everything ceased.

She halted, pivoting slowly, straining and listening for that single pin-drop through the stillness.

The back porch door thundered, exploding. Wood splinters flew in all directions. A fire log hung half in, half out. The door boomed and shook, crackling in vertical fissures that ran top to bottom, expanding in girth with each blow. Another log shot in and through, followed by two more, sending it into a massive convulsion, blowing it, shattering it into bite size pieces, taking along the adjacent stained glass window for championship.

Emma's mouth turned up in a slight smile. She had expected them to come through the window. A tad cleverer than credited.

She raised the shotgun, aligning the sights onto the gap the kitchen steel door should have sealed off. The one space she had forgotten.

Glass crunched. Wood snapped.

She stepped back.

They rampaged into the kitchen, mouths frothing, teeth bared, fingers snarled. One carried a firewood club, one a mossed over rock, one an old arrow. Their eyes, as if synchronized, rose. It was like looking into the face of death.

They lunged.

"Bless me ... Great Spirit ... For I have sinned," she said with a calmness that pushed alarming over into frightening and frightening over into terrifying.

She pulled the trigger catching the one in front directly in the middle of the forehead, clearing away everything from his nose up. She pumped the gun.

"It has been never since my last confession." She fired into the middle of the seconds' chest, blasting a fist size hole clean through, knocking his feet out from under with the force. She pumped the gun.

"I have killed." She shot the third directly through the left eye, splattering three quarters of his face, skull, and brains onto the upper kitchen cabinets. She pumped the gun. Another leaped through the doorway. She fired, blowing his head off. She pumped the gun.

"Three plus one is four," Emma said matter of fact.

She remained transfixed, gun raised, ready, her tuning forks rotating, searching for the slightest misplaced arc, a twitch of breeze, a snapping twig, a rustle.

Nothing.

She reloaded the shotgun, again pumping one into the barrel, swinging it onto her back, leaving the safety off. She skimmed the four bloodied, lifeless piles on the kitchen floor. They stunk like decay as if they were directly akin to the vulture, carrying the fumes of eating the dead. Every portion of their nakedness, encrusted with something; grass, dirt, ash, blood, urine, feces, and ooze. The fecal matter was rancid onto itself, moving with white plump maggots that seemed to duck in and out of the folds, where it had matted onto the skin like rolled dough.

These things were not human. They were a species of their own, two legged creatures spawned of the darkness.

She stepped in amongst them, carefully plucking up the spear and examining it. The metal arrowhead was dirt encrusted, the wooden shaft old, weathered. She tapered her eyes snake-like knowing exactly from where it had come. She lodged it into the side of her belt, striding out onto the back lawn.

Emma instantaneously sheltered her eyes, looking up through the crack between her index and middle finger. The light was worse than blinding.

The entire sky seemed to have been consumed, vampirized by the three enormous spheres that seemed to be hovering rather than suspended in the sky like earlier. They appeared joined and locked down, hanging close to the ground like an alien mother ship, awaiting the return of her scout vessels that had been sent to sample the ground cover as a prelude for the next menu item.

A sonic boom blew through the air. The tree branches wavered. The ground trembled. Emma whirled, about facing in the direction of the farmhouse down the hill. Another boom rocked out.

'I am ... Too old a soul ... There is no death ... Only a change of worlds ... In the generations of time ... The past, the present, and the future all co-exist in the spirit world,' whispered out from her soul.

The earth shuddered, reverberated.

'Must understand the beginning, to draw aside the veil of unborn time, for the gift of the future, while in the present.'

Emma hurdled across the lawn.

'The burial site of Mother Earth has been exposed, the iron-mask jar has been exhumed and taken, its mouth unplugged, it is speaking.'

She jumped the fence, swinging the shotgun forward.

'Beware the five days of the Waning Moons ... When humanity turns against itself ... And the sun becomes three ... The earth will heave, break the mirror ... Set the nineteen dead free.'

She flew through the field, her feet skimming the soft earth not leaving a trace, her Chiricahua blood riding high, pulsating throughout her veins.

She broke through the bushes.

Threw the stock to her shoulder.

The seven were as before, immobile, linked with flesh, lying on their sides around the fire.

Emma stopped, point-blank firing and pumping the gun, playing a ghoulish form of ring around the rosy. She reloaded, pumped the barrel, leaving the seven, immobile, linked, on their sides around the fire.

She shifted to the smaller second blaze in back where two of the head bobbers were tending it. She raised the gun, firing directly into mid chest, one right after the other. They wavered like two starter dominoes, stiffened, tipping, one over top of the other smacking skulls, dropping where they stood.

She moved into the farmhouse. The one hunched on the kitchen counter jerking the intestines out of some kind of furry dead thing did not move, seemingly oblivious to Emma's presence as she started to feed from inside the soft underbelly.

Emma sighted, pulling the trigger and pumping in one fluid motion. The girl blasted sideways into the window shattering it, rebounding, plopping into the sink. What was left of her skull rested neatly in amongst the piles of dirty dishes on the counter.

"Four plus seven, plus two, plus one," she murmured. "Fourteen," she breathed.

She walked through the remainder of the house, the filth of it way beyond the other side of revolting. The mounds of feces. The urine stained walls. The blood pools. The decomposing leavings of indistinguishable flesh heaps. The piled decaying human remains, arms, legs, heads, all a crawling and buzzing.

She exited the house way she came. Walked to the garage. Raised the shotgun. Flung the door open.

Her eyes tracked through the interior, lingering in every nook and cranny. Empty of life. She lowered the gun and stepped in.

The improvised shrine was front and center. Small logs were roped and tied to form a crude tabletop. Cement blocks the base. Metal rusty arrowheads on wooden shafts encircled the shrine; driven into the dirt floor and angled toward the table making them appear like big wooden fingers with fat metallic nails. In front of the arrows, lay heaps of mangled carcasses as if botched sacrifices. Some partially eaten, others mutilated so badly it was hard to tell what they once were, except for the ones that sported fingers or toes.

Hanging on the walls were sloppily gutted scalps of mice, squirrels, cats, dogs, deer and humans, most still bloodied and dripping. The dirt floor was mucky moist, clouded and stained in an abstract mosaic art that would make any gallery owner proud, except for all the blood and body fluids.

Dead center of the table, amidst a pile of leaves as if a makeshift bedding, rested a rusty metal jar with a mask overlay of a rudimentary human face. A metal oval shaped wad lay off to the one side.

'The burial site of Mother Earth has been exposed, the iron-mask jar has been exhumed and taken, its mouth unplugged, it is speaking.'

Emma stepped forward.

The arrowheads turned, the shafts leaned, moving of their own volition, aligning, pinning together, blocking.

Her eyebrows rose in disbelief. She stood motionless, digesting thoughts that made little or no sense.

She booted the nearest arrow, watching as it quivered back and forth. She booted it harder, purposely knocking it against the one to the right. They both wavered, shaking. Her eyes flashed to the ground, the base soil about the shafts, disturbed, loosened, ringed with minute dirt crumbles. She disguised her smile by way of a sneer.

The jar pivoted, detailing her every movement, swivelling its masked face, staring, intimidating with its dark eye holes.

The hair on the back of her neck prickled, embedding into the nap of her sweater. She rotated her shoulders unprickling, mentally pushing it aside, adding it to her growing collection of bizarre oddities.

She crouched, ducking beneath the sight line of the tabletop. She could hear leaves rustling, dry crunching.

Emma crept through the carcasses, wedged between the arrows, straightaway orbiting the shrine, unearthing and whipping shafts. She gathered them into a pile, cut a length of rope, bundling them along with the one from before.

"Nineteen arrows," she said. She tied them to her belt with a slipknot.

'Nineteen dead souls ... Nineteen crazies,' her thoughts stopped mid-way between A and B equals C.

She snatched the jar from its blindside. With the other hand, she grabbed the plug. She twirled the jar face forward, fitting the plug into its mouth, throwing it to the ground mask up. She repeatedly rammed the shotgun butt against the plug collapsing the metal onto itself, erasing its mouth. She followed suit with the eyes, ears, and nose completely obliterating its facial features.

Emma foot tossed it up into the air like a soccer ball, catching it, examining her handy work. She wove it in and out the loops of rope, securing it in amongst the arrows.

The earth pulsated and throbbed. A thunderous blast followed rocking the air currents, setting the wooden planks of the garage vibrating as it soared through. Her hair blew back.

She stepped from the building, the extraordinary light, all at once show casing her silhouette as if the star of a big budget Broadway production with casting extras as small foot long shadows that mirrored her in every minuscule detail like an entourage of cloned midgets.

Another boom shattered the atmosphere, not unlike a thundercloud, collapsing, falling to the earth. For a second time, her hair blew.

Emma darted over the front lawn and paved road, crisscrossing through the meadow. Droning whispered through the long grass, there and gone with diminutive displacement. The songbirds silenced. Emma halted.

Once more the humming came and went, undemanding, stealing space, disbursing the common molecules. Emma stealthily crept through the grass.

Then there it was ... Out from the closet ... Murmuring.

She closed in, shotgun slung across her chest, knife sheaf unlatched. The murmurs folded into slurred chants. Emma stepped over the tape, standing unobserved on the inner rim staring down at the five on their knees, their arms fully extended, the top half of their torsos bobbing on and off the ground, mouths jabbering in tongue. White steam wound in and out, under and around their bodies as if encompassed in a dry ice field.

The earth juddered and shook.

A high-pitched wail tumbled out from the soil vibrating through the steam vapours.

They all at once stood, clasping hands, yelling, howling, commencing with stiff, corpselike movements, working them over into a feverish dance routine, heads whipping round on their necks like they were made of rubber, feet kicking up and stomping down, hips rotating and swaying, chests heaving and bouncing. All the while, slipping and sliding atop a sparkling black ice like surface that was clicking and crackling like cold window glass.

The black surface heaved, bellowing at an ear-piercing level. The top layer slit and fissured tumbling them sideways.

They immediately regrouped, resuming their bizarre motions, stepping forward, tightening, and closing the circle's circumference.

The black started to lurch up and down in tune with their rotating hips. They unclasped hands, dropping them in unison, grasping and cupping the genitalia of the one in front, rubbing furiously.

Emma widened her stance, took aim ... Fired, pumped ... Fired, pumped ... Fired, pumped ... Fired, pumped.

The fifth bobbed his head childlike as if totally lost. He turned it one direction then the other, and then bent like a cautious animal sniffing, inspecting the carnage. He got down on all fours, slowly circling, stopping every three or so feet, cocking his hind leg and spraying urine as if marking his territory. He circled again dipping his fingers into the blood, raising his hand to his mouth, lapping it slowly from his flesh as if taste testing. He went round a third time, digging his thumbs into the eye sockets, popping them like over ripened grapes, scraping out the insides, swallowing them whole. He clambered into a crouch, grunting, hooting, cooing ape-like, and hopping about shaking the bodies.

He shrugged his shoulders, stood, gradually backing from the black substance, dragging his feet through the soil, bending his toes backward. He trudged right through the pegged off caution tape of a square, plunked down cross-legged, embarking immediately into dirt consumption, never once gazing in her direction.

Emma examined him. The blank facial expression. The glazed over eyes. The filth. His humanness so long departed.

Her heart held no remorse for the thing she was silently approaching; descending unseen, in full view. She squatted within a hair's breadth of him.

He seemed completely absorbed, his fingers working, sifting soil, plucking good size pinches, rolling and rerolling them into perfect rounds with his thumbs and index fingers, shoving them two at a time into his mouth, gulping them back.

Emma shook her head.

She rose, stepping out and into another area, where the soil spit and bubbled, like a pot full of water on high, around nineteen gaping holes. She untied the arrows, setting one aside. She drove the wooden shafts, arrowhead first, deep into the earth, erasing them from external existence.

Emma slapped the metal jar into her leg, restraining it from its fanatical swinging and loop-de-loops, within the roping as if this had been its pretence for escape.

She returned to first area, careful not to step on the downed yellow tape where he sat cross-legged, dining.

She dropped the jar, topside down, into its hole. A tortured scream channelled out from the fizzing dirt. She shot her hand in, pulled it back, rolling it over to recheck the jar.

Nothing ... No eyes ... No ears ... No nose ... No ... Mouth.

She shoved it back, covering it completely over with soil.

Emma crouched directly in front of Gary.

He raised his head, his deadpan eyes locking onto her face. "Em?" ... "Em?" ... "Is it really you?" he garbled through the mouthful of dirt.

She nodded.

Gary smiled, closing his eyes.

Emma drew the hunting knife.

"You've come home," he whispered.

"Yes."

The blade of the knife sparked silver-white as it flashed across his throat slicing the jugular. Deep red heart blood pumped out in spurts, coating his chest. His head bobbed once, dropped, his body folded in half, slumped to the ground.

Emma ran the knife along her palm, allowing her blood to mix, to seek, to expel the evil from the dead, to give back the consecration to Mother Earth.

The land drank of the blood.

She rose, slowly, precisely. She could feel the soil commencing to cool beneath her feet as she walked across it. She could see the steam withering, whiffing out smaller and smaller puffs as she fetched the nineteenth arrow from the dirt that had changed in color from ruddy black to dark brown. As her arm whipped up then down jamming the final wooden shaft home, the black surface wrinkled and sunk below the soil leaving her alone with the silence of nothing.

'The outline of the stone is round, with no beginning, no end.' Emma ascended the hole.

'It is a perfect work of nature, strong and true.' She stepped over the tape.

'Its power is endless. She fished the stone from her pocket, lifted her left leg bending it at the knee, pulled her right arm back, and propelled the stone straight up.

'It is the connection of the earth to the spirit.' The stone fell to earth at the precise time the three spheres jostled, separated, sucked in, imploding and shattering into jagged particles that rode the skies on reddish-white fireballs, exploding like fireworks upon impact.

A sudden rain shower doused the earth.

The corners of her mouth turned up ever so slightly. The sign had come twice over. She bowed her head in silent acknowledgement.

The skies whirled, changing colors as if a giant was playing with a kaleidoscope.

The rightful sun rose from under the horizon. The sky turned pale blue. White fluffy clouds formed.

Emma fetched the stone, removed the belt, carving thin strips of rawhide from its underside with the hunting knife. She fashioned it round the stone securing it within, tied and knotted the ends, slipping it over her head.

She sauntered across the meadow, crossed the roadway, and strolled up the laneway. The smile her mouth still embraced blustering out into laughter.

'Aftermath'

"County Road 507 is not well traveled." The officer motioned to the coroner to fold the white plastic back.

Sara stepped forward. "But, eight days?"

"As I said ... It is pretty deserted out there,"

Sara glanced at the corpse. Blinked slow, purposeful, and then nodded.

The officer raised the recorder to his mouth, speaking matter-of-factly. "Let the record show corpse number nineteen has been identified as Gary Stokes."

"Number nineteen?" Sara's voice shrilled. "I ... I ... didn't realize there were so many."

"I am sorry for your loss Miss." The officer nodded for the coroner to rezip. "Will you be attending the residence today?"

"Yes. We are going there now. My aunt and uncle had four cats." Sara watched the cold gray steel slab regress into darkness, the door close, heard the mechanized latch bolt. "I ... I ... am going to take them back home with ... with ... me," her words slurred and stumbled from her lips, her eyes still on that gray steel.

"Are you all right miss?" the officer asked. He pulled a chair from the wall.

Sara sat with her head on her knees, the room swimming in lazy circles.

"Whenever you're ready," he touched her shoulder. "I will radio ahead for you ... It is still considered a crime scene."

Sara nodded, not knowing, not caring what he meant, attempting not to faint or lose her breakfast.

"Was it bad?" Simon asked.

"Yes," Sara croaked. She reached over and grabbed her husband's hand, clinging onto it as if for dear life.

They rode the rest of the way in silence.

~~~

"Can you pull a board off?" Sara asked.

"I thought you said they were radioing ahead for us." Simon's eyes traced along the bright yellow tape that read 'Police Line Do Not Cross.'

"That's what he said."

"Did he say anything about letting us in?"

"Well ... No ... But, that's what I assumed."

Simon sighed, mentally picturing them both in jail for breaking into a house and disturbing a crime scene.

"Si ... We can't leave the cats," she pleaded.

He sighed again. 'Jail it is.'

They both ducked under the police tape.

Simon circled the farmhouse, turning knobs, pulling doors, jimmying window bottoms. He widened his circle starting again, abruptly stopping and gazing up at the open kitchen window. The beginning traces of a grimace filtered across his mouth.

"Hey! ... Sara! ... Over here!"

Within an instant, she was there, staring upwards along with him. "How? ... It's so high."

"Come here ... I'll boost you."

"Throw me is more like it ... That's got to be nine, ten feet up."

"It's all we got." He interlocked his fingers fashioning his hands into a step. "Come on girl, climb me." He swung his hands back and forth then hoisted them to his shoulders demonstrating what to do.

Sara smiled. "Okay, here goes."

She stepped onto his hands, grabbed his shoulders, and hoisted herself up to a stand. She punched in the screen, hauling herself awkwardly through the window, crawling onto the counter.

The smell of salt, copper, and rot smacked her full on. She dry retched, and then cupped her nose with her hands. She wiggled to the edge, jumping to the floor carefully avoiding the dried blood ponds, puddles and smears, and the small bits and pieces of greyish-green something buzzing with flies and crawling with maggots.

She walked through the bottom half of the house calling for the cats.

Silence.

She unlocked and opened the front doors to Simon standing on the porch, taking long draws from his cigarette. "Want to come in?" she asked.

"I'll wait."

"Okay chicken, suit yourself. It's really not that bad."

"Then, why are you talking through your hands?"

She did not honour him with a reply.

Sara called for the cats naming each in turn. She stood silent, holding her breath, straining, listening.

And ... There it was ... A soft echoing mewing.

She climbed the stairs, repeatedly calling out their names. The mewing intensified.

She checked all the rooms, her feet momentarily deadlocking, refusing to move out of the master bedroom doorway, as if she was meant to see something. She took in the room, eyes dashing over the bedding, the dirt encrusted stains, the balled up bedside rugs, the drawn drapes, the muddied footprints alongside the bed, the pile of neatly folded clothing atop the antique dresser.

She backed from the room toting oversize goose bumps.

"Bur ... Ba ... Bre," she stuttered. She started over. "Bear ... Hansen ... Steffi ... Garbie!" she called.

More mews.

Sara followed the sounds, all at once stopping, looking up, eyes zipping back and forth across the wooden ceiling.

Scratching.

"There you are," she murmured.

She retrieved a chair from one of the rooms, stood, felt along the ceiling and dug out the pull-cord lodged in between the joists, tugging it to lower the hidden staircase.

Something dropped, tinkling as it danced across the floor. She picked it up, a smile tickling at the corners of her mouth. She climbed the ladder coming face to face with a padlock.

"This isn't like Uncle Gary," she said quietly. She unlocked the padlock, flipped the latch pushing the door up and open. All four cats mewed in unison. Sara popped her head up through the opening, grinning at the blankets, beds, litter box, the two super sized bowls of food and five dishes of water.

"Not at all ... Like him," she whispered.

She fetched the cats, carting them gently one by one to the second floor landing. They purred rubbing and twisting round her calves, then scampered off down the hall in the direction of the master bedroom, all suddenly halting halfway as if prompted by something, turning, gazing up at her as if she was meant to follow.

She did.

~~~

"Sara? ... Sara! ... Did you find them? ... Sara? ... You've been in there over an hour and a half ... SARA?" Simon stepped into the front foyer, tenting his hands over his mouth. "S ... A ... R ... A!" he shouted.

"I'm out here," she called.

He strode back out onto the front porch.

"OVER HERE," she yelled. She burst out through the smaller trees of the woods, jogging across the back lawn, the four cats in tow.

He leaned at an off angle, unable to move, eyes like over cooked eggs, mouth open, forehead wrinkled with shock.

Her printed lace blouse was gone along with the dress pants. She wore a faded blue, oversized plaid shirt, gathered and tied in a knot just above her bare mid-drift and snug fitting, whitewashed old jeans with ripped out knees. Her long dark hair, pulled back in a single loose braid that tossed from shoulder to shoulder as she ran towards him, barefoot. The fine, gold hoop rings that always adorned her earlobes, replaced with long hand-beaded earrings. Around her neck hung a single stone, rawhide necklace. The only thing missing was the feathered headband.

His mouth silently flapped in place, opening and closing like a ventriloquist's dummy without the ventriloquist.

Sara halted on the front lawn. Held out her arms, twirling in circles, singing something he had never heard the likes of before. She bunny-hopped over to the porch, went up on her tiptoes and planted a soft kiss on his nose.

"Where's your shoes?" he garbled over top of a tongue that suddenly felt six inches thick. He mentally kicked himself. Where's your shoes? Why on earth, had he asked that? Of all the things swimming around in his head ... he asks about shoes. He tried to clear his throat.

"Oh those ... I kicked them off somewhere."

'You kicked them off somewhere?' he repeated silently. 'You just kicked off designer shoes ... Somewhere? ... Somewhere!' He stepped back giving himself personal space. A stupid answer to a stupid question. Before he could sift through his list sorting out the proper questions, starting with 'what in hell are you doing?' ... And, 'why are you doing it?' she was there. Right there in his face, so close he could feel her breath, talking up a storm, non-stop.

"You know I was thinking, before I went off in the woods, instead of moving the cats to our house why don't we move here, to the cats' house? After all, we have been saving for a suburban home for years and this is already a suburban home, well country really. Which is by far, way better than suburban. Don't you think? To be out in the country? And you know as well as I, it will still be many, many, many more years until we get a down payment together. Moreover, my aunt told me long ago when I was little, that this farm would be left to me. She wanted it to stay in the family. You know this place has been in our family for generations upon generations upon generations. And, also, as you know, she was the one who finished raising me. Raising me right here, right here on this here farm, after my mother, her older sister, passed away. Though, she was really more like a sister to me, but she did teach me stuff. You know all the important stuff, like dreams, peace and the sky. And ... And I am the only blood family left. You know the last of the line. And I do love this place. I have always loved this place. You'd love this place. It is just so grand and beautiful. It has over five-hundred-fifty acres alone, and its own lake. We could have a garden and a dog and horses and chickens, for fresh eggs. And, maybe even children someday if we are so blessed. Half bloods, but still. And I work from home anyway. You could work in the city and come here on weekends until you find something closer. Or maybe not, maybe just quit and write your novel like you always wanted to. We would have no mortgage payment, no water bill, just the taxes and hydro, and phone if we want one. And the cats could stay in their own home. All the dirt, blood and crawly stuff will clean up in a flash. Surprising what a little bleach will do. Don't answer anything right now we can ..."

Sara grabbed onto his arm tugging him inside, carting him on a quick house tour as she continued talking and talking and talking. The only three things that stuck were, 'Before I went off into the woods' ... and ... 'Move here to the cats' house' ... and ... 'Surprising what a little bleach will do.'

He felt like his eyes were going to burst out like popcorn and stick into one of those blood pools they had stepped over during the live running commentary.

"Well ... So ... What do you think? ... Yes? ... No? ... Yes? ... Maybe? ... Yes? ... Yes?" She said. She abruptly silenced, standing in front of him, her deep brown eyes gazing directly through him and on out the other side.

He tossed his head back and forth. He could still hear her talking up a storm, as if her voice had somehow crept inside him still going and going like a hamster running its wheel in the middle of the night, practically unstoppable. He shook his head again, opening his mouth shooting out one syllable words that squeaked and pitched, as if some oddball foreign language. He felt like smacking his head off one of those trees outside.

Who in the hell was this person? he wondered. And what has she done with Sara? Left her out in the woods? Moreover, What the hell was Sara doing in the woods in the first place? ... Now, if he could only say all this ... Aloud ... But he couldn't ... Why he couldn't defied logic ... But he just couldn't.

His eyes rolled over her. Every pocket was stuffed and overflowing with bright, florescent yellow plastic strips. Her eyes seemed as if embedded in his, trailing along with them, seeing what he was seeing. She immediately drew her lips into an odd, incompatible smile, as if she had splashed it on with paint just for his benefit.

She smacked her palms together. "Okay it's settled then," she chirped. She pulled him back out on the porch, positioned her hand into the small of his back and guided him in the direction of the car.

He stumbled and tripped as he walked, his head cocked at an awkward sideways angle totally focused on those pockets.

She opened the driver's door.

"Is ... Is ... That ... That the police tape?" He stuttered. He had never had a problem speaking in his life. Now he had mental problems and a class one stutter.

"Yeah! ... Why?" Her hands were on top of his head, gently shoving him down into the seat.

"You're ... You're taking down the police tape?" His voice was two octaves higher than normal.

She lifted his legs, swivelling his torso, planting his feet down on the car mat.

"You're taking down the ... the ... the Tape?" he repeated.

"Of course, silly," she whipped back so nonchalantly they could have been deciding between peas and carrots for dinner. She closed the car door.

He rolled down the window. "But ... But ... But ..."

Sara cut him off. "We can't live in a house with all this ridiculous tape all over the place. Now can we?"

Her eyes suddenly flashed to the forest and back.

"But ... But it's police tape!" He sounded more like a child than a full-grown man. 'Crap Simon ... For Christ's sake ... Get it together!' he yelled inside his head. He clenched the steering wheel, whitening his knuckles, rocking himself violently back and forth.

Sara hissed through her teeth, "Police tape is only stretchy plastic. It comes down in a pinch."

Her eyes dashed again to the forest.

"But ... But the house ... The ..."

She cut him off again. "Make no mind, I'll clean it."

"But ... But the murders ... People ... People died ... Your ... Your Uncle died."

She leaned in through the open window. "Well ... Just maybe they deserved it ... Ever think of that? ... Or better yet, maybe they weren't people any longer. And my uncle died," she whipped her arm up over her head, bending it at the elbow, pointing across the road. "Over there, not over here, not that it matters none,' she whispered.

Again, her eyes drew into the forest, her lips forming the hint of a smile, then suddenly pulling straight as if she had caught herself.

He gagged on the large sudden lump in his throat. 'What did she just say?' He stuttered nonsensical words that even he could not understand. He drew his hands across his mouth, rubbing hard at his lips, hoping he could get it all to work right. 'We can't live in a house with all this ridiculous tape all over the place ... Just maybe they deserved it, ever think of that? ... Or better yet, maybe they weren't people any longer ... My uncle died over there, not over here, not that it matters none,' floated to and fro in front of his face ... 'Ridiculous tape? ... Deserved to die? ... Weren't people? ... He died over there?' shoved at him again.

He took a gulp of air suddenly coughing, choking, dry retching.

She stepped back from the car waving cutely.

"You're not coming?" He felt like biting his tongue off. Another ludicrous question ... Did she seem like she was coming? ... No. Did she look like she was coming? ... 'No.' Why was he even going? ... He did not have the answer.

He wanted to dart from the car go into the forest, and find his real wife, go home, roll back time and start this day all over. But for reasons unknown, other than a possible alien abduction, he just sat there, car keys in hand, preparing to leave with the full knowledge he-they were about to move.

She waved again. "Just pack what we need and I'll see you in a couple days," she shouted. "Don't forget to put a change of address in," she added.

He started the car.

She watched it trail slowly down the drive, turn, pull out onto the pavement, climb the hill and disappear from sight.

"Wow! ... I'm so glad that's over," Sara said. She plunked down into the wooden rocker on the front porch, straightening out her legs.

"Me too," said Emma. "I thought for a moment or two there, you were going to have to be committed ... The looks going across that white man's face ... My ... Oh... My!"

"Are you saying you had a problem with my delivery?"

"Is that what you're calling it?" Emma started to laugh.

"White man?" Sara cut up, chuckling wildly. "White man! ... Yours was a white man too, if I remember right."

Emma's hearty laughter stilled. "White ... Yes ... Man ... Maybe ... Once upon a time ... But, unlike the stuff of fairytales, things don't always turn out as we would wish ... Evil is consuming, all encompassing."

"Is that why?" Sara turned in the rocker, fastening onto Emma's eyes.

"Yes."

"The eighteen as well?"

"Yes."

"The police won't find you?"

"No."

"Do they even know it was you?"

"No."

"Where will you go?"

"The forest."

"Will you be okay?"

"Yes." Her lips drew into a warm smile.

"Will you tell me one last time about this stone?" Sara gently pulled it out from her neck fingering it. "I want to make sure I've got it right."

"The outline of the stone is round," Emma began.

Sara returned Emma's smile. "The outline of the stone is round," she repeated.

"With no beginning, no end," Emma continued.

"With no beginning, no end."

"It is a perfect work of nature."

"It is a perfect work of nature."

"Strong and true."

"Strong and true."

"Its power is endless."

"Its power is endless."

"It is the connection of the earth to the spirit."

"It is the connection of the earth to the spirit." Sara held up her right index finger, repeating it, in its entirety. "The outline of the stone is round, with no beginning, no end. It is a perfect work of nature, strong and true, its power is endless ... It is the connection of the earth to the spirit."

Emma smirked. "You got it kid ... Remember, you are the last of the Chiricahua's, the final guardian to walk the soft earth with clear eyes to see, the wisdom to understand, and the power to face evil winds." She pointed across the roadway, "For underneath that meadow lays the entombed burial site of Mother Earth."

Sara nodded, tucking the necklace into her shirt.

Emma abruptly, speedily rose. "Someone's coming up the lane," she said. She stepped from the porch.

"Will you come back?" Sara asked.

"But, of course."

Sara went up on her toes catching the glints of the sun on the squad car's dark hood.

She turned, focusing on Emma's image, full bodied in great detail, her long dark hair blowing backward in the wind, the green of her sweater, the well-fitted blue jeans, the confidence of her gait. She watched one hand over top of the other clutching her chest as Emma slowly dissolved into the shadows of the forest.

A smile tickled the corners of her mouth showing off her hereditary dimples as she strode towards the vehicle. "Good day officers," Sara said. "What can I do for you?"

~~~

Emma traveled swift and silent through the forest, her bare feet not so much as disturbing a single blade of grass. The 'Ichabica' followed closely scooting behind the bushes and trees each time she turned.

She knew they were there.

She grinned, catching the aromas of black tea, bergamot, and vanilla beans on the wind. She crossed the small clearing, turning right, and following the cobblestone pathway.

The Chiricahua Chief handed her an over-size cup filled to the point of overflowing. "I've been keeping the tea warm for you," he said softly. He left the door to the one room cottage open.

They pulled their rockers adjacent to one another, the fire sizzling and crackling within its stone hearth warming their backs. The marine shotgun, shells, hunting knife, belt, and lengths of rope lay neatly in a pile in the corner.

"Sara wears the stone?" he asked.

Emma nodded, pushing up the sleeves of her green sweater.

"You did good grasshopper," his eyes sparkled over top of the cup rim.

Emma rolled her eyes. "Grasshopper?" she questioned.

He bent his head playfully.

"You been watching reruns again?" she quipped.

"Do you see a television set?" he asked.

"As if that would matter!" Emma took a sip of tea. "By the way ... Just in passing."

"Yes," he retorted. He knew what was coming.

"When I prayed and asked for a sign," she paused rearranging her cup within her hands. "I hoped it would be, you know, right in my face."

"It was right in your face. Twice over, might I add."

"Rain! ... Rain! ... You call that a sign?"

"What did you expect? ... Purple snow? ... Falling fish?" His grin broadened in amusement.

She gave a slow exaggerated shake of her head. "But come on, rain?"

He sipped at his tea trying to contain his laughter. "By the way ... Just in passing."

"Yes," she said.

"In answer to your question, no you're not a little slow."

"Yeah right." Her dimpled smile could have scored a ten out of ten. "So now what?" she asked barely above a whisper.

"We wait ... We have all the time in the world ... Until the next," he added in between sips.

"Until the next?" she countered.

"My Emma ... Like the fat man says 'there's always a next time'."

"Shouldn't that go ... 'It ain't over till the fat lady sings'?"

"What-ever," he muttered. "Maybe I should watch more television, update some."

"You don't have a television," she retorted.

"As you most eloquently stated, as if that would matter."

They took of the remainder of their tea in silence, both rocking back and forth, barefoot, in tune with the crackle of the fire.

~~~

Simon drove the first sixty miles with windows down, staring blindly along the paved roadways. The next forty with windows down, staring blindly, with the radio blasting. The last fifty, windows down, staring blindly, radio blasting, deep in amongst thoughts.

The day seemed blurred, like an instruction manual purposefully doused in a pail of hot water, left closed out in the hot sun to dry for a month ... Hard to open ... Clumped together ... Ink blurred ... For the most part undecipherable.

He mentally rolled around the few things that remained on the back cover. A five-hundred-fifty acre farm in the country with its own enclosed private lake. The fully restored house, a rambling giant, rich with heritage, ornate woodwork and stained glass. All free and clear, no mortgage, no nothing. A garden, a dog, horses for the barn, and yes maybe even chickens. To be able to withdraw from fast passed city life, and write his novel.

And the big one, maybe someday children.

Then there was Sara, this new Sara, this new improved Sara. The tied above the waist cotton shirted, tight jean clad, braided haired, beaded ear ringed, barefoot, suddenly un-shy, vibrant, full of life, Sara.

A brand new Sara with a remarkable, uncanny resemblance to Emma, the beautiful, free spirited, sharp-witted Emma, whose cup was always half full. The Emma he'd had a secret crush on, no doubt like many others, from the very moment he had laid eyes on her. She carried a presence that seemed to defy words.

He had forgotten so much.

It had been just past a year now that she had died along the shoulder of the roadway. The police said she had crawled damn near a mile, most of her major bones broken, her collarbone sticking clear through her shirt, bleeding profusely, trying to get home, trying to get help.

The car accident, that should never have happened.

A hit and run by drugged up teenagers, not even old enough to hold a license.

Emma had stopped to help a snapping turtle across the road.

He remembered the funeral, heart breaking beyond measure. Her burial clothes; true to form, an emerald green sweater, blue jeans, and of course the bare feet.

And following her traditions.

Ina Louise Jackson

Gary setting her ashes free into the winds on the farm homestead.

Simon wiped the tears from his cheeks, pulling into the underground parking.

Somewhere deep inside him from the bottom most layer, Emma's voice rose, soft and delicate, very much there.

"There is no death ... Only a change of worlds ... In the generations of time ... The past ... The present, and the future all co-exist in the spirit world," she whispered.

COUNTY ROAD 507

Epilogue

The thing about legends is,
Sometimes ... They're true.

TROLLING

Dedication

For my sons:
Always be ... the best you can be
For ... What will be, will.
And it will always find a way ... To be.

Prologue

Didn't your mother,
Ever tell you not to talk to strangers?

Ina Louise Jackson

TROLLING

"Trollin' ... Trollin' ...
Trollin' on the river.
Ta ... Toot, toot, toot, toot,
Toot, toot, toot, toot.
Ta ... Toot, toot, toot, toot,
Toot ..."

Intermittent high-pitched metallic laughter bounced and echoed dancing in-between the growls and squeals.

Run ... Run run ...
Run ... Run run run ...
Run ... Run run run ...
Run ... Run run ...
Run.

The sun rose, cascading ribbons of light across the fields, stretching and falling where it shouldn't, missing where it should. Soon they would come. Soon they would know, but for now, all was well. The quiet stillness need not give it up.

The grass was long in the field like elongated willowy straws with tufted ends. They stood at bay strong and silent, not giving off the slightest quiver with the tantalizing breezes.

As the dewdrops warmed they let go, melding together forming into a trickle, which grew bottom heavy and slid down the cold flesh, dropping and pooling in the place where there had once been an upper and lower jaw. The one remaining eye dangled free and clear of the socket, swaying lazily on its rosy bungee cord. Dark red spatters mixed with the lumpy blue granite like coils coloring them purple. The earth had also joined in the macabre collage outlining the shadow of the still figure in dark red liquid.

The field lay to the right of Yardley Park. It would be quite a time, with the on-coming rain showers, before anyone walked hand in hand through there again. Time is always relevant to all things, living things anyway. After the rains, it would take the better part of a week or so to find all of and prove identification of the teen boy once called Bill Biltmore.

~~~

Beth Knowles flipped off the hall light, tapping then opening each of the three bedroom doors in turn. "Come on, computers off, lights out, its bedtime," she said.

She entered her own room dressing for bed. Ten minutes later, she retraced her steps, walking backward down the hallway again tapping and opening doors. "Bedtime," she repeated.

She tucked Rachel and teddy bear in, snuggling and pulling up the petal pink coverlet, cocooning the six-year-old want-to-be ballerina. She flicked on the night-light. "Sweet dreams my angel," she whispered. She kissed her cheek.

"'Night mommy," Rachel muttered sleepily.

The next room in line belonged to Riley. Beth made her way through the obstacle course of the day's clothing, runners, soccer balls, basketballs, and footballs amidst the schoolbooks. She fluffed and pulled his covers smiling to his disapproving rolling eyes. She kissed his forehead. "Goodnight handsome prince."

"'Night mom," Riley shot back yawning and stretching trying to appear drowsy.

She turned towards the doorway stopping, smirking at the blue blinking neon light under the carefully placed and draped tee shirt. She shoved it aside opening the laptop, her eyes immediately flashing over the two crumpled cars and body bags. "More crash scenes? ... I thought we talked about this?"

He sat bolt upright. "But mom ... It's all made up ... It's not real ... It's just movie props and stuff." He was lying through his ten-year-old teeth.

Beth hit the off button.

"Mom," he complained.

"Mom nothing," she countered. "Next time it's gone."

"M ... O ... M," he whined.

"'Night."

The last room on the left housed her first-born, Nikki, the thirteen-year-old going on twenty. She turned off the overhead light, clicked on the bedside lamp, then pointed to her watch. "Ten o'clock, no later ... Okay?" She planted a kiss atop her daughter's head. "I'll be back to check."

"I know ... You always do," Nikki said offhandedly.

"And don't close the door all the way."

"What's with you and like doors lately?"

"Did you hear what I said?" Beth pointed at the door.

"You shut yours!"

Beth's eyebrows abruptly rose. "Excuse me!"

"Whatever." Nikki waited until she heard her mother's bedroom door hinges squeak then shoved hers shut. She reopened her laptop watching her auction. Her latest sale of the worn and perfumed purple lace thong undies was hitting an all-time high.

"'Night guys," Beth called out.

"'Night ... mothmey," Rachel muttered into her pillow.

"'Night mom," Riley returned.

"'Night mother," Nikki retorted.

Beth smiled standing in her bedroom doorway, waiting for the rerun of 'The Waltons.' 'Night Riley, 'night Nikki ... 'night Rachel, 'night Nikki and on it went. Priceless it was, totally out and out priceless.

Beth dialled the all-familiar telephone number. The one she had been dialling for years. The one that bypassed the night time answering service.

"Hello," said Doug Knowles. His voice sounded tinny and far away.

"When will you be home?" Beth fidgeted with the belt on her housecoat.

"Soon."

"When is soon?" She drew the belt into a loose bow fussing with the ends.

"Soon is shortly ... I'm just wrapping up here," He swivelled his big overstuffed leather office chair side to side then pivoted round and round in lazy circles.

Beth looked up at the bedroom ceiling, nodding her head mouthing, 'Soon is shortly,' until her know it all smirk widened taking over her entire face. "Of course darling, I understand completely. You're just wrapping up, then will get a last minute call keeping you for hours, as always" she whispered too low for him to hear. "Okay then ... Your dinner's keeping warm in the oven."

"Thanks hon." He spun himself one more time, then clutched the under edge of his desk pulling himself tight to the desktop ogling the picture on the computer screen. He traced his index finger across it then pressed the save. The photo of the eight year old in full make up, stockings and garters, smiling provocatively out at him with her school tartan hiked up shoving off her bare bottom was a keeper. He locked all the office doors, poured himself a stiff shot, and settled into his chair scanning again. Being the last to leave the office did have its perks.

Beth dimmed the lights in her bedroom, put some music on, and poured a glass of white wine, curling up in between the pillows on her bed and logging into private chat room nine-six-x-six-nine.

'There you are,' Bob typed. 'I've been waiting for you, my sweetness.'

She smiled. 'I've missed you so ... You're all I've been thinking of for hours,' she typed.

'Really? ... Tell me more ... Any certain part you been thinking of more than others?' he typed.

Ten p.m. came and went. As the hall cock chimed twelve a.m. Beth sent a screen full of hugs and kisses Bob's way, with an invitation to meet same time, same place, the next night.

Beth washed up, pulled back on her pyjamas, unlocked her door and trundled off down the hall.

Nikki's door was tightly closed ... Yet again.

"Nikki ... Nikki?" she said quietly. "You asleep?" She opened the door slow and silent.

Nikki shoved the computer in between the mattresses, turned on her side, and snapped her eyes shut.

"Nikki ... You sleeping?" Beth whispered. She bent over running her fingers softly through her daughter's hair, fixed the blanket pulling it up over her shoulders. 'All good,' she thought. She turned off the night side lamp. "Have good dreams my love," she kissed her forehead lightly and left the room.

Run ... Run run ...
Run ... Run run run ...
Run ... Run run run ...
Run ... Run run ...
Run.

~~~

"My God! ... Hey Hon? ... They've found another one!" Doug didn't say anymore. He pushed the morning newspaper aside and started to eat his eggs and toast.

'Another?' she mouthed. Beth knew what he was referring too. The papers had been full of it. This one brought the count into the double digits. Young teens, boys and girls, found dead, heads smashed in, their body cavities slit open bow to stern and empty of all organs, from lungs on down to reproductive. The upper and lower jaws crudely hacked off and missing as if they had been taken as a trophy or memento of the kill. The bodies always on their right sides curled in the foetal position knees to chest, all of them left lying in the long grasses of fields or parks.

Beth sat down across from him at the kitchen table. She scooted the paper over starting to read.

Riley munched away on his cereal, smiling, watching his parents' futile attempts at camouflage. He already knew. It had been all over the streets and school like wild fire, from the start, long beating the newspapers to the punch. There had been, and still was, a lot of speculation and scenarios for the kills, even that they were linked to an underground satanic cult. He knew different. He studied many, many cult kills and these weren't like those. He wished they had posted more on the net, it was difficult to tell this time if the pictures were a hoax or the real deal, if there had been more it wouldn't have been in question. The close ups of the kid were blurred and the others had been taken from too far back, and if memory served him right the body seemed to be lying in a different position than at the time of the kill. He smiled. He knew a lot more than anyone.

Beth folded the newspaper in thirds closing it. She turned to face her husband. "Will you be late again?"

"Worse Hon ... I have to pull an all-nighter," he replied quickly, too quickly.

He opened the refrigerator pulling out his lunch. An on-line friend of his 'The Happy Hammer' had told him about this foreign site launching tonight where none of the kids were over five and it was no holds barred, anything went, sex, blows, confinement, whippings, torture and it was live. He could barely wait. The web fee was a little hefty, but his bonus would cover most, the credit cards the rest, it would be just another business luncheon he had forgotten to tell Beth about when the bill came in. It had worked for years. Besides; the boss always paid him back one way or another; a little book fudging might be needed, but hell who didn't fudge figures now and then. Moreover, sleeping on the leather sofa in the office wasn't so bad either, especially when that girl from typing stayed for an hour or two. He so loved the smell of her on the leather.

"You stayed all night last week and the week before and the week before that and before that. This has become a routine," Beth said. She was so used to his long hours that his staying for the night was now a commonplace event. For her, the excitement of their marriage had died long ago, probably for him too. The arrival of the kids had changed things for them both. Her being, the fulltime work from home mom, always near and there for the kids, and him, the aloof work away from home dad, never near and there for the kids.

She smiled inwardly thinking about Bob, her private new lover, all with just the touch of a button on the computer keyboard, safe, secure, and she never needed to dress up or leave the comfort of her bedroom.

"They're pushing us pretty hard with all these new contracts, advertising has gotten to be a bitch, it's not what it used to be, but it pays the bills." He grabbed a bag of potato chips from the cupboard stuffing it into his plastic lunch bag.

Beth had stopped listening; he was spouting the same old, same old tried and worn excuses. She was reading again. "Oh my," she blurted. "I wouldn't think they'd be allowed to print so many of the details. Would you?"

"It sells papers, Hon," Doug answered.

"I feel sick," Beth rolled the paper and threw it in the trash.

Nikki had been watching her mother intently as she read, her body language, the flickering of her eyes, the color draining from her face, the pushing back from the table. She tore the wrapper off her cereal bar with her teeth, jamming over half of it into her mouth.

"Nikki come straight home after school and walk the streets don't take the short cut through the park and field," Beth said.

"I can't, I have volleyball practice," Nikki garbled through her over stuffed mouth.

"Well then straight away after that. Don't cut through the park or field."

"Yardley Park and field I presume?" she sputtered, open mouthed, spraying cereal bits into the air.

"Yes ... And you and your brother walk together!"

"You don't have to be so over protective mom ... We're not like little kids ... We already know all about it. It's all around the school and like the news and the net and the mall and everywhere else." Nikki gulped back a glass of juice.

"Don't go through the park or the field," Beth ordered, this time sounding more like a drill Sergeant than anything else.

"Whatever! ... Come on Riley, we'll be late." Nikki picked up her backpack.

"I'm coming ... I'm coming." Riley dipped his head, trying to contain his amusement at his mother and sister squaring off.

"Remember do as I said," Beth instructed.

"Christ mom! I got it the first time!" Nikki jammed the last of the cereal bar into her mouth.

"NIKKI! ... WATCH IT!" Beth yelled.

Riley rushed the kitchen screen door unable to keep his laughter in check.

~~~

"So, you'll wait for me?" Riley asked.

"You'll be back here exactly an hour after my practice ends, right?" Nikki retorted.

"Yep."

"And you'll be like right here in this spot?" Nikki pointed to the tree.

"Yeppers," Riley chirped.

"Where in hell are you going that's so God damn important anyway?"

"Me and my friends are going to posse up in the field of that last kill after school. We're going to hunt for blood and body parts and stuff. We're taking some specimen jars from science class with us. You swear you won't tell mom?" He swished his feet side to side; he'd made up enough of a story

277

in case he got caught over there. She didn't need to know the real reason he was going to the field. Nobody did. "You swear?" he repeated.

"Please," Nikki rolled her eyes. "You got the twenty bucks?"

"Yep," Riley pulled the crumpled bill from his back jean pocket.

"Then I swear ... Give it."

Riley handed it over. "You won't ever tell?"

"Nope, my lips are sealed." Nikki fanned the twenty back and forth in front of Riley's face. "But ... Next time it'll cost you thirty."

"Thirty? ... Come on ... Thirty? ... Really?" Riley scoffed.

"Inflation," Nikki countered.

"Where would I get that?"

"Same place you got this ... Out of mom's purse." Nikki shoved the bill into her backpack, walking off down the pathway towards the school.

"RACHEL YOU READY?" Doug yelled down the corridor.

"She's slow," Beth interjected.

"Rachel ... Get a move on dolly," Doug walked half way down the hall.

"'Kay Daddy," Rachel tucked in her tee shirt, prancing towards him.

"Are you picking Rachel up Hon?" Doug held out Rachel's backpack motioning for her to slip into it.

"Yes, of course." Beth planted soft kisses on both their checks locking the back screen door behind them.

"Like my skirt daddy?" Rachel swished the frilly edges back and forth.

"Yes doll, you look like a little princess." Doug rounded the corner then slowed, entering in behind the long line of vehicles waiting to pull into the school drop off zone.

"I like the skirt too. It used to be Nikki's. Mommy fixed it up for me on the sewing machine," Rachel said softly.

"I'm glad sweetheart," he said. "I'm very glad."

Rachel pressed the ruffles of the pink skirt flat with her palms. "It used to be white but mommy dyed it orange for me." She smiled sweetly over at her dad.

"That's nice," he turned kissing the top of her head. "Better go honey, the bell's going to ring any minute."

Rachel walked backward waving cutely bye at her dad, then turned and skipped up the walkway to the school.

"Such a good kid," he muttered. He pulled out onto the roadway. He wondered when she'd lose her sweetness and start mouthing like the other two. Nikki and Riley had sure turned into handfuls. Beth had wanted kids from the day they first met. Well she got what she wanted. Three times over. It sucked to be her. He smiled, it was in the having kids and watching them grow and evolve that his new interest had taken wing and come to the forefront. He had them to thank for the child porn. There was really nothing else like it. Their smooth skin and unscathed bodies ... Their tantalizing eyes. Soon he would take the step and buy one for himself, but for now the sites on the net were good and of course that new girl in the office. She had lied about her age when she had applied for the summer job saying she was eighteen, but he knew she wasn't a day over fifteen. He started to laugh; she was serving him well.

~~~

Riley pushed himself from his desk running full tilt down the corridor and out the front double glass doors, snaking his way through the bikes, across the schoolyard and into the clearing just before the field and Yardley Park. He had an hour and a half to find what he'd lost. He prayed it was still there and the police had not picked it up. He had never been fingerprinted that he could remember so if they ran everything found through their database, he might be safe. But still ... As his mom always said, an ounce of prevention is worth a pound of cure. He slipped off his backpack, went down onto his hands and knees crawling in under the crime scene taping.

~~~

"You're like late," Nikki said.

"Am I?" Riley knew he was but, with his older sister, acting stupid worked like a charm.

"So, did you and your buds find what youse were hoping for?" She picked up her backpack slinging the one strap over her shoulder, walking beside him.

"No," he replied, which was the first thing in this whole scheme that wasn't a lie.

"Police tape still up?" Nikki asked

"Yep," Riley replied. It was still up, moved about twenty feet, but still up.

"Thought it might be. Anyone around guarding it?"

"Nope."

"Thought that too," she said.

They turned from High Street cutting across the top half of the field before Yardley Park.

"Nikki?"

"Yeah," her eyes swept over the long grasses in the field.

"Who do you think is behind all this?" Riley wanted to feel her out.

She hunched up her shoulders. "Don't know, don't really care," she flippantly answered keeping her tone light, lying like a son of a gun. "Like ... Should I even go there with you?"

He beamed. "I have my theories."

"You do ... Do you?" This she wanted to hear.

"Yeah." His heart nervously thumped in his chest seeing the Yardley Park plaque sign in the field come into view. Would Nikki notice the moved tape? He knew she went in there quite often. Had she been lately? The dark side she tried to keep so secretly hidden dictated so. He also knew, she knew, he went in there as well. There was a line in one of 'Stephen King's' movies that went, 'a person without secrets is like a scarecrow without stuffing.' And ... How they both had their secrets.

"Spill it!" she quipped.

"A serial killer, or a cannibal, a zombie, a thrill slayer, the devil, or an escaped croc from the zoo, or even better, an alien beamed to earth like from the movie 'Predator'."

"OMG! ... Riley! ... Enough already!"

"You asked," he quipped. He had watched for a change in her pupils as he spoke. There'd been one.

"Yeah I guess ... I did." She scrunched up her eyebrows. "An escaped croc?" She started to laugh.

"Are you laughing with me? ... Or at me?" He started to giggle too.

"At you ... You Moron!"

They knuckle bumped, cutting across the remainder of the field into the park in silence, heading for home.

~~~

"LIGHTS OUT IN HALF HOUR GUYS," Beth yelled. She crossed her bedroom making comfy in the middle of her bed.

'You're back ... I see ... XOXO,' Bob typed.

'Not for long though,' Beth typed.

'Awe.'

'You're so sweet ... Back at you ... XOXOXO,' Beth typed.

'Can you come back for another tête-tà-tête?' Bob typed.

'Hum ... Okay,' Beth typed.

'I'll be waiting and thinking of you as always.' Bob stood adjusting his web cam to focus directly between his legs.

Beth giggled like a schoolgirl. 'You're so bad,' she typed.

'That's part of why you like me ... Isn't it?' Bob typed.

"Maybe,' she typed.

'XOXOXO.'

'Be back ... Soon ... XOXOXO,' Beth typed.

'XOXOXO.'

Beth drank back the remainder of her wine sitting the glass on the dresser beside the laptop. She ran her fingertips slowly across it thinking of Bob. She drew the belt on her housecoat knotting it at the side, entering Rachel's room. "'Night Sweet Pea," she whispered kissing her forehead, and cozying the comforter up about Rachel's shoulders.

"'Night Mommy."

Beth tiptoed from the room striding into Riley's next. She gently pulled the laptop from between his stilled hands setting it on his desk beside his schoolbooks. She fluffed his covers kissing his temple. "Goodnight my little man," she cooed shutting off his lamp. Beth stood and watched him sleep. She smiled then left the room.

Riley listened to his mom's usual preludes to Nikki, the time warnings, the closed door, the whatever-elses. He opened his eyes counting her steps as they trailed back down the hallway. He sat up hearing the click of her bedroom door locking. He sprang from his bed grabbing the laptop from the desk smiling as he flipped it back open. His mom had forgotten to turn it off. He clicked on the zoom feature of the dialog box tracing the pointer arrow slowly over each and every detail of the new, very clear image of the mangled, gutted body found in Yardley Park Field. He smiled, a toothy, full, almost sneer-like smile, stretching out the sides of his lips; the body had been repositioned again. He could hear his older sister's voice droning away on the telephone as he settled in under the covers, tenting them with his head, just per chance he missed the sound of the footsteps coming down the hall later.

"OMG! ... Like are you serious? ... No! ... No! ... I'm all in ... Thanks ... Think I'll pass on it for tonight ... Yeah really ... See ya tomorrow ... 'Kay bye," Nikki depressed the button disconnecting the call, depressed the button a second time, listened for the dial tone, leaving the phone on ... And off the hook to the outside world.

~~~

Computer log in nine-eleven p.m. ... Teen chat ... 'What's up?'

Private chat request ... 'All male-All buff!' ... Nine-thirty-one p.m.

'Hey you!'

'? ? ?' All male-All buff typed.

'How you doin, you Buff hunk?'

'Who are you?' All male-All buff typed.

'Guess?'

'Gina?' All male-All buff typed.

'Nope ... Guess again?'

'Rhoda?'

'Nope ... Better!'

'Desiree?' All male-All buff typed.

'Nope ... Not even warm.'

'Who?'

'Give you a hint ... Sixth period math.'

'Are you sure you go to the same school? ... We only have five periods.'

'Typo.'

'Lol ... So come on ... Who are you?' All male-All buff typed.

'Fifth period math.'

'I have math second period.'

'Silly me, she says in the red lace bra and red thong ... Lol ... Typo again!'

'Lol ... Lol ... Red huh? ... So ... Give it up?' All male-All buff typed.

'New girl.'

'Deb? ... No way?'

'Way!'

'Hum ... I've had dreams of you!' All male-All buff typed.

'Tell me more, All male-All buff.'

'Hot dreams.'

'More ... More ... More!'

'Really, Really ... REALLY! ... Hot dreams!' All male-All buff typed

'Lol ... Guess what I'm wearing now?'

'What?'

'Nothing.'

'Nice ... Wish I could see that nothing ... Deb.'

'You can.'

'How?' All male-All buff typed

'You know that park near the school?'

'Jessup?'

'Yeah.'

'What about it?' All male-All buff typed.

'Wanna meet? ... There?'

'When?'

'Eleven tonight, I'll bring my nothing on and a six pack of beer.'

'Shit that's late! ... But ... Can I cop a feel? ... Hey, you're bringing beer?'

'Yep to both.'

'How will I get out?' All male-All buff typed.

'Got a window?'

'Yeah.'

'Open it and jump, says Deb with the nothing on.'

'Lol.'

'See you there?'

'For sure!' All male-All buff typed.

Run ... Run run ...
Run ... Run run run ...
Run ... Run run run ...
Run ... Run run ...
Run.

~~~

Nikki cracked opened her bedroom door listening, taking note, fine-tuning in above the normal house noises. She stood for the longest while, quiet, reserved. She shoved her feet into her slippers scuffling down the hall towards her mother's bedroom. She drummed her fingernails up and down the wood of the door. "Mom? ... Mom?"

"Yes darling?"

Nikki leaned against the doorframe waiting for the door to open.

"Mom you didn't have to get up. I just wanted to tell you," Nikki paused looking around her mother at the open laptop on her bed, the scattered pillows, and the empty wine glass on the nightstand. "I just wanted to tell you I'm going to bed."

Beth glanced at the clock, then at her pyjama-clad daughter. "It's barely past nine-forty. Something wrong honey?" She instinctively formed fitted her hand to her daughter's forehead.

"Just feeling a bit off."

Beth checked both cheeks then her forehead again. She did feel warm. "Is it your tummy?"

"No mom ... Just like, you know, girl stuff." Nikki stepped back from her mother not wanting another check-up.

"Oh okay, Hon ... Well come on," Beth moved in behind Nikki placing her hands on both shoulders guiding her gently down the hall. "I'll tuck you in."

"Like aren't I a bit old for this?" Nikki shuffled into her room.

"Never, ever, ever my darling."

Nikki flapped her elbows loosening the maternal wrapping, and turned on the television channel surfing. After while she turned up the volume, locked her bedroom door, pulled the black jeans and black hoodie from under the bed, threw off the pyjamas, dressed, formed her pillows end to end on the bed covering them with the blanket, opened her window, removed the screen, and jumped out.

~~~

Doug threw the newspaper onto the kitchen counter. "Another one!" he exclaimed. "What in hell is this world coming to?" He plunked into one of the kitchen chairs clasping his hands directly in front of him on the table.

"Where?" Beth blurted.

"Jessup Park." He shook his head slowly back and forth, rearranging his breakfast cereal in the bowl.

"Still no leads?" Beth pushed the cereal box towards Riley.

"Not a one," Doug replied.

"Do you think it's some kind of cult like they say?" Beth dipped her toast in her tea.

Doug screwed up his face, blending his eyebrows together. "Cult?" He spooned cereal into his mouth chewing slowly. "I don't know, seems pretty far-fetched."

"But, isn't all the murders and the way they're done far-fetched?" Beth dunked her toast again.

"But why teens?" Doug countered.

Riley cut in, "maybe because they're young and juicy and tender." He held his bowl to his mouth gulping the left over milk down.

Beth flipped her half piece of toast onto her plate. Had she heard right? "What did you just say?" She stared at her son.

"You know ... Young ... Juicy ... Tender ... Just saying," Riley stated matter-of-factly as if they were discussing anything else but what they were.

"Go to your room," Beth ordered.

"It's Saturday, I have soccer practice in an hour," Riley said smugly. For the life of him, he could not figure out what was wrong with what he'd said.

"Then go to your room for an hour!"

"But I have to be there in an hour," he pushed his chair from the table teetering it up onto its back legs.

"RILEY!" Beth yelled.

"Jeese! ... I'm going all ready, okay." He pushed his chair forward banging it hard into the table.

"RILEY ... KNOCK ... IT ... OFF!" Beth watched him fist punching the air as he trailed down the hallway into his room.

"I know why the teens," Nikki interjected.

Doug and Beth simultaneously turned in her direction, their wide-eyed stares mirroring one another.

"'Cause they're easy targets ... They're like stupid," Nikki's eyes flickered back and forth between her parents.

"You go to your room too!" Beth pointed to the hallway.

Nikki rose slowly, cleared away her plate, put the orange juice carton back into the fridge kicking it shut with her foot, and then shoved her chair towards the table. "Whatever ... But like at least think about it."

"Nikki go ... Now!" Beth commanded.

Nikki paused in the doorway whirling around, studying the astonished expressions flashing on her parents' faces. "Jesus Christ," she muttered. "You treat me like I'm a little kid." She slid her sock clad feet along the hardwood floor in the hallway mocking a figure skater, slamming her bedroom door shut behind her.

Doug held up his hands in the 'got me' pose; all the things he had wanted to say and discuss had rolled up into a tight ball of their own and refused to move.

Beth sighed heavily.

Doug opened and closed his mouth. He ran his hand through his hair then knocked his head to the right repeatedly.

"Is it all over the front page again? ... What about safety factors? ... Did they say how ..." Beth halted mid-sentence her eyes following the direction of Doug's head knocks. She cupped her hand to her mouth. 'Oh my goodness,' she thought. 'Rachel.' She had been so quiet; she had honestly forgotten she was still at the table. She mouthed thank-you to her husband. She had been so ready to jump in with question after question.

Beth cleared her throat. "And you my little miss, all done with your breakfast?"

Rachel nodded yes cutely. "Mommy?"

"Yes baby girl."

"I know why the teens," she offered up.

"I beg your pardon?" Beth choked out, her voice shrilling and vibrating. What had her six-year-old just said? ... She could rationalize this from Riley and Nikki but Rachel? ... Little Rachel. She looked at Doug for help. He seemed congealed around the edges and farther away as if he had somehow pushed himself far, far back from the table.

"I know why," Rachel stated again.

Beth gawked at Rachel unable to speak.

Rachel looked sweetly back and forth between her parents twirling the curls of her hair around her fingers. "It's the age."

"What?" Beth blurted.

"The age ... Mommy ... That's all." Rachel got down off the chair and skipped down the hall into her room.

Beth and Doug stared at one another across the table.

"Did she just say? ... It's the age?" Beth spit out.

Doug nodded.

"So that's it then ... It's confirmed ... All three of them are from the same pod."

Doug nodded again.

Beth worked her jaw back and forth grinding her teeth.

Doug pursed his lips together holding up his right index finger. "Just in passing," he paused attempting to clear his throat.

"Yes?" Beth's voice squeaked.

"Before you get all bent out of shape," he paused again watching her shoulders tighten.

"Yes?"

"It is all over the news and probably the schools and everywhere else and Rachel maybe doesn't say much, but she does listen to her brother and sister, and has no doubt heard them both trying to figure out the who done it and why," he paused once again reflecting Beth's slight smile back at her. "So ... If I were you I wouldn't pay this any mind."

"Hum ... You're probably right," Beth got up from the table plugging in the kettle. "Rachel really got me there," she said quiet and distant.

"Like I said don't worry, she's like a little walking tape recorder ... And the other two, well, they're probably just caught up in the frenzy of it all, you know how kids are?" He didn't believe a word of what was leaving his lips but it sounded good. He didn't know what the hell was wrong with the three of them. They all gave him the creeps at times lately, so much so the hair would stand on the back of his neck and his skin would goose-bump. They were not normal by any means.

"Coffee or tea?" Beth fetched the mugs from the table.

"Coffee."

They drank their drinks chattering back and forth about nothing in particular.

"Going to cut the grass today?" Beth asked.

"No." Doug was reading the paper again.

"No? ... It's been over two weeks." Beth rested her chin into her palms reading the article underneath the newspaper headline about the Jessup Park slaughter.

"I know it's been awhile," Doug muttered from behind the paper. "But I still can't get that damn shed open. The doors are as if they've been cemented shut and it reeks like hell on fire back there," he continued without looking up.

"Okay ... I'll try, but if I get it open ... You have to cut," Beth said.

"Deal," he flipped pages then started to read again.

Beth shoved on her rubber garden shoes and crossed the back lawn. She yanked on the door handle. Stuck wasn't the word. She hiked over to the garage coming back out dragging a crowbar. She shoved it in through the door handle using her weight to pry. The door popped giving a hair and then sprang back into place, huffing out a thin wisp of air in the process. Beth locked her hands around her knees abruptly vomiting. The trailer of air was rancid, vile, putrid, and seemed to have lodged inside her nose and throat. She vomited again. She left the crowbar and walked slowly back to the house.

"Get it open hot shot?" Doug was grinning like the 'Cheshire Cat.'

"No."

"Told you," he quipped.

"I think some kind of animal's died in there." Beth hung over the kitchen sink swishing her mouth with water.

"Probably a squirrel or something."

"A squirrel? ... It's far too putrid for a little squirrel ... I'm going to go with the 'or something'," Beth said. "Maybe we should just borrow Sandy and Ben's mower and forget about getting into the shed till the smell wears off some."

"Works for me, theirs is a rider."

~~~

Doug picked up the car keys. "Riley let's get a move on, we've got twenty minutes to get there."

"Dad?" Riley rolled the passenger side window fully down hanging his arm out.

"What?"

"Do you know what the stats are on missing teenagers?" Riley's head swivelled, gazing backwards at the stop sign his dad had just driven right through.

"What on earth are you talking about?"

"Stats Dad ... They say ... Forty-three percent are dead in one hour ... Sixty-four percent in the first three, and ninety-nine to one hundred percent in twenty-four."

Doug slammed on the brakes rocking them both forward into the dash. He stared open mouthed at his son. "What in hell is wrong with you?"

"Nothing," Riley chirped.

"Christ! ... All this morbidity has to stop!"

"All this what?"

Doug pulled to the curb. "Get out!"

"But it's still two blocks to the soccer field!"

"Riley ... Just get out!" Doug leaned over him flinging the door open.

"Will you be back in two hours to get me?" Riley pushed the door shut. The car was already starting to move.

"Your mother will."

"Okay ... Then Dad ... Whatever." Riley hiked along the sidewalk, cutting across the well-traveled pathway up the side of the empty small stone house, jumped the back fence, and criss-crossed the dirt laneway coming out at the top side of the soccer field. His dad had sure been weird these past years, even weirder than weird. He had seen him more than once out back in the middle of the night with the binoculars focused on their neighbour's daughter's bedroom window. What was she five? ... Six tops? He kicked small rocks thinking thoughts he did not want to about his dad. Next time he had a shower he was locking the bathroom door, rules or no rules.

~~~

Beth took a break from damp mopping the floor to check in on Rachel. The kid had been quieter than usual lately. She poked her head round the doorframe. All her dolls were out. She smiled to herself watching her daughter playing.

Rachel redressed one of the dolls, picked up another, turned her head and grinned up at Beth, she then squealed and started slapping and banging the two dolls against one another. "Take that ... And that," she gurgled in a low voice smacking the dolls harder and harder together. "And that!"

Beth froze, her eyes ringed in white.

Rachel pitched her voice, "help ... help ... help me!" She made the one doll run from the other. She turned the running dolls head backward as if checking on the one chasing, and then made it trip and fall to the ground. She rammed the other doll directly on top beating it on the lower knocking its head off. She lifted off the top doll making it hop away. "You no good to me," Rachel gurgled in the low voice. "You looked young but you're too old ... You've ripened." She brought back the doll that had hopped away making it kick the one on the ground and then hopped it away again. She made the doll lie down behind her shoe as if hiding, then paraded another doll across in front of the shoe. "There's a good one," she gurgled out, totally focused.

Beth grabbed the doorframe turning her knuckles white. "RACHEL ... WHAT ON EARTH!" she screamed.

Rachel picked up the first two dolls smiling sweet and innocent up at her mother. "Mommy ... Look ... This one killed that one."

"Rachel ... Why?"

Rachel shrugged, her non-blinking eyes fixating onto Beth's. "Too old," Rachel muttered.

"Too old?" Beth repeated. Her eyebrows were arced so high if there had been a wind she could have hovered off ... 'Too old?' she repeated inside her head. The too old question just sat unattended, her brain still too heavily bogged, attempting to wrap around the dolls killing one another.

She cleared her throat. "Sweetheart," she began. "Dolls don't kill one another because they're too old."

"But, they're no good for nothing."

"No good for nothing?" Beth's levels of understanding seemed to have flown the coup and did not appear to be coming back any time soon. 'How could a doll be good for nothing?' She re-worded and tried again. "Don't you like your dolls anymore honey?"

Rachel's demeanour suddenly changed. She stood and wrapped her arms around her mother cuddling close. "Yes I like them, Mommy ... But I'm playing slaughter in the park."

Beth was glad Rachel was tight against her; she could not begin to mask the expression on her face. "Well ... Honey ... I ... I," Beth broke off, she was in trouble.

Rachel patted her mother's back. "I know what you're trying to say Mommy ... It's all right."

Beth ran her hands over Rachel's hair. "You do ... Do you?"

"Yes," she pulled back and looked up at Beth. "You're going to tell me slaughter in the park isn't a good game to play and I shouldn't do it any-more."

"Wise beyond your years, huh kid?"

"Yep," she smiled sweetly.

"Rachel ... I need to know why you were saying the things you were?'

"What things Mommy?"

Beth bent down coming face to face. "You know the things the dolls were saying?'

"What things Mommy?" Rachel said again.

"You don't remember?"

"No," she swung her skirt back and forth swishing the material.

"No?" If she didn't know better she would have sworn her daughter had read the situation and was playing her, just like the other two did ... Only better.

"No," Rachel repeated.

"Sweetheart ... Where on earth, did you get the idea for this ... This game?"

"Slaughter in the park?"

"Yes."

"Oh ... From Daddy and Riley and Nikki at breakfast. Daddy said there was another and he didn't look good. Riley said the slaughters were because they were young, juicy, and tender and Nikki said because they were easy and stupid and that it was the age.

"I see," Beth drew a heavy breath. "I see," she repeated. Beth remembered the conversation well, almost too well, and she was sure it had been this little one here that said about the age, not Nikki, but maybe she was wrong. The shock and horror of her children's words and speculations had all run together like a tie-dyed tee-shirt left spinning in the washer too long. Beth picked up the broken doll. "I'll try and fix this and Rachel?"

"I know Mommy; don't play slaughter in the park anymore," Rachel blurted.

Beth put her hands on her hips, shaking her head, she had just had an awkward conversation with a six-year-old and the six-year-old had come out on top. She went into the kitchen laying the doll out on the counter and commenced searching through the drawers for the plastic glue.

~~~

Computer log in one-nineteen p.m. ... Teen chat ... 'LOL.'
Private chat request ... 'Blondie Bombshell' ... Two p.m.
'Hey ... How you doing?'
'Who is this?' Blondie Bombshell typed.
'XO xo XO to you!'
'Thank you ... Now I gotta know who you are?' Blondie Bombshell typed.
'Guess, sweet-sweet princess?'
'Luis?'
'Give me a break.'
'Okay ... Marc?' Blondie Bombshell typed.
'Please ... '
'Clue?'
'Science lab.'
'Mr. four eyes Bogwarth's lab?' Blondie Bombshell typed.
'Yes.'

'*OMG! ... You can't be Mad Max can you? ... I wouldn't be that lucky ... Lol!*'

'*It's your lucky day then.*'

'*OMG! ... OMG! ... !*' Blondie Bombshell typed.

'*Wanna hang later?*'

'*You want to hang with me? ... With me?*'

'*Don't be so surprised.*'

'*OMG! ... OMG! ... Like yeah ... I wanna hang later!*' Blondie Bombshell typed.

'*You know that park, the one right near the school.*'

'*Sir MacDonald's?*' Blondie Bombshell typed.

'*Yes ... Susie.*'

'*You know my name! ... OMG!*' Blondie Bombshell typed.

'*Of course ... Silly ... I'm in you science lab.*'

'*Oh yeah ... Lol ... Forgot.*'

'*Susie? ... Beautiful-sweet-beautiful, Susie.*'

'*Yeah?*' Blondie Bombshell typed.

'*My folks are going out tonight and my Moms car will be here, so I was thinking there's a full bottle of tequila under the kitchen sink. Hum ... How about it?*'

'*Never drank tequila before.*' Blondie Bombshell typed.

'*Then girl ... You haven't lived.*'

'*You can really drive?*" Blondie Bombshell typed.

'*Yes sir ... We on?*'

'*What time?*'

'*After dark ... Ten ... Eleven?*'

'*I don't know ... How would I get out?*' Blondie Bombshell typed.

'*Door ... Window ... That's what there for ... You know.*'

'*Lol ... Can we go for a drive?*' Blondie Bombshell typed.

'*Sure.*'

'*Lol.*'

'*Susie ... Did I tell you how hot you are!*'

'*Okay ... I'll come ... See you at ten.*' Blondie Bombshell typed.

'*I'll be waiting ... XO xo XO.*'

Run ... Run run ...
Run ... Run run run ...
Run ... Run run run ...
Run ... Run run ...
Run.

~~~

Riley tumbled in through his bedroom window landing in a tangled heap on the floor. "MOM?" he screamed, startled.

Beth was sitting on the end of his bed. She closed her book placing it aside her. "Hi son," she said quietly, unnervingly. Her eyes flickered over him. He was covered in dirt and leaves and small twigs, and something that looked a lot like half-dried blood. She leaned into him inspecting one of the ruddy-brown splatters. It was blood all right. She ran her tongue along her lips wetting them, settling her eyes on his face.

"I can explain," he said.

"I bet you can ... Do you know its twelve-thirty a.m.?" Beth glanced at her watch. "Correction," she said. "Actually it's twelve-thirty-four a.m., to be exact."

Riley could feel the coldness of her glare slicing right through him and out the other side. He pressed his back into the wall. She was starting to unnerve him.

"No ... No ... No." Beth made a clucking noise with her tongue after each no. She shook her head back and forth. "For goodness sake don't back away ... I want to hear all of what you have to say ... I wouldn't want to miss a single solitary word ... Uh ... Uh ... No-way." She forced a smile. "SIT!" she ordered.

"Mom, I'm not a dog." He kicked himself for opening his mouth when he should have kept it shut. He knew he was in very deep shit. She was way, too calm.

"Lucky for you! ... One can kill their own dog without much to-do, but killing your own kid they kind of frown on, you know what I mean?"

He nodded.

She pointed to the floor in front of her feet. "Sit! ... Now!" Beth folded her hands neatly into her lap. "Well ... I'm waiting."

"I ... I ... We ... We ... Um ... Ah ..."

She cut him off. "Quit the bullshit Riley!"

"My three ... Three friends ... You know Stan, Luke ... "

She cut him off again. "And Morley whose nick-name is Link, yes I know." She leaned over and grabbed the front of his sweatshirt twisting it tightly about his neck. "I'm not going to say this again! ... Quit with the God Damn bullshit crap! ... You hear me kid?" She released his shirt, flipped her hands palm side up, and made a disgusted face, wiping the residue of whatever it was from his sweatshirt, off on his sleeves.

"My three friends and I have a secret place and we've been doing magic experiments a lot lately and tonight was a full moon and we needed it to conclude this one potion to drink to make your-self invisible. We were using candles and Stan accidentally backed into them and knocked them over and Link ... Link slipped in the wax and cut himself ... Bad ... So we kind of dragged and carried him home and that's how I got all the dirt and stuff and blood all over me. We all had it on us ... I guess we all must of lost track of time ... I ... I'm sorry Mom ... I'll never do anything like that again." His knees started to vibrate, knocking his legs up and down into the flooring.

Beth slowly ran her index finger back and forth across her lips, ducking her head glancing up at the cloud-covered skies. They had been like that since late afternoon. She sucked her lips into her mouth chewing on the bottom one.

Her silence seemed longer than forever. He sure wished he'd come home earlier. Much earlier, and he could have, but didn't.

"Riley ... I'd rather you be a thief than a liar," she said coolly ... Too coolly. "Do you wish to adjust any of your details or are you happy with them?"

"I'm not lying, Mommy."

"Mommy? ... Really now?" Her smile was toothy and full.

Riley shivered head to toe with fear. His goose bumps were so huge he felt like his skin was about to burst open.

"Seeing as you're sticking with the bull-crap lies," Beth paused, she had to think hard and carefully for the second time this day, before she spoke.

Riley broke into her pause. "Why do you think I'm lying? ... Which I'm not."

"When it sounds too good, to be true ... It usually is. ... And, I know you're spinning bull-crap ... And besides ... People, you included, always look up and to the left when they lie," she smiled the same smile again, pulling her lips farther back from her teeth. "It's a proven fact," she added.

"Did I just do that?"

She nodded slowly and deliberately. "Have you ever noticed where the characters look when caught by the police and interrogated on those crime shows you're always watching?"

"No."

Beth puffed out her cheeks. "Figures," she scoffed. "Guess you're too absorbed in the blood and gore" She picked up her book slowly making her way to the door. "Riley ... Just so you know."

"Yeah?"

"Yes not yeah," she corrected.

"Yes."

"You're grounded."

"How long?"

"Rest of your life."

"You're not going to tell Dad are you?"

"Already have." Beth snapped her figures, whirling round and walking towards his desktop. "God ... I almost forgot," she muttered. She tugged the computer cord from the wall charger, taking both with her.

"Mom ... That's not fair!"

"Fair? ... Fair? ... I'll tell you what's not fair!" She bent directly over him into his personal space. "Not fair is your mother hearing an odd noise and checking in on you to make sure you're all right and safe at nine-forty-five this evening ... Only to find your window all the way open with the screen removed and you ... shall we say ... missing!" She moved right into his face. "Not fair is searching all over the place inside and out, then driving round the neighbourhood and not finding any sign of you! ... Not fair is telephoning every one of your friends including Stan, Luke, and Morley, might I add, and no one knows where you might be! ... Not fair is calling the police and finding out you have to be missing twenty-four hours before being declared a missing person! ... Not fair is your mother pretending to read this 'GOD DAMN BOOK!'" She heaved it hard into the wall breaking the spine, and then continued, "While sitting on the edge of your bed looking out the window every two seconds, praying and hoping you're okay! ... Then breathing a sigh of relief when I see you sneaking across the side lawn, only to have you tumble in through your frigging window, full of muck and blood and who knows what else! ... THAT'S WHAT NOT FAIR IS!" She shoved the computer up under her arm. "What's your asshole of a password?"

"Severed head," he said quietly. He had been wrong; he was in more than deep shit, he was wallowing in it.

She shook her head. "Why does that not surprise me?" she muttered sarcastically. She walked out of the room slamming the door behind her, sending his darts and board flying in all directions across the room.

Riley listened to her retreating steps. Hopped out the window, picked up the plastic bag, opened it and retrieving the scalpel he'd lifted from the science lab. He wiped the blood from the blade off on the rose bush leaves, tumbled back through the window sprawling out onto the floor, and shoved bag and scalpel deep between his mattresses.

"RILEY," Beth yelled from her doorway. "Shower and wash that muck off and get in bed. You've got five minutes."

"I can't that fast ... I,"

Beth cut him off cold. "FOUR AND A HALF!"

Riley ran for the bathroom whipping off his clothes as he went.

Beth was in his room as soon as the bathroom door closed, opening drawers and cupboards, checking under the bed and the piles of stuff that seemed everywhere. Coming up empty, she sat on the side of his bed, legs crossed, humming the same tune repeatedly, waiting.

Riley ran down the hall into his room. "You're in here," he spit out, unmasked alarm showing on his face. His eyes flashed to the open drawers and cabinets.

"Where did you expect me to be? ... Moon?"

"Mommy, I just meant ..."

Beth interrupted him. "Riley, knock it off with the mommy shit! ... Knock it off with everything! ... Okay? ... You're treading a very fine line with my temper."

Riley went around the other side of his bed, pulled back the covers and crawled in.

Beth rose, walked slowly to the door, pushed it shut, pulled the screwdriver from her housecoat pocket and took the hinges off.

"Aren't you going to tuck me in?" he asked cutely.

"Nope."

He watched her take the door out of the room, heard her drag it into the kitchen and out the back door. He huddled under the covers waiting for her to come back in from outside. "'Night Mommy," he called out hearing the click of the latch locking on the kitchen door.

She didn't reply.

He counted the florescent stars on his ceiling while she rummaged around in the kitchen, finally closing his eyes and tuning into the sounds of her movements as she strode down the hallway towards her bedroom, the computer cord dragging and bouncing making small echoing clickity-clacks behind her. He sprang from his bed, lifted his mattress, shoved his arm in and grinned. They were still there, unlike his door and the computer his mother was probably turning on this very moment. He mentally patted himself on the back, having more than one password was meant for times like these. He turned and faced the wall closing his eyes. For a reason he could not put right in his head, he really missed being tucked in and kissed goodnight.

Beth typed in his password going directly into his document file. She flashed over the homework files then clicked on his pictures. She scanned the crash scenes finding nothing dead, other than the vehicles. His remaining files contained normal boy stuff. Had she misjudged? ... Or ... Had he outwitted her? ... She suspected the latter ... She closed the laptop.

A peculiar noise echoed throughout the house, as if winding in and out of the rooms. Beth had dismissed it as the house settling the first couple of times she heard it, but did houses only settle late at night?

She strode quickly down the hallway checking, making mental notations as she went. 'Rachel sound asleep with teddy bear' ... Check ... 'Riley appearing sound asleep or sound asleep' ... Check ... She opened Nikki's door, glancing at the unmoving lump with the tufts of long hair sticking out every which way from under the covers. 'Nikki sound asleep or as Riley appearing so' ... Check ... She walked through the entire house ... 'All okay' ... Check.

Nikki waited until her mother was back in her room. She reached out and shoved the door, silently closing it. She whipped the covers back springing from the bed, removing her black runners, black jeans, and black sweater. She pulled the folded, oversized paper bag from under her bed, jamming her clothing inside. She pulled on her pyjamas, picked up the bag, lifted the window, jumped out, stole across the street, shoved the bag into the garbage can at the curb, retraced her steps, and jumped back into bed pulling the covers up over her head.

Beth placed Riley's laptop at his spot on the kitchen table, pulled a bottle of wine from the rack, and went back into her bedroom pouring an over-sized glass, curling up in the window seat. She sipped slowly staring out into the darkness that blanketed the backyard and ravine with the trail that lead into Yardley Field and Park.

She had always loved the darkness, the peacefulness of it, but not anymore.

She fetched the phone checking in on Doug at the office. It went straight to voicemail. She smiled. He must be busy. 'Yes right' she thought, busy with one of the five list she attached to him. Number One: The computer searches of child porn sites, she had known for a good while now. Number Two: Another affair to add to his on-going collection since the kids were born. Number Three: Chatting on line with those creepy, odd buddies he accumulated in cyberspace. Number Four: Pointing that telescope at the office at things he should not be. She counted the home binoculars in with this one. Lastly, Number Five: The exploration of the after- hour's alternative clubs where men dressed as women.

She shook her head, more for herself than anything else. Marriage was an institution, so she had been taught, and one takes the good with the bad and stays for the sake of the children. She almost had enough money saved to make a new institution of her own, one without the adult male half with the five list.

She poured another glass of wine. It was two a.m. She flipped open her laptop logging into her email account. There were seven messages from Bob. She sat the laptop beside her, topping up her wine glass. Bob, she thought. She sighed heavily. The guy she was having an on-line affair with, the guy she had never met, never spoken to or seen his face. She didn't even know if Bob was his real name. Kathleen, sure was not hers. From the beginning, she rationalized their contact as pure fantasy, not hurting anyone or anything, and still did if she did not think about it too much. In a way, it was all she had in her life that was solely hers and hers alone. Her life seemed to need a good healthy dose of daily unreality.

She tipped her glass back guzzling the remainder of the wine, pulled the machine towards her, lifting it onto her lap, balancing it on her knees. She bypassed the in-box with his seven emails, checking into their private chat-room nine-six-x-six-nine. She smiled. It was two-twenty a.m. and there he was, logged in, on-line, somewhere. She waited for him to come.

'Well hello ... My fair lady,' Bob typed.

'I so hoped you'd be in here,' Beth typed.

'Miss me?" Bob typed.

'You could say that.'

"Something wrong love?" Bob typed.

"You could say that too."

"Bad day sweetness?" Bob typed.

"That also."

'Let's see if I can turn this day around for u-you ... Okay?' Bob typed.

'Okay,' Beth refilled her glass.

'Have you checked your emails?' Bob typed.

'No ... I came straight here.'

'I sent you something special,' Bob typed.

'Ah ... You're so sweet.'

'Sweeter with honey drizzled on certain parts.'

'Lol,' Beth typed. She pressed her back into the cushions settling in.

'Smiling yet?' Bob typed.

'Starting to.'

'Go check your emails ... I'll wait.'

'Okay ... Be right back,' Beth typed.

Beth logged out of the chat room and into her email account. Now there were eight messages from him. She chuckled softly, opening them one by one reading the 'I miss you's ... The hopes of chatting later's ... The x's and o's, saving the message entitled 'surprise' for very last.

She fetched the wine bottle shaking the remaining dribs and drabs into her glass. Anticipation set deep smile lines each side of her partly open mouth. She flipped her feet up and down waiting for the download to complete. She fumbled with the mouse pointer totally missing the open now bar the first time. She giggled, watching the picture starting to filter in and down the screen.

Her mouth dropped the same instant the wine glass fell. She cupped her mouth with both hands, her smile abruptly vanishing, her mouth opening wide and full as horrified wrinkles lined her forehead, her wide grape-like eyes flashing back and forth across the color photo of her and the three kids on the porch of the house. Their house. Underneath the photo 'For You Beth,' was typed in bright red. She tried to swallow, choking instead. She snapped the lid closed.

"OH MY GOOD GOD!" she wailed. She ran into the bathroom ramming up the toilet lid, hanging over it, the wine feverishly erupting out from her stomach, splashing down both sides of the bowl, back splattering onto her face. She slunk to the floor, wrapping her arms tightly around the toilet base, sobbing.

The telephone rang ... Stopped ... Then rang and rang and rang.

Beth crawled across the bathroom floor on vibrating limbs, face planting into her bedroom carpet. As the telephone rang again, and again, she worked her way over to it. She had already assumed Doug was not coming home this night ... Why couldn't he just leave her a message. By the time she got to the bedside table it had quit again. She pulled herself up onto the bed, rolled onto her back, grabbed the phone from the receiver holding it to her chest ... Waiting ... Minutes later she said hello.

"Hello Beth." The voice was slurred, abnormal, and not familiar.

"Who is this?" She glanced at the clock. It read two-fifty-three a.m.

"Did you like your surprise Beth?" the voice asked.

Her eyelashes felt like they had glued themselves to her eyebrows. "B ... O ... B?" she sputtered out in broken gasps.

"Yes,' he stated. "Were you expecting someone else?" he asked, and then started to laugh like some demented creature out of a horror movie.

She pitched the phone across the room. It slammed into one of the dressers, the back coming loose, sending the battery tumbling across the carpeting into the bathroom where it skidded to a halt in front of the garbage can. Her entire body started to shake like someone not taking too well to their detox program. She dry-wretched over and over again. She tumbled herself awkwardly to the floor crawling in under her bed. She held no semblance of thought, no nothing of nothing, only unadulterated fear.

~~~

The front door banged and thunked so hard it jostled the doorframe. Beth wiggled out from under the bed, grabbing her housecoat. The door banged again.

She ran down the hallway sure whoever it was, was going to break right through if she did not get there soon.

She peeked out the side window. Two tall, bulky men dressed in uniform stood at the stoop.

Beth unlocked and threw open the door. "Good morning officers," she said. She pulled her housecoat up onto her shoulders tying the belt snugly. She glanced down at her watch.

It was barely six a.m.

"Morning ma'am." The one officer flipped his notebook open. "Beth Knowles isn't it?"

She nodded. She watched him write something in the notebook.

"Sorry to disturb you at this hour ma'am"

She hid her smile. 'Disturb her? ... Really?' She was so far the other side of disturbed; she probably had her own complete section under that word.

"We are canvassing the neighbourhood," the officer with the notebook began. "There was another body found in Sir MacDonald's Park this morning."

"This morning?" she blurted. "But it's barely morning!"

Both officers glanced at one another. The one with the notebook stepped back, writing again.

Her thoughts had jumped to Riley so quickly ... Too quickly. She still had too many cobwebs in her head, from him and his late night excursion, from Bob and his surprise, from not sleeping a wink. "I just meant ... I don't know what I meant ... I guess it's just shock talking ... Sorry."

The officers glanced at one another again.

She pulled at the ties on her housecoat, untying then retying them.

"It's quite all right ma'am," the other officer said. "As my partner was saying ... We are canvassing the neighbourhood requesting a curfew be observed, and all doors and windows to be locked." He handed her an official looking piece of paper.

Beth put her hand to her throat.

"Ma'am ... Can you account for your family's whereabouts last evening between ten p. m. and one a.m. this morning?"

"Yes," she sputtered, shoving her shaking hands deep into her housecoat pockets.

"My ... My three children were at home here with me."

"That would be Rachel Knowles, Riley Knowles, and Nikita Knowles?"

"That's correct" she lied. She had no idea where Riley had been, and in all honesty had not even checked in on the other two, until way after the officer's time frames.

"And your husband Doug Knowles?"

"I'm sure he was at work, he's been working a lot lately, working overtime you know." Her voice was starting to shake like her hands; her nerves were getting the better of her.

The officer with the notebook who had been writing constantly stepped forward and took Doug's details. His cell phone number, his work address and telephone numbers, car make, model, and plate number. They bid their goodbyes striding side by side along the pathway to the sidewalk.

She watched them speak briefly with the officer in the squad car sitting directly in front of her house, and then walk next door to Sandy and Ben's. The squad car crawled along the roadway staying close to the curb, stopping in a direct line with the officers.

Beth went into the kitchen, plugged in the kettle, and then retrieved the telephone calling Doug at the office. It went directly to voice mail, as did his cell phone. She hoped for his sake he was there and alone because she had the feeling he was about to get some company.

~~~

Computer log in three-ten p.m. ... Teen chat ... 'The Good Die Young.'

Private chat request ... 'Very Naughty Boy' ... Three-thirty p.m.

'Hey ... What's up?'
No response.
Log out three-forty-two p.m.
Computer log in three-forty-three p.m. ... Teen chat ... *'Sweet.'*
Private chat request ... 'Muscles' ... Four p.m.
'Hey MUSCLES ... How you doing?'
'Who's this?' Muscles typed.
'I sit near you in class.'
'Which?' Muscles typed.
'Math.'
'R ... E ... A ... L ... L ... Y?' Muscles typed.
'Really.'
'Who are you?' Muscles typed.
'Ah come on ... You don't know?'
'No ... And SHITHEAD! ... I'm home schooled ... So who the hell are you?' Muscles typed.
'An admirer from your old school.'
Computer generated message ... 'Muscles' ... Has signed off.

~~~

"Where's Dad?" Riley asked chomping on his burger and fries. He held up both hands making invisible quotation marks in the air. "Work again?"

Beth shrugged her shoulders. 'Hope so,' she thought.

"Mom?" Riley said.

"Yes," Beth swirled two French fries into the ketchup pod.

"I took my laptop back."

"I know."

He grinned. "Didn't find nothing ... Did you?"

"Eat your supper." Beth ignored his question taking a huge bite of her burger. 'No I didn't find anything,' she thought. She studied Riley, chewing slowly. She knew he had done something to it so she could not see the things he had in there. For all she knew maybe he had more than one password. She wondered how old kids had to be before they would figure out their parents were not totally stupid.

"You didn't ... Did you?" Riley's grin had turned to a smirk. He knew he would have never seen it again if she had. And, there was no way she could, without that other password.

"Eat your supper," she repeated.

He chuckled. He'd won out.

"Mommy?" Rachel said.

"What darling?"

"Can Nikki walk me over to Susie's after dinner?" Rachel nibbled at her hamburger.

Nikki waved feverishly, pointing from Rachel to Riley chewing and gulping frantically trying to unpack her over stuffed mouth.

"I'll take you," Riley said. He watched his older sister still fighting with the food. "How much did you stuff in there Nikki? ... Half the thing?"

Nikki scowled at Riley giving him the finger.

"Mommy did you fix my dolly?" Rachel asked.

"Still working on it honey."

"The same thing happened to more of them ... Could you fix them too?"

"Pardon?"

"More of them lost their heads ... Can you fix them too?" Rachel asked.

"Don't look at me," Riley shot out. "My doll days are long done."

"And I thought they were just starting," Nikki broke in.

Beth held out her arms pointing her index fingers at Nikki and Riley. "You two ... Knock it off!"

"Rachel ... What did I tell you about playing that game?" Beth shoved her plate away from her. She turned in her chair facing Rachel square on.

"But I didn't Mommy. They were like that when I woke up this morning."

"Must have been the doll headless horseman again," Riley piped.

"Enough!" Beth ordered raising her voice.

"Mommy ... I really didn't do it." Rachel's eyes were starting to water.

"See it *was* the doll headless horseman," Riley said. He covered his mouth with his hand pretending it had just slipped out.

"RILEY!" Beth snapped.

"Just saying." Riley tried to contain his laughter, losing, running from the table down the stairs into the family room.

"Bring them here then." She cuddled Rachel in her arms. "Don't play that game anymore ... Okay?" Beth whispered.

Rachel nodded her head and ran off into her room gathering the dolls.

"Mommy thinks we played that game again," Rachel whispered to the dolls. "But we all know I didn't ... Don't we?" Rachel made the headless dolls nod yes. "I saw youse playing that game all by yourselves last night ... Remember?" She made just the heads nod again. "It was after Nikki and Riley came back in through their windows ... Right?" She made the heads nod yet again. "Okay ... Come on. Let's get you all to mommy." She gathered them up trundling down the hall into the kitchen.

~~~

Computer log in seven-forty-five p.m. ... Teen chat ... 'Doobie.'

Private chat request ... 'Happily Stoned' ... Eight-ten p.m.
'What's up?'
'Not much and you?' Happily Stoned typed.
'What's your name?'
'What's yours? ... Lol,' Happily Stoned typed.
'Sherry.'

'Anton,' Happily Stoned typed.

'No way?'

'Way ... Do I know you?' Happily Stoned typed.

'Yeah we go to the same school.'

'Right on! ... Hey, wait a minute! ... Are you that new exchange student?'

'That would be me.'

'Wow! ... You're hot!' Happily Stoned typed.

'Wanna hang out? ... I can scoop a six pack from my folks.'

'Yeah! ... For sure! ... Wanna meet downtown?' Happily Stoned typed.

'I'd rather be alone with you and the six pack of beer I have.'

'Wow!'

'How about that park near the school?'

'You're funny ... It's more like part of the Sir Bishop schoolyard where we practice football,' Happily Stoned typed.

'Okay schoolyard. I call big fields parks ... Lol.'

'Lol ... When you wanna meet up?' Happily Stoned typed.

'Say ... Ten p.m.?'

'Hum,' Happily Stoned typed.

'We don't want to get caught drinking under age or anyone to see your roaming hands now do we?'

'You bring the beer ... I'll bring the blanket,' Happily Stoned typed.

'Lol ... See you at ten.'

'Can't wait ... Can't wait ... Hey is it ten yet?' Happily Stoned typed.

'Lol.'

Run ... Run run ...
Run ... Run run run ...
Run ... Run run run ...
Run ... Run run ...
Run.

~~~

The running figure with the blanket tucked under his arm halted, holding his arms up in the white blinding lights as instructed.

The officers lunged from the cruiser, one going each side.

"Name?" the one officer asked.

The second scanned him with the flashlight then aimed it onto his face.

"An ... Anton," he stuttered. He felt like he was about to piss himself.

"Full name," the same officer instructed.

"Ant ... An ... Anton Holl ... Hollingworth." His knees were slamming on and off one another so badly he thought they were going to give way.

"Address?"

"Three-twenty-six Avondale road ... It's not far, it's ... "

The other officer cut him off. "We know where it is. Are you not aware of the curfew?"

He nodded confirming he was, not meeting their eyes.

"Would you care to explain then, what you are doing out here past the curfew?"

His nervous energy almost had him blurt no. "I ... I ... Wa ... Was ... Oh brother."

The officer put his hand into the small of Anton's back. "Just, take your time Lad," he said.

"I ... I ... Was going to meet a ... a ... a girl," he lowered his head staring at the ground, shuffling his feet back and forth.

"And where were you meeting this girl?" The officer's eyes went from him to the blanket on the ground and back.

"The ... th ... the schoolyard." Anton looked from one officer to the other.

"Get in the back seat." The officer opened the door closing it after he was in.

"Are ... are yo ... youse arresting me?" Anton asked.

"No ... We are driving you home."

The officer in the passenger seat got out of the car four houses down from Anton's, opening the back door. "Go right home now, we'll be waiting and watching," he said.

"You're not telling my parents?"

The officer smiled. "No, not this time. If we find you out here again we will," he smiled again. "Anton, we were teenagers once too ... Now say thank you and be off."

"Say ... Thank you?" Anton reached and grabbed the officer's hand in both his giving a limp handshake. "Thank ... Thank you for bringing me home."

The officer held onto his hand. "Wrong thank you, Anton."

"I ... I ... Don't unders ... Understand."

The officer gave his hand a firm handshake, then let go. "The thank you is for quite probably saving your life."

Anton's eyes ringed in white all of a sudden cluing in. 'The murders ... The murders in the parks.' "Thank you ... Thank you," he blurted. He ran across the four front lawns into his house.

The cruiser slowly crept down the road turning left at the corner.

~~~

Computer log in Ten-forty p.m. ... Teen chat ... 'Things That Go Bump After Dark.'

Private chat request ... 'Odd Boy' ... Ten-forty-one p.m.

'Hey ... How you doing?'

'Okay and you?' Odd Boy typed.

'This room's quiet huh?'

'Yeppers, just me,' Odd Boy typed.

'You, waiting for someone special?'

'Maybe,' Odd Boy typed.

'Lol ... Mysterious ... I like that.'

'You do ... Do you?' Odd boy typed.

'What's your name?'

'Odd Boy ... What's yours?' Odd Boy typed.

'Odd Girl.'

'Well then ... I guess we got that over with,' Odd Boy typed.

'Lol ... You're funny.'

'So I've been told,' Odd Boy typed.

'What school you go to?'

'Eastdale ... And you Odd Girl, where do you go?' Odd Boy typed.

'Lol ... I go to Eastdale too! ... Wow! ... What a small world!'

'Lol,' Odd boy typed.

'Hey ... I've got some fireworks ... Wanna meet in behind the school at the edge of the park and set them off?'

'Yardley Park?' Odd Boy typed.

'Yeah.'

'When?' Odd Boy typed.

'How long it take you to get there?'

'Ten minutes tops,' Odd Boy typed.

'Ten minutes, then.'

'Lol ... You're on,' Odd Boy typed.

'See ya soon ... Odd boy.'

'Likewise, Odd girl,' Odd Boy typed.

Run ... Run run ...
Run ... Run run run ...
Run ... Run run run ...
Run ... Run run ...
Run.

~~~

He hunkered down, crouching off to the side of the slide in the schoolyard at the park's edge waiting. He looked over one shoulder, then the other, sensing he was not alone.

Eleven-ten p.m. came and went, as did eleven-thirty p.m.

314

He knew something was out there. He could feel it. He stood wiping his sweating palms onto his jeans. He stared out into the darkness. He drew his hoodie up covering his head. He slowly circled the slide then sat on the outer edge of the metal run. "I know you're here," he whispered.

The tufted ends of the long grasses quivered. He stepped forward.

The grass rustled, bending, then poked back up wavering back and forth twenty feet farther back.

"It's okay," he whispered, taking a couple steps forward. "You can come out." He could feel eyes watching, observing. "It's okay," he whispered again. "Really it is."

The grass whipped, flattening, and then springing back into place as if something was tunnelling through it backwards.

He moved forward entering into the grasses. He stopped, held his arms stiffly against his sides and planted his feet, peering into the darkness.

The breeze shifted course. A vile stench smacked into his face tearing his eyes. He cupped his nose and mouth gagging and dry retching uncontrollably. He took another step, then another, then another, advancing slowly into the field.

A figure lean and supple slowly rose at the outer perimeter, directly in front of the tree line, as if purposefully cloaking its self in darkness.

He could sense the intelligence, the power, the monitoring, the taking him in, the studying of him as if he was a smear on a microscope slide. He didn't move.

The figure abruptly turned, backed, starting to deploy slow at first, then like lightening, weaving in and out and around the trees, making not even the slightest of ripples in the silence.

He watched mesmerized. It was like nothing he had ever seen before. And, in the blink of an eye, it was gone.

He blew out a long stream of air suddenly aware he had not drawn one single breath during the figure's examination.

315

Was this what he had been searching for? ... And ... If it was ... Then why was he still standing and not gutted like all the others? He chewed at his bottom lip. He had missed something ... Something very, very important.

He stared out into the blackness. Had it been there all along, silent, camouflaged, watching? ... Had he sensed right? ... He thought so. But ... Had it really left? ... Or, just moved where he couldn't see or suspect? ... He didn't know. He suddenly started to shake head to toe, fear wrapping around him, clinging like a wet bath towel. It took two tries to shove his hands into his pockets. He staggered back to the slide, slamming down in a half assed sit, fearful his stick-like legs had lost the ability to hold up his body's weight.

A cold shudder shot through him. He looked side to side and over both shoulders. His thoughts took wing again. Had it doubled back? ... Had it even left? ... Would Yardley Park be the first to have a return visit, making the body count two? He bolted from the slide running wildly for home, unaware of something dogging his every movement.

~~~

"HOLY SHIT!" Riley screeched. He whipped round in a semi-circle his feet going air-borne, his arm pinned behind his back, his body sling-shot forward in a full frontal body check into his mother, sending them both down to the ground.

Beth quickly right sided herself, crawling across the lawn and latching onto Riley's arm again.

"JESUS CHRIST MOM! ... THAT HURTS!" he screeched. He twisted his body pulling backwards, trying to get out of her grasp.

She forcefully dragged him from underneath his open bedroom window, round the front side of the house. "Riley ... Just shut ... The hell up," she said between breaths. He'd knocked the wind out of her. She pointed to the front door. "Go ... Sit ... At the table ... I should be in shortly." She let go of his arm.

He wanted to ask how long shortly would be, but thought better of it. He had never ever seen her this angry. He went in the house purposely leaving the front door ajar at a formidable eavesdropping distance and sat at the table as he had been told.

Beth repositioned herself on the lawn, hunkering down out of sight. Minutes later there was a snatch and grab front yard rerun with the added extras of shrill screams and swearing.

"GET IN THE GOD DAMN HOUSE ... NOW!" Beth shouted.

Nikki ran into the kitchen knocking over one of the kitchen chairs, taking her place at the table.

Riley and Nikki glared at one another, eyebrows raised, mouths open. The front door slammed shut and locked.

"Don't either of you dare move a muscle," Beth ordered. She went into the garage from the laundry room, banging the door shut behind her.

Nikki and Riley could hear knocks and thumps and bangs and yelling in between the crashes and smashes. They did not move.

Moments later Beth slipped into one of the kitchen chairs looking as if she had just survived a tornado. She scooted the chair over directly across from the two of them. "That's much better," she whispered. She took a deep breath smiling oddly at them both, holding it and stretching it into a grimace, turning her neck back and forth as if she was trying to get the kinks out.

Their eyes followed hers to the kitchen clock that read twelve-twenty-nine a.m.

Beth smiled that same unnerving smile again. She folded her hands neatly in front of her on the tabletop interlocking her fingers. "So," she said, calmly, structured. "Isn't this nice, all of us gathered at the table for a late night chat ... Who would like to go first?" She stared them both down, her eyes narrowed and snake-like.

Nikki and Riley simultaneously launched into squirming and fidgeting.

"Well?" She tapped her foot, unclasped her hands, drumming her fingernails like a galloping horse back and forth in front of her. "All righty then," she pushed herself back from the table. She held up her right index finger. "Actually ... Just give me a minute okay?" She wavered her finger back and forth using it like a makeshift pointer. "NOD" she ordered.

They nodded in unison.

"I'll be right back ... Besides ... It'll give the two of you extra time to get your stories straight in your heads ... You know get the bugs out ... So to speak." She leaned on the table right up close and personal into their faces. "Between you and me ... I just can't wait to hear this." She smirked and went down the hall into Rachel's room.

That little thing that pops up and nags one way down deep had been there inside her for quite a piece. Now it had moved front and center. Checking would send it back to where it lived.

Beth's eyes flashed over the bed with the little lump covered up head to toe in baby pink coverlets. The only thing sticking out from under was a teddy bear arm.

She went back into the kitchen. "Okay ... Where were we? ... Oh yes ... One of you," she paused getting up from her chair abruptly slamming her fist down on the table making the salt and pepper jump. "ONE OF YOU!" She repeated, yelling. "WAS ABOUT TO TELL ME WHAT THE HELL," she paused again, blowing and swishing the hair from her face, sitting back down. "About to tell me what you were up to," she said more calmly. She brought herself tight up to the table refolding her hands. "NOW WOULD BE GOOD!" she bellowed, losing again to temper.

She glared at them both in turn.

"Well, well no one want to go first?" She shook her head slowly back and forth holding her hands palm side up. "The

two of you, always have so much to say about everything ...
So what gives?" She tutted then stood, smacking the table
directly in front of Nikki with the flat of her hand. "Okay! ...
You're first!"

Nikki opened and closed her mouth soundlessly.

"That's nice Nikki, next time try it with sound." Beth
twirled her thumbs round one another without unclasping
her hands. "Nikki, my child, as you've probably noticed, I
don't have much patience right now and I really don't feel
like going back into the garage and yelling and throwing
more stuff, but then and again, taking you with me and
bouncing you off the walls might prove interesting. Oh and
before I forget ... hold on here," she went to the hall closet
pulling out a large paper bag throwing it onto the table. "I
believe this belongs to you." Beth forced an odd smile, that
looked as if it had been drawn on with pink crayon. "No need
to thank me child."

Nikki's eyes widened, flying from the bag to her mother,
back to the bag full of the black clothing and sneakers she
had shoved into the neighbour's trashcan.

Beth smiled the same odd smile again.

"Wasn't that nice of the Landrys across the street to
assume you'd dropped it and someone walking past threw it
into their garbage can, thinking they were doing a good deed.
Next time, you should choose a trash can farther away and
make sure you have cut all the name labels off. You know the
ones your mother sewed in them in case they got mixed up at
school in the locker rooms ... Now if I recall correctly you
were about to turn your sound on and start talking ... Were
you not?"

"I ... I ... I," Nikki began. She gulped back the mouth full
of warm saliva that had pooled under her tongue. She felt
like she was about to throw up.

"I? ... I? ... What? ... Well?" Beth's voice simmered with a
wrathful overtone of something one could not put into words.
"Seeing as this is so hard for you to wrap your head around,

let's do it this way, starting with why the hell you're dressed in all black?" She flicked the paper bag, "again?"

"I ... I ... I," Nikki stuttered.

Beth sucked in a deep full breath. "So you've said," she hissed.

"To go out?" Nikki's eyes flickered to Riley and back.

"Really? ... I wouldn't have guessed." Beth slammed her fist down on the table again. "QUIT THE BULLSHIT!" she yelled.

Nikki watched her mom's eyes turn icy as they slowly traced over every inch of her face. She felt as if her tongue had somehow dehydrated in the process, collapsing, folding over backward. "I ... I ... Didn't ... Didn't ... Want anyone to ... To see me ... When I ... I went out."

Beth sucked her bottom lip into her mouth. "Somewhat better," she said. "But first let's clear up why you were even going out in the first place, via your bedroom window at twelve midnight ... Shall we?"

"It was eleven-ten," Nikki corrected.

Beth's glare spoke volumes.

"I ... I ... I," Nikki's entire body was pulsating. She death gripped the edges of the chair.

Beth drew her hand slowly across her mouth, stood, shoved her chair in place, and started to hum while moving slowly, step by step, around the table in her daughter's direction.

"Okay ... Okay," Nikki blurted. She glanced at Riley.

Riley was fixed, immobile, eyes wide like eggs in a frying pan. His clenched hands sported knuckles drained of color. His forehead carved out in rippled fear lines ... Unadulterated, motherly fear lines.

"I'm waiting," Beth bent over placing her elbows on the table resting her head in her palms. "Well?"

"I went out ... 'Cause I ... I ... Was looking for ... For something." Nikki's voice pitched and wavered, making sounds like a little kid just learning to talk.

Beth's eyebrows drew into a single raised line. "You went out because you were looking for something?"

"Ye ... Yes Mommy."

"And the something was?" Beth scooted her elbows across the table to Nikki, bringing them face-to-face.

"Riley ... I ... I ... Wen ... Went looking for ... For Riley?"

"Nikki, that sounds more like a question to me," Beth swivelled her head Riley's way. "Doesn't that sound like a question to you?" she asked.

Riley shook his head back and forth.

"No?" Beth asked.

Riley nodded his head up and down.

"So ... Riley ... Tell me, did you need looking for?" Beth asked.

"I ... I ... I," Riley stuttered.

Beth again banged her fists on the table. "ENOUGH!" she screamed.

"I ... I ... Went out back, came back in, then went out back to find Nikki, which was what I was doing before, but I didn't find her 'cause I was out back and not near her room, to go in her room, but when I came back in, I did go in, but she wasn't there, so I went back out," he blurted.

"Say again?" Beth screwed up her face. "I don't think, I got that."

An odd low whine swept through the house, haunting, hollow, more constructed and mechanical than as if something of blood and breath.

All three of them abruptly halted as if caught up in a macabre game of 'Simon Says.' The three sets of eyeballs clicked back and forth clock-like as they shifted around the room on a search and seizure mission for that minute particle that contained the common denominator of logic.

It was nowhere to be found.

The whine crept through again, this time lower in volume, almost hushed as if it was trying to steal through unnoticed.

The sounds were like nothing they had ever encountered, even in horror movies. Beth's mind tugged at her, she had heard this before but had pushed it too far back into her brain's cobweb filled, inner storage compartment, passing it off as anything other than what it was ... Unnatural ... Inhuman.

"Stay here," she whispered. She hurriedly slid her socked feet along the hardwood floors not making so much as a sound entering Rachel's room. She clutched at her chest, her pounding heart easing, dissolving the irrational fear, that the whatever it was had come from within her room. She was, as she was, a little lump covered head to toe with a protruding teddy bear arm.

Beth stepped back, slamming into something solid, warm, four footed, usually referred to as Nikki and Riley.

They grabbed at her as if seizing the opportunity to bond themselves in like over-sized appendages.

"Mom," Riley whispered into her ear. "Did you ... You check ... Her ... Her?" he asked. His knocking knees needed to know that Rachel was all-intact under there ... And that it was still Rachel.

Beth raised her eyebrows questionably.

"Check Mom," he wove his arm through hers pointing towards the bed. "Please ... there's just so ... so much weird ... going on." He stared at the little pink hump. "What if there's something under there with her? ... Or ... What if the lump is the 'Grim Reaper'? ... Or ... What if it's a thing making that weird sound?"

Beth lunged forward whipping the covers back. Rachel uncurled, rolled onto her back grabbing her teddy bear, clutching it to her chest.

Beth let her held breath slowly seep out through her teeth. She mentally gave herself a shake; she had let herself get caught up in Riley's imagination again. She re-covered her daughter, and then tiptoed from the room.

The three of them walked in a close, short apron string, single file back into the kitchen.

Beth pulled out a chair and sat, instantaneously both knees were taken. She smiled, angry or not she just could not help it. She wrapped Nikki and Riley within her arms drawing them close. "You know how very much I love you both, don't you?"

Riley nodded, Nikki whispered yes.

"What the hell are we doing here? ... Hum?" She gave them a squeeze. "What on earth were you both doing outside after dark? ... Again?" Beth kept her voice a hair above a whisper.

Riley and Nikki starred at one another. The words ... 'She knows,' silently flying back and forth between them.

"Come on guy's ... I'm your mother ... Mother's always know everything sooner or later ... Like ... Open windows with missing screens ... Like things stuffed between mattresses ... Like sales of intimate under garments on the internet ... Like lost items being returned by friendly neighbours." She moved her arm from Riley reaching over and dragging the brown paper bag containing the black clothing across the table. "You know, how it is," she paused patting their backs gently. "Shall I go on?"

They both bowed their heads shaking them in a slow no.

"So come on? ... Out with it ... What on earth were you up to?"

Without warning a hiss like whine rose, then fell, sounding far off yet near all at the same time. Six wide eyes trailed the floor, walls, and ceiling.

Within seconds, the hiss-whine shot through again, the burst short, the sound falling back onto its self like a misplaced echo. They stiffened, immobilized.

The third time was the charmer, the duplication, the low whine, haunting and hollow, mechanical.

What it was? ... They didn't know ... Where it was ... They did know.

They scrambled from the chair, banging and bumping into one another in sheer unadulterated panic. Riley and Nikki jumped up on the kitchen counter standing side by side in the double sink, hands clasp, knees vibrating, whacking their legs into one another. Beth ran to the hall closet retrieving the broom, waved it back and forth as if testing its weaponry fortitude, ditched it grabbing the biggest carving knife from the drawer. She clenched her fist around the handle whitening her knuckles, posing her arm to strike, standing dead center of the kitchen and slowly pivoting three-hundred-sixty degrees.

Run ... Run run ...
Run ... Run run run ...
Run ... Run run run ...
Run ... Run run ...
Run.

Tires screeched outside. A vehicle door banged. Hurried footsteps thundered up the walkway. The front door boomed, roared, and shook. The latch mechanism squealed, cracked, let go. The door whip lashed back and forth then halted, spraying out drywall particles as the doorknob jammed through the wallboard, anchoring it.

A police officer stepped into the front hallway, quickly moving through the house into the kitchen, flashing his badge. "Ma'am, someone in this household has broken the curfew." He smoothed back his dishevelled hair. "I saw two figures running across your front lawn, followed by what appeared to be a short scuffle." He eyed up Riley and Nikki who were still standing in the sink, hands clasped, knees knocking. He turned to Beth, who was also still posed, clenching the carving knife. "Anyone else in the house ma'am?"

"Just my ... My little one ... One, but she's ... She's sound ... Sound asleep," Beth's voice vibrated in her throat.

She felt nervous and helpless and violated and caught red-handed and whatever the words were for holding a knife up ready to strike. The officer had seen her children outside. Maybe even followed them home. Seen her, bring them down. Heard the yelling and screaming. In addition ... He had broken open their front door. Fear suddenly sprang up, adding itself to her list.

"Get her," he instructed. His eyes had turned dark, haunting.

"Can ... Can ... I see your ... Your badge ... Again?" She lowered her clenched fist knife arm, reaching toward him with the other.

"No time right now ma'am. This is a matter of grave importance. Get her now."

Beth sat the knife on the edge of the kitchen counter, motioning for Riley and Nikki to stay put. She scurried down the hallway, wondering why police uniforms made people scurry, but they obviously did. She was living proof.

Scream after scream after scream rocked the house.

Beth could hear the screams, the high pitching shrillness, the utter purity of the terror contained within them, the realization they were hers was far removed. Her eyes rolled back, her knees buckled, and her breath shallowed as she folded in sections like a piece of perforated paper. Her head smashed off the corner of the dresser midway down. She felt no pain. Her lights were already out.

The room ... Rachel's room was littered in butcher's cut red meat hunks individually wrapped in eggshell-white coloured gloopy ooze. A massive load of vomit covered the entire bedside mat. Maggots and bloodworms wriggled in and out of the partially digested human organs that lay within it. The overpowering smell of rot and decay hung like a dense fog about the room. Dark red blood splattered in varying degrees, thin, thick, close, spread, along the walls, ceiling, and floor as if someone had tried to spray paint the space with an old aerosol can that did not work quite right. Shards of bone imbedded in the walls and furniture like shrapnel. Strips of muscles and tendons lay scattered across the once baby pink coverlet. Tufts of hair with scalp hung off the ceiling fixture. An eyeball floated in the water of the small glass on the nightstand. Part of a foot lay in amongst the dolls.

It was as if someone had blown from the inside out.

The window was wide open, the screen missing.

Beth eyes moved violently back and forth under the lids, as if lost deep within 'Rem' sleep. Seconds later they shot open, closed, flickered, blinked, fully opened.

A piece of scalp with a long curl of hair slid from the overhead light splattering down onto Beth's forehead. Blood dripped and balled, rolling down her temples into her ears. She opened her mouth belting and shrieking screams that bounced and ricocheted inside the room.

She could hear sets of footsteps running, coming nearer and nearer.

She turned her head. The piece of scalp slithered into her hair. Her eyes flashed back and forth at lightning speed scanning the objects under the bed. Comprehension was at a premium. She could not process the signal. She left the world again. No matter though, the multiple sets of upper and lower jaws, all clean as a whistle as if boiled for hours, bound together in their peacock blue kitchen twine would still be there in full technicolour for her viewing pleasure upon her return.

Nikki stopped dead in the bedroom doorway, her screams jumping around the hallway like an over anxious kid with their first go at a 'Yo-Yo'.

Riley was to the side, nails clawed into the doorframe, mouth open and dry, tongue hanging, a small puddle of urine in between his feet.

The officer pushed between them, stepped over Beth, crossed the room, and hopped out the window.

~~~

"Ma'am? ... Ma'am?"

Beth was suddenly conscious of something cool on her forehead, her cheeks being tapped with the flat of a hand.

"Ma'am? ... Are you all right?" the officer asked.

She could feel someone starting to pull her into a sit. The facecloth slid from her forehead down across her closed eyes, then disappeared as if plucked away.

"Take it easy now ma'am ... When you're ready." The officer was crouched to her right, his arm behind her, supporting her weight.

Riley and Nikki were changed into pyjamas and were squatted down on her left.

Beth blinked twice, opening her eyes.

She was in the kitchen.

"You gave us quite a scare there," the officer's voice was soft and gentle. He helped her into one of the kitchen chairs, taking up one himself. "It's going to run until no one remembers, and then it will begin again, hunting through the Internet," he said. "This is its pattern," he added.

'It? ... It?' she thought. What was he referring to? ... What was it? ... It? ... Wasn't it blown apart in Rachel's room? ... Rachel's room with all the authentic horror? ... The room that was minus her six-year-old daughter, whose new favourite game was slaughter in the park ... Scratch that ... Now she could play slaughter in the bedroom ... For real ... When she came out from hiding! Her eyes whipped back and forth, like a digital clock hit by a power surge ... 'What a terrible thought ... Why did I think that? ... What on earth is wrong with me?' The vision of the blood-bathed room came into full mental view, complete with the sets of jaws underneath the bed.

She started to shake head to toe as if she was caught in the middle of a blizzard with nothing but a bathing suit on. "What ... What ... The hell are you talking ... Talking about?" she mumbled. Her head slowly sank to the tabletop, flattening out her nose with the sheer weight of it. "Can someone get me a blanket?" she muffled.

The officer dashed his eyes over top of the back of Beth's head studying Riley and Nikki in a way that made them want to run from the room. He pushed himself from the table. "Where's your blankets?" His eyes floated between them.

Riley's hand was trembling so badly he pointed to the ceiling.

"The ha ... haff ... hall," Nikki was having trouble talking, her mouth seemed to only want to open halfway and her tongue didn't move.

Warmth draped about her shoulders. Beth groped at the blanket, wrapping it tightly about her. She lifted her head, resting her chin on the table, attempting an unsuccessful thank you smile at the officer.

The officer dipped his head table level looking directly into her eyes. "If your son here hadn't gone to the school yard, or your daughter been in the field, I would have had it."

Beth's body beaded with sweat. This officer, who bore witness to all their goings on and probably more ... Who had broken open their front door ... Walked through the house like he knew the layout ... This officer ... Was ... Was ... She couldn't find the words ... There was just something ... Something unnerving, off, not right.

"As I was saying ... I was onto that flesh sucking, organ eating varmint. The media never tells the real stories, or the truths, but I am sure you are mighty aware of that ma'am. When it ran in here just before your son and daughter, I knew this was the lair."

"It? ... It? ... Ran in here? ... Lair?"

"Yes to both ma'am," he said.

Beth had been watching him, watching his eyes. They did not appear to blink. Who had eyes that did not blink? Her head started to swim. She dropped it onto the tabletop again.

"It assumed the one you called Rachel," he said.

"It what? ... It what?" His words were not making any sense. She sucked up all the available air on the tabletop, held it, blowing it back out in one long steady stream.

"I'm sorry for your loss ma'am," he said. His face was on the table, cheek down keeping eye contact with her.

Her mushed up mouth opened and closed in rapid-fire succession. Tears flooded down her one exposed cheek, lifting the dried blood from her skin, mixing, dropping off and pooling it into miniscule puddles on the tabletop. "Rachel is okay though, isn't she?" she croaked. She did not understand what he was telling her. She did not want to.

"No ma'am."

"But ... But ... I drew her bath, put her to bed, tucked her in, kissed her good night, kissed her teddy bear goodnight."

"There's no teddy bear in the room ma'am. It must have taken it with it."

"It? ... It? ... It took Rachel's bear?" She started to cry again. "I just got that bear for her a little while ago ... She picked it out herself." She lifted her head from the table. "I can't understand any of this ... Can you please find my Rachel?" she pleaded. "And the teddy bear," she added.

"Ma'am ... I know this is difficult for you ... Your daughter Rachel is gone," he paused searching for different wording. "Rachel has passed. When it assumed her, it took over her in entirety, ceasing what was. The thing you have been living with for the past few months looked and sounded like your daughter, but was totally something else ... If it is any consolation ma'am, it must have liked it here. I've never known it to stay in one place so long."

"Can you say all that again? ... Only slower? ... I don't think I got it right," Beth mumbled through tears.

"Ma'am ... Your daughter Rachel has passed on ... When she was assumed, she ceased to be. The thing you have been living with, looked and sounded like Rachel, but wasn't."

"Does that mean you aren't going to look for my daughter and her teddy bear?"

"Ma'am ... There is no Rachel to look for ... And it would seem it took the bear with it."

Beth dropped her head to the table, landing it face down, sobbing. "Rachel ... My baby girl ... Is dead?"

"Yes ma'am." The officer sat back in the kitchen chair and folded his arms, waiting.

"Who are you?" she asked almost too quietly for him to hear.

"Internal Earth Investigations," he answered.

Beth jolted up from the tabletop. "You're what?"

"Internal Earth Investigations," he repeated.

Beth hung her head, shook it back and forth. Dropped it to the table, hitting her forehead on and off it, then sat back up.

She turned sideways glancing at Nikki. She seemed like a statue. Her face white, drawn, her lips gone, sucked into her mouth. Her cheeks hollow. She looked like she had died and been brought back in *Dr. Frankenstein's* laboratory.

Beth swivelled in the other direction. Riley was much the same with a few minor tweaks, his mouth was open, his eyebrows a single line, and he was leaning off kilter in the chair.

"You're what?" Beth said again.

"Internal Earth Investigations ... Ma'am ... I know it's a lot to digest."

"Really ... You think?" escaped her lips before she could stop it. But, between something that looked and talked like Rachel, but wasn't, exploding all over a bedroom and a cop from internal earth what-cha-ma-call-it in her face, she did not think she was doing too badly.

The officer smiled slightly. "I'd like to chat longer, you all seem like pleasant people," he stood and pushed the chair into place. "But I have to get on it, before the trail goes cold. You understand ma'am?"

Beth nodded. 'Pleasant people?' she thought. 'We seem like pleasant people? ... Okay then ... Has he blinked yet?'

"Oh and ma'am, you've got a dead cat in your shed out back. I'd be taking care of that soon if I were you." He tipped his head in the direction of the three of them. "Good day ma'am, sir, miss." He left the kitchen, hurriedly disappearing out through the opening the front door used to fill.

Beth, Nikki, and Riley rose slowly, wobbly as if they were made of jelly, weaving and wavering, bumping and slamming into the walls, following his trail through the house like he was a voodoo priest and they were his zombies.

They gathered out on the front stoop, huddling together, each grabbing and wrapping into a section of the blanket as they watched the patrol car turn from their drive out onto the roadway, pick up speed, and disappear into the darkness.

They stood for the longest time, then abruptly, as if cued, their legs intertwined, swayed, quavered, and then buckled, sitting them where they stood as if they'd been suddenly anesthetized.

They clasped hands, staring blankly.

The older model car directly across the street, motor running, windows up, was seen, but not.

Beth ever so slowly started to think, taking baby steps at first, frilling and fluffing them out as she went. By the time she could skip without tripping, she went onto Rachel. Rachel who two months back suddenly wanted to become a ballerina, who wanted to be taken to watch the classes. The classes of early teens, where she sat cross-legged studying them intensely, class after class as if sizing them up ... And she was! The new teddy bear she had seen in a store window and wanted more than anything, and received for doing Saturday and Sunday dish duty for a month. The bear she had professed to love far more than any other toy and had taken everywhere ... Even now! The room she'd never tidied before but had been keeping spotless, just like the accumulating sets of jaws under the bed ... Spotless. Her doll games growing more and more violent, 'Slaughter in the park?' The same sweet smile always, never altering, never changing up. Her sudden overwhelming interest in computers; learning so impressively that they had bought her one of her own. All the baths she'd had, two and sometimes three a day, locking the door, telling her with the same sweet smile the noises that sounded like retching, gagging, and regurgitating was the toy she'd taken in to have a bath with. Her eyes changing color, deepening, growing a depth and wisdom, wisdom beyond her years, and had they blinked over the past few months? ... She wasn't sure ... But thought, not.

She felt sickened, irresponsible, brainless, taken in. Her daughter had not been advanced for her age ... Her daughter had not been her daughter. She had been something else entirely. Why had she not seen it? ... Why had she not sensed it? ... Or gathered all the bits and pieces up and lay them out in front of her ... Surely she would have noticed they didn't fit together any more ... But, she hadn't. She hadn't even been looking, hadn't been looking at any of her children for that matter. She had been totally self-absorbed, totally self-indulgent, playing into superficial fantasy games on her own computer, and getting half-sloshed, to boot.

She suddenly hated herself.

She wrapped her arms around Nikki and Riley drawing them closer. She breathed in their warmth, their smell. The start of a smile etched at the corners of her mouth.

Beth raised her head, her eyes flashing over the older model car, motor running, windows up, parked directly across. The one she had noticed earlier but hadn't ... The one that was still there. She studied it, bumper to bumper. A cold chill abruptly shot up her spine.

The horn beeped. The driver's window started to descend. Another cold chill shot through.

She stood, bringing Nikki and Riley to their feet, all of them scooting inside the entranceway.

"HEY BETHY! ... IT'S ME! ... BOB! ... HOW YOU DOIN'?" the man yelled.

Beth whirled round, standing statue-like half in, half out the opening. The driver's window was all the way down. A man was leaning out the window. A man she could smell the sweat, urine, and alcohol on, from where she stood. A man with no front teeth, greasy long hair, and a tattered shirt so filthy she could not make out what color it was.

"BETHY!" he called out. He hung his left arm out the window swinging it back and forth purposely showing off a handgun. "SHOULDN'T HAVE TURNED YOUR BACK ON ME LIKE THAT BETHY!" he yelled.

Beth's knees clouted off one another as she stepped back.

"Aren't you goin' invite me in? ... We've a score to settle! ... I thought, maybe me and you could play us some 'Russian Roulette?' ... Course now I'll have to change it up a bit ... How many kids you got again?" He clicked the safety off the gun. "What do you say Bethy?"

Beth grabbed at her throat pulling the skin of her neck ... She couldn't breathe ... She backed into the front entranceway. The front entranceway without the door.

"Come on, Bethy ... Don't be like this," he called out.

The driver's door sprung open.

Beth frantically jerked and pulled at the front door. Nothing.

She propped her left foot against the wall, braced the other behind her reefing with all she had. "RILEY! ... NIKKI!" she screamed, rattled, panicking, hearing the car door slam shut. "RILEY! ... NIKKI!" she screamed louder. "COME! ... HELP!"

They instantaneously appeared, one latching onto the knob, one her.

"Do you know that guy with the gun walking towards the house Mom?" Riley asked propping both his feet against the wall.

"YES! ... NO!" She wailed. "PULL! ... FOR GOD'S SAKE ... PULL!" she screeched.

The knob made a hollow popping sound, puked out plaster, unleashing the door belting it forward, knocking all of them backwards and smashing them into the wall.

"The gun guy's walking across our front lawn Mom," Riley's voice jumped an octave.

The three of them slammed the door shut. Riley shot the dead bolt across. It hit air. "MOM ... THE DOOR WON'T LOCK!" He yelled.

"RILEY COME!" Beth screamed from another room.

"WHERE ARE YOU?" He ran into the kitchen and back. "DINING ROOM!"

Beth and Nikki were pushing their grandmother's heavy antique buffet across the floor. Riley ran between them shoving with all his might. "Where we going?"

"Door," Beth huffed.

They wedged it tight against the front door just as the knob started to twist back and forth. The door thumped like someone was pounding it hard with their fist, and then the doorbell rang ... And rang ... And rang.

"Both of you ... Get in the car ... Run ... Now!" Beth was pulling boxes down from the top cupboard, dumping them on the floor, snatching up things, ramming them in her purse. Riley and Nikki took off through the laundry room into the garage.

Beth grabbed the car keys from the holder, pulling the entire thing from the wall. She untangled the key chain, pitching the brass plaque that said 'Home is the key to my heart.'

She ran into the garage jumping into the driver's seat and starting the car.

"Mom ... Mom," Riley hung over the back seat pointing at the garage door. "Want me to pull it up?"

Beth revved the engine then floored it, ramming right through the wooden door. "What did you say?"

"Nothing," he was grinning ear to ear. "Where we going?"

"Airport," Beth glanced over at the house as they sped past. Bob was trying to get in through the front door.

"Airport?" Nikki and Riley asked in unison.

"Yes."

"Like ... Where?" Nikki said.

"You guys pick."

"We can pick?" Riley fist punched the air mouthing 'yes'.

"Yes ... As long as it's ... Far ... Far away." Beth glanced at them through the rear view mirror.

"Spain?" Nikki said.

"Yeah ... Spain?" Riley chirped.

"Spain it is!" Beth said. She pulled out onto the highway on ramp.

"Are we coming back?" Riley had his face pasted onto the side window fogging it, drawing stick aliens with the tip of his index finger in the mist.

"No."

"Not ever?" Nikki asked.

"No."

"What about Dad?" Riley said.

"Forget him."

Nikki and Riley looked at one another, shrugged, then started to smile.

"Mom?" Nikki smoothed out the kicked up ruffle on her baby-doll bottom.

"Yes."

"We're all in our PJ's." Nikki folded her hands into her lap.

"That's okay." She turned on the right hand signal, changing lanes into the one directly under the sign with the picture of a plane on it.

~~~

Bob leaned on the front door. He lit a cigarette and blew smoke rings in between hacking up mucus and spitting it onto the flowers in the pots that graced each side of the entrance. He urinated through his jeans where he stood.

"Maybe I'll go have a look around," he said. "Can't hurt none." He stepped from the stoop, jammed the handgun into the back of his jeans, and strolled around the house pulling and pushing at each window in turn, stopping, smiling up idiotically at the baby pink drapes spattered in red dots flapping in the breeze from the wide-open window without the screen.

~~~

The officer traveled the dirt road to the very end, pulled into the middle of the field and stopped. He locked the patrol car with the keys in it and walked a hundred yards, disrobing. He opened his mouth rounding his lipsm uttering a hiss like whine, tinny, hollow, and mechanical. He coughed throaty at first, and then harsh and full using his stomach muscles. His body trembled. His insides rumbled. He dry retched time after time like a cat expelling a fur-ball, then regurgitated phlegm and white gloopy mucus. He firmed his footing, bending in half, pressing his palms into the soil and rocking his weight. His teeth flew from his mouth, his eyeballs shot from the sockets, blood sprayed from his pores as he all at once exploded, splattering out bite size meat hunks in a wide three-hundred-sixty degree circumference.

It shook its self, rolling its thick leathery skin side to side, then horizontally rippling it the length of its body. Its slitted, amber, effervescent eyes opened, scanning the darkness.

It could hear the radio calling for Officer Handlin. It tapped the hood on the way by thanking him for the loan.

It crossed the dirt road, climbed the knoll, standing dead center and silent. It cocked its head listening. It flared its nostrils, smelling for traces. It lowered its head starting to run, picking up speed, moving as if winged, far removed from the human scope of vision.

Five hundred miles away it halted, climbed the radio tower its nostrils spreading, flickering, detecting the scent.

"Medatrica," it growled. "Making your boomerang look like a flying saucer, or whipping up crop circles, or throwing spit balls down onto the earth like meteorites is one thing." It descended the tower. "But ... This ... This! ... You know eating humans' innards makes us sick ... Remember last time?"

It started to run again.

"Why earth was picked to raise you through your early years will always be questionable," it hissed. "MEDATRICA!" it shouted. "I WILL FIND YOU!"

~~~

A flying saucer shot directly in front of the plane.

"Did you see that?" The pilot pivoted his seat facing the co-pilot, locking onto his eyes.

He nodded slowly. "They won't believe us," he said.

"No ... It will be like last time ... A lot of examinations and counselling and time off ... Unpaid time off," the pilot added.

The co-pilot pursed his lips. "Did you see anything?" he said.

"No."

"Me neither," the co-pilot said shaking his head back and forth. "Me neither," he repeated.

~~~

Riley's excitement was cooling. His first ever airplane ride was not what he'd thought. He had pictured more of a thrill ride with rolls and dips. Even the window held little interest now, just light blue, light blue as far as his eyes could see. Even the wing he had been staring at had not once jumped, turned, or lifted its flaps, like in the movies.

He grabbed the earphones, tearing them from the plastic package deciding to tune into the film.

He turned his head, flattening his face into the window for one last look. All at once ... The blue blurred ... Darkened ... Obscured ... Disappeared.

Something was out there ... Out there on the outer side, pressing back ... Something ... With effervescent amber eyes

... Slit, effervescent amber eyes ... Non-blinking ... Staring out from a hideous face.

'Something ... Was out there ... Outside ... Outside the plane ... Pressing its face, into the windowpane.' His mind over-loaded. He beaded in sweat. His entire body trembled. He pushed himself from the armrest lean to, jolting backwards toppling directly onto Nikki.

"Riley ... What the hell?" she snapped.

He curled up into her lap, kicking the back of the seat in front in the process. "There's ... There's ... Something ... Something in the window." He lifted his right arm, shakily pointing towards the glass.

Nikki looked around him, there was nothing. "There's nothing," she said.

He peeked at the window. "But ... But there ... There was ... There was something looking at me ... I swear there was."

Nikki had her hands under his butt trying to lift him off her. "Riley, we're in an airplane!"

"You don't think I know that?" He wrapped his arms tightly around her neck holding on for dear life.

Nikki tugged at Beth's arm. "Mom? Mom!"

"What?" Beth folded the magazine, shoving it into the seat pocket. She had been lost in the article she'd been reading, a bomb could have gone off and she wouldn't have noticed. She glanced over at Nikki ... She looked like she'd sprouted Riley, like a tree sprouts new branches and leaves in the spring ... They were so intertwined they appeared to be Siamese twins.

Nikki started thrashing and kicking. "Get off me ... You ass!"

Riley clambered across the seat gluing himself onto Beth.

"Jesus Christ ... Riley!" Nikki pulled at her baby dolls fixing them. "You ever do that again, I'll swat you one! ... You almost pulled my PJ's off!" She untangled her headphones putting them back on.

Beth put a finger underneath her son's chin gently lifting his face. Eyes, huge, wild, terror filled latched onto hers. "My sweetheart, what-ever is wrong?" Beth whispered. She guided his head to her upper chest, neck tucking him tightly against her. She gently drew her fingers through his hair. She could feel every ounce of him vibrating so much that the seat was shaking.

"Mommy?" he whispered into her neck.

"Yes honey."

"There's ... There's ... Something out there."

"Out where, darling?" Beth kissed the top of his head.

"Out ... Out there ... Outside there." He pulled his hand loose, quickly pointing a finger towards the window and then shoving it back in behind her.

Beth sighed heavily; this kid had been through so much. Hell ... They had all been to the 'Outer Limits' and back, a couple times, for real. She wrapped her arms around him asking the passing flight attendant for a couple blankets. She bit at her lip not wanting to ask him where exactly, outside there was, but did.

"Out ... Outside the window," he blurted in a three-year-old, high-pitched squeak.

Beth studied the window. She rested her chin on top of his head. Was there something out there? ... She didn't know ... Common sense dictated the words ... No ... No ... And ... No ... Completely, utterly impossible ... Common sense also dictated ... That little six-year-old girls didn't get possessed by something and then blow apart all over their room either ... Or ... Odd, unblinking police from internal earth something, didn't come to your house in the middle of the night ... Or ... Someone called 'Bob' from the safety of an internet chat room didn't come to your home with a loaded gun.

"You believe me Mommy ... Don't you?" He was sucking his thumb.

"Nikki pull the blind down over that window!"

Nikki looked from the movie to her mother to the window and back to her mother.

"NOW!" Beth yelled.

Nikki threw the headphones down, jolted sideways and pulled as ordered ... Fear suddenly welling up inside her ... Her mother was not Riley and not crazy ... She snapped back into place, eyes directed anywhere ... But on that window ... That same window her brother had said something was outside of and ... She didn't finish her thoughts ... Her skin had goose bumped so badly it hurt ... She pasted herself to Beth.

"Mommy, you believe me, don't you?" he said, again.

"Yes, my handsome prince ... I believe you," she whispered. And her words were never more true ... She did.

Beth pulled the blanket up, tucking and covering him up to his nose. She glanced at Nikki; she was already cocooned within the other.

"You won't let it get me ... Will you Mommy?" Riley said.

"Never."

"Or Nikki?"

"Not ever."

Riley shut his eyes.

Beth tucked the plastic knives and swizzle sticks in between the seats. It was the closest to weaponry the airplane kitchens had to offer. She watched the window, guarding, protecting them as they slept. She repeatedly told herself that the flickering and pausing dark shadows, on the other side of the drawn blind, were just clouds.

~~~

It couldn't see past the blind. It moved to the right, then the left. It still couldn't see. It wanted to watch them as it had done over the last couple of months. It liked watching them.

It moved down the wing, sitting mid section, dangling its feet over the edge. It fussed with the teddy bear's bright red ribbon, plumping up the bow.

It turned its head in the direction of the window. The shade was still drawn. It could wait.

It thought of Riley. He was almost ready.

Intermittent high-pitched metallic laughter bounced and danced back and forth over the metal wing in between the rushes of air.

Ina Louise Jackson

TROLLING

Epilogue

The difference between
Good and Evil
Is ...
Perception.

AUTHOR'S NOTE

The greatest gift a person can give to another is that of their
time.
Thank you for yours.

Sincerely
Ina Louise Jackson

The Left Side of Wrong

By Ina Louise Jackson

Julie Porter's life is much like everyone else's, until the day that everything begins to go downhill. Her husband isn't the man she married, there is something about the basement, and who keeps planting the roses?

This gripping tale of abuse portrays one woman's slow descent into madness and will keep you on the edge of your seat.

*Contains graphic scenes and language.

The Left Side of Wrong, eBook ISBN 978-1-926898-55-1, www.pinelakebooks.org
The Left Side of Wrong, 6x9 trade paperback, ISBN 978-1-926898-56-8 www.pinelakebooks.ca

www.ingramcontent.com/pod-product-compliance
Lightning Source LLC
Chambersburg PA
CBHW051329020726
47501CB00007B/1991